DEPTHS OF THE REBELS' STONE

I0588039

Dreamweaver Diaries

BOOK TWO

Eric Johnson

 Broken Table Press

First printing, 2021.

Broken Table Press
Belchertown, MA, 01007

www.ericjohnsonwriter.com

To Amanda.

ACKNOWLEDGMENTS

This book would not have been possible without all the help and support I received from my family and friends throughout the years. My wife, who put up with my long hours of disappearing into the words that I create and who patiently listens to my excited non-sequiturs about characters and events totally disconnected to anything in our lives. My children, equally patient with my writing hours, inspire me to be the best that I possibly can. Bob and Lee, my folks, have supported my passion for writing for as long as I can remember and are probably my biggest fans. I love you all.

Jamison, my alpha reader, who gives such great advice, I'm truly grateful for your help which was equally important on book two as it was on book one. My editor, Ellen from Em Editing, whose professional eye helped pull together all my lose ends.

DEPTHS OF THE REBELS' STONE

ONE

"W hen looking at rocks under the microscope—" Mr. Hunt, Isabella's Earth Science teacher, was droning on again about the grain structure in sedimentary stone. As usual, Isabella was staring out of the window. Outside, the sun shone down through the early morning fog, which drifted lazily through the trees. Even though it was just early October and the temperature outside was only starting to get to sweater weather in the mornings, the heat kicked on in the classroom. Summer was still fresh in Isabella's mind, and given the summer she'd had, she was sure it would be at the forefront of her memories for a while longer.

Her notebook was already full of small sketches of foxes – more appropriately, one specific fox. Although she had not been able to get back into the dream world since the night she went after her brother, she felt it taunting her at the edge of her dreams. She missed Finn and his enthusiasm for everything. She hoped that Ajay had been right, and that Finn was safe. The last time she had seen him, he had been fighting the shadow congress with Wren and her dad.

That part was the craziest to her, and she still couldn't be positive that it was really him. The sight of her mild-mannered father—the man who rarely rose his voice and would sing to her and Tucker at night—wielding a sword and fighting beside a massive wolf still was hard for her to believe. He had confirmed everything that night: the dream world, the hunters, the weavers. It was all part of his family heritage, her family heritage, and now she was supposed to start her training this weekend. They were going to go camping so her mother wouldn't wonder what was happening or why they were disappearing at night.

"Miss Shaw." Hearing her name snapped Isabella out of her reverie and back into the stuffy classroom. "Are we interrupting something?"

"Sorry, Mr. Hunt." She could feel her cheeks warming, and it wasn't to do with the heat of the room. Isabella had always been a good student but paying attention in first period freshman year was not easy. "I promise I was paying attention." She was not.

The teacher nodded his head and continued to stare at her. She felt the eyes of every classmate boring into the back of her head, but she refused to look around to meet them. Two kids in the back of the class snickered as Isabella frantically searched the board for any sign of a question. Nothing. Mr. Hunt didn't write on the board; he talked at the class, and they were supposed to take the notes down. It wasn't fun, but she usually tried. Today was another story.

"Well," she began. Isabella had next to no clue what was being discussed, so she went with the last thing she'd heard him say. "Well, the grain structure would—"

The classroom door opened and a boy she had never seen before slunk in. He stood for a moment, scanning the room. His brown hair hung just past his ears and had a slight curl out near the ends. He wore a red t-shirt with the Pizza Planet logo on it under a coal gray cardigan. Over his right shoulder was his backpack and in his left hand was a piece of paper. Most importantly for Isabella, his entrance had drawn attention away from her.

"Is this Earth Science?" the boy asked the room.

"It is," Mr. Hunt said. His voice was higher in pitch than usual, a telltale sign of his annoyance. "Can I help you?"

"I'm your new student."

"Okay." Mr. Hunt scanned the classroom for an empty desk, and his shoulders visibly slumped. "Why they insist on overloading my classes, I will never know," he said, motioning to the back of the room. "Grab a spot on the radiator for now. I'll get you a desk for tomorrow," he said, before adding under his breath, "although I'm not sure where I'll put it."

"Whatever." The boy shrugged and started to the back of the room.

"I'm sorry, I didn't catch your name."

"Evan Byrne," he replied. He made it to the back of the room and took out a notebook.

Isabella, hoping she was forgotten, pretended to write something in her notebook but was really drawing a flower next to one of the little doodles of a fox.

"So, Miss Shaw," Mr. Hunt turned his attention back to her, "back to our question from earlier. What is the main cause of sedimentary rock formation?"

Not forgotten, but thankful she had done the reading from the night before, Isabella perked up and began to answer with a bright smile. It was a softball question, but if it hadn't been for Evan coming in when he did, she would have had to have admitted that she wasn't listening. Not the worst fate imaginable, but an embarrassment she didn't want right now. She reminded herself to thank him for his timing. Besides, she told herself, glancing back at him as the class continued, it would give her an excuse to talk to him.

The rest of the class was uneventful, but before she could catch the new kid, he escaped from the door at the back of the classroom and into the hallway. By the time Isabella had packed her notebook and headed into the hall, he was nowhere in sight. She watched for him in her next two classes, but he never showed up. By the beginning of fifth period and lunch, Isabella had all but forgotten about him and was busy sharing the latest gossip with her friends at their usual table.

"Have you seen that new kid, Evan?" Kisha said, her curls seeming to bounce with the excitement of her own voice.

"Earlier," Isabella said, but her response was drowned by those of her friends who excitedly told their stories of what they knew about him.

"He looks like he stayed back," Cora said, already bored by the conversation.

"I heard that his father just got a new job and they moved here from Italy." Dina officiously pushed her long blond hair from her face and took a bite of her sandwich.

"He didn't sound Italian," Isabella said, eating her own lunch.

All three girls stopped and stared at her.

"What's wrong?" she asked, wiping her chin with her hand before remembering to look for a napkin. "Do I have something on my face?"

"Izzy," Kisha said, grabbing her arm and staring at her, "have you talked to him?"

"Not really," she shrugged. "He's in my second period, though. Saved my butt from having to answer a question when I wasn't paying attention."

"You know you can say *ass*," Dina said, rolling her eyes.

"You know you can be an ass," Isabella retorted.

"Okay"—Kisha leaned in conspiratorially—"Izzy is our girl on the inside."

"What does that even mean?!" Isabella shook her head. Kisha could be a bit over the top sometimes, but she meant well.

"You're going to talk to him, find shit out, and tell us about it," Kisha smiled. "None of us have classes with him, so it just makes sense."

"Whatever." She packed up what was left of her lunch. "I need to go to the bathroom. I'll see you last period, okay?"

"Don't forget, you're on a mission!" Kisha called after her.

Isabella rolled her eyes as she headed out of the cafeteria toward the bathroom. On her way, his red shirt caught her eye. Turning, she saw Evan bump into another boy whose name she couldn't remember. He was easily half Evan's size and stumbled forward, dropping his lunch and his bag. Evan caught him by the shoulder and the boy just managed to stay on his feet. Isabella couldn't hear what he said to the kid, but then he laughed and the boy bent down to pick up his books and spilled food.

For a moment, Isabella wanted to go and see what happened, but the bell rang to dismiss lunch and she still needed to use the bathroom before her next class. Leaving the scene, Isabella assumed Evan had gone to get napkins to help clean up. Coming out of the girl's room, Isabella saw the kid picking up the last of his food from the floor and looked around for Evan. A flash of red went around the corner toward the gym, and Isabella figured she'd catch up to him later. As annoying as it was to admit, especially to Kisha, Izzy did want to talk to him. There was something about him that she couldn't quite make fit. But for now, that would need to wait. First, she had French, History, and English to get through.

By the time English class rolled around, Izzy had forgotten about Evan and her friends' mission. Instead, she thought about the camping trip with her dad as she sat staring at the pages of the book she was supposed to be reading. Nothing in the book even came close to the excitement of traveling in the dream world. Her father had promised to let her try again, but he said if she couldn't, then he'd take her to his old training ground. There were ways that weavers could bring people along. He'd only done it once before, but he didn't like to talk about it too much. This weekend, though, that was what this weekend was all about. Training her to become a Dreamweaver like him.

Besides, it was the end of the day on Friday. There wasn't much left she could focus on, so when the bell rang, she threw the book into her bag and was first to the door. Stepping into the already teeming hallway, she walked right into another student.

"Oh, I'm sorry!" She glanced behind her to make sure she wasn't blocking traffic, then moved out of the doorway to help pick up the papers she'd knocked out of his hand.

"Hey, don't worry about it," he smiled as they both crouched down to pick up the papers. "I'm Derek, by the way."

"Izzy."

"In a hurry?"

"Little bit," she said as she handed him a stack of papers and went to grab one of the books. Next to the book was a red Adidas sneaker. She looked up and saw Evan standing there, looking down at her.

"Izzy, right?" he asked.

Isabella stood up, forgetting what she was doing, and brushed a stray strand of hair behind her ear. She could feel the warmth beginning to spread up her neck as she smiled at him. His eyes were a greenish-gold, and when he smiled, his teeth glowed white. "Yup, that's me." She hated her answer as soon as she said it. "Evan, right? You're in my—"

"Science class? Yeah, Mr. Hunt seems like a dick," Evan said.

"He's okay most days," she shrugged. "Just don't get caught not paying attention. He likes to spring things on you if he thinks you're not focused."

"Got it," he replied with a nod. "Are you busy later? My dad and I just moved here from Florence, Massachusetts, and I thought maybe you could show me a good place to get a pizza?"

That's why Dina thought he was from Italy! Izzy bit her lip to keep from laughing. She didn't want to have to explain that her friend had thought he was from another country; Dina would be mortified, and she wasn't going to do that to her.

"Uh, excuse me," a voice from the floor interrupted Izzy's thoughts. "You're standing on my book."

"Oh," Evan said as he took a step back. "So, pizza?"

The watch on Isabella's wrist buzzed with a text from her dad.

I'm outside.
You coming?

The familiar excitement that had been building around her all day burst back to the surface. "Sorry," she said as she scrunched her face, "Another time, maybe?"

"Works for me," he said, shrugging. "See you Monday."

Isabella spun on her heels, almost colliding with Derek who clutched his books to his chest so she wouldn't knock them out of his hands again. "Sorry," she said without looking. She headed to the doors, quickly tapping out a return text to her dad.

This was going to be a great weekend. She needed to get home and pack, but that was just to fool her mom. She'd spend the whole weekend in the dream world with her dad, and he'd begin her training. While her friends didn't really understand her new-found excitement for camping—something she'd sworn off after the fiasco in seventh grade—they seemed to take it in their stride. At least she knew they'd never ask to come along again.

Outside, she ran to her father's Ford Focus and tossed her backpack into the back seat before getting in the passenger seat.

"Ready to get your stuff, then hit the trails?" he asked.

"Is it going to be a long hike to the campsite?"

"Nope, we're parking in it," he said, turning the key to start the car. "Once we get started, well, that's another story."

TWO

Isabella had been through her pack four times at this point, once in her room a week ago when she first packed, twice more last night before going to bed, and again in the morning. Sifting through the contents for the fifth time, she worried about forgetting something important. It wasn't like she could just run to Target and pick up something she needed. The last time she went, she had nothing with her, just the nightgown she'd worn to bed that night. Things had turned out alright, but this time her father wanted her to be prepared. This time they would be training. Training for what, she didn't know, so that's why it was so hard to pack.

"What the heck do you pack for dream training?" she wondered out loud as she surveyed the contents spread out in front of her. Her dad had been vague, to say the least. He said to bring whatever she thought she'd need. So, Isabella packed what she had found last time she was in the dream world, a small dagger with gems in the handle, and a dream catcher that she had used to get out of the dream world. Besides that, there was a change of clothes, a leather jacket with a hood, and food.

"Ready?" her dad asked as he tossed his own backpack in the back of his blue Ford Focus hatchback.

"I guess." Isabella threw her bag in the back and opened the passenger side door. "Tell me again why we're bringing a tent and stuff?"

"Because we're going camping." Her dad raised an eyebrow at her over the top of the car. "You do understand that, don't you? No running water, no computers."

"I have my phone," she replied, rolling her eyes at him. "Besides, you said we were going to train. You know, you were going to bring me into the dream world and show me how to use my powers like in some crazy superhero movie."

He looked over his shoulder as if someone might have overheard, then, turning back to her and grinning, he shrugged and got into the car without answering her question. She followed suit and buckled up. Pushing the start button on his car, the radio blasted to life, pumping some alternative music that someone thirty years older than her would have loved. Isabella rolled her eyes again, put her earbuds in and cranked her own music. It wasn't until they were on the highway that he reached over and turned down the music, popping one of her earbuds out in the middle of Taylor Swift's "End Game".

"Okay," he started out of nowhere, "about the training." Isabella turned off her music and watched her dad as he drove through traffic. She tried, as she had been trying to for the past six months, to match the image of her quiet father with the guy she had seen fighting the shadow congress. They hadn't talked about it. There was never really a time, but she was going to get the story this weekend. She'd make sure of it. "Once we go under, I'll meet you on the other side."

"In the dream world?"

"Yup, and we'll see what you can do."

"How are we going to get there? I mean, I know you told me not to, but I've been trying for the past few weeks. I just can't seem to do it."

"I know."

"What do you mean you know?" Isabella scrunched her face, and her shoulders tightened. "Are you mad?"

"No," her father chuckled. "I knew you'd try. That's why I had Vígolfr keep an eye on you."

"Your wolf was spying on me?" Isabella had met Vígolfr the first time she went into the dream world. He was a terrifyingly large white wolf who'd helped her find Kimi. He also fought alongside her father as his companion.

"Not spying." He smiled at her incredulity. "Let's just say he was watching out for you without you knowing."

"You do know the definition of spying, right?"

"He didn't like the idea either, but you're my girl. It's dangerous in there. You were lucky when you rescued Tucker that you didn't run into anything worse than a shadow."

"What do you mean worse than a shadow?" She remembered the feeling of being surrounded by five shadows when trying to rescue her brother. Afterward, her father had explained shadows to her. Shadows are, or at least were, people who died in their dreams and became trapped by their regrets or their anger. These emotions pulled them deeper into their own darker natures, dark natures that everyone possesses, until all that was left was their pain or anger or regret. They became a shadow of their former self. They then wandered into people's dreams and tried to drag them in with them, hoping to someday fill the void inside themselves. It was the shadows that created nightmares and dream traps.

"For now, let's just count our blessings that you don't know that and feel comfortable knowing that Vígolfr is going to keep the rest away from you. For now."

"Has he heard from Kimi?" she asked, careful to keep the worry out of her voice. Kimi was her own companion, unbeknownst to her father, but things hadn't gone well in their first meeting where Isabella had repeatedly pushed her away and insulted her. In the end, Kimi was injured during the battle with the shadow congress. Isabella had helped her, but when she left, Kimi still didn't look good. Ajay, one of the hunters she'd met in searching for her brother, had promised to get her help.

"Still nothing," he said with a sigh. He put his hand on her knee and gave it a squeeze. "I'm sure she's fine, Izzy. From what you said, she was with the Champion's clan when you left. They're good people, Wren's people. We'll find her."

"But—"

"We'll find her."

They rode in silence for several miles until her father pulled off the highway and onto one of those two-lane country roads that winds through miles of forest before it gets to something that could, with some imagination, be called a town. The monotony of endless trees lulled Isabella into a trance as she stared out of the window at the landscape. For a moment, she thought she could hear Kimi's voice calling out to her and the air in the car began to feel chill and damp.

The Focus jerked quickly to the right and then back left, causing Isabella's forehead to hit the window and wrenching her back into the present. Rubbing her sore forehead, she asked, "What was that?"

"Sorry, Izzy. Some yahoo just pulled out of a blind trail in the woods back there and nearly t-boned us. You okay?"

Isabella nodded and they drove on in silence. After a couple miles, she said, "Where do they come from?"

"Who?"

"The hunters. Ajay and Finn, people like them?" She hated how little she knew about the world she had gone to. After she'd rescued her brother, she'd talked to her father about the dream world several times. What he'd given her was all pretty general and focused on what he called Dreamweavers – something he was, and what he believed she was too. "There were so many of them, and they were all so different, nothing like what I see around town."

He laughed easily. "Oh, you can say that again. They're not all that different from the shadows, really."

"But they seem so different. They're kinder. They like to help people."

"Well, yeah, in that respect they are very different, but they are also people who died in their dreams, as are the denizens. You said you'd gone into a town near where you ended up the first time, so I'm assuming you met some denizens."

"The people who lived in the town?" Isabella shuddered involuntarily. "They were like zombies just going through the motions of living. They didn't even acknowledge I was there."

"That's unusual, but you said that Finn was investigating something when you met him, so it could be that something was up. Most denizens I've met are just like regular people. They live day to day lives in the dream world."

"What do they do in the real world?"

He took a deep breath and sighed. "Remember how I said they were like the shadows?"

She nodded, then remembered he was driving and said yes.

"Well, they're like the shadows because they are dead too. They don't come back into the real world, though I'm not sure calling it the real world is right. The dream world is just a real and just as dangerous. I call this world the waking world. It reminds me that both worlds are real in their own ways."

"They're all dead? Like they're ghosts or something?"

"Not ghosts so much as souls or intelligence, if you prefer."

"But why aren't they shadows then?"

"It all depends on how they die in their dreams and what their last thoughts are. The shadows, their last thoughts are of sadness or pain or loss. The denizens, when they passed, their thoughts were of love and hope."

"What about the hunters?"

"They're special." Her dad smiled at the windshield. "With them, it wasn't their thoughts that defined what they became. It was their actions. Hunters died trying to save someone else. They are some of the best souls in the dream world, and the fact that you found them, or they found you, says a great deal."

"So, Ajay and Finn, all the people in their camp, in that town, they're all dead," she said, not so much a question as the idea settling in. "There are so many of them, and they're all so different. Different ages, ethnicities, how do they all speak the same language? Everyone was speaking English."

"The world's a big place," he said with a shrug, "and while most of it speaks English, to them you were speaking their language. The dream world is an interesting place like that. It doesn't matter what language you know, everyone speaks the same one."

"So, the dream world is like heaven?"

"No, at least I don't think so. It's just another reality, bigger and more diverse than ours, and we are lucky enough to be able to live in both." He turned off the paved road and bounced along a dirt path. "But enough questions for now. We're here. Let's get the tent set up and get your training started."

They pulled into a clearing in the forest. It was obviously a campsite that had been used before; a small fire pit was set up in the middle, and a path led off deeper into the woods. When Isabella climbed out of the car and stretched, she heard the babbling of a river nearby. It was peaceful, except for the bothersome flies and the impending swarm of mosquitoes she knew would come at dusk, like they always did when the family was camping.

"You never answered my question about how we were getting into the dream world," she asked as she set up the tent.

Her father was wandering the edge of the camp to gather wood for a fire. He claimed they needed to come back smelling like campfire smoke or her mother would never believe they went camping. Isabella was pretty sure it was more that he just loved campfires. "Well, every culture does things differently. Some Native American cultures make a tea used a plant called peyote. Others used certain mushrooms or smoked. I heard of one culture out in the Himalayas used fermented yack urine."

"What are we going to use?"

Her father pulled a small bag of something green from his back pocket and shook it before putting it back in.

"So, you're going to let me smoke? Is it like pot or something?"

Her father dropped the bundle of sticks he'd collected next to the fire. "Are you crazy? First off, you're fifteen. Secondly, you're my daughter. There is no way you're going to be smoking pot. And you can forget about peyote and mushrooms. I see that twinkle in your eyes. What is the world coming to," he sighed and shook his head.

"What's in the bag then?"

"This, my dear," he said as he pulled the bag out again, "is fresh ground sage. We are going to go in the old-fashioned way, meditation."

"Oh," she said, going back to the tent. She had hoped for something a little more exciting when her dad had started his description.

"Don't be so disappointed," he chuckled, "I'm sure you'll get a chance to try another method eventually. Just not on my watch, baby girl."

THREE

O pen your mind to the dream world," Isabella's father instructed. He sat on the other side of the fire from her, the light making shadows dance across his face. He looked different, bigger almost, in the firelight.

"What does that even mean?" She scowled at the flames. This was pointless. The sun was beginning to set when they started meditating, but now the moon was well above the trees and still nothing. "Open your mind"—she stood up and kicked dirt at the fire—"sounds like some hippy shit."

"Watch your mouth, young lady." He opened his eyes and watched her pace on the other side of the fire.

"Sorry, Dad." Isabella picked up a stick and peeled off some of the bark, tossing them into the fire. "I'm just frustrated." Her dad watched as she threw another stick into the fire and squared herself to him. "But what do you *mean* by open your mind?"

"Well, I guess it means something a little different to everyone." He leaned back, putting his hands in the dirt behind the blanket he'd been sitting on. "The way I do it, I literally picture a door in my mind, and I simply open it. That gives me some sort of entrance. Then after I relax sufficiently, I expand the door until it fills my entire consciousness." He smiled wistfully at the moon. "It helps me for it to be nighttime."

"A door?"

"Yup, just a door. It was my grandfather's suggestion. It helps when it's something that you're familiar with, and we've all seen doors. My door is a heavy wooden one with a book engraved on it. It looks just like the one that led into my grandfather's library back in Sweden. You've never been there so that probably won't help you, but it was an amazing room."

"So Grandpa was a Dreamweaver too?"

"My dad," he said slowly as he shook his head, "not that I know of. I suppose he could have been, but he never mentioned it. I asked Farfar once—that's what I called my grandfather—but he just shook his head and quickly changed the subject." Isabella wanted to ask more, but her father closed his eyes again and said, "Now, busy Izzy, let's try it again."

Looking at her old *Finding Nemo* beach towel, she took a deep breath and sat down. Folding her legs awkwardly under her in what she imagined was a meditative pose, Isabella closed her eyes. In a few moments, her left foot was falling asleep and she grunted in frustration. Shifting position, she started rubbing her foot through her boots.

"It might help to be more comfortable," her father said. "I wouldn't go so far as taking your boots off or anything. Most weavers can't change their outfits once they're in the dream world. That's why we try to have everything we need on our person. Sit however you're most comfortable; that might help."

She shifted her position until she sat with her feet pulled in close to her bottom, knees together, and arms around them. She rested her forehead on her knees and tried to picture a door. Nothing. Blank and empty. At first, she'd had glimpses of something just at the edge of her consciousness, an urgency, but the harder she tried to picture a door, the less she saw. At this point when she closed her eyes, she saw nothing. "I can't do it," she burst out in frustration.

"Sure you can," her father encouraged confident, as if her success was a foregone conclusion. "Just relax."

"But I can't see a door or anything."

"Then don't picture a door. I said that worked for me, but that doesn't mean it's going to work for you. Try something else, or try nothing."

"Well, that's not helpful."

He laughed. "Sorry, hon. Some things just take time."

Isabella closed her eyes again and took a deep breath. She tried to picture a door, but that led to nothing so she began running through everything could be entered: a hole, a slide, a window. Still nothing happened. She didn't feel any closer to opening herself to the dream world; she just felt like she was getting a headache from the roaring in her ears that kept getting louder. She opened her eyes and looked at her father sitting across the fire. "Do you hear that?"

"Hear what, baby girl?"

Isabella listened to the sounds of the night. She could hear a slight breeze rustling the leaves of the trees, some night animal scurrying in the underbrush, but no roaring. "Nothing, I guess I was hearing things." She closed her eyes again and relaxed, focusing on her breathing, and the roaring sound came back. Louder this time, closer, but when she opened her eyes, it was quiet. "Every time I close my eyes, I hear this roaring sound. It's loud, like a river or something."

"Do you see anything?"

"No, just hear it."

"That could be your ticket in." He smiled apologetically, "Makes me kinda sorry you never learned to swim."

"I'm not sorry," she said as she pulled her knees closer to herself. "I don't like water anyway." Closing her eyes, she tried to imagine moving closer to the roaring sound. She could feel a spray of water on her face and hands and once again opened her eyes to see if it had started to rain. "I can't do this."

"Here, just try listening to my voice. I'll talk you closer to it." Her father began to talk through moving forward, his voice calm and soothing, and soon, just like when he'd used to read her bedtime stories, she found her eyes beginning to close. She could see the water as he described it, but he described a river; what she saw was more like a wall of water, falling out of nowhere and into a small pool. She moved closer to it and stuck her hand out into the waterfall. It was wet, which shouldn't have surprised her, but this was her imagination.

She looked into the pool, her father's voice lost to the roaring waterfall, and imagined it swallowing her up. Her pulse quickened and she took shallow, ragged breaths. The waterfall and pool in front of her began to fade from view. Calm down, she told herself, you can do this.

The water came back into focus, like when you turn the dial on one of those coin-operated viewers at state parks. Conscious of her breathing, she walked around the pool, but the view in front of her never changed. She stood at the edge of a small pond, and at the far end was a waterfall. Putting her foot in the water, she felt it soak into her boot, wetting her sock and making it stick awkwardly to her foot. Her heart pounded and she drew in a sharp breath.

Her eyes shot open, and she saw she was sat across the fire from her father. He was watching her expectantly and, though he tried to hide it, she could see disappointment flash across his face. The look passed so quickly Isabella was almost sure she'd imagined it.

"You seemed close there for a moment," he said. "What'd you see? Was I right with a river?"

"Waterfall." She could hear her pulse in her ears and her shoulders ached from the tension. "There's a small pool that I think I need to get across. I don't think I can do this."

"Let's try it again. I know you can do this. I mean, you've been there before. You have most early weavers beat already."

"Okay," Isabella said with resignation in her voice. Going into the water didn't appeal to her because there was no way of telling how deep it was or if she could even touch the bottom. This could be some sick joke her mind was playing on her that had nothing to do with getting into the dream world. Following her father's directions to the edge of the pool again, she was careful to keep her breathing as calm as possible as she stepped into the water.

The ground dropped quickly in the pool. Barely halfway across and the water was already up to Isabella's knees. Stepping carefully across the invisible but rocky bottom, Isabella kept moving forward, the water rising with every step. First to her waist, then up over her stomach, to her chest, then shoulders. She could almost touch the waterfall, the spray getting in her eyes as it crashed furiously into the pool, still a couple feet in front of her. Her breath was coming in short gasps now. She couldn't hear her father's voice over the roaring water, but she could feel the sense of urgency that she'd noticed the first time she tried. She let the urgency drive her forward, and with as deep a breath as she could take with the water lapping against her ears, Isabella closed her eyes and dove toward the waterfall.

She felt the force of the waterfall push her under and she held her breath as her lungs burned. She flailed with her arms, trying to grab hold of anything, her feet splayed out behind her kicking uselessly. The ground pushed up against her and the water pushed her down from above.

Trapped in between, Isabella felt the air being compressed out of her. She wanted to cry out but knew that the water would fill her lungs and she would drown. Her hands pushed against the rocky bottom and felt a sharp stone slide across her skin. Despite the pain running down her arm, she managed to get her feet under her and push. When her head broke the surface on the other side of the waterfall, Isabella gasped for breath. Eyes still closed against the stinging water, she flailed for something to grab on to. Her sore hand hit something hard and rough, causing her to wince in pain as she slipped back under the water.

She hadn't managed to get a good enough breath. She could feel her lungs trying to burst from her chest as she was once again pushed below the surface of the water. She scrambled with her legs but couldn't get her footing on the loose rocks at the base of the pool. Instinctively her eyes shot open, ignoring the pain of the water against them, and she saw light above her, dappled by the surface of the churning water. A shadow moved, blocking the light, and for a moment she froze. If she made it into the dream world and needed to face a shadow immediately, Isabella didn't want to think about what that meant for her.

The shadow grew more prominent and then the surface of the water broke, whatever was up there coming down toward her. She tried to fight as arms grabbed her under her armpits, but the angle was wrong and she couldn't get a good hit on her attacker. She remembered the moment in the boat with Finn and Kimi, the bloody hand where Kimi had bitten her to release the hold of the shadow, but this felt different. When she'd fallen out of the boat, she'd felt comfortable, safe. Now she was terrified.

As the water broke around her head, the sun shone down through the trees and she heard a grunting sound as she was dragged up and out of the water. Whoever had pulled her up fell back with a thud and let out a choked sigh. Isabella covered her eyes from the brightness and coughed. Wearily she turned to see who was there. Dripping wet and smiling ear to ear, her father sat in the grass a few feet from her.

"You did it," he said breathlessly, eyes shining in the sun. "But promise me something."

Relief flooded through her at the sight of her father sitting there. Gone was the fire, gone was their camp, the truck, the old towel—which, honestly, she kind of wished she had—and in their place was an emerald pool with a peacefully trickling waterfall. The water in the pool was barely a foot deep all the way to the stone edge. "What's that?" she asked.

"Never try that when I'm not there."

She looked back at the innocuous waterfall and the small, sparkling, emerald pool. "Don't worry. Remember, I hate water."

FOUR

I still don't understand why I couldn't just try to fall asleep and go in like last time?" Isabella asked after she had dried off by sitting in the sun at the foot of the waterfall.

"You can't control where you show up when you do that."

"But I did last time?"

"You did?" Her father cocked his head to the side and smiled. "So you ended up right next to your brother?"

"Well, no," she conceded, "I ended up in some sort of trap."

"A dream trap," he said with a nod, "set up by the shadows to catch people and turn them into shadows too. Was that where you were planning on ending up?"

"Well, no. But—"

"Exactly." He patted her on the shoulder. "But now you're here." He swept his arm out toward a field with a small log cabin built at the edge of a forest. An empty stable and corral were on one side of the cabin and a stack of chopped wood on the other. Grazing peacefully along the edge of the field was a small herd of deer, one of which had large antlers and stood watching them warily. "Come on," he said as he grabbed her hand, "I'll show you around."

The cabin had been built by her great-grandfather, her father explained as they walked around the outside. Inside was easily twice as large as it was on the outside, a trick of the dream world. They entered a great room through the front door. The plush furnishings looked enough to comfortably seat at least twelve and were centered around a massive stone fireplace. Looking up, Isabella saw a towering cathedral ceiling that disappeared into a darkness so deep the burning candles couldn't penetrate; ornate support beams spanned the width, and five equally ornate doors lead off of the main room.

"This is yours?"

"Well, it's our family's. My Farfar built the cabin, but this has been our family's land and training ground in the dream world for generations," her father explained as they settled into the couches. "Though I can't tell you how many, Farfar was never clear on that. He explained that it was built like the shadows build their dream traps, but just without the trap part. I've never been able to figure out how he really did it, but unless it burns down, I don't think I'll ever need to. Even then, most weavers don't have a home base like this. They have training grounds in the capital that most of us use."

"Why didn't you bring me there then?"

He looked around as if worried someone was listening, concern washing momentarily across his face before he smiled and shrugged. "I like it here. So"—he clapped his hands and rubbed them together as if he were cold—"speaking of training, let's get to it. First thing, we go outside and try to contact your companion. Once you contact them, we can get started."

Isabella's heart beat faster as they walked out the front door. The last time she had spoken to Kimi, they had been on better terms, but Kimi had said more than once that she was done with Isabella. Honestly, Isabella couldn't blame her for it either; she had been selfish and cruel toward the poor little fox, but that was because of several misunderstandings. Kimi had to forgive her. If not, she'd become what Finn, a hunter she'd met her first time in the dream world, had called a stalker. She didn't want to work for the shadows, but if Kimi didn't forgive her, that's just what would happen. Or at least that's what Finn had told her would happen.

"What happens if my companion doesn't come?"

"I'm sure it'll come," her father said, dismissing her concerns. She hadn't told him how she'd treated Kimi. As a matter of fact, she kept a lot of that trip a secret from him. There were parts that she wasn't proud of and, honestly, she was afraid if he knew how close she'd come to failing then he wouldn't let her come back. "Based on what you told me, you never even ran into them. I'm surprised really, most weavers meet them almost immediately."

"Dad..." Isabella looked at the grass surrounding them and fidgeted.

"Maybe Vígolfr scared them away." He chuckled at some unshared memory. "Wouldn't be the first time."

"Dad."

"I bet you were a little surprised at him," he said with another chuckle. "When I first met him, he was just a small pup. Oh, we had some fun then—"

"Dad." Isabella took a deep breath and looked up at him, but he was looking off at the forest's edge.

"There was this one time when I was first training with Farfar." He laughed in a way that was unfamiliar to Isabella. For a moment, she feared that this was one of those dream traps. However, the laugh was still distinctly him, just freer than she'd seen at home. "He could barely see above the grass, and he was just bounding through and ran right into this old tree stump. He sat down on his hind legs and shook his head, then glared at the stump like it had insulted him by being there."

"Dad, I've already met her," she blurted out as he took a breath to continue his story. Isabella felt her stomach drop into her knees as she waited for her father's response. It took a moment for her words to hit him, but as they did, they didn't dampen his excitement.

"Great!" He turned to her and smiled. "That makes this easier. What's her name? Where is she? They don't tend to stay away long when you're new here." He looked up in the air and then scanned the edge of the forest. "So, what are we looking for? Knowing you, I'm sure it's a bear or something fierce like you."

Collapsing to the grass, Isabella buried her face in her hands. She knew how badly she'd messed everything up last time. Her father's hand on her shoulder didn't give her the comfort he seemed to hope it would. Instead of leaning into it, Isabella shrugged him off and took a moment to regain her composure. Pushing the heels of her hands into her eyes, she willed the tears away and with a ragged breath, stood up, turning toward her father and lifting her chin to look him in the eye. For his part, he watched and gave her the space needed. He was always good at knowing when she needed space.

"It's Kimi, she's not another hunter I found," Isabella started, her voice quivering slightly, "she is a small red fox. I didn't told you before because"— she took a deep breath and clenched her hands in fists— "Because things didn't go very well. She washed her hands—er, her paws, I guess it would be—of me. We got into a fight because I thought she was keeping me away from Tucker."

"That's crazy—" he began, but she interrupted him.

"I know that now." She examined her fingernails to avoid the disappointment that on her father's face. "But at the time, I was convinced that she was working against me. Finn, I told you about him and his hunters, right?" He nodded. "Well, Finn explained everything to me. She'd bit me because she was trying to rescue me like she did time after time when the shadows were surrounding me. When I left, she was injured"—Isabella fought back tears again—"and I left her. I don't think she's going to come."

"I know," he said smiling at her, "Vígolfr told me. I was just wondering when you were going to let me know."

"But—"

"Turn around, Izzy." He turned her and pointed at the waterfall she had come through to get here. "You see that beautiful waterfall?" It was her turn to nod. "That was you." He moved around in front of her and looked into her eyes. "That wasn't there before. That used to just be a stone cliffside. You made your entrance. If Kimi had given up on you, well, that wouldn't be there. Plain and simple."

"Are you sure?"

"Positive." He put his hands reassuringly on both of her shoulders and gave them a firm pat. "So let's give her a call and see what her side of the story is."

"How do I—"

"Just close your eyes and call her name. Simple as that."

Isabella smiled; she'd tried to get back into the dream world several times over the past few months, but she'd been unable to. Every time she thought about Kimi, there seemed to be a hole in her heart and an ache that just wouldn't go away. Now her heart fluttered at the thought of seeing her again. Taking a deep breath, Isabella closed her eyes. "Kimi," she called. She swelled with hope, but still something nagged at her, the same urgency she'd felt when she was trying to come into the dream world in the first place.

The two stood in the field watching the grass around them, waiting for the telltale signs that a small animal was coming through. As the light breeze caused the grass to sway evenly across the field, Isabella's heart sank. She closed her eyes and tried again, louder this time, the urgency that she felt pulling at her coming through in her voice. Still nothing. After a third and fourth try, she turned to her father. His image blurred with the gathering tears, but she bit her lip to keep them from falling. He wasn't looking at her. Instead, he was squinting off into the distance.

"I don't think she's coming." Isabella could feel the hollowness that she'd felt in the forest all those months ago. "This was a mistake."

"Hold on," her father said, a smirk coming to his face beneath his squinting eyes. "What's that out there?" He pointed out in the distance.

Although still too far away to tell for sure, Isabella thought she could see what her father was pointing at. A distant section of grass swayed opposite to the breeze, rustling in a meandering line from the forest's edge toward Isabella and her father. Isabella felt uneasy and her hand moved toward the jeweled hilt of her dagger. She felt the cool gems beneath her fingers and quickly pulled her hand away. If Kimi came through the grass, Isabella didn't want the little fox to think that she wanted to hurt her.

"See"—her father's posture relaxed as he watched the movement of the grass—"nothing to worry about."

The urgency still pulled at Isabella. "Okay, but when she shows up, don't move too quickly. She was really skittish the first time I met her."

"Nonsense!" He rolled his eyes at her. "Companions play games sometimes, but they are not skittish. They are good judges of character," he added, "so if she was skittish the first time you met, there must have been something nasty nearby, like a shadow or a nightmare or something."

Isabella wanted to ask what a nightmare was, but before she could, the grass in front of them waved erratically. A small red squirrel emerged, almost bumping into their feet as it gulped down air like it was drowning. Isabella tried, unsuccessfully, to hide her disappointment that it wasn't Kimi who'd come. The squirrel rested its tiny hand on Isabella's pink boot and held the other one up as if it were asking for a moment to catch its breath. True to its name, the squirrel's fur was a rich reddish-brown, and it sat with its tail running closely up its back until about halfway up, when it made a perfect arc back toward the ground. The fur on the tail's upper side splayed out and looked almost white in the sun, while the underside darkened to nearly black. The fur along its chest and around the nose was white though clearly dirtied from its journey. The ears drew Isabella's attention the most because they were topped with wispy tufts of fur, alternating between red and black. Its eyes were as black as night, but they held an intelligence that reminded her of Kimi.

"That doesn't look like a fox." Her father raised an eyebrow and bent down closer to the squirrel. He waited as its breathing slowed to normal, or at least what Isabella thought normal was for a squirrel, before asking, "So, what can I do for you?"

"Are you Allan Shaw?" The voice was small but sure. It took Isabella a few moments to realize that it was actually the squirrel talking to them.

"Sure thing." He held his hand out and the squirrel hopped into it. He stood up and motioned toward Isabella. "This is my daughter, Izzy. What can we do for you?"

"I'm Skia," the squirrel said, bowing down in her father's palm. "My weaver, Wesley, told me to find you."

Her father scrunched up his face and looked up and to the left. "I'm at a bit of a loss here. I'm sorry," he said, "but I can't remember a weaver named Wesley, nor you, I'm afraid."

"We only met once," Skia said, smoothing out the long hair that sprouted from his ears. "Wesley is a chronicler for the council. He took a report from you years ago about a promising boy lost to the shadows. I think he became a hunter or something."

Recognition lit her father's face. "Oh! Scrawny, bookish kid? With glasses?"

"You could describe him like that." Skia brushed something from his nose before continuing, "I'd prefer the intelligent gentleman."

"I'm sorry," her father chuckled good-naturedly, "of course. Though I don't remember seeing you."

"That beast of yours looked hungry, so I kept to the shadows."

"Vîgolfr's completely harmless."

"From your reputation, I respectfully doubt that."

Isabella's father raised both eyebrows and then with a smile, but no further explanation, added, "I suppose you have a point. So, again, what can we do for you?"

"I'm not sure about your daughter, but Wesley needs your help. He's trapped in the northern territory."

"That's on the other side of the capital. Surely there was someone closer that could help."

"He was very clear in his instructions that I find you specifically."

"Well." Isabella's father turned to her. "What do you say, baby girl? Up for a trip to the north?"

Before Isabella could answer, a voice from behind interrupted them, "No time."

When she turned around, Isabella saw the familiar shape of the white wolf sulking through the grass. Isabella had known his guttural voice in an instant.

"Vígolfr," her father called out, "it's about time you stopped over to see me. I've been here for hours already."

Isabella wasn't sure if her father was exaggerating the amount of time they'd been in the dream world. She couldn't get a grasp on it. It hadn't felt like hours since coming through the waterfall, but the had thoroughly dried and toured the expansive cabin, including the library. Realizing her mind was wandering, Isabella brought her attention back to her father and Vígolfr, the latter of whom was talking about a crisis in the south that required her father's immediate attention.

"I'm sorry, Skia," he said, setting the red squirrel back down in the grass, "I need to take care of this. Izzy, it's too dangerous for you to come, but you'll be safe here. Take a look around, maybe read some of the books in the library, and I'll be back after we take care of this."

"But Mr. Shaw," Skia insisted, "I assure you Wesley is in most desperate need."

Vígolfr let out a low growl before turning to Izzy's father. "It's poised to take the whole town of denizens. I'm afraid the bookworm will have to wait."

"I knew you'd remember them. I still can't place the kid's face," her father said, then turned to kiss Isabella on the top of the head. "I mean it, Izzy, stay here. It's dangerous out there." Without waiting for an answer, he spun quickly on his toes. He sprinted off behind Vígolfr, leaving both Izzy and Skia to watch dumbly as they disappeared past the waterfall.

Isabella looked down at the little red squirrel, still shaking from its close encounter with the white wolf, and said, "If he can't help, I will. Just lead me to him."

FIVE

It took the better part of an hour—at least what Isabella thought was an hour—to get the supplies for their journey to the capitol from the cabin. It didn't help that she'd been there all of a few minutes before her father had literally run off. Still, the pantry was surprisingly well-stocked with jerky, dried fruit, nuts, and some other odds and ends. Gathering her pack, its contents now dry after nearly drowning, she began to shove stuff into it. Skia was pacing back and forth along one of the beams overhead. He'd been on edge since her father had run off, but to be honest, he'd been on edge since he showed up. He'd scurried up into the rafters almost as soon as he'd come inside and jumped down just as Isabella put on her pack to begin their walk to the capitol.

"Are you sure you can do this?" Skia asked, perched on the back of one of the leather couches. "I mean, without your companion?"

"Your person needs help, right?"

"Wesley," he said quickly.

"Right"—she shrugged dismissively—"he needs help?"

"But I was supposed to bring your father." Skia scurried down to the arm of the couch and back up again.

"Well," Isabella said as she held her hand out for the squirrel to jump onto, "you've got me."

He hesitated until a banging on the door made both of them jump. Skia scurried up Isabella's arm and hid under her hair. It felt strange to have the little claws pricking into her neck, and she winced every time he moved.

"Do you mind?" she snapped, rolling her shoulders. "Your claws are digging into my neck." He moved onto her hood but stayed under her hair. "Better."

He trembled slightly as she walked to the door. "Are you sure this is a good idea?"

Another knock at the door. "If someone is knocking, it's important to answer the door. It's only polite."

"But what if the person on the other side is less than polite."

"You worry too much," Isabella said, throwing the door open.

On the other stood a thin woman with long red hair wearing a sweater with a giant rainbow and a unicorn galloping across it. The shoulders and forearms were reinforced with leather. Across her chest was a bandoleer with six knife handles sticking out in front. On her shoulder, looking imperiously into the room, was a deep brown hawk, its head turning side to side, eyes sharp and intelligent.

"Wren!" Izzy shouted, making Skia start behind her. She threw her arms around the severe-looking woman as if they were old friends; Wren stiffened at the show of affection. "I haven't seen you in months."

"And I suppose I'm not to be spoken to then," the droll voice of the hawk answered.

"I'm sorry." Isabella quickly backed up. "Mentu, it's good to see you again." She bowed slightly as a joke to the overly formal animal.

"Finally," he said, exasperation clear in his voice, "one of the Shaw's has some propriety. Your father is entirely too informal for my taste."

"Enough out of you, you old fuddy-duddy." Wren looked askew at Mentu. "Izzy," she said with a curt nod in greeting, and suddenly Isabella could feel the heat creeping up her cheeks and began to feel very small. "Is Allan home?"

"Why?"

"There's a problem to the south. A band of renegades has taken control of one of the towns under the capitol's protection. The council needs him and Vígolfr there to negotiate."

"Oh, Vígolfr came by not long ago and they headed south, so maybe they're already on their way."

Wren nodded at the backpack on Isabella's shoulders. "Where are you going?"

"Skia needed help rescuing his weaver."

"No." Wren reached in and took the backpack from Isabella's shoulders, throwing it onto one of the couches. "Too dangerous."

"But he needs help," Isabella replied as she tried, unsuccessfully, to coax Skia off her shoulder. "He came here looking for my dad."

"This isn't some lost wanderer we're talking about here." She looked around Isabella into the room behind her. "This is a trained Dreamweaver. If he's trapped somewhere, he's going to need more than a little girl to rescue him." Wren shifted her focus to the squirrel. "Skia, is it?" she asked, causing the squirrel to shiver. "You should know better. Besides, where's Kimi? You weren't thinking of going off without her, were you?"

Isabella mumbled an answer under her breath, but she couldn't meet Wren's eyes.

"What did you say?"

"I don't know where she is."

"Then definitely not." Wren gently pushed Isabella into the cabin. "You are staying here. And Skia," she said, her voice holding a clear warning, "if I hear that you and Isabella headed out together to save your weaver, I swear I will feed you to Mentu. I'm serious, you two. It's safe here; this cabin has always been a haven for your family and their trainees. Stay here, stay safe." With that, Wren twirled around and Mentu screeched and took to wing. Wren looked back over her shoulder. "I'm serious. I have a feeling more is going on here than it seems, and Allan would kill me if I let you go." With that, she closed the door and was gone.

Isabella went over to the couch and grabbed her bag.

"What are you doing?" Skia asked. "You heard that scary woman; if we leave, she'll feed me to that hawk of hers."

"She didn't mean that," Isabella said. At least, she thought Wren hadn't meant it.

"You don't know Wren very well then." He climbed off Izzy's shoulder and onto the back of the couch.

Isabella paused, one hand on the strap of her backpack, and considered what Wren had said before leaving. If Wesley wasn't just some bookish guy like her father had made it sound, but instead a weaver like her father or Wren, she wasn't sure there really was anything that she could do for him. "What will you do?"

Skia stood on his hind legs and reached a paw out to Isabella. "I'll get help in the capitol. There are other weavers there like your father, none quite as good, but..." He let his already small voice trail off.

"I can help." Isabella was less sure the more she said it. Even to her own ears, she sounded like a child begging to be treated like a grown-up.

"No," Skia sounded dejected but resolute, "Wren is right. It's too dangerous. Thank you for the offer, Isabella Shaw, but I will find another weaver. You should find your companion ... Kimi, was it?"

"Yeah." Isabella looked off, worry bubbling up inside of her. Something was wrong. She hadn't been able to shake the feeling of urgency that resurfaced when she tried calling for Kimi. At first, she thought it was just Skia, but now she wasn't so sure. "She's a red fox. Maybe you've seen her?"

Skia shivered. "No, I haven't," he said, then added, "What is it about you Shaws and your predators. Why couldn't, just once, one of you connect to one of those nice deer that are always wandering in the fields?"

Isabella didn't know how to answer that question, so she just shrugged and set her bag back down on the couch. They said their goodbyes, then she watched as Skia pushed open one of the windows and hopped out into the long grass. In the distance, she could see Mentu, or who she assumed was Mentu, circling. Seeing the squirrel leave alone, the hawk gave a screech and veered off in the direction her father had gone.

Alone in the cabin, Isabella took a deep breath and dropped down hard into one of the overstuffed chairs. Burying her face in her hands, she screamed in frustration. She was not a kid. She'd survived this place before, and she didn't need to be protected. She thought back to rescuing of her brother, facing off against the shadow that was disguised as her father in the dream trap. There were tells, things that were just slightly off. She knew how to react to those things, but here, now, things weren't off. They were just different. It made sense that her father wanted her protected, and it seemed everyone needed him. So here she was, on a camping trip with her father instead of hanging out with Evan, and now her father had bailed.

After a while of staring at the ceiling brooding over the unfairness of life, Izzy got up and wandered the cabin, eventually ending up in the library like her father had suggested. The fact that there was even a library in this cabin didn't make sense. Every time she tried to read anything in her dreams, she never could as the words had been rendered indecipherable scribbles; that's how she'd known about the last dream trap. She'd Googled why once, and found something about the creative side of the brain ruling when dreaming while the logic side that made sense of letters was dormant or resting. Wandering around, she ran her fingers along the spines of the old books that filled the shelves. The corner of the room was a series of cubbies, each with a rolled-up piece of paper sticking partway out.

Walking over and hoping there would be some pictures to look at, Isabella pulled one of the rolls out of its cubby. She placed it on a nearby table and unrolled it, revealing a hand-drawn illustration of the cabin that she was in with an older man and a young boy standing in front of it. She assumed that it was something her great-grandfather had done. Her own grandfather had been a great artist when he'd been alive, but since he was never a weaver, he'd never have seen this cabin. She knew her own father hadn't drawn it, so it must have been something his grandfather, Farfar, had done.

She rolled up the paper and put it back into the cubby, pulling out the roll under it. But when she unrolled that paper, Isabella's breath caught. She was staring at a map. Tucking one corner under the table lamp, she reached behind her and grabbed a statue of a bear cub, setting it on the diagonal to hold the map flat.

Looking at it, Isabella could only assume that it was a map of the dream world. In the center of the map was a huge city. The label on it clearly read The Capitol. She scanned other areas of the map, hoping to find something that she recognized, but she was unsuccessful. When she was about to give up and put the map away, she moved the bear, revealing a small cabin drawn on with pencil, and a picture of a buck with large antlers. She squinted for a closer look and then noticed the placement of the cabin on the map, the curve of the woods. It had to be the cabin she was in. She traced her finger south. The land there was expansive and varied. Towns with names like Banos, Loja, Gaziantep, and Hajrah next to names that were more familiar to her, like Marble Falls. Tracing to the north brought more towns. She looked to see if there was anything else she was missing when the realization hit her.

Putting the bear back onto the map, Isabella walked over to the bookshelves. The titles of the books were written clearly on the spine: *Maps of the Old World; Discovering Your Lineage; What to do About Walkers; Powers and Myths: Dreamweavers; Dream Traps and Nightmares.* The list went on. Isabella scanned the titles, butterflies in her stomach as she read each of the names out loud as if to prove to herself that she could. She didn't know why, but here she could read. She reminded herself to ask her father about it later, but at least now she had something to do.

The titles seemed to focus on anything and everything she could think. One title in particular had caught her attention. She walked back to the book and pulled it off the shelf. *Powers and Myths: Dreamweavers* seemed to be the most promising of the titles and a good enough place to start as any. After some of the stories Finn had told her about what weavers could do, she figured there could be some real answers in here, and since she was here to train anyway, she might as well start now.

Isabella tried to concentrate as she flipped through the book, but the nagging urgency kept itching in the back of her mind and she could only manage to read the chapter titles before getting distracted. It wasn't until she caught the title "Losing Your Companion" that she was able to focus. Isabella read the first few pages of the chapter and then slammed the book closed, tears welling up in her eyes.

She grabbed the map from the table, rolled it up, and brought both the book and the map out to the great room. She tore open her bag and shoved both the items in, tossing an extra sweater onto the couch to make room. She tore a slip of paper off a pad on the counter and grabbed a pencil next to it. She scrawled a note to her father and set the pencil down. She looked at the note on the counter, then grabbed the pencil again and put it in her bag with everything else. She gave the cabin one last look before slinging her bag over her shoulder, walking out the door and closing it behind her.

SIX

After hiking up a hill for the better part of the afternoon, Isabella had the map spread out on a fallen tree, weighed down by two small rocks. She looked between the picture on the map and the valley laid out below her. The images on the map didn't make any sense with what she was seeing, and it didn't help that she couldn't even figure out what direction she was heading in. The wind picked up and, grabbing a corner of the map, flipped one of her rocks to the ground, causing the map to threaten flight. Isabella scrambled to catch it before it sailed off the mountain and into the valley. With an exasperated grunt, she rolled the map back up and shoved it into her pack.

This was crazy, Isabella thought to herself. She was crazy for thinking she could do this. Walking off into the woods to help a talking squirrel who didn't even want her help. Folding her arms against the cooling temperatures, Isabella watched the sun begin to touch the tops of the trees on the other side of the valley. Somewhere out there was a weaver who was trapped, his companion desperately seeking help. Somewhere, Finn and the other hunters were protecting the denizens. Her father and Wren were off saving the world, and somewhere else was Kimi doing whatever Kimi was doing. But not Izzy, she thought ruefully. *Isabella is standing on a mountaintop in the cold wind, incapable of even helping herself.* She picked up a stone and threw it out into the valley. This sucked. That was the best she could say about it. It just sucked. She wanted to be a Dreamweaver. Her father had told her so many stories about his time weaving, but she couldn't even help herself off a mountain.

A noise on the trail she'd just come from pulled her out of the wallow of self-pity she'd been patiently crafting. Instincts kicked in and she moved, crouching down in a low bush near the side of the clearing she'd stopped in to check the map. Without taking her eyes off the path, she unbuckled the knife from its sheath and drew it about half an inch in preparation.

The noise was awkward, like someone flailing their way through the undergrowth. She knew from experience that the shadows were mostly silent as they floated through the forest. The noise didn't sound like any animal she knew, except maybe a bear, but it didn't sound big enough for a bear.

She took two deep breaths to steady her heart as it threatened to leap from her throat. With each breath, she felt the world come into sharper focus. The wind through the branches rustled the leaves of the trees while a bird called out in the distance. Then there was the pounding of two feet against the packed dirt and stone, the sound of gravel and a grunt as whoever it was overbalanced on the loose rocks of the path. Isabella was sure it was a person, but she wasn't ready to give up her cover just yet.

A young girl burst into the clearing, looking over her left shoulder. She paused in the clearing, eyes darting around for someplace to hide as she leaned on her knees panting, the sweat dripping off her forehead onto the dry dirt at her feet. She looked to be about sixteen or so, with short, dark hair matted against the side of her face and her thick-rimmed glasses barely staying on her nose. Isabella watched as the girl slowly caught her breath and spared a moment to look over the valley at the setting sun. The colors had just begun to glow in the distance and looking at it seemed to calm the terror in her eyes for a moment while she stood wrapped in its beauty.

"If light is in your heart," the girl said to herself, "you will find your way home." Then she turned her back to the setting sun and surveyed the scenery again. She looked at the bush Isabella was crouched in and, for a moment, Isabella thought the girl had seen her. The moment passed and the girl's body tensed seconds before Izzy sensed an intense feeling of anger and resentment begin to permeate the clearing, the temperature dropping further.

After stopping like a deer on the roadside, the girl swung away from Izzy's hiding place and hurried further down the trail. The feelings of anger and resentment grew more potent, and Isabella knew why the girl was running. She didn't know what the girl saw or where she thought she was—her father had told her that dreamers experience the dream world differently, seeing images from their own subconscious—but whatever this girl saw, Isabella knew what was truly after her even before the shadowy figure flowed into the clearing. It flinched in the sunset and quickly flowed down the same path the girl had taken. As it passed, Isabella felt the waning of the resentment but the anger lingered, like an afterimage in negative.

As the feelings of anger began to dissipate, Isabella let out the breath she hadn't realized she was holding and relaxed her shoulders. She'd almost forgot how overpowering the feelings flowing from the shadows were. Now that it was gone, Izzy thought of the girl it was chasing. She had no idea what she was up against. In her dream, this darkness could be anything, but there was one thing Isabella was sure of: if it caught her, there wouldn't be anything she could do. That thought got her moving moments before a scream ripped through the otherwise silent air.

Careful to try to keep the element of surprise, Isabella stepped into the clearing and drew her dagger. The sun was barely above the treetops as Isabella moved across the clearing and onto the path already swathed in the evening's drawing shadows. Although she was confident it was going to be a huge mistake, like everything else she'd done since coming into the dream world, Isabella couldn't leave this girl defenseless against a shadow. Even if she wasn't a Dreamweaver, she should help. Finn would, and he didn't even know what was at stake. Isabella moved down the path quickly. She wasn't as quiet as Finn, but she'd been hiking with her family since she was three years old, so she knew how to move quickly—even if not so quietly—on a trail.

Before long, she began to feel the anger swell up again around her as if the trees themselves would take up arms and start batting at her, like the Whomping Willow from *Harry Potter*. What was up ahead, she knew, was far worse than that. The emotions began to overwhelm her as she turned the corner in time to see a shadow looming over the dimmed figure of the girl. The shadow was not as big as the ones that had formed the shadow congress, but it was still at least six feet tall and had one arm raised above its head, readying to strike the cowering girl beneath it. There was no time to think through her plan, so Isabella did the first thing she could think of.

"Hey!" she called out to the shadow. "You leave her alone."

The full force of the shadow's emotions flooded toward her as it turned and began to glide in her direction. With the element of surprise gone, Isabella dropped her weight and flipped the knife, pommel side up, in her hand. It wasn't ideal, but better this thing come toward her than the defenseless girl. As the shadow approached, a low sound emanated from it, almost a vibration. Isabella raised her dagger defensively; the yellow jewel in the pommel caught a stray ray of light and seemed to glow. The shadow raised its wispy arm to block the light, but it was like trying to cover a window with a sheer curtain, and the light from her dagger pierced the shadow all the way through. With a painful cry and an increasing wave of resentment, the shadow turned from both girls and fled deeper into the forest.

Keeping a wary eye on the edges of the woods, Isabella sheathed her dagger and crouched next to the girl. "Come on," she said, reaching out a hand to help the girl to her feet, "let's get back to the clearing. There'll be more light there. It won't last, and that thing will probably be back once the sun sets, but at least we can figure out how to get out of here."

"Thank you," the girl replied. There was a look of confused recognition on her face, but she didn't reach for Izzy's hand. Instead, she pushed up from the ground with her left arm, keeping her right arm tucked tightly to her side.

Isabella knew that the girl saw someone else, someone she thought she recognized and trusted enough to follow. Reaching out again, she grabbed under the girl's arm to help her up. When Isabella touched the girl, the world around her wavered like heat radiating off the road in the summer. In its place, a different world settled in her mind, one of sadness and destruction. A few other people stood milling around. They were dressed in jeans and t-shirts, similar to the girl, but they each held a gun pointed away into the woods. On the ground next to where the girl had fallen lay a headless corpse in a dirty, blood-smeared suit. Its head lay a few feet away, eyes the color of cottage cheese staring at the sky.

"Thank you again," the girl said, leaning into Isabella's help. "Do I know you?"

"I don't think so." Isabella looked around, trying to get her bearings. Much of the surroundings looked the same as before, except for the people and the decapitated corpse, of course. This must be the girl's dream, she thought to herself, then aloud she added, "I'm Isabella, but everyone calls me Izzy."

"Rumi. Glad you came by when you did. I would have been toast." She motioned with her head to the corpse on the ground. "Damn walker got the drop on us. Where'd you learn to fight like that?"

Isabella was playing catchup, but she thought she had all the pieces she needed. She didn't feel the weight of her knife on her belt and, glancing around her, she saw a thin sword lying on the ground. The blade was ornate and curved and glinted in the setting sun. She didn't recognize it, but the handle was clearly her knife's handle. "You good to stand for a second?" she asked.

"Sure." Rumi shifted her weight. She was clearly worn out from the run up the path, and this strange dream seemed to be taking a toll on her.

Isabella let go of Rumi to bend down and pick up the strange sword. When she removed her hand from Rumi's arm, the world began to become wavy again, and she almost lost her balance. When her vision cleared, Isabella looked down at her knife, sitting in the leaves at her feet. Gone was the decapitated body of what she assumed was part of some zombie nightmare Rumi was having. Gone were the men with guns. It was just Rumi and Isabella standing on a dirt path in the woods.

Rumi flinched toward Izzy. "You might want to hurry up."

Quickly, Izzy crouched down and picked up her dagger, waiting for another shadow to come from the forest. After a moment of nothing happening, she relaxed her stance but kept the blade ready.

"We're moving out," Rumi said, some strength and authority to her voice, the voice of a leader.

When Isabella reached out and touched the girl, the world shifted again. The sound of gunfire was in her ears, punctuated by a low moaning. The weight in her hand was different. Instead of the dagger that Ajay had given her, she held the sword by her side.

Together Isabella and Rumi limped to the clearing at the top of the mountain. The valley looked utterly different in Rumi's dream. Instead of the forest below them, a ruined city smoldered, the smoke of forgotten fires obscuring the colors of the sky. Up here, Rumi seemed to relax a little. Looking around, Isabella could see why. They were surrounded by more people with guns and other people milled about or climbed up and down ladders descending from the trees.

To test her theory, she helped Rumi to sit down on the rocks and then let go of her arm and stood to admire the view. The transition was less disorienting but, as expected, she was looking out over a pristine forest once her vision cleared. No smoke, no burning city, just the reds and oranges of a setting sun painted across the sky. She sat down next to Rumi and rested a hand on the girl's knee. "It's nice up here," she said.

"Thanks," Rumi replied, some pride in her voice, "we set this up a month or so ago. The ladders help. These things are too clumsy to climb them, so we're mostly safe up there, but I like to come down here to watch these sunsets. There's something normal about sitting on the ground watching another day go by. I just can't believe I was stupid enough to not see that damn walker."

Isabella wasn't sure what to make of everything, so she sat in silence and enjoyed the gathering colors through the smoke.

SEVEN

H e got me, you know?" Rumi said as they sat on the mountain, looking over the smoke rising from the city below. "Just like they got my hometown. Soon, I'll be just as ruined as that infested pit smoldering down there."

"Let me see." Isabella knelt in front of Rumi to get a better look, leaning on the girl's leg to keep contact.

Rumi moved her left hand away from her side and Isabella could see teeth marks on her flesh. There was some blood, but the most disturbing part was the tissue around the bite that had turned a pale gray color. She knew this was just the girl's dream and that in reality she was laying in a bed somewhere, safe and sound. Isabella reached out to touch the wound, curious if she would feel the dying skin or the girl's actual healthy skin.

"Careful," Rumi warned, flinching away from Izzy's touch. "I don't want you to get infected too."

The movement was enough to off-balance Izzy, who reached back to keep from falling over. Isabella shifted back into the dream world when the touch broke and saw the actual wound for the first time. Four clear lines of darkness corrupted the exposed flesh along Rumi's ribs. Isabella rushed over to her pack and rifled through it for a first aid kit to get some antiseptic cream, hoping it could stop the spreading infection. Pushing the book aside, she rummaged through the granola bars and jerky she'd brought but didn't see the first aid kit.

She'd set it on the bathroom counter before leaving her house—her real home—to go camping with her father, but Tucker had to go potty and she was shooed out of the bathroom before she was able to pack it. She must have left it at home. Cursing herself for the careless mistake, she switched gears. When Kimi had been hit by a shadow, they'd used honey to slow the infection. She wouldn't have time to smoke the bees this time. The tendrils of shadow were already creeping under Rumi's skin and the trees up here were low, not the type bees tended to use.

"I can't believe I was so stupid," Rumi muttered to the air, Isabella forgotten. She seemed to be talking to someone else in her dream, someone in her own subconscious. "You told me not to go in there, but I did anyway. I know I put everything at risk. I'm the one who got bit, so don't give me your crap."

Isabella could hear the regret in Rumi's voice; it was almost palpable as the temperature began to drop in the clearing. At first, she thought the shadow had returned, but the feeling came from the clearing, not the woods. Rumi looked strange, too, like she was fading. For a moment, Isabella hoped that Rumi would just fade away and wake up in her own bed, but something in the back of her mind told her that wasn't likely.

"Don't yell at me," Rumi screamed to the air, "I did my best." Clearly, someone from her dream was talking to her, blaming her for getting attacked.

Isabella grabbed a handful of leaves and dirt from under one of the trees and hurried over to Rumi. She placed her hand on the girl's shoulder and rode the wave back into the dream. People were standing around them again. They were angry, yelling at the girl about how she had put them all at risk. Isabella didn't know if this would work, and she was sure it wasn't going to save the girl's life, but she wanted to do something to at least stop her from being surrounded by so much anger. "I've got it," Isabella said, setting the leaves down next to Rumi. "The rest of you get back on patrol." She tried to sound authoritative, like Rumi had, but ended up just sounding as scared as she felt inside.

"Who are you to tell us what to do, little girl," one of the rougher-looking men said, taking a menacing step toward them.

"You heard her." Rumi's voice sounded tired, the authoritative edge Izzy had heard gone now. "Make sure you got the rest of them before they get to the camp. Remember how bad it was last time."

He mumbled something in response, but the group that had been standing around them dispersed, leaving them alone with the sounds of people going about their daily lives in the trees behind them.

"Were you with us when the hoard attacked?"

"I was." Isabella didn't know what story she was playing into, so she tried to be vague. "I joined you just before. I was lost, and you took me in."

"Right." Rumi still looked confused but didn't argue. She moved her hand and winced.

"Does it hurt?"

"What do you think? I got bit. Of course, it hurts."

"This should help with the pain." Isabella looked next to Rumi where she'd put the dirt and leaves; instead, there was an open first aid kit, complete with antiseptic cream and gauze wrap. She moved to grab the supplies, but as soon as she was no longer touching Rumi, they shifted back into the pile of leaves and dirt they actually were. She picked them up anyway and placed them on Rumi's blackening side. A dark-gray mist seemed to rise as the leaves touched her. "How's that?"

"Better." She looked at Isabella and smiled weakly. "Thank you." Then she turned to the sunset and fell silent. Her breathing labored as the black tendrils wound from her wound over her shoulder and onto her neck.

Isabella watched in horror. There was nothing to be done, or at least there was nothing more she could do. If she had moved quicker, if she hadn't hidden when Rumi first came up the path, if she had cared more about helping than keeping the element of surprise, then maybe she could have done something. Now, she could just watch as the shadows took this innocent girl. Somewhere on the other side of this girl's closed eyes, there was someone who loved her, someone who didn't know that she would not wake up. They would never have a chance to say goodbye, never hug their daughter again.

"I can't feel my arm." The words came between gasps of air.

"Don't worry," Isabella said, trying to keep her quivering voice steady, "that's normal." She inhaled slowly, fighting the tightness in the back of her throat. "You'll be back to doing your thing by morning."

"That's good." Rumi's voice was beginning to slur and her gasps became more like wheezing. "My mother asked me to finish helping her fix the car in the morning, so I'll need that arm."

"You'll have it," Isabella's voice broke a little, and she cleared her throat to cover it, "I promise."

"I'm getting tired," she said, "but I want to see this sunset. It's why I'm up here."

"I got you." Isabella shifted herself so Rumi could lean against her and still see the setting sun. When Rumi weight was on her, the scene shifted back and the tendrils of smoke rose more strongly against the sky. The leaves and dirt were now bandages wrapped neatly around Rumi's ribs and chest, but even in this illusion Isabella could see the black tendrils of the infection snaking out from under the bandage. "I'm here." She wasn't sure why she said it, but this girl, this stranger, needed to know she wasn't alone.

"Thank you, Izzy." More wheezing.

They sat silently for a few minutes and Izzy watched Rumi's chest rise and fall as the sun dipped below the horizon, blasting the last of its rays in a dramatic effusion through the smoke and sky. Rumi shifted a little and pulled something from her front pocket. "Here," she said, placing a round, metal object in Isabella's hand. "I want you to have this."

"No"—Isabella tried to hand it back to her—"you're going to need it. You'll be okay."

Rumi laughed weakly and pushed Isabella's fingers closed around the object. Pulling her hand away, the scene shifted in front of Isabella again to the pristine hillside and valley below. "My uncle gave me this when I was a kid," Rumi said before pausing and wheezing in another labored breath. "He said to use it if I'm ever lost." She closed her eyes and exhaled.

Isabella opened her hand and saw an old metal compass with a delicate filigree pattern flowing over the outside edge of the case. Tears gathered behind her eyes. She tried to say thank you, but the words caught in the back of her throat. Not wanting her to be alone, Isabella put her hand on Rumi's shoulder, and they sat in silence for a while.

"If light is in your heart, you will find your way home," Rumi said.

"What's that?"

"Just something my Nai Nai used to say," she wheezed, gasping a breath in. "You said you were lost. I don't know, it seemed—"

"It seemed like what, Rumi?" Isabella looked at the girl in her lap. Her eyes were closed, the black tendrils wrapping around behind her ear and over her eyelids. Her chest rose, then fell. Rose again. Fell. The last rays of the sun dropped their color, the clear and cloudless sky taking a deepening purple of the coming night. Below them, the undisturbed forest swayed.

Isabella didn't move until the last rays of the setting sun faded into darkness. Her eyes were puffy and her cheeks wet. She had failed. Because she wasn't good enough, quick enough, Rumi would not be waking up in her warm bed tomorrow morning. She would not enjoy another sunrise or a hug. She would not get to grow up, or help her mother fix the car. Instead, in the waking world, her parents or friends would find her, they'd try to revive her, and ultimately they would drop flowers on her casket.

"I'm so sorry." Isabella choked on the words even as she said them, stroking Rumi's hair. The words felt small, and Isabella felt small as she looked over the valley stretching out to the darkening horizon. Somewhere, a little squirrel was searching desperately for help for his weaver, and a trained Dreamweaver was trapped. Somewhere, Kimi, who she'd wronged again and again, probably wanted nothing to do with her. Finn, Delson, Ajay, and the hunters were out there doing what she couldn't.

She thought about the words she'd read in the book tucked neatly in her backpack.

If the weaver's companion and the weaver are both free and in the dream plain, but willfully separate and choosing not to reunite, both must suffer consequences. The weaver will lose their powers on the dream plain, and the companion, if unable to be paired again, will, in time, go through the shivering, a painful process by which the companion reverts to ether wherefrom all companions rise.

If Kimi was staying away from her, it would be like a death sentence for the fox. Kimi would simply fade away and cease to be. Isabella closed her eyes. As the book said, there was only one solution that wouldn't lead to Kimi being evaporated or *shivering*. Isabella needed to go back to the waking world and wait for her father, explain everything and never come back again.

Looking around one final time, Isabella took a deep breath and closed her eyes, willing herself to wake up.

She focused on her breathing, counting her breaths. *Seven, eight, nine, ten.* She pictured the waterfall and the small pool it fell into next to her family's dream cabin. She saw herself approaching the water, felt the coolness of it wash over her, but all the while an urgency pulled her back away from the water's edge. She ignored it; that was for someone else to deal with, not the girl who sat on a mountain with the cooling head of her victim in her hands. She pushed past the urgency and through the waterfall. A breeze brushed her hair against her cheek and she opened her eyes, expecting to see the coals of their fire.

Instead, she looked over the dark valley, same as before, with the weight of her deeds literally in her lap. She tried to wake up and get out of the dream world twice more, but both were unsuccessful. She couldn't even save Kimi from her fate. Isabella screamed into the darkness. She screamed because she couldn't help Wesley and Skia, for her failure to help Rumi, for the inevitable loss of Kimi, and for herself. When she was done and even the echo had died down, she apologized to Rumi's body once again. Isabella lifted the girl's head and set it down gently on the ground. She rummaged through her pack and pulled out the blanket she'd taken from the cabin.

When she turned and looked at Rumi's prone body, gray ash was rising from it like in the dead forest she'd followed her brother into—the land where the shadow congress had set up their battle with Wren and the hunters. She didn't know what it meant, but nothing connected to that land was good, so she feared the worst. What happened to people who died in their dreams? It seemed like a question that Dreamweavers should know the answer to, but standing there watching the ash rise from her body, Isabella had no answers.

Isabella used her blanket to cover Rumi's body, pulling it up to her chest but stopping before covering her face. She wanted to remember this poor girl's features. She needed to have that failure drilled into her to remember to never again fail anyone like she had done this time. Rumi's eyes were closed and the shadow's infection had sent spirals of itself throughout her face. She was still a beautiful girl and her youth had not been robbed by death. It was her mouth that drew Isabella's attention more than anything else. One corner was buried in the still-expanding shadow, but the other corner was slightly turned up like she was about to laugh at some private joke. It reminded her of her grandfather at his funeral. She had insisted on looking at him lying in his coffin, and he had had worn that same bemused look too.

"I feel like I should say something for you here, but I just don't have the words. I'm sorry that I let this happen. I could give you excuses like I'm untrained or I panicked, but the truth is, I made a choice. I made a choice to wait and see what would happen, and you paid the price for that choice. I will carry you with me forever because of that. I don't know any prayers or churchy stuff like that, but you remind me of my grandfather, so maybe the blessing my mother said at his funeral will do. I don't know if you're religious. If not, sorry about the whole God thing in it, but yeah, here it goes:

May you see God's light on the path ahead
When the road you walk is dark.

May you always hear,
Even in your hour of sorrow,
The gentle singing of the lark.
When times are hard, may hardness
Never turn your heart to stone,
May you always remember
when the shadows fall—
You do not walk alone."

When Isabella finished talking, she folded the blanket gently over the girl's face. She turned to head back down the path she had first come up, back down the way that would take her to the cabin and to the waterfall, and hopefully back to the waking world where she wouldn't be responsible for anything except going to school and getting halfway decent grades.

EIGHT

T he pebble made contact with the surface of the emerald pool. It quickly disappeared beneath the water, causing ripples to emanate from the spot until they bounced off the edge by Izzy's feet, turning back on themselves and disturbing the smooth rhythm of the undulating water. She had been elated when the roof of the cabin came into view through the trees because it meant that she was mere minutes away from going back to the waking world. The problem was, she remembered having to come here through the waterfall, and if her dad hadn't been there to help her, she'd have drowned. Sitting here on the edge of the pool, Isabella had no reason to think that going back would be any different. The difference was that this time her father wouldn't be there.

Faced with another addition to her long line of spectacular failures, Isabella took to throwing small pebbles into the water and watching the ripples until they decayed. The sun had long since gone down, but the moon was full and bright as it cast its pale light over the scenery. She threw another pebble at the reflection of the moon in the pool and watched the ripples course through it. The waves of the water distorting the reflection of the sky reminded her of the changing reality when she'd touched Rumi. The book that she'd taken from the library was still tucked in her bag, and while it probably had the explanation for what she'd experienced, her determination to leave and never come back made that information useless. Why learn about something that you will never see, or do, again? So here she sat, unable to go forward and help Skia but unable to go back home to the waking world. Nothing to do but sit and count her mistakes, like ripples on the water.

"After seeing your note, I didn't expect to see you back so soon." The voice behind her was friendly and familiar.

Isabella shrugged and continued to stare at the pool.

"Wow," Wren said as she settled into the grass next to Isabella, "very different welcome than last time."

Isabella pulled her knees to her chest and buried her face in them.

"Right, so you're not looking to talk." Wren lay back in the grass and put her hands behind her head. "That's cool. It's nice here. Mentu likes it, lots of game for him, though this is new," she said as she pointed her foot at the water.

After sitting silently for a while, Isabella couldn't take it anymore. "I couldn't do it"—she threw another stone into the pool—"so I was going to leave. Go back home."

"And you're still here?"

Isabella said nothing. The rings from the pebble expanded outward, and overhead Mentu circled.

"Look," Wren continued once it was clear that Isabella wasn't going to say anything, "you're still a kid. If you want to leave, leave. Honestly, you shouldn't be here anyway. You're still too young."

"I can't."

"Can't leave?" Wren sat up and looked at Isabella, "Sure you can. Just stand up and go back through your portal. I'm assuming that's what this is."

"You wouldn't understand." Isabella pushed up violently and stomped off toward the empty paddock. The grass was shorter here than in the fields surrounding the cabin, like someone maintained it. She climbed a fence and sat on the top rail. This part of the cabin confused her. She saw the deer in the distance again. In the moonlight she could see the buck watching her cautiously, but when she didn't come closer than the paddock fence, it went back to grazing in the moonlight. She idly picked at the wood on the fence rail, tossing splinters that came off into the grass in front of her.

"I don't know what's going on with you," Wren said from behind her, "but I came here for a reason. If you don't want to talk, whatever, but I need you to tell me if you know anything more about where your dad went."

"I already told you, Vígolfr came by and they both ran off that way." She motioned away from the front of the cabin. "Why do you keep looking for him anyway?"

"What do you mean?"

"You're—I mean—you're you."

She leaned against the top rail of the fence that Izzy was sitting on. "I'm going to need more than that."

"You fought the shadow congress, you run around the dream world like you own it, bantering with your bird, and people are in awe of you. Heck, I'm in awe of you." Isabella turned to look at Wren. The woman was a force; her features were both sharp and warm. Her fiery red hair was pulled back into a pony-tail, and her eyes burned with an intensity Isabella never saw in the waking world. She wore a ridiculous neon blue sweater with a rainbow and a unicorn on it, but the leather on the shoulders and arms made it look as incongruous as the rest of the woman. "You're confident and strong and deadly, and I'm—" Isabella motioned down at herself. Her jeans were filthy from sitting on the ground next to Rumi while she died. Her shirt, once white, was the dingy gray of sweat and dirt.

"You look like you've been doing."

"I've been failing, more like it."

"Okay, so you've been failing."

"Just like that." Isabella felt like she was shrinking.

"What do I know," Wren said forcefully, "I wasn't there. You said you were failing, so fine, what of it?"

"What do you mean what of it?"

"So, you say you failed, and now you want to leave, but you say you can't leave, so you're sitting here sulking. You want to have a pity party, fine, enjoy. I'll leave you to it." Wren shrugged and turned to leave.

"The great, Wren." Isabella could hear the petulance in her own voice, but she didn't care. "Off to save the world."

"You sure have a chip on your shoulder, little miss 'this is all my subconscious'." Isabella turned to glare at her. "Yeah, I remember that conversation. I thought the last time you were here you would have learned a thing or two."

"Well, I guess I haven't."

"I guess not." Wren stormed back to the fence and Mentu swooped down and perched on a post not far away, watching the two of them. "You know what your problem is?"

"No," Isabella spat back at her, "what's my *problem*?"

"You still think that you can do this all by yourself."

"What does that even mean? You do it all yourself."

Wren laughed bitterly. "Do you even hear yourself? 'You do it all yourself'," Wren mocked Isabella's voice. "What was I doing the first time you met me?"

"Defeating a shadow congress that I ran from."

"No, I wasn't," she scoffed. "I was looking for help from the hunters. What am I doing now?" She didn't wait for Isabella's answer before storming on, "I'm looking for your father's help with something."

"But when I saw you fighting the shadow congress—"

"I was fighting alongside *your* friends," Wren interrupted her. "Finn, Delson, Ajay, the Champion. Besides, when am I ever alone?" She looked over at Mentu, who took flight and lighted on Wren's shoulder, taking the cue. "I'd be lost without Mentu."

"You can say that again," the bird said as it imperiously locked its eyes on Isabella.

"Okay, mouse breath," Wren shot back at the bird. "The point is, what we do is hard, and we don't do it alone."

Isabella looked down at the moonlight-bathed grass of the paddock and thought about all the times she'd pushed Kimi away. Now, because of that, if she stayed here then Kimi would end up going through the shivering and ... Isabella couldn't even bring herself to think the rest. She pictured Rumi, laying there covered in her blanket, imagined her family waking up in the morning and finding her lying cold in her bed. Her tears broke through silently. She hoped Wren couldn't see from where she was and turned further away from her.

After a few moments of silence, Wren started again. "There's this stalker. Do you know what those are, stalkers?"

Isabella shook her head.

"Stalkers are—or at least used to be—Dreamweavers, but they made some bad choices along the way. You probably should hear this from your dad, but you need to know to understand what's going on here, so whatever, right?" Isabella didn't respond, so Wren continued. "There are lots of different types of people in the dream realm. There's weavers, like us, hunters, like the Champion and his group, there are denizens and dreamers. But there are also darker things here, shadows, nightmares—let's hope you never have to go against one of those, but of course, you are a Shaw, so—" Wren didn't finish that thought out loud, "and there are stalkers. Stalkers are like us, except for whatever reason, they never connected with their companions. The companion goes through the shivering." Isabella shuddered at the word and Wren noticed in the pale light. "I see you've heard of that at least. Good, because I did *not* want to explain it. So, their companions shiver and something in them breaks. The weaver, I mean. It doesn't happen immediately, but it happens nonetheless.

"It's little cruelties at first, easily overlooked callousness. A withheld favor at a key point, or some spiteful jealousy, a secret told, you know, petty things. But it doesn't stop there. Soon those petty things become bigger and more important. The shift is hard to watch because there's nothing you can do about it. Harder still if you knew them before."

Isabella felt her shoulders tense. It seemed like Wren knew something about her and Kimi, but she was afraid to ask, so Isabella sat there and watched the deer at the edge of the forest.

"That's why I need your dad, you know." The paddock's rail shifted as Wren climbed up, perching next to Isabella. "There's a stalker out there using a group of shadows to torment a town of denizens. They've been attacking people who go out after dark. When you said your dad and Vígolfr went south, I hoped they'd heard about that and were there helping, but when I got there, no such luck, so I set up a curfew and came here hoping he'd be back."

"And you're stuck with me," Isabella said bitterly.

"You're still a Shaw, kid." Wren patted Isabella's shoulder. "When it comes to having someone watch my back, that matters."

"Why?"

"Your family has always been something of a legend in the capitol. They rarely go there, and when you see this"—she motioned at the cabin and surrounding grounds—"it's no surprise. But not everyone has something like this, and quite frankly, I'm not even sure if this is legal."

"There are laws?" Isabella couldn't help but turn toward Wren.

"Of course there are laws," she said with a laugh that sounded warm and safe. "Why else would there be a capital?"

"I just figured—"

"The lawless land of your dreams?" Wren laughed again, "Not quite. Either way, your family is special, and I've known your father since I became a Dreamweaver. He trained me, so when I have a problem I can't handle alone, like the shadow congress or this stalker business, he's the first person I turn to. And as you saw with that squirrel, I'm not the only one."

"Why do you need his help with this stalker?"

"We have a history, this stalker and I."

"Wren," Mentu chimed in, "I am quite sure the girl does not need to hear this."

Wren looked from Izzy to Mentu and back again. "I disagree with you there, buddy. I think this is exactly what she needs to hear."

"If you say so," he said, then, cocking his head to the side, flapped his enormous wingspan and took to the sky, "but I will not be party to this." Izzy and Wren watched quietly as Mentu circled above them until he was lost in the night sky.

"Why doesn't he want you to tell me?"

"He can be a bit of a stuffed shirt at times," she said warmly, watching the starry sky, "but I think he doesn't want to scare you."

Isabella's curiosity was piqued.

"So, story time," Wren said as she rubbed her hands together.

✣ NINE ✣

WREN'S STORY PART I

A t eighteen years old, Wren is in the training ground as Mentu circles overhead, crying out and occasionally swooping down to investigate something in the forest nearby. She stands crouched down, knives in each hand, facing another eighteen-year-old. His brown hair is pulled back into a small ponytail near the top of his head, and across his broad shoulders rests a long wooden quarterstaff. A black bear stalks along the edge of the field, occasionally casting glances toward the two people squaring off in the center.

"Any luck getting through to that wing nut up there?" the man asked as he moved slowly clockwise in the clearing.

Wren matched his movements, keeping the exact distance between them. "He has a name," she said, feinting a strike with one of her knives.

He dodged. "Yeah? What is it?"

"Mentos"—she scrunched her brow—"or something like that."

"Nice." He swung the staff off his right shoulder with one arm, pivoting and drawing it across in front of him. "You don't even know feather-brain's name?"

Wren jumped back and spun, bringing her right shoulder around toward the man. She slashed with the knife in her right hand but missed as he stepped quickly to his left and brought the other end of the staff up in defense. "How 'bout Bluto over there?"

"Her name is Geduld." He turned to face her, not letting her stay on his flank.

"So," she said as she dropped her guard for a moment, "you finally spoke to her?"

Seeing his opportunity, he took a step forward and swept the low end of his staff as if rowing a canoe, performing a rudimentary leg swipe. Wren didn't see it coming in time and, unable to avoid it, took the full force of the staff behind her knees and fell backward to the ground hard.

"That was a cheap shot, Oskar," she said, reaching for his proffered hand. "But seriously, when did you speak to her?" Wren motioned toward the stalking bear with a nod of her head.

He pulled her up and they both sheathed their weapons. Geduld was beginning to make her slow way across the field, and they stood watching for a moment before Oskar said, "Just before I went back to the waking world last time, here in the training grounds. I didn't get too close, but we said hi, did the whole names thing. Seemed like she was gonna say something, but my alarm must have gone off 'cause I was torn out."

"That's the worst. You guys almost done with school over there?"

"It's Germany," he scoffed, "not the dark side of the moon. We still go until June."

"Hey, I don't know." She shrugged. "I'm still new to this crazy dream world stuff." She looked up at Mentu circling above them. "He still hasn't said much to me."

"Probably scared off by your sweaters." He shielded his eyes and squinted in humor. "Why do you wear those ridiculous things?"

"What do you mean?" Wren looked down at her favorite pink sweater emblazoned with an oversized golden *maneki-neko*. "This is the lucky cat. These things are awesome."

"Whatever you say." Oskar shook his head, reached out about shoulder height and closed his hand around something Wren couldn't see. When he drew his hand back, he held two bottles of mineral water. "Want one?"

"That is still crazy to me," Wren said, taking one of the bottles. Gerolsteiner was written in blue across the top of the label, a blue lion inside something that looked like a compass rose below it. "How do you pull stuff out of the air like that?"

"I don't know. Allan said he'd heard of people who could do that, but he'd never actually seen it. Guess it's not that common." He opened his bottle, which made a satisfying sound of carbonation escaping its confines, and took a deep drink.

"What do you think of him?"

"Allan?"

"No, the lion on the bottle." She playfully shoved at his shoulder. "Of course, Allan."

Oskar shrugged. "He's fine, I guess, a bit of a *besserwisser*, though."

"Bezervizer?"

"A *besserwisser*. You know, the type of person who always has an answer or can always tell you more about whatever you thought you knew."

"A know-it-all?"

"Yeah, that's it." He smiled, keeping a wary eye on the large black bear that still lumbered toward them.

"He is our trainer," Wren said as she followed his gaze behind her and turned to watch the bear with him, "I think he's supposed to know more than us. Plus, he's old guard. His family has been doing this for something like fifty generations." Wren moved in and lowered her voice. "Word is, they have some sort of illegal compound or homestead or something from before the council existed. It was grandfathered in or something."

"I wouldn't put it past him."

She motioned to the bear as it came to a stop a few feet away. "Looks like Bluto wants to talk."

"Come on, Wren," he replied with a roll of his eyes, "be serious for once. You'll offend her." He stepped toward the bear. "Geduld." He nodded his head toward the beast as she reared up on her haunches. "It's good to see you again."

When she spoke, her voice was softer than Wren had expected from the hulking form. It had a warm, motherly tone to it. "There is a dreamer in trouble nearby. We should go and assist them."

Wren looked up at the hawk flying overhead. "Why hasn't my companion come to tell me?"

"I cannot answer that for you, weaver," Geduld rumbled warmly, "but sometimes the newer companions have trouble sensing these things. I have been with the Schäfer family for three generations. Oskar is my fourth." The bear looked to the sky. "Besides," she continued turning her black eyes on Wren, who flinched under the appraising gaze, "would you even know how to call him?"

Wren didn't answer. The hulking bear simply came down on all fours and turned back toward the forest, lumbering her slow way across the field. When she had moved out of earshot, Wren let out a breath and shook her head. Until then, she hadn't realized Oskar's family had a legacy in the dream world or that there was even such a thing, besides the rumors of the Shaw family.

Noticing her discomfort, Oskar put his arm around Wren's thin shoulders. "Sorry 'bout Geduld, she can be rather abrupt."

"She has a point." Wren looked up to the sky. "I wouldn't know how to call him down from there. I'm scared to. He reminds me of a poem I was forced to read this year in English. 'Turning and turning in a widening gyre, the falcon cannot hear the falconer'. What if he doesn't hear me when I call?"

"What if he does?"

"I think that thought might scare me more."

"Well"—he looked from Mentu in the air to Geduld on the ground—"I've gotta get going. Finish this match later?"

"Let me come with you."

"Wren." He paused. "You don't even know your companion's name. You can't help until you get better with him."

"I won't get in the way," she pleaded, trying not to sound desperate. "I need to get out in the field. All this training without doing anything is driving me crazy."

"Promise to stay out of the way?"

Wren, Oskar, and Geduld made a strange trio. Mentu kept his distance, but he seemed to be following along as they searched the forest for the dreamer being pursued by a shadow. At that time, Wren had never even seen a real shadow. She'd had bad dreams growing up—most people with the potential to become weavers have more than their share of nightmares when they're younger— but she'd always seen them as whatever her subconscious was whipping up that night. A real shadow, as Allan had described them to her during one of their training sessions, was more like a vaguely human-shaped smoke that leaked feelings. Despite the description, she wasn't ready for what they came across.

When they found the dreamer, a little dark-skinned girl with pigtails in a pink princess nightgown, she'd fallen flat on her back and was crying out for help. Wren rushed toward her without thinking, sweeping the girl up in her arms and using her own body as a shield against her assailant. When she touched the girl's arms, the air in front of Wren's face seemed to shimmer momentarily, and the sounds behind her changed, but she didn't dare look. She'd ready about being transported into dreamer's dreams, but the experience was more disorienting than she'd expected.

When she'd curled around the small child, the full force of the shadow bore down on her. There was a wave of anger effusing the air, but there were other emotions: regret and blame, the two strongest. The former of the two was almost palpable, beating at her back so hard that she could feel the tears forming in her eyes as she looked back on her own life and her petty failings rose to the surface of her memories.

She heard the fight behind her, but from her position she couldn't see anything. There were grunts of exertion from Oskar, the heavy sound of something sharp landing on his wooden staff, and the roar of Geduld which caused even Wren's blood to run cold. Meanwhile, the girl in her arms whimpered and pulled closer to her, fresh tears soaking into Wren's sweater. Then there was a yelp, clearly a cry of pain from some animal, and the heavy thud of flesh falling to the ground. Oskar cried out. Wren's back tensed as she heard his staff bounce off the rocks to her left moments before he fell next to her and rolled over, groaning in pain. She could feel the shadow looming over her and tried to prepare herself for what she knew would come next.

The sound, a howl echoing through the trees, was so haunting that even the shadow paused and looked around. The girl in Wren's arms screamed and scrambled desperately away, breaking Wren's grasp and crashing through the underbrush like nothing was there. Wren was about to go after her, but realizing the girl was already out of reach, she rolled over and drew her knives. Fighting on her back was far from ideal, but Wren could at least defend herself now that the girl was gone. Looking at the undulating shape of the shadow, a new emotion, hopelessness, flooded toward her. She had prepared for the regret so this came as a surprise and she lowered her guard slightly. The shadow advanced, its tendrils beginning to envelop her hiking boots, and she heard the knives drop from her hands.

The movement was quick, like a flash of light from the shadows of the forest followed by footsteps and the sound of something skidding against the dry leaves. When Wren could finally see, the tears having left her eyes, standing before her was a white wolf, terrifying yet familiar, and off to the side was a man crouched over one of Oskar's legs.

"Vígolfr," Wren breathed out in relief, "thank God you're here."

"Thank Mentu," the wolf said matter-of-factly, "he found us and said you two fools had gotten into trouble again."

"But Geduld—"

"Geduld should have known better than to bring you both out here," the man said, walking over next to the wolf and offering Wren his hand.

"Oh God, Geduld." Wren looked around but didn't see the hulking form of the bear. "Is she—"

"She's fine," Allan said, looking down at his trainees, "and you two got off lucky."

"I think Oskar got hurt." It felt lame to even say, but Wren didn't know what else to say instead.

"He did." Allan looked over at the prone man. He looked more like a child laying there, his leg wrapped in some sticky substance that was already picking up leaves. "He'll live, but healing will take time." Allan sighed and looked suddenly older. "I'm not sure how well he'll heal, but he'll heal."

In the waking world, Oskar Schäfer was a football player who had been scouted by American colleges to play for their teams. After that day, the offers dried up, and the next time Wren saw him on the training grounds, he was still walking with a cane and he carried a pistol on his hip. It wasn't the most efficient weapon against the shadows, but he practiced day and night on the range, ammo never being a problem because he would grab more from the air any time he needed.

Wren waited at the shooting range, watching the people with their bows and crossbows. There weren't any rules against modern weapons that she knew of, but most people went for the more traditional shadow fighting weapons offered at the training grounds. When Oskar walked in, she tried to start a conversation, but he walked past her as if she wasn't there.

"Have patience, child," Geduld had told her when she'd seen the bear sulking in the distance. "He is young and hot-headed." Almost apologetically, she added, "He blames you for his leg and the loss of the scholarships."

"But that's not fair," Wren whined, falling back against the bear's side. "I was just trying to protect the girl."

"You should not have even been there," Geduld sighed. "Allan was correct when he said I should have known better. You have not yet bonded with Mentu, though by the tears in the shoulder of your sweater, I see you are at least working on it."

"He went to get them."

The bear didn't answer but rose slowly to her feet, giving Wren time to stand. Then as she walked away, she added in a voice tinged with sadness, "Give it time. He will come around."

 TEN

Isabella didn't want to get drawn into conversation. She wanted to sit there and be left alone, but Wren was not getting the hint. Instead, she'd told a story about her early days as a weaver. As much as it was a struggle to imagine someone getting the better of Wren in a sparring match, it was even more of a stretch to think that was the same woman who so flawlessly faced the shadow congress, her knives flashing in the sun as she spun and swiped at the impending darkness. Even as she was running for her own life and trying to usher Tucker to safety, Isabella had thought that Wren looked like a thing possessed out on the battlefield. The thought that she would freeze in front of a shadow gave Isabella some comfort, and because of that comfort, she felt indignant that Wren was blamed for being afraid.

"That's not fair," she said, looking at Wren, who took her own turn staring at the grass at their feet. "Neither of them should have blamed you. You were protecting that kid."

"I thought that too"—Wren paused—"at the time."

The two sat there in the silence of a field at night. The crickets and cicadas rang out, an owl called in the distance. Some of the smaller nocturnal animals announced their dinners were found, and above it all, Mentu circled.

Isabella looked up at the starry sky. "Why are you telling me this?"

"People aren't born strong or weak," Wren said, her voice soft enough that if Isabella didn't know better, she'd have thought Wren was talking to herself. "We're not born brave or cowardly. These are choices we make in a moment, and one choice, while it influences the next, doesn't define us. This stalker I told you about, the one I need your dad's help with, I knew him. He was a good guy once, a weaver. They all were," she looked up at Isabella for a moment, "the stalkers, I mean. They weren't born stalkers. At some point, though, they made a choice, the wrong choice, and they let that choice define them. That's what happened." Again, their silence filled the field but it wasn't until it began to feel uncomfortable that Wren spoke again. "You said before that it wasn't fair, and I agree, none of this is"—she swept her arm across the landscape—"but I'm not sure that I shouldn't be blamed."

"For what?" Isabella squinted at Wren.

"This stalker," Wren said as she dug her heel into the ground, "that's causing so much trouble. It's Oskar, and I think what I did, or rather what I didn't do, made it happen."

"How?"

"It was probably a year after that day on the training grounds when he was injured by the shadow . . ."

ELEVEN

WREN'S STORY PART II

It was spring in the dream world, about a year after the incident on the training ground, and Wren still wasn't sure how the seasons worked in here. Where she lived, winter had a complete hold on the landscape, so the warm sun was a nice change of pace. She was practicing seeing through Mentu's eyes while he flew above her. The first time had been very disorienting, like with the girl in the forest when Wren had entered her dream. They'd been at it for a week now and, while the transition was getting easier, Wren still found it hard to stay connected and was disoriented when Mentu was flying, like some out-of-body experience. At the moment, she saw through Mentu's eyes while he soared over the forest, and while the feeling when he dove was terrifying, the freedom of the air through Mentu's feathers was freeing; Wren was giving herself up to the feeling.

"The council wants us to check out a dream trap that some shadow set up east of here," the familiar voice sounded far away. For a moment, Wren didn't react. "You in there?"

Wren pulled out of Mentu's consciousness and crossed her arms, scowling at the person who interrupted what was probably her best session with her companion yet. Oskar stood before her, one hand on his wooden cane and the other resting on the handle of his pistol. She hadn't stood face-to-face with him since the day they'd saved the little girl, the day he'd been injured. Outwardly he hadn't changed much in the year, but something about the way he held himself had. Instead of the broad-shouldered, upright confidence he'd had before, now Oskar was slightly hunched over, Wren assumed from walking with his cane, and he squinted more. Instead of his quarterstaff resting across his shoulders, he had an old western-style holster for for silver pistol with its dark mahogany-colored handle. His right hand never seemed to stray far from the gun, and it rested on the grip as he stood waiting for Wren's reply.

"Earth to birdbrain, you with us?"

"I didn't know we were on speaking terms." Wren's voice was cold but she was working hard to keep it that way. Ever since Geduld told her that Oskar placed the blame on Wren's shoulders for everything that happened, Wren had been pissed.

"The council specifically requested both of us"—he looked impatiently at the forest's edge—"though honestly, I don't know why. Geduld and I can take care of this if you want to keep staring off into space."

"I'm training." Wren stepped back defensively. "Connecting with my companion. Something you should try once in a while." Wren hadn't been the only one Oskar had blamed for his injury. He had limited his contact with Geduld and on several occasions she'd seen the old bear wandering the training grounds alone.

"Whatever." He turned and started off toward the forest. "I'm better off without your help anyway. I won't tell if you don't."

Wren watched him walk toward the forest, but she made no move to follow him. She told herself that they were better off working alone because their current mutual dislike wouldn't get them far. Geduld turned to look over her shoulder before following Oskar into the shadows. The old companion seemed worried, but Wren chalked it up to going alone with Oskar, something she'd be worried about too at this point. He wasn't the same carefree guy he used to be, and while she couldn't fault him for changing after losing his scholarships and having a persistent limp, she did think he'd taken it too far.

The wind blew her red hair into her face as Mentu gracefully came into land on her shoulder. "Should we not follow him?" The hawk's imperious tone annoyed Wren from time to time. This was one of those times.

"No, we should not," she mocked his tone and turned her back on Oskar and the forest.

Without another word, Mentu launched himself into the air, ignoring Wren's call and her attempts to share his sight. She watched him circle out in the direction Oskar was heading then, shrugging her shoulders, went to the library to do some research on Dreamweaver powers. She'd been at the table for some time, the books stacked at least five high, a record for her. She never did like the book learning aspect of things. Most of the people here had smaller, land-based companions like squirrels and mice, but primarily domestic animals like dogs and cats sat curled near their weavers. That made the fluttering entrance of Mentu all the more noticeable as he hopped through an open clearstory window and glided to perch on Wren's stack of books.

"What brings you fluttering in here?" Wren asked, leaning back in her chair, happy with the slight dig at the all-too-proper bird.

"I do not flutter," he said, his talons kneading the binding of the uppermost book, a heavy tome about something called Nightmares which, if the book was to be believed, were like shadows on steroids.

"Sure thing," she chuckled warmly, "whatever you say, Sir-Flutters-a-Lot."

"My name is—" Mentu ruffled his feathers and let out an exasperated squawk. "Why do I even bother? We need to go."

"Where?" Wren stood up, bumping the table and causing the books Mentu was on to slide awkwardly over. He hopped off as the first book began to move and walked across the table. "Is the council sending us on a mission?"

"They already did, in case you forgot." Mentu glared at her, the yellows of his eyes catching the sun and reflecting it back, giving them the effect of glowing. "You decided not to go."

"Oskar can handle a simple dream trap." Wren carelessly opened one of the books on the table. "Besides, I'm busy studying."

"No, you are not"—he hopped up on the book she was reading—"or else you would have the book right way up."

Sure enough, the book in her hands was upside down, but Wren was not going to cede the point. "On purpose," she exaggerated her tone, "I'm looking at it from a new perspective."

"After you said you weren't going with them, I followed them from the air and kept an eye on them."

"You little sneak."

"I take exception to that, but in this case, you might be right."

She raised her eyebrows. "See. I'm rubbing off on you after all."

If birds could sigh, Wren was positive Mentu would have let out a doozy. As it was, he rolled his eyes before he went on. "Doubtful. Now pay attention." It was Wren's turn to roll her eyes. "I followed Oskar and Geduld until they got to the dream trap. Once they entered it, I found a branch to wait on. Something was strange when they came out, though. Geduld was backing away, growling lowly at Oskar. I think there is some trouble that we could possibly help with."

"Probably rubbed her the wrong way," Wren said. Mentu hopped off the book and she set it down. "We get in fights from time to time."

"Because you are insufferably immature."

"And you're a stuffed shirt!" She poked the bird good naturally in the chest.

"I do not know about all of that," he huffed, puffing his feathers out again, "but this was different. It felt wrong."

She looked at the stack of books on her table. "Fine. I guess we don't have time to clean up." She shrugged. "Awe shucks," she added with mock sincerity.

Wren followed Mentu as they wound their way through the paths. She was sure that the hawk was misreading the situation. Geduld was an experienced companion, more so than any of them. Mentu also seemed like a rules-follower to her; she wasn't sure why they had gotten paired, but Allan had explained that companions were a reflection of an underused part of the weaver's personality. The best weavers eventually figured it out and either accepted that part of themselves or at least came to terms with it. She'd asked him what happens if the weaver rejected that part of their personality, and he had avoided answering the question.

Lost in these thoughts, she almost ran into the side of the black bear as it stood resolute in the path, body tense, teeth bared, and staring directly at Oskar while a low growl emanated from her throat. Skidding to a stop, Wren looked between the two. They looked to be at a stalemate, but one that should never have been possible. Oskar's pistol was out with a light puff of smoke beginning to dissipate.

"I told you to get out of here," he spat the words at Geduld. "Your service to my family has come to an end."

"Don't listen to them, Oskar," she growled, her usually smooth voice filled with aggression. "You're better than this."

"I gave you a warning shot." He pulled the hammer back with his right thumb and leveled the gun toward Geduld's head. "I didn't have to miss, and you know that."

"You will come to regret your choice." The matronly bear's voice lost its guttural rage. In its place was a sad resignation.

"I don't think so." He noticed Wren standing frozen on the path near Geduld. "But what do we have here? Did you finally decide to deign to follow the council's command?"

"What are you doing, Oskar?" Wren struggled to put any sense into what she was seeing.

"Something I should have done a year ago," he scoffed. "Honestly, I'm glad you didn't come. I probably would have been too busy saving you from your own incompetence to have found my new friends." Wren hadn't noticed the wispy shapes behind him until now, but now that she had, they were all she could see. The two dark misty figures standing behind Oskar began to move forward, and as they did, Wren could feel the emotions wash over her. Greed and envy and emptiness filled the forest around her. "Matter of fact," he chuckled and looked up unto the sky, "I don't see that pompous feather pillow that hangs around. Maybe I should let them come over there and play with you."

Geduld growled again, her white teeth glistening in the sun. "That would be a mistake, you fool. I may not be willing to hurt you, but I will destroy them."

"Not willing to hurt me?" Oskar laughed ruefully and held up his left hand, balancing himself on his good leg. "What do you call this?" His hand was wrapped in a bloody cloth, and from the looks of it, he was badly injured.

"I was trying to save—"

"Save it." He cut her off, aiming the pistol at her again. "You served my family for three generations"—the venom in his voice made Wren flinch—"in honor of that, I will give you until the count of three to get out of here. If I get to three and you haven't turned your lardy self around, I will shoot you."

"Those are shadows, Oskar," Wren pleaded, "they're not your friends."

"And you are? If it weren't for you, I'd still be able to walk without this damn thing." He waved his cane in the air. "I'd be playing soccer in the States at a good college, with a good future. Without the scholarships, they sent me to Berufsschule instead of university. No soccer, no American university. You destroyed that for me. Such a friend."

"But the girl—" Wren felt hot tears gather in her eyes.

He looked over his shoulder at the two shadows. "The girl got away regardless, though I don't know that we helped her at all anymore."

"What are you talking about?" Wren's head was spinning. "Of course we did."

"Look at me, Wren," he commanded as he pointed the gun toward her. "Out there, I'm nothing. In here, I'm a god. The council keeps us down, only trains the weakest of skills. Allan knows that. Why do you think he has that secret compound?"

"That's a rumor." She didn't know why she felt the need to defend Allan against Oskar. They had mocked their mentor together countless times during their first year, but it felt different now.

"Now that I think of it"—he shifted his finger toward the trigger—"maybe I put a bullet in you now and get this over with. I'm giving Geduld to the count of three, but you haven't earned that privilege. Say goodbye, you worthless feather—"

A screech from the trees above drew everyone's attention as Mentu came in like a fighter jet. His talons were extended and he dug them into Oskar's right hand before flapping his mighty wings and taking to the sky again, shreds of skin dangling from his now red talons. Oskar screamed and fell to the ground, cradling his right hand against his chest. The gun tumbled to the rocks at his feet and went off, the bullet burying itself harmlessly into a tree.

In the chaos, the shadows advanced on Wren and Geduld. The bear let out a roar that turned Wren's blood cold. The shadows paused their advance. "Get on," she said, the power back in her voice, "we need to get out of here."

Wren grabbed a handful of fur and pulled herself atop the large bear as she reared up and turned in one motion. Then, without warning, Geduld thundered deeper into the forest. Her powerful legs took them away from the screams and curses of Oskar and the feelings of hollowness and greed emanating from his new friends. After a few hours ride, the two stopped at the entrance to a cave with a small clear stream trickling from its mouth.

"We will be safe here," Geduld said, the matronly edge of her voice coming through once more.

"What about Mentu?" Wren was frantic. "I've tried to see through his eyes, but I can't. Is he okay?"

"I wouldn't worry about him," she said, curling up and putting her nose beneath her massive paw, "he is wiser than his years."

"Well, I should surely hope so," the officious voice spoke from the branches across the stream. With the grace that only a bird in flight can have, Mentu glided to the ground and bowed his head to Geduld. He'd managed to clean his talons, and except for a small red spot on his otherwise white underbelly, there was no evidence of his daring rescue. "If I were not, then poor Wren would be in sore trouble."

"You know what," Wren said, "I think you may be right."

After that, Geduld insisted that Wren return to the safety of the training grounds and stay there for the next week when she wasn't in the waking world. Mentu planned on staying with Geduld for a time but he was sure to check in with Wren at least once a day, except for her sixth day. On the seventh day, Wren was preparing to go back to see Geduld in the cave and find out what had kept Mentu away when she saw him circling overhead. She waited for him to come down, offering her arm with new leather attached to the sleeve. He landed gently and hopped up to her shoulder, nuzzling his head into the nape of her neck, something he had never done in the two years they'd been together.

"I missed you too." Wren giggled as his feathers tickled her neck. "I know you probably came back from there, but I stayed away for a week like Geduld asked. I miss her, and I'm going to see her. There is nothing you can say that will stop me."

"She is gone." His voice was tired, heavy in his own way.

"Where'd she go? I'll search the forest without you if you don't tell me, but I'd much prefer to go together." Wren was serious on both counts. Not being with Mentu for a full day had worn on her, and she began to miss his dry humor.

"She shivered," he said and leaned into Wren's neck again.

Confused by the affection, Wren leaned into him as well. While his feathers tickled and his razor-sharp beak was cold against her carotid, it felt good to have him so close. "So, she went someplace warmer?"

"No." His voice and that simple refutation made the realization sink in. That afternoon in the library last week, when Mentu had come to get her, Wren had read something about companions who were separated from their weavers willingly. Tears came unbidden to her eyes and she reached up, caressing Mentu's feathers. The two stood in the warm sun, huddled together with memory against the painful truth of the present.

❧ TWELVE ☙

L istening to Wren talk, Isabella couldn't help feel the hollowness of missing Kimi. They had never had the bonding moment like what Wren and Mentu had after their experience with Geduld and Oskar. "What happened to her?"

"Mentu told me later that he'd stayed with her for some time, only leaving to gather food or come see me. He didn't come on the sixth day because she had begun the shivering." She looked up at the starry night sky. "I didn't know what that meant at the time, and Mentu didn't want to talk about it. It wasn't until a few months after that when I found a book in the library."

"*Powers and Myths?*"

"You know it?"

"I found it in my dad's library"—she motioned toward the cabin with her head—"thought it might be useful."

"The problem with that book is that it doesn't say which are myths and which are powers." Wren absently picked at the fence rail. "Some of that stuff is pretty unbelievable, and I kinda hope that some of it is exaggerated."

"I read that chapter," Isabella said as she hopped off the railing and fished the book out of her bag. "Kinda brutal."

Wren didn't answer. She continued to look up at the sky and then, wiping the back of her hand across her eyes, said, "The next time I saw him—Oskar—things weren't any better. I was headed out on a walk. Sometimes I wander the forests of the southern lands as the sun always feels better here for some reason, and Mentu dropped down to tell me about a little boy being chased by shadows, two of them working together.

"I followed him immediately because I'd learned my lesson early. Mentu's judgment is often better than my own. We wound through several difficult paths. I'm not sure how much of the dream realms you've seen since you first came, but some of the deeper sections of the forest can be pretty dense. Anyway, we were hacking our way through a particularly dense area when I heard a scream and crying. We double-timed it best we could, but by the time I got there, it was too late.

"I saw the shadows looming over a boy and a man. The boy's eyes looked frantic and angry and he was literally spitting his words at the shadows. And the man, well, he was egging the boy on. There was something familiar about the man, but I couldn't place it right away. When we got closer, I could hear what the boy was saying.

"He was cursing the shadows, calling them werewolves which was probably how his subconscious was seeing them. I knew them. It was a feeling I'd had before—a hollowness, with both sorrow and regret. Once I centered that, the rest of the chips sort of fell into place. Instantly, I knew that Oskar was the man with the unfortunate dreamer. I managed to avoid the shadows and get around to the other side of the boy, but there was nothing I could do even then.

"He had a large wound on his left arm. There was some blood, but it's not the blood that gets you in the dream realm, it's the infections. The shadow infection drew its tendrils deep into the boy; black lines ran out from his arm across his body, some curling into his ears, his eyes, even up his nostrils. You see, these infections are insidious. They crawl from the actual wound and find other ways into the body. The boy was spewing insults and curses at the shadows and at his parents for not protecting him. My heart broke for him, and I wanted to do something.

"Oskar saw me and stood up, leaving the boy writhing alone on the ground. He gloated that, once again, I was helpless to do anything. He had claimed the boy for the shadows, and I couldn't stop him. I ignored him, of course, and tried to talk to the boy, but I couldn't get him to acknowledge me; it was like he couldn't even see me. Then he started to change. He began to fade before my eyes. I'd never seen anything like it. First, the infection began to fade, almost like it was evaporating, and I thought I was getting through. Then there were the ashes rising from his body, ashes like in that forest where we fought the shadow congress. You remember that, right?"

"You saw me there?" Isabella was surprised Wren not only noticed her in the middle of the battle, but she also remembered her.

The woman nodded sadly. "So you remember?"

"Yeah." Isabella felt like Wren thought she was missing the point, which was possible.

"Well, the ashes rose, leaving behind a pulsing wispy shadow, and they didn't stop. Eventually, the boy's body was either pulsing shadow or floating ash, and the emotions he'd been yelling about, grief and anger, began to fill the area. Oskar laughed, not a practical joke type laugh, but like he found it genuinely funny. Before long, it wasn't a boy I was holding anymore; it was a shadow. I should have taken it out right there, I still don't know why I didn't, but there are times when the why of things doesn't matter. I let that boy suffer, and as far as I know, he's still suffering today."

Izzy was silent. She had always thought of adults as these people who have it all figured out. Her dad, her mom, the teachers at school, they always had the answers. But if Wren, this confident, mighty warrior, had these doubts, had made these mistakes and had gotten past them, then maybe she could get past what happened with Rumi. One question still burned in the back of her mind, and while she had her suspicions, and could probably find her answer in one of her father's books, she had to ask. "What happens to people who die in the dream world?"

"If they die in here, they die out there too." Wren sighed heavily. "That was one of the hardest things for me to deal with at the time. My slowness had cost that boy his life. His family lost their son, and his friends will never be the same. One moment touches so many people."

Thoughts of Rumi's family came to Isabella's mind, of her father or mother walking in and finding her dead in her bed. "So that's it," she asked, hoping that there was more to the story, "they die in real life and turn into shadows in here?"

"Not always." Wren looked at Isabella, who quickly looked away to avoid eye contact. "Why do you want to know?"

Isabella blushed. "Curiosity, that's all." She didn't know if her voice was convincing or if the lie was written on her face, but Wren, while she seemed unsatisfied with Isabella's answer, didn't probe further.

"Asking for a friend, eh?" Wren paused, but when it was clear that Isabella wasn't going to explain further, she continued anyway. "I'm not an expert on this by any means, but I've seen my fair share. Turns out, losing people is part of the gig when you hunt nightmares."

Nightmares. Isabella remembered hearing or reading something about them before, and she still didn't understand what they were or how they were different from shadows. She was afraid that if she interrupted Wren to ask, she might not get the first answer. So, with great effort, she bit her lip closed to keep from interrupting.

"Far as I can tell, you've got three types of people living in the dream realms full time: shadows, denizens, and hunters. There are others: weavers who have given up the waking world to be here, stalkers like Oskar—thought I don't know if they're here all the time or if they're more like weavers—and the dreamers. What you're asking about dying in dreams, for that we only need to know about shadows, denizens, and hunters.

"Seems to me, what they're thinking about or feeling defines what they become in here. If they're like that boy and are filled with anger, sadness or bitterness, then they become a shadow, consumed by those feelings. If their last thoughts are happier, they become denizens."

"What about the hunters?" Isabella's thoughts turned toward Finn.

"Hunters died in here too." Wren seemed to be able to read her mind here. "Even Finn. But they're a special breed. To become a hunter in the dream world, the dreamer needs to have died trying to save someone else. Hunters possess intense selflessness unlike most of us."

"How'd he die?"

"Finn?" Wren thought a moment. "Don't know. When they wake up, any of them, except maybe the shadows, they don't remember anything from their former life or from their death. It's like a blank slate, a fresh start." She was quiet again. "I guess it's kinda like reincarnation in a way. They get to have a new life; it's just in here."

"But don't some hunters work *with* the stalkers? I remember Finn saying something about that."

"I've heard rumors from time to time, but nothing I believe." Wren's confidence came through in her voice as she said, "No, the hunters are the best of us."

"What about weavers when they die?"

"Same thing. A weaver can become a shadow as sure as they can become a stalker."

Thoughts of Rumi flooded Isabella's head, along with questions about what she'd become. She had been cursing the zombies and herself before she died, but then there was the sunset and that thing about light and finding home. Isabella needed to know for sure. She wanted to ask Wren, or beg for forgiveness, but the thought of confessing her failures terrified her. What if Wren tried to keep her safe by locking her in the cabin, or worse still, forbade her from becoming a Dreamweaver? Isabella wasn't sure if she could even do that, but the thought of not seeing Kimi again, although a real possibility getting more real every minute, made that place in her heart ache.

Mentu screeched above them, and Wren seemed to be shaken out of some reverie. "Anyway, I've stayed here longer than I should have. I still need to find your father." Noticing Isabella's vacant expression in the pale moonlight, she asked, "What's on your mind, kid?"

"Nothing." She knew she should tell Wren about Rumi. After all, hadn't Wren just confessed the same mistake? Wren's mistake was speed, whereas Isabella's was fear and self-preservation. In Wren's first dreamer rescue, she had used her own body as a human shield to protect the little girl from the shadows. Izzy had hidden in a bush until the shadow was safely past. Wren was selfless, Izzy selfish. No, she decided, she wasn't going to tell Wren about Rumi and the shadow. That was her cross to bear. And while there was little chance of Wren knowing Rumi's fate, it would have been nice to share the load, share the memory. "Just thinking about whether or not my dad will be mad that I left the cabin after he told me not to."

"You're back now. What difference does it make? Just destroy the note you left on the counter."

"You're not going to tell him?"

"Nope"—Wren shrugged—"not my place. I do need to go. Be safe, Izzy Shaw. I know you'll be a great weaver someday, even if your dad is beginning your training early."

With that, Wren and Mentu headed back to the south, leaving Isabella with still more questions but a little more hope than she'd had before.

THIRTEEN

When Isabella sat up on the couch, she couldn't figure out where she was or how she'd gotten there. At first, she assumed this was home, that none of the previous day had happened and she needed to get ready for school. It was only after slamming her shin into the coffee table that Isabella realized where she was. The soaring ceilings, the earthy scent of the leather sofa, and the big stone fireplace should have been dead giveaways, but it was her backpack that had doubled as a pillow the night before, which was now tucked tightly into the arm of the chair, that cemented it. Of all the disorienting things that had happened to her in the dream world, waking up was definitely in the top five.

The sun had risen over the tops of the trees and cut warm golden lines through the dusty air. She started the water for hot chocolate, her favorite morning beverage, and opened the front door to let some fresh air into the cabin. Birds sang happily in the forest. While she knew animals were wandering around, she wondered if all the animals in the dream world were companions or potential companions, or if some of them were just animals, and if so, how they got there.

Based on Wren's story from last night, all the people living in the dream world had died in their sleep. Most were the victims of shadows, though she assumed some might have been accidents too. Isabella wondered if the same was true for animals or if something else brought them here, or if they had always been in the dream world. There was so much she didn't know about this place, so many questions she wanted answered. Then she remembered Rumi, and that memory brought with it all the pain and feelings of failure again.

Because of that memory, Isabella had planned on leaving the dream world and her possible future as a Dreamweaver. Wren's story had helped her sleep easier, but it had also given her an ultimatum. Without realizing it, Wren had put a timeline on any chance Isabella had of meeting up with Kimi again. Based on what she'd read in *Powers and Myths*, if she and Kimi were both in the dream world but chose to say apart, then Kimi had six days before the shivering. One of those days had already passed.

She considered her options while she poured the water into the cocoa mix she'd found in the cabinet. It was surprising that there was any at all because her father hated cocoa. It must have been left by her grandfather. They'd had cocoa parties when she was younger, but no, she thought, her grandfather was never a Dreamweaver, only her great-grandfather. This was all too confusing. Shaking her head to clear the cobwebs from sleeping inside the dream world, Isabella walked out into the cool morning air, her cup of cocoa steaming in her hand.

The buck was still grazing in the distance, along with the herd of deer he watched over. The dew on the grass occasionally caught the rays of the rising sun, making it look like someone had tossed handfuls of diamonds on the field. Everything was still and quiet, except the birds singing, so the quick movement near the corral caught Izzy's attention. She called out Kimi's name, not expecting anything to happen but hoping it did anyway. The grass moved by the corral fence, and Isabella's heart leaped. After all this time, all this worry, Kimi hadn't rejected her. Kimi had forgiven her for the undeserved blame and rejection that Izzy had pushed her way last time she was here.

Almost unable to restrain herself from running out into the field to embrace the little red fox, Isabella sipped on her cocoa, burning her tongue a little in the process. She kept herself rooted to the porch of the cabin, trembling with a mix of excitement and nerves. The unfairness of her own actions toward Kimi, reflected in Wren's story of Oskar, made Isabella feel she didn't deserve the forgiveness that she so powerfully wanted. With hope and fear warring inside, Isabella stepped off the porch, setting her cup on the railing, and headed out to meet her companion.

The grass shuddered quickly by one of the posts, and then out of the grass a flash of red came. Isabella's heart soared for an instant before her eyes told her what her heart didn't want to hear. Sitting on the top of a fence post, its tail bouncing, was a small red squirrel. The squirrel sitting on the fence, a familiar sight, shattered her hope and brought her to her knees on the wet grass as the reality of her situation came crashing in. She had lost everything. Something else floated below the surface, though, something that screamed at her for attention. The urgency that had nagged at her consciousness since she'd first heard the water-fall.

"Skia?" She knew it was a long shot. A squirrel is a squir-rel, she thought, unless it's not. "Is that you, Skia?"

Isabella stood up, dirt and dew clinging to the knees of her jeans, and took a wary step toward the squirrel. It was acting like any other squirrel, nibbling on an acorn it held between its tiny paws. Another step caused the squirrel to flinch, pausing its breakfast, before dismissing the threat and returning with zeal to the nut.

"Skia," Isabella said again, although she was almost posi-tive that this was not Wesley's companion. "I'm going to help you, whether you want me to or not. And then," she added hopefully, "you can help me find Kimi." She thought back to when Vígolfr had mentioned Kimi's name, calling her his sister. Later he'd said that all companions shared a bond. Isabella hoped that would be enough to find the little fox. If it wasn't, then Isabella was no bet-ter than Oskar, no better than a stalker. And if that was the case, she had no right to ever come back to the dream world. If she was honest with herself, she liked this world and enjoyed the people in it. She longed to see Finn and Ajay again, but to do that she would need to find Kimi first and, if Wren was right, she had five days to do it.

Her decision made, Isabella marched back into the cabin and grabbed her coat and backpack. She was not going to hide from her responsibilities, no matter what people wanted her to do. She wrote another note for her father, having thrown the pre-vious one into the trash the night before, and shrugged into her jacket. Something in her pocket bumped against her right hip and

Isabella dug her hand into the pocket to see what it was. Her hands found the cool, stout cylinder with its delicate ornate decorations; an undeserving gift from Rumi as she lay dying. Isabella opened the compass and watched as the needle spun toward the north. The north, toward the capitol, toward Skia's trapped weaver. Leaving her abandoned cup of cocoa still steaming on the railing, Isabella started north, down the path she had followed Skia the day before.

Isabella stopped on the trail before the top of the mountain. She knew that up there, under her gray woolen blanket, lay the body of a girl who would not see her graduation because Isabella had failed her. Taking a deep breath, Isabella steeled herself for visiting Rumi's body once more. Stepping out into the clearing, she saw the sun wash over the valley through a cloudless sky and she was once again taken by the view. The mountain she was standing on cast a shadow on the forest below as the sun worked its way up and over the stunted trees, but this unblemished forest was a sight rarely seen in the waking world, and Izzy counted herself lucky to be able to see it now. The second thing that she noticed was the emptiness of the clearing. There was no blanket, no body, and barely any blood. What she did see was a pile of leaves and dirt that she had used as bandages to calm Rumi.

Wren's story, her tale of watching someone turn into a shadow, surfaced in her mind. The ashes rising from the body, the swirling dark infection from the shadow's wound—even as Wren had described them, Izzy had pictured Rumi and this mountaintop. Now, the lack of body seemed to be confirmation of her worst fear. Isabella felt the hopelessness and emptiness rise within her but fought them off. Wren had made mistakes too. Wren had survived them, and so would she.

"Rumi, if you're out there, I'm sorry," she told the air, thinking of the feeling of relief that emanated from the shadow she killed trying to save Kimi. "I will do everything in my power to make this right."

Isabella had not been further than this spot before and now she stopped, unsure of which way to go. Happy her father had insisted on her learning how to use these things on one of their yearly camping trips, she pulled the map from the cabin out of her backpack and Rumi's compass from her pocket, and found the right path. A path that would lead her to the capitol and, with any luck, to Skia.

It took another couple of hours and, based on the sun, it was close to noon when Isabella walked into the town labeled Evenstar on her map. The town looked like something out of a magazine or a textbook, one of those older European cites that Isabella had never been to. Most of the houses were made of stones and some were wooden with plaster, but they all had reddish tiled roofs. Wooden carts piled with all sorts of items, everything from toys to meats to clothes, lined the dirt streets and people—denizens, she presumed—were milling around. Unlike the last town she had been in in the dream world, these people seemed to take notice of her. Her clothes were clearly different than theirs, and although they didn't gawk, nobody ignored her either. Being honest with herself, she wasn't sure which greeting she liked better.

Not wanting to draw too much attention to herself, Isabella looked around for someone who was not busy buying or selling at one of the carts. One person stood out. A girl, maybe a little older than herself, was playing fetch with a grey, wire-haired puppy. She laughed as the dog, running back with a stick far too big, tripped over its own feet and tumbled to a stop in front of her. After shaking itself off, the puppy yipped and jumped up, licking the girl as she squatted down. She pushed her short dark hair behind her ear to retrieve the stick for another throw.

"Excuse me," Isabella said as she approached the girl, "I was wondering if you could help me?"

When the girl turned around, leveling her vibrant green eyes on Isabella, time seemed to stand still. Isabella had to will herself not to react, but inside she wanted to simultaneously run away and hug the girl in front of her. Although there was no recognition on the girl's face, Isabella knew her. "I'll try," the girl said, "what do you need?"

Her heart was pounding. "My name's Izzy, and this might sound weird, but I was wondering if you've seen a red squirrel named Skia come through here?"

"A squirrel?" The laughter was light and airy, as if she had no cares in the world. "No, no squirrel named..." she trailed off.

"Skia," Izzy's face reddened slightly as she realized how odd this question must seem. "No problem, but maybe you could tell me how to get to the Capitol from here?"

The girl shrugged. "I'm sorry, Izzy. I'm new around here. I just came over the mountain last night myself."

"It's alright. I'll ask around. Thanks." Isabella was positive she knew who this girl was, but she was hoping that she'd get confirmation.

"I'm sorry, that's rude of me." The girl stuck out her hand toward Isabella. "I'm Rumi, pleasure to meet you."

"It is." When Isabella shook Rumi's hand, she felt a slight shock that lasted less than a second.

"It's strange," Rumi said, squinting at Izzy, "but you seem very familiar." The puppy, tired of being ignored, grabbed the cuff of Rumi's pants and tugged while letting out a playful growl.

"Cute puppy," Isabella commented.

"Thanks." Rumi brushed the hair out of her face again and looked lovingly at the puppy. "He looked lonely, so I figured I'd play with him for a bit. I guess he wasn't done."

Isabella said goodbye to Rumi, happy that she was happy but still sorry she would never again wake to her real life. Asking around, she eventually found someone who pointed her in the direction of the right road. Isabella, bolstered by seeing Rumi happily living as a denizen and not languishing as a shadow, set off with the hope that she may still be able to put something right.

⊰ FOURTEEN ⊱

T he capital city, when seen from a distance, was a mess of domes and spires. The sun, now well on its way toward setting, gleamed off polished glass in several places yet seemed to be absorbed by other sections. When Isabella first saw the city in the distance, she couldn't make sense of the baffling mixture of modern and ancient sprawl, but as she reached the tightly packed outskirts of the city, she realized that the true grandeur of the capitol couldn't be experienced from a distance.

Entering the city by the road she had taken was like the old story of the frog in the boiling pot; you didn't know you were in the thick of things until it was too late. Most of the buildings on the outskirts looked like they were built a long time ago, stones worn smooth by years of exposure, but there was glass in the windows and modern-enough looking doors that the incongruity of it all distracted Isabella. She almost walked into an old man leaning heavily on a cane.

"I'm sorry," she said after narrowly avoiding the collision.

"Sorry?" he groused. "You should be sorry. Wandering around with your mouth open like that." He shook his cane at her before continuing on, still mumbling to himself.

Most people in this section of town looked older, like the buildings themselves, but there was a buzz of life in the atmosphere. Isabella thought again about Rumi and the life she would live now as a denizen of the dream world. She wanted to know more about them, more about their daily lives, because she felt somehow responsible for Rumi's future. It was, after all, because of Isabella that she was stuck in here.

Before she'd noticed, Isabella emerged from the tight streets with their stone walls onto more of a cobblestone path which dropped quickly, affording her a view of the entire city spread out beneath her. All the roads were similar and all the buildings close together with their red terra-cotta tile roofs and glass domes. Some of the buildings further off had tall towers, almost like spires of a medieval castle. Several were topped with statues depicting angels, birds, carriages pulled by eagles, bears, and wolves. The view was breathtaking, but one building in the center of the city caught her attention more than any other.

The central building was columned and easily dwarfed the surrounding structures. The four corners were topped with gleaming golden roofs and Isabella saw lights beginning to turn on on some of the upper floors. The building itself seemed to be made from a light colored stone, polished until it was almost as reflective as the glass dome adorning the middle. She had to see it closer, but there were no direct paths except for a winding river which cut the city in half and ran past the side of the impressive structure.

Making her way to the river, Isabella followed along the streets on the eastern side. Even with the buildings between her and the river, she could hear people and boats going back and forth. She was forced to cross the river several times on one of the many bridges that connected the two sides. As she crossed, she marveled at the sheer variety of vessels on the water, ranging from a man in a canoe to an extremely large boat that looked like it would barely fit under the bridge, causing Isabella to hurry to the other side and the safety of the road.

By the time she reached the massive stone steps, Isabella was exhausted and had to rest for a moment before attempting to climb the palatial entryway. The building, which she could now see was made from some sort of pink quartz, sported two giant bronze statues in front of the stairs. One was of a young boy, probably no older than nine or ten, sitting at a desk surrounded by books. On top of the books sat a mouse, so lifelike that Isabella half expected it to jump down and splash through the surrounding fountain. The other statue was of a woman about her mother's age, maybe older, standing on a pedestal and holding up a scroll. Beside her on the pedestal was a shaggy looking dog.

People streamed in and out of the building, jogging up the steps, sometimes with several books in their hands and occasionally empty-handed. When she began to climb the steps, Isabella was surprised to find them less of a struggle than she'd expected. Although she was still thankful when she reached the top. A stone transom loomed above the imposing wooden double doors that adorned the top of the stairs. Carved on the stone in large block letters were the words 'Central Library', and under that in smaller but still impressive lettering was the phrase *A Nobis Errata*

Discimus. Isabella had no clue what it meant, but she liked the sound of the words when she read them aloud before she walked inside the open doors.

While the foyer was crowded, it did not feel cramped. The ceilings soared above her, and beyond the foyer, Isabella could see shelves and shelves of books filling the rest of the building. It looked to Isabella like every book ever written was housed somewhere in the cavernous space, and yet as full as it was, people moved around easily, seemingly finding the book they wanted quickly. On the lower levels, which Isabella could view from the balcony beyond the foyer, several people were seated, stacks of books awaiting their studious eyes. While Isabella felt that a poor way to spend such a beautiful day, they seemed happy to do it. But the people and their books didn't draw Isabella's attention for much longer as she spotted a small red flash of fur leaping from table to table, pausing momentarily before being shooed away. Isabella smiled to herself and ran down the curved staircase on the right-hand side of the balcony. She ignored the grumbles of protest from the other people in the library as she rushed to the latest table where a red squirrel was making its case to the person sitting there.

"—desperate for someone's help. My friend Wesley is trapped. You might know him. He was here all the time."

"Skia!" Isabella couldn't withhold her excitement at finding the companion so easily, but the wary looks from the library patrons reminded her to lower her voice. "Skia, I've found you."

"Miss Shaw?" Skia looked confused at seeing her again. "I thought we decided—"

"No." She put her hands on her hips to emphasize her point. "Wren decided, you decided, and I just gave in."

"But you changed your mind?"

"I'm allowed," she said as she scowled at the squirrel, "besides, you need my help."

"I told you I would find someone else."

"And that looks like it's going great." Isabella motioned to the annoyed-looking girl sitting at the table where they were talking. "She looks *so* ready to help."

"She can't hear me."

"What do you mean she can't hear you?" Isabella noticed that the look the girl at the table was giving was directed at her, not Skia.

"Well," the squirrel chittered in what sounded a little like a laugh, "only Dreamweavers and hunters can actually hear companions. So to her, you look a little like a crazy person."

Isabella looked from Skia to the girl at the table and smiled sheepishly. Then, holding her hand out for Skia to climb on, she said, "Now let's get out of here before they cart me off somewhere."

Skia hopped from the table onto Isabella's arm and climbed up to her shoulder.

"Thank you," the girl said with a breathy exhale, "your squirrel has been hopping around here chittering at people all day."

"Sorry," Isabella replied. Not knowing what else to say about it, she turned and headed out into the streets, hoping that she would look a little less crazy talking to a squirrel on the steps than inside the library. When they were outside, Skia hopped off her shoulder and onto one of the wide stone railings of the stairs. Isabella frowned at him, dropping her backpack to the ground between her feet and rolling her shoulders to get rid of some of the tension. "Why didn't you tell me? That girl probably thinks I'm a crazy person."

"I did tell you."

"Only after I was talking to you." She grunted in frustration. "You could have warned me before."

"Most weavers already know, besides, I figured your companion would have told you. By the way, where is your companion?"

"I'm still new at this," Isabella replied, dodging the question. "Do you want my help or not?"

Skia sat up on his hind legs and ran his short arms over his face, his tail twitching as he did. Then he settled back to all fours and said, "You had a point in there. I wasn't actually able to get any help."

"Why were you in there anyway if none of them could hear you."

"I was looking for a hunter or a weaver. Most of the weavers tend to use the library at the training grounds, but Wesley liked this one better."

"Let me guess, it's bigger?"

"How'd you know?"

Isabella looked up at the towering columns. "Good guess."

"Anyway, I already tried the library at the training grounds, and nobody was willing to risk it." He seemed a little embarrassed by the admission. "He's not all that outgoing."

"You sure are," Isabella mused. "Do hunters hang out in libraries a lot?"

Again, he rubbed his face and smoothed his tail before answering, "No, but it's all I know. Where else would I go?"

Isabella could tell Skia was embarrassed, so she changed the topic. "We need to get going if we're gonna save him. If you're willing to accept my help, that is."

"Miss Shaw"—Skia bowed down—"it would be an honor to accept your help."

"Well, I don't know about that, but—"

"No, no, no," a voice, gravelly with age, said from behind her, "this will never do."

Before she could turn around, Isabella felt something hard tap lightly on the top of her head. Without thinking, she closed her eyes, scrunched up her neck, and reached up with her hand to try to stop a second tap.

After a moment of disorientation, Isabella rubbed the top of her head. Something was wrong. The air felt different, less charged with sounds of people moving around. More serene. Quieter. Then she heard birds chirping and felt the warmth of the afternoon sun. Opening her eyes, Isabella's breath caught in her throat. She wasn't on the steps of the Central Library anymore. Instead of the imposing pink quartz railing, she was looking at a stone firepit. The fire had long since burned itself out, and the coals had stopped smoldering. Across from the firepit sat an empty yoga mat.

Looking down, Isabella saw her old ragged *Finding Nemo* towel and knew if she turned around, she'd see their tent. At first, she thought her father not finding her at the cabin had somehow pulled her out of the dream world, but one quick look around showed her how wrong she was. The tent was there, the truck was there, and the cooler with food hung from a nearby tree—her dad had called it bear-proofing the site, the food there in case they got tired of training—but he was nowhere to be seen.

As she realized she was alone in the woods in the waking world, the implications of her situation began to surface. Nobody was there to help Skia find Wesley, and while Isabella didn't know either of them very well, she didn't want the poor little squirrel to have to shiver out of existence. Then there was the matter of finding Kimi. The choice was clear. She needed to get back.

FIFTEEN

Hoisting the cooler back up into the tree was a lot harder than her father had made it look, but Isabella refused to give up. This was her food she was talking about, and no bear would get a free lunch on her. Thinking of bears brought Wren's story back to her, and as she sat on her blanket slaking her hunger with a sandwich, she thought about Geduld and the shivering. It wasn't fair that companions' lives were tied so closely to their weavers. She thought of Skia, alone again in the dream world, his time ticking away while she sat out here. Kimi was safe, according to the book anyway, but Isabella still missed her. Whenever she thought about the warm fur and the cold nose of her fox—she wasn't even sure if it was right to call Kimi her fox, but she wanted to—she felt an intense urgency, like finding her was a matter of life and death.

There was a way to get back, she knew that, but she also knew that she'd never be able to go back through the waterfall without her father there. There was no way. Maybe, she thought as she popped the last bite of sandwich in her mouth, she would be able to imagine something more manageable to go through. Her father imagined a door, the door to his grandfather's library. Isabella thought about doors she could imagine. There was that colossal library door, maybe the cabin door, or those blue doors in the dream traps which let her get back into the dream world from inside the traps. Perhaps they could work here.

"Only one way to know," she said aloud.

In her head, she ran through the meditation her dad had used. Closing her eyes, she focused on breathing—breathe in, breathe out, breathe in, and breathe out. Think about the feeling of yourself on the ground. Feel the unevenness of it against you, your weight against it. Breath in, breathe out. Feel the air entering your lungs and leaving your lungs. With each exhale, let go of one thought, one worry, one concern. Breathe in, breathe out. Empty the bottle of your mind, and when it is empty, climb inside yourself. Inside you will see a door. Breathe in, breathe out. That door will lead you to the dream world. Picture your door. Visualize it.

Isabella visualized the blue door of the cottage where she'd first met Kimi, the door that Kimi had helped her find. It was a six-paneled with chipped blue paint. The frame around the door was white. The handle was a tarnished bronze with some white paint, long dried. The door was vivid to her. She reached for the handle and felt the familiar shock. This was working, she told herself. She told herself that she didn't need the waterfall, but once the door was open, it didn't lead to the now-familiar cabin in the dream world. Instead, she saw her waterfall, the ground in front of the door wet from its spray. Her concentration faltered and she was back sitting on the fraying towel, looking at the ash pit.

Isabella breathed in and breathed out. She worked through the steps and visualized the door again. She could even smell the air in the kitchen, dusty and stale, but there was something else too, a faint rumble and the smell of moisture. Once again, the door opened to her waterfall. So did the cabin door, the library door, her parents' bedroom door, and the classroom door. Each one opened to the same waterfall, and each time her concentration broke and Isabella sat alone on an old towel in an empty campsite.

There was no getting around it; if she was going to get back into the dream world, Isabella knew that she would need to get through the waterfall. The thing that pissed her off more than anything was the unfairness of it all. Her father got an ordinary door, one he'd probably gone through hundreds of times, and she needed to swim through some morphing waterfall that grew deeper whenever she got near it. Her father, who could conquer anything, gets it easy, and she had to struggle.

"Oh, stop complaining, you baby. People are counting on you." Isabella's own voice surprised her. Her words sounded so strong, so confident, so not her. "Okay, waterfall, I'm coming for you this time."

She ran through her breathing once again, only this time she didn't fight picturing the waterfall. Isabella felt the spray from the rushing water before she could see it, and she heard it before she felt it. Now she stood at the water's edge. Forward was toward her almost certain death, and back meant Skia would almost certainly die. Picking up one of the larger pebbles from the water's edge, Isabella tossed it into the pool. She watched as it almost immediately hit and settled on the bottom.

She remembered going through the first time. The water had gotten up to her chest before she'd leaped into the waterfall, barely missing some sort of tree branch or root, though she didn't remember there being a tree beside the small pool and waterfall. She began to wade out into the water. Her only chance was to leap farther and grab that branch so she could pull herself to safety. If that failed, then she drowned, but there was no other way. The water was up to her waist now, churning with the force of the waterfall. She could feel it pushing and pulling her, trying to take her feet out from under her, trying to swallow her alive.

Isabella's heart began to beat faster. She could feel it in her ears. Her breath came in short gasps. Breathe in, breathe out, in, out, in, out inoutinout. She tried desperately to wring the oxygen out of the seemingly thinning air, unable to capture enough of it. Her legs began to shake, first from the stress of the pushing and pulling water, then just from the stress. Her arms were next. This was a mistake, she told herself as she took another few steps into the water.

Now submerged up to her chest, Isabella shook violently. It was the cold, she told herself, just the cold. Her teeth chattered as she gulped at the air, still unable to get enough oxygen to feed her quivering muscles. Her right foot slipped first, and Isabella could not get it planted again before the left was pushed back by the waterfall. Able to take one last gasp before plunging into the water, Isabella felt panic flooding her system. This is it, she thought to herself, I'll die trying to get into the dream world, killed by my own imagination. Struggling to get her feet under her, she wondered briefly if being killed by your own subconscious was considered suicide. Just as the thought floated to the surface, she was able to get her knee under her, then her foot. Soon, she pushed her head up through the water and gasped for air.

Breaking her concentration, something she couldn't do while under the water, Isabella returned to the blanket and the cold firepit. She dug the heels of her hands into her eyes, and with a grunt of anger and frustration, she let herself plop back against the dirt behind her. Think, Isabella told herself, think. Her hands flopped over her head and she stared at the dappled sun coming through the trees. She had no idea what day it was or what time it was, and her phone was locked in her dad's car since he'd said that stuff didn't work in the dream world. The sun was almost directly above her, so it had to be close to noon.

Watching the branches sway back and forth brought her mind back to the branch sticking out into the pool below her waterfall. If she could manage to grab onto that branch, she could pull herself free of the waterfall's grip and make it safely to the dream world. That was a big if to rest her life on, and she had missed it last time. Isabella lay on her back in the woods watching the branches sway and hoping that the cooler dangling from the rope overhead didn't fall on her.

She sat up suddenly. "Of course," she said out loud, getting up to get to work. She felt so stupid for not thinking of it before now. She rushed over and untied the box from the tree. Pulling the rope over the branch, Isabella examined the ends. Nothing was fraying—her dad took good care of his ropes. All she would need to do would be tie a loop that she could then pull closed on the branch, then she could use the rope to pull herself out of the water. The problem was that her father was the knots person. He'd tried to teach her, but by then she was more interested in her phone than in anything outdoors.

If she had her phone, she could easily Google knots and watch a video, but her phone was in the car. Briefly, she thought of taking a rock and breaking the window of the truck to get at her phone. Her dad would be mad, especially if he found out it was her, but she could always lie about that. The minute the thought entered her head, she dismissed it. She didn't want to lie about his window. She wanted to learn to become a Dreamweaver, and for that, she needed his trust.

Doing the best she could from memory—something about a bunny going around a tree and back in a hole—Isabella twisted the rope into some strange mess, but she was able to get a loop into it. She would have to leave the cooler on the ground. "Welcome, bears," she said ruefully before sitting back down to breathe and visualize.

This time, as she approached the waterfall, Isabella held the rope out like a shield against some dragon and waded out into the water. When she was chest high, her breathing coming in short gasps and her arms shaking, she tried to throw the rope through the waterfall. Instead, the water pushed it down and back toward her. Isabella rewound the rope and moved closer. She threw the rope against the wall of water but had the same luck as if she'd thrown it against an actual wall. She moved forward and repeated the ritual until she was close enough to almost touch the water with her hand.

When the rope first went through, Isabella almost let go of her end, but she caught herself at the last moment. Now to see if the rope snagged on the branch. Isabella pulled on the rope with a quick jerk and it came smoothly back through the waterfall. Rolling her eyes, she coiled the rope and tried again. "Come on," she said, "come on, come on."

It was the fifth time she threw the rope that it caught on something. Isabella pulled gently on the rope, then a little harder. Finally, she pulled with all her strength. Each time it held. Isabella's heart pounded in her chest for a different reason now. Instead of fear and intimidation, Isabella felt accomplished. She took another step forward, then another, each time moving closer to the cascade of water. Finally, standing neck-deep in the water, Isabella took a deep breath and leaped through the waterfall, holding tightly to the rope. The waters shifted when she crossed over, growing stronger, deeper, and then she was being pushed under. With a death grip on the rope, Izzy tried to pull herself forward. Flashes of Finn in the river when they'd first met came unbidden to her mind.

The water pushed against her back and as her feet crossed over from the waking world to the dream world, Isabella got the full force on herself. The water pounded on her back, pushing her down into the pool below. Frantically, Isabella flailed her arms, trying to move through the water. The rope was momentarily forgotten in her panic. Once her mind cooled, Isabella remembered the rope still clutch in her left hand.

Hand over hand, she pulled herself out of the water, but as soon as her head broke the surface, the waterfall's power seemed to redouble. Isabella was hit square in the back and pushed hard against the sharp rocks at the bottom of the pool, knocking the rope from her hands. Precious oxygen escaped as she involuntarily grunted, but she kept herself from inhaling. Isabella panicked again, her hand searching for the rope, first here then to the left, then back to the right, hoping that it had been long enough to reach the bottom of the pool. Isabella's lungs burned and her eyes felt like they bulged from her face. She was running out of oxygen and needed to do something fast.

SIXTEEN

The water pounded on Isabella's back, pushing her into the sharp stones at the bottom of the pool. As much as she tried to push back, her burning lungs screamed for action. Her hands, pinned beneath her, were scraped and raw, and rocks dug into her right hip. The hypnotic rhythm of the waterfall was threatening her consciousness as lights danced behind her eyelids.

Pushing back against the water, Isabella extricated one of her hands and began to search the bottom for the end of the rope, despite having no idea if it was even long enough to reach her at the bottom. She had to believe it was.

Her hand scurried over rocks and gravel and grasped what she thought was the rope, but it squirmed in her hand. Only with a great effort did she avoid taking in a lungful of water to scream. Silt bloomed in the water around her as her free hand ran frantically over the bottom.

Isabella felt the rope's fibers just at the edge of her reach, but it slipped out of her fingers and twirled away in the water.

Stones were jutting from the bottom of the pool, and while at first she had viewed these as obstacles between her and the rope, now she realized they could be handholds, ways to pull herself closer to it. Grabbing the closest one, the edges biting into the skin of her palm, Isabella moved forward one rock at a time. Another stone, and a few more inches, then another, and repeat. The gravel on the bottom scraped against her, but she persisted. Eventually, with the pressure of the water still pushing down on her, Isabella was able to get her hand on the rope.

With the rope in her hand, she allowed herself to hope this might actually be possible. Hand over hand, like she'd seen Finn do before, Isabella pulled herself out from under the battering of the waterfall. Her lungs wanted to burst, begged her to release the pressure and inhale. Her body rebelled, her grip slipped on the nylon rope, and her arms shook, but Isabella didn't let go. Soon, the angle changed, ever so slightly at first, then with increasing pitch. She stopped dragging herself and tried to get her feet under her, but they slipped on the loose stones.

The light danced on the surface of the water, teasing her senses, but it didn't look like it was getting any closer. Her body convulsed and focusing on the rope became harder. Twice, she stopped moving, realizing only after letting go of the rope and slipping lower into the churning waters. Isabella focused on the point where the water met the land on the surface. A darker spot moved up there. It was small but distinct, and while the dark spot could be anything from a shadow to a burst blood vessel in her eye, it gave her something to focus on. Hand over hand, she climbed closer to the light, and hand over hand she pulled herself, gasping, through the surface of the water and onto dry land, where she fell to her back and stared into a cloudless cerulean blue sky. Her vision was still blurry and her chest ached like a full-grown man had stood on it, but Isabella laughed at the sky.

At first, Isabella dismissed the pinpricks on her arms as the oxygen returning to her system through the large gulps of air her lungs still greedily drank. But as they moved up toward her shoulder and then to her chest, Isabella hoped it was something else, someone else.

"Are you alright?" Skia's high register voice chittered in her left ear.

"Skia!" Isabella gasped. "I'm so glad … to see … you. I was —"

"Sent back, I know. It was Kasimir. He saw us talking and deemed you too young to be a Dreamweaver. He sent you back, assuming you had come by mistake."

Isabella nodded but didn't trust herself to speak yet. She had stopped gasping but could still feel the adrenalin coursing through her body, coupled with exhilaration as much for what could have happened as for what did; from being thrust out of the dream world so suddenly, torn from the middle of a conversation, to now ungracefully coming through the waterfall. But she was back, and that was what mattered.

"How long … has it … been?"

"Just one night."

The sun peeked over the treetops. Suddenly, Isabella realized something was missing. Sitting up, an action she immediately regretted because of her now splitting headache, she looked around for her bag. It wasn't there. She tried to remember if it was at the campsite but couldn't picture it. "My bag." Her voice had an edge to it that made her feel almost out of control. "I think—"

Skia laid one of his tiny paws on her knee reassuringly. "It's on the porch. I was able to get a friend to bring it back on their way south. I'm sorry I didn't see Kasimir in time to warn you."

"We have to go back."

"But we'll need to avoid the capital." Skia backed up slightly. "The council gives one warning. That was yours."

"What happens after a second warning?"

Skia smoothed his tail. "No one knows. Nobody whose gotten more than one warning is ever seen, except maybe your father."

"My father has gotten in trouble?"

Skia laughed; it was a warm sound. "You're funny."

Isabella smiled despite herself. "So he doesn't get in trouble." That seemed more like it because her father followed the rules. He didn't even speed when they were late.

"Oh, Izzy," Skia said with a hop forward and a chuckle, "your father gets in a lot of trouble. The thing is, no one is willing to cross Vígolfr. You have seen that thing?"

"My dad's wolf?" Isabella shrugged. "Seems harmless enough. You didn't get in trouble, did you?"

"When there is trouble for one—so the saying goes."

Isabella hadn't heard any saying that started that way but simply nodded and watched the edge of the forest. "We have a long way to go then." She stood up, careful not to fall on her wobbly knees. "Let's get the map from my bag." Isabella patted the metal cylinder in her pocket.

Skia played with his tail. "I'm not sure it's going to matter. It's been a long time, and the path north, without going through the capitol, will take a few days. I'm not sure this is a rescue mission anymore."

"Don't say that." She walked over and held her hand out for Skia. "You would know if he was dead. You'd feel it."

"How do you know?"

"I-I just do, you know. It's like Kimi; I know she's out there but not willing to come. I deserve it too."

Skia didn't respond, but he hopped off Isabella's shoulder and onto the railing when they got to the cabin. The cocoa, now cold and congealed, sat on the railing, still waiting for someone to drink it. That girl isn't here, thought Isabella. Maybe she never was. As promised, her bag sat tucked up against a log couch on the porch.

The contents were a little mixed up, but everything seemed to be there. Isabella began to take things out until the book, her knife, the dream catcher, food, and the map were all laid out. Figuring where they needed to go would be as easy as finding the path on the map, then using the compass to follow it. Nothing could be done about the time they'd lost, but it was in her power not to make it worse. She began talking through the path they could take but noticed that Skia was no longer looking at the map with her. Instead, he was rummaging through her pile of stuff.

"What's this?" Skia pushed the dream catcher with his nose.

"Nothing, just something I picked up from a peddler last time I was in here."

"Peddler?"

"You know"—Isabella turned her focus back to the map—"an old lady pushing a cart with all sorts of junk on it. I was bummed because I couldn't find Tucker, so she gave me that to make me smile.

"Weavers' charms." Skia sounded like he was in awe of something.

Turning around, Isabella saw the dream catcher in the squirrel's paw. "Finn always used to say that. Said it was an expression or something."

"It is." Skia reverently set the dream catcher down and hopped over to the book, resting his front paws on it. "But that is a weaver's charm. Do you know what it does?"

"Does?" Isabella was confused why Skia seemed so excited about this turn of events. "It opened a portal to get me home once."

Skia jumped up and down and danced from paw to paw. "Portal?" The word seemed to make him so excited he ran around the porch in circles. "Don't you understand what this means?"

"No?" Isabella watched Skia shake so much it looked like he was going to explode. Oh no, Isabella thought, I'm too late, and this poor little thing is going to go through the shivering. "Could you stop running around a second and explain it to me?"

"Just pick it up! Pick it up, and we'll be there!"

Isabella picked up the dream catcher and, like last time, spun it around her finger in a circle. Then she tossed it in front of her, where it fell silently to the grass and lay there. Skia hopped over and touched it, then turned back to Isabella. "When does it open?"

"It doesn't," she said, sitting down on the stairs of the porch. "I've tried it a bunch of times at home, but it falls flat."

Skia hopped up the stairs to the book that Isabella had left sitting next to her bag, sniffed around it, and then looked at the spine. He made a chittering noise that drew Isabella's attention. Turning around, she watched as he worked his way under the cover of the book and turned a few of the opening pages. She cocked her head to the side as the squirrel ran his paw down what looked like the table of contents and mumbled something to himself.

"What are you doing?"

Skia didn't answer as he turned the page and seemed to scan the next one.

Isabella moved closer and crouched down next to him. Glancing up from the book, Skia shifted slightly and then looked back at the page. He shifted again, then looked up at Isabella. "Could you move over there"—he pointed to the other side of the book—"you're in my light."

"Are you reading this?"

"It's a table of contents," he said after she moved, "it's not very hard to read."

"But no, I mean, you can read?"

"Wesley practically lives in the library when he's here." Skia tapped on an entry in the table of contents. "What do you think I do all day, sleep?"

"Well, no." Isabella had not expected that answer and stammered to find a response. "It's just, you're a squirrel."

"I'm a companion"—Skia put his hands on his sides, above his hind legs, and looked up at her—"and *most* Dreamweavers respect that."

"I'm sorry, I—"

"Now help me turn to this page." Skia pointed to the book again. "I could do it, but you'll be quicker."

Isabella looked at the entry in her book: "Charms and Trinkets". Turning to the page, she read the opening paragraph.

Some people in the weaver society maintain that the use of charms and trinkets is a myth purported by the shamanistic cultures and their contemporary counterparts in the waking worlds to sell these trinkets to tourists and spiritualists. Much of the literature suggests using such items was indeed a vital part of ritualistic dream weaving in the earlier sub-culture of physical weavers, until the Great Purge of 1882 when the council, then a fledgling body, deemed the practice unsafe and banned the use of charms thereafter.

"It doesn't sound like something that is supposed to work." Isabella walked over and picked her dream catcher off the grass. Her fingers traced the intricate weaving, lingering on the stones that hung from sections of it, unsure what she'd expected. The first time had been simple. When spun, the dream catcher started sparking blue light, then the portal opened and she could safely get her brother home. Since then, when trying to use it to get back into the dream world, nothing happened.

"Right here," Skia called from the cabin's porch, "I remembered it being a couple pages into the chapter. It says that the stories describe weavers wielding great power by using trinkets and charms. Among those powers is the ability to travel between worlds *and* across great distances in moments."

"But how?"

Skia sat down on his hind legs, the excitement leaving his voice as he said, "It doesn't say."

Looking at the squirrel who was sitting on his haunches with his tail flat against the floor of the cabin's porch and his ears drooping, Isabella was almost brought to tears. Skia, who had been so happy, so energetic, looked like he was about to give up. Slinking back to the book, he began absently flipping the pages. Either he was looking for the answer, or he was trying to pass the time. Either way, Isabella knew she needed to do something.

She spun the dream catcher around her finger and watched as each revolution changed nothing. By now, the sun had climbed over the trees and was well on its way to afternoon. Day three, halfway. Three more days to find Kimi and fix things before it was too late. The sun's rays bloomed on the mountaintop, and Isabella found herself thinking about Rumi laying in the dirt at the top of the mountain. Although happy she'd found her as a denizen, that didn't change the fact that it was too late for the girl, too late to graduate high school or get married or wake up. Isabella was screwing everything up again. She pictured the last sunset Rumi had watched, sitting on the top of the mountain, the valley stretched out in front of them as the colors exploded on the tops of the forest below.

"Isabella." Skia's voice was soft, but something in his tone pulled her from her memories and the dream catcher, which she'd been spinning on her fingers, slipped off. The air filled with a crackling sound and a blue flash, and Isabella took a step back, almost tripping over the steps behind her. "You did it!"

On the grass before the cabin stood a circle of blue light, sparks of which occasionally arced from the outside. In the middle of the ring, Isabella could see a mountaintop overlooking a forest. Just to the right of a large stone sat a small pile of leaves and some darker ground. The scene looked exactly as she remembered it, but it wasn't home. She walked closer to the image in front of her.

"You did it," Skia said, a mix of surprise and admiration clear in his voice.

"I was thinking about that mountaintop," she said, leaning around to look at the other side. "It's the same over here, same image and everything."

"Come here." Skia started pushing some of the smaller items back into Isabella's bag. "Get your bag, and let's go through before it closes."

Quickly shoving everything back into her bag, Isabella slung it over her shoulder and held out her arm for Skia to climb up. She looked back over the field and noticed metal by her feet glinting in the sun. Bending down, Isabella picked up the compass that Rumi had given her and stuck it back in her pocket. With a deep breath, they stepped through the portal.

At first, it was like walking into a picture; everything was flat, two dimensional, but before Isabella even had time to panic, the world seemed to expand out from the center, taking on dimension. Air rushed past her, then with a flash of blue light, the portal back to the cabin closed and the dream catcher fell to the ground.

"That was amazing!" Skia said as he hopped onto a nearby branch. "I've read about accounts like this in old books, but I never thought I'd actually experience it."

"I was spinning this around my finger and thinking of this mountaintop and the valley," Isabella explained, feeling her pulse quicken. "That must be it. I have to picture where I want to go, then I can get there."

"So we can't use it to get to Wesley?" Skia said quietly, his excitement short-lived.

"I don't know." Isabella smiled and looked up at the clear blue sky. She was feeling good, a rush of adrenaline; this felt like a significant win. There had to be a way they could use it. "My mom always says I have a great imagination. Maybe if you describe the place to me, I can picture it." She shrugged. "Worth a try, right?"

Skia described the cave that he had watched Wesley go into, and the land around it. While he spoke, Isabella lazily spun the dream catcher around her finger and tried to imagine the scene he was painting. Closing her eyes, she pictured walking down the trail Skia and Wesley had taken to the cave, an unusual trip for the typically sedate and bookish weaver. They had read about a collection of books lost in a cave structure during an expedition several years ago. The books were the last of their kind. All other copies were destroyed during the Great Fire, which happened over a hundred years ago and cost the Dreamweavers much of their ancient knowledge and archives. Isabella shook her head; the history of the Dreamweavers Skia was intermixing into the story was distracting her. Once again, she focused on the path, the feel of the forest, the thicker shadows as they neared the cave's entrance.

The entrance was set in an average gray mountain. A series of vines had grown over it, disguising it from the casual eye. There was a detail about the vines, a trumpet-shaped flower with purple petals that grew on them, and Skia's description reminded her of the morning glory vines that grew at her grandmother's house. Isabella shook off the images of her grandmother's and focused on a cave covered with morning glory vines.

The air around her crackled in the breeze as blue sparks arced off the dream catcher. Isabella flinched back, accidentally throwing the dream catcher over the edge of the mountain. It hovered about a foot from the drop-off, spinning in the air. The blue circle around it expanded, and inside Isabella was looking down at a tangle of morning glory vines covering a dark opening. She turned to Skia who was holding his tail in front of him, his little mouth hanging open.

"You did it," he said, hopping over to the drop-off and looking down. It was steep, and the portal was a foot away from the edge, hanging in mid-air. "Can you make that jump?"

"It's only a foot. I could probably step into it."

"That's not what I mean." Skia pointed at the image in the clue circle. "I mean that."

It took Isabella a minute to realize what he was talking about, but when she did, her heart sank. The picture in the middle of the circle was not at ground level. Instead, it seemed that the portal was dangling from the top of some trees. There were branches visible in the lower portion of the image, but they looked small and Isabella wasn't sure they would hold her. Judging from her limited experience, once the portal closed the dream catcher was on the other side, so Isabella assumed this was going to be their only chance to use it.

"I don't think I have a choice. Come on," she said, her voice much more confident than she felt, "it's now or never."

Skia hopped from the edge back up Izzy's arm and to her shoulder, his nails pricking through her sweater, and together they jumped from the edge of the drop-off and into the portal.

ᕙᕈ SEVENTEEN ᕈᕗ

A s troubling as jumping into a flat image, only to have the world then pull out into three dimensions, can be, when those three dimensions include a thirty-foot drop from a treetop, the difficulty rating goes way up. Skia didn't seem to have trouble with the transition. He simply hopped off Isabella's shoulder and, after grabbing a branch, scurried toward the tree trunk. Isabella was not so lucky. During her free fall, as branches whipped past, lashing her arms and face, she twisted her body, trying to grab one of the many branches speeding past. After almost immediately missing the limb she had scouted out through the portal, Isabella crashed into three others, succeeding only in slowing herself down, before she finally grabbed one that was about an inch and a half thick. The branch bowed under her weight and the sounds of splintering wood, reminding her of windstorms back home, told her the branch might not hold under stress. Her feet, on the other hand, were dangling in the air, unable to find anything to settle on as she frantically kicked, the branch complaining with each bounce.

"Skia, what do I do?" Isabella yelled.

"Just work your way to the trunk," Skia said, resting comfortably on a thick branch near the tree's trunk. "The branches are safer there."

As good of an idea as moving toward the trunk sounded, that meant letting go of the branch with one hand. "I can't."

"Sure you can, use your legs."

"I can't reach anything with my legs." Isabella flailed more wildly, her fingers and her right arm beginning to ache, but she still couldn't get her feet to land on anything solid.

"Not like that." Skia sounded annoyed, as if Isabella were making the most obvious mistake. "Swing your legs up onto the branch, then you can scurry along it."

Between the choices of letting go with one hand and possibly falling, dropping down and definitely falling, or swinging on the branch like a monkey and perhaps falling, Isabella was not sold any of the ideas. With a lack of other options, she kicked her legs up toward the branch anyway. On her first swing, her left hand slipped off the now swaying branch, and she screamed. Getting ahold of the branch again, she was now farther out from the trunk. The branch creaked under her weight, but Isabella tried again. This time, she used the momentum of the swinging branch to help her, still falling short but keeping her grip.

"Third times a charm," she grunted, swinging herself up toward the branch and managing to hook her legs around it for a moment before they slipped off. Her weight jerked at her arms, causing more pain to lance through her left shoulder. Despite the pain of the bark biting into the palms of her hands, Isabella forced her burning muscles to respond. It took two more goes before she was able to get her legs wrapped around the branch.

"Good," Skia called from the trunk of the tree, "now scurry."

"That's easy for you to say," Isabella said, "you're a squirrel. You can climb down the stinking tree trunk." Isabella pushed her legs toward the trunk despite her grumbling, crackling sounds from the branch coming with each movement. With more support for her body, moving her hands felt marginally safer and eventually she used her arms—one over the other—when the branch became more expansive. By the time she reached the tree's trunk, Isabella climbed on top, drenched in sweat, and collapsed against it.

"Nice work," Skia said as he hopped to the next branch down, "now go branch by branch until you get to the ground."

"Give me a minute, will you?" Isabella closed her eyes and let her breath even out. She exhaled and looked at the sky but could feel something drawing her to the cave. That was the way to Wesley and hopefully her ticket to some help finding Kimi.

The climb down the tree was not as bad as Isabella feared it would be. The branches were close enough together that she could dangle from one and just about reach the next. As they got closer to the ground, the branches spaced out so she had to drop a few inches, which was harrowing at first but soon became a bit of a game to her. The last branch ended about nine foot from the ground, but that reduced to about four foot when Isabella dangled from the branch , and she landed on a bedding of pine needles.

Now on the ground, everything looked different. Isabella and Skia weren't on a path, but instead were in the middle of the forest. Shadows loomed despite the blazing sun that shone above the canopy. Isabella shivered at the temperature change. Skia wasn't faring much better. As soon as it was apparent that Isabella would make it down the tree, he'd hopped on her shoulder, his nails making tiny pinpricks on her skin. For the last drop, he had hopped off and crawled down the trunk to the ground. Now that they were both on solid ground, the little guy was back up on Isabella's shoulder, only now he tucked himself under her hair.

"I don't like this," he chittered behind her right ear. "Something doesn't feel right."

"You described this place," Isabella reminded him, worried that he was beginning to back out. "This is where you said that Wesley was. We need to find the cave."

"I know," Skia said shakily, "but—"

"But you need to step up." Her voice was on the edge of breaking. If Skia gave up on Wesley, what hope did she have with Kimi? "If we don't get to him soon, who knows what will happen." Isabella couldn't get the idea that Skia might go through the shivering at any time out of her mind. The poor little squirrel's shaking was making that seem more and more likely by the minute.

"That's not what I mean," he quickly corrected her. "I'm planning on rescuing Wesley, he would do the same for me, but this place doesn't feel right. Something's off."

They emerged from the edge of the forest into a small clearing at the base of a cliff. A little off to the right was a trailhead, and to the left was a tangle of branches with some small, purple trumpet-shaped flowers growing on it. They weren't quite the morning glory she'd thought, but they were close enough. She started toward the branches, the smell of honey floating on the light breeze.

"Stop," Skia said as he dug his nails into her shoulder.

Isabella did as she was told, but looking around she didn't see any reason why Skia was so jumpy. "There's nothing here"— she pointed toward the trumpet-shaped flowers—"so we're gonna go up there. Wesley's through there, right?"

"I think so, but something's not right here. I don't want to go in there. It's not right."

"I'm scared too," Isabella said gently, not used to being the brave one but liking the feeling, "but people never get trapped on a nice bright beach somewhere."

"I'm not—I mean—I'm not going in there." Skia hopped off Izzy's shoulder.

"Come on." She stopped and looked down at him. "Let's go to the entrance, then we'll decide. You're feeling wired from going through the portal."

"Okay," he said, eyeing her warily, "but I'm not making promises. Squirrels are meant for trees, not caves."

"Don't be a baby," Isabella said and started toward the flowers again. Soon the squirrel was bounding along behind her. If she was honest with herself, something did feel strange about the cave, but it might have had more to do with not knowing how to light her way through its darkness. She mentally kicked herself for not having thought about it until now, when it was too late to do anything about it. She would just have to make do.

The cave's mouth was cooler than the rest of the clearing, and Skia climbed partway up the trunk of one of the nearby trees, refusing to get any closer. The branches around the entrance had purple flowers, but they were too small to be morning glories. Other than the wrong flower, the entrance looked like any cave entrance. Isabella stood at the edge looking down and could hear nervous tittering from the tree behind her.

She turned her back to the entrance of the cave and faced Skia. "See, nothing strange. Just a cave. Now let's go in and find Wesley.

"I'm not going in there"—Skia flinched as he said the words—"it's not right."

"You want me to go in there myself and rescue *your* weaver?"

"No," he said with a tremble, making Isabella worry that their time was almost up, "you shouldn't go in there either."

"But then how are—" Isabella stopped and turned toward the cave entrance. "Did you hear that?"

"Hear what?"

"That sound." She leaned into the darkness to try to hear better. "Sounds like someone calling out for help."

"I don't hear anything."

Isabella dropped her backpack by the tree Skia was nervously clinging to and walked back over to the entrance. The opening was too small to wear the bag through, and she wanted to get closer so she could hear better.

"Someone is definitely down there." Isabella faced Skia and put her hands on her hips. "Are you coming to help me or not?"

"I can't." He scurried further up the tree as if worried she might try to snatch him off and drag him inside.

Isabella took the compass from her pocket and ran her fingers across the filigree, imagining Rumi getting this gift from her uncle. She opened the cover and read the inscription: *When you can no longer see the sun, let this guide you home.* The needle rocked to the right and stopped. Isabella turned herself to face the direction of the needle.

"I'll go in a little. Be right back." Turning her back on Skia, Isabella began to head into the cave.

"What if you get lost?" Skia asked, perched on Izzy's pack.

"I just got my bearings. That's north. The entrance here is west. If I get lost, I'll use the compass and head east." She patted her pocket with the compass. "Don't worry so much." Moving a branch aside to let more light in, Isabella descended into the darkness. For a moment, she felt like coming in was a mistake, but she pushed that thought aside when the cry for help came again, knowing she'd made the right choice.

The cave was dark, but enough light came through the opening to allow Isabella to make out some shapes. The call came again. She considered answering but remained silent instead. The light began to fade as she descended deeper. The ground was damp and slippery, and the air had a fetid smell like something had been using the cave for its own personal bathroom.

"No." The male voice was familiar, but she couldn't place it. "Please no, I'm sorry, I'm sorry, I won't do it again."

Whoever it was, he was close. Isabella drew her dagger from the sheath at her belt and crouched low as she continued toward a corner. Around the corner, a light flickered, possibly from a fire. The shadow of a looming figure took up most of the wall in front of her.

"Please," the voice said again, "somebody help me."

She stopped at the corner and rested her back against the wall. She hadn't expected to find someone guarded by whatever loomed on the wall to her right, but she couldn't let someone else down like she had Rumi. Determined to save the boy despite the threat to herself, Isabella rounded the corner, holding her dagger in front of her, and found herself staring at the back of a massive shadow. The emotions of despair and greed flowed off it like water, flooding the small room. Isabella could see a small cot in the back of the room, a dresser, and a smokeless fire burning in the center of everything.

Isabella took a moment to scan the shadow's back. The core was easier to spot with the fire on the other side, and Isabella crept up to the back of the shadow. Its arm was raised over the boy, ready to strike, its claws dripping a black substance that ate away at the floor beneath it. Knowing she couldn't delay, Isabella raised her dagger and slashed down at the core. With a solid hit, the shadow dissipated, clearing the room of the negative emotions, but Isabella didn't feel the sense of relief she had with the last shadow she'd gotten rid of.

The boy had brown hair that hung past his ears with a slight curl near the ends. His skin was pale, and he wore a dark-colored cardigan, not typical for denizens of the dream world. A dreamer, Isabella thought to herself, and, sheathing her dagger, she approached him slowly. He was backlit, so it was hard to see his face, but something about him seemed familiar.

"Hey." She stopped a few feet away and crouched down in front of him. "Are you okay?"

"Izzy?" The boy lifted his head and seemed to stare at her for a moment before his shoulders relaxed slightly. "Is that you?"

She couldn't place his voice, and with the poor lighting of the fire, she couldn't see his face. "Yeah, it's me."

"Evan," he said, seeming to relax a little more now his suspicion had been confirmed. "From school."

"Evan!" How she could be lucky enough save the cute boy she was supposed to go on a date with on Monday confounded her, but she had to suppress a giggle all the same. "Are you alright? Did the shadow hurt you?"

"What was that thing?"

"What did you see?"

"It was this huge dark-fog-monster-thing." He grabbed his shoulders. "It had like claws and these glowing eyes."

"It was a shadow," Isabella said, trying to figure out why he was here. "Most people see them as whatever their subconscious works up."

"Subconscious?" He squinted at her in the dark. "Am I dreaming or something."

"Well, yeah, basically." She didn't know how much to tell him, but she needed to say something. "This is a dream, so most people would see this as something out of their subconscious."

"If this is all a dream"—he stood up and looked around the room, Isabella following suit—"are you a dream too?"

"No," she said, resting her hand on the hilt of her dagger. "I'm a weaver. I'm someone who weaves dreams for people. I can affect the course of a dream too once someone is already in."

"Weird," he said, looking around. "Can we get out of here? This place gives me the creeps."

"Yeah." Isabella reached out for his hand, planning on leading him out of the cave. Best first date ever, she thought to herself. "The entrance isn't far. You never answered me though, did the shadow get you?"

"No," he said, giving himself a quick pat-down before taking her hand. "Thanks to you, it didn't get me with those claws. How'd you get rid of it?"

"I have my ways." She felt a little stupid having only slashed at it with a dagger, and she doubted he needed to know the finer points of killing shadows, so she went with mysterious. He didn't answer, and almost immediately Isabella wished she could take back the mysteriousness. They walked in silence for about a minute before the sun outside became visible in the distance.

Hoping to break the now awkward silence, Isabella asked, "How'd you get here?"

"To the cave? I don't know, I went to bed, then I was walking in the woods. Saw the flowers and thought I'd investigate. Then came down to see what the light was and boom, that thing materializes out of nowhere and starts waving its claws around."

"The entrance is up here—" A rumbling in the cave around them cut Izzy short as the ceiling and the walls started to send pebbles down to the floor. "Let's hurry!" She pulled on Evan's arm, but he must have missed a rock in the darkness because suddenly his hand pulled from hers and he slid to a stop.

"Go on without me," he called from the ground, yelling to be heard over the cacophony of crumbling rubble.

Isabella turned back to Evan and, jogging over, smiled and reached down to pull him up. "I'd have to find a way back in to get you."

The noise became deafening and soon large boulders were rolling off the side of the mountain, blocking the light from the entrance. By the time Evan had upped and turned around, the final boulder fell into place, blocking the light from outside and leaving them holding hands in the darkness.

EIGHTEEN

"What happened?" Evan's voice was tumbling. He grasped her hand so hard it hurt, but Isabella didn't mind. Actually, she was kind of enjoying it. "How are we going to get out of here?"

Isabella looked around her, but she might as well have had her eyes closed. The darkness in the cave was complete; what little light had been coming through the entrance was now blocked off as smaller stones filtered down over the newly fallen boulders. There was a vague musky smell as Isabella moved closer to the rocks, dragging Evan with her. The closer they got, the more dust was in the air. As they had began navigating some larger boulders, the ground got slippery and they had to stop.

"Skia," Isabella called out, "are you out there?"

She waited, but there was no answer. Another rumble and some of the looser rocks above them shifted, sending a new shower of pebbles onto their heads. Isabella put up her free arm to protect her face, then pulled Evan back through the boulder-strewn floor deeper into the darkness.

"Are you sure we should go this way?" he asked. "What if the shadow thing comes back?"

"It won't." Isabella didn't remember the feeling of gratitude when she'd gotten to the core of the shadow, but wrote it off as being distracted. "I have a theory about them."

"You have a theory?" He sounded surprised. "How do you even know enough about them to have a theory."

Isabella didn't know what to tell him. "Well, let's say I've seen them before."

"You've what?"

"Long story," Isabella said dismissively. Now wasn't the time to get into it. "We need to find a way out. Have you been here before?"

"I don't even know where here is," he said, still holding on tightly to Izzy's hand.

Isabella moved farther into the cave. One shadow was dealt with, but who knew if more were hiding in the depths of this place. If she could get to the fire, at least they'd have light. At the same time, something about the fire had felt off; there was no smoke. Working along the wall, her hand running over the cool, wet stone, she got to the corner where Evan had been. The light that should have been coming from around the corner was gone. The fire was out. Isabella silently cursed her luck, then, in a more chipper voice, said, "Don't worry, we'll get some light."

"How? That fire was burning when I got here."

"How did you get here anyway?" Isabella was naturally suspicious of people, but something about Evan made her want to trust him.

"Honestly, I'm not sure." His voice was close in the darkness. "There were these flowers, purple ones that smelled like honey, then I saw the cave and thought I'd explore."

"Okay, but why do you see all this and not something from your subconscious like the other dreamers?"

"Is that what this is?" he asked. "I'm really dreaming?"

"Probably, but not exactly." Isabella tried to find the words, before settling on, "It's hard to explain."

Evan pinched himself, then frowned and rubbed where he had pinched his arm.

Isabella watched him for a moment and then laughed. "What did you do that for?"

"I heard that you can't pinch yourself in your dream."

"Did it work?"

"Depends." He shrugged. "If this is a dream, I heard wrong. If I heard right, this isn't a dream." He looked at her, then furrowed his brow.

Isabella was caught by the deep green of his eyes. They shone with an inner fire but looked like they could be soft and caring, like eyes of a doe or a puppy. His hair was down over his forehead and when he leaned over like he was now, it would whisk around his eyelashes, drawing her back into his big eyes. It was only after admiring his eyes once more that Isabella realized she shouldn't be able to see him at all. She looked around. "Where is that light coming from?"

His voice was tentative as he answered, "Your belt, I think."

Isabella looked at her belt and saw that the pommel of her dagger, the one Ajay had given her the last time she was here, was glowing with a warm yellow light. She pulled it from the sheath for a closer look. The yellow faceted gem in the pommel seemed to have a luminescence coming from deep within it. Isabella examined the other gems in the handle, but there was nothing special about them. On closer inspection, the stone in the pommel looked to be a topaz or something similar, except that within the cushion cut stone there were two dark flecks, one of which seemed to be glowing.

"So," Evan said, reaching for the dagger, "is that some strange flashlight thing?"

"No, it was a gift from a friend." Isabella didn't hand it to him. Instead, she held it pommel up and began looking around the cave they were in.

"What now?"

"Now"—she pointed down a dark passageway leading deeper into the cave—"we go deeper. The way I see it, there must be more ways out, so if we choose one path and keep following it until we see some light or hear something, then we should be alright."

"I think we should dig ourselves out."

"Bad idea." Isabella started walking down the path she'd chosen. "Take one wrong rock out, and the whole thing could collapse on us."

Evan stood in place for a moment. Once it was clear that Isabella was continuing down the path with or without him, he jogged to catch up. They walked in silence for a while, but with each step, Isabella's shoulders tensed. She wondered where Skia was and if he'd gone through the shivering. She worried that they would not be able to find Wesley quick enough. Her pace slowed as the urgency that had started her down this path faded, leaving her feeling hollowed out and helpless. There was no point in this, she began to tell herself. Soon Skia would go through the shivering, then Kimi, and all the while Isabella would be stuck wandering down here lost and alone.

The last thought jarred her out of her oncoming stupor of self-pity. She wasn't alone. Why had she thought that? Not that wandering around here forever with company was any better, even cute company like Evan, but still, the desperate feeling didn't make sense. Then the other emotion hit, loneliness, and suddenly Izzy thought about leaving here and maybe losing Evan's attention. Here she had him to herself. Out there, in the waking world, she had a date with him, but who knew what would happen after that. She wanted him to herself. Perhaps wandering here with him wasn't so bad after all.

Isabella stopped in the middle of the path. Something was wrong. She thought about the feelings surrounding her, and then it hit her. She hadn't felt the relief when rescuing Evan because the shadow wasn't killed; she'd simply scared it away. Fighting the emotions swirling around in her, Isabella dropped into a fighting stance, holding the dagger pommel up.

"What are you—" Evan started.

Shushing him quietly, Isabella listened. Shadows didn't make noise when they walked, but sometimes they would bump into things. At least, they had in the dream trap version of her house. Isabella didn't hold out much hope for that, but tried anyway. The shadow could be coming from anywhere, so she tried to concentrate on its emotional eddies of despair and greed. Focusing, her hand tightened on the handle of her knife and Isabella closed her eyes. She pictured the cave in her mind and concentrated on those two emotions like a homing beacon. Giving full reign to the feelings within her, she tried to follow them to their source.

"What's wrong?" Evan's voice shook.

Isabella shushed him again and opened her eyes, trying to look as far as she could down one path, then the next. It was coming, but she didn't know where it was coming from. If the shadow snuck up behind her, who knows what would happen to her. It would almost certainly scratch her with those claws, then she would join Rumi and any thoughts of being a Dreamweaver, or graduating high school for that matter, would be forgotten.

"Where are you?" she whispered. The handle of her knife was glowing softly. The light was enough to see by but not enough to see far. When the shadow came, Isabella knew it would come quietly and quickly as if it had materialized from the darkness.

The voice she heard behind her was breathy. "Give me the boy, weaver." It was close, but not close enough that it had come into the light. "You can leave."

"Don't let it take me," Evan murmured, grabbing her shoulder with one of his hands.

"No one is being taken here." The steadiness of Isabella's own voice surprised her. "Get out of here, shadow. I'm not afraid of you."

"But maybe you should be," the breathy voice wheezed in laughter, "you don't know who else I have down here."

"I rescued Evan from you." She stood taller. "I'll rescue whoever else you have."

"But at what *cost*, weaver?" the shadow asked.

"Why don't you come here and find out." Isabella tightened her hand on the dagger and she loosened her elbows and
shoulders in preparation.

When the shadow swept into the very edge of the light, it
seemed to wince as if in pain before it regathered itself. The
tremulous dark fog that made up its body spun and wavered as it
moved patiently but inexorably toward Isabella. She watched the
shadow, trying to time her strike so its core would meet her blade.
She watched its soul bounce inside the darkness, a small, darker
ball.

When the shadow was within a foot of her, Isabella knew
it was time to act. She lunged forward, leading with the knife.
Her body tugged to the left and, thrown off balance, she spun and
fell to one knee. The shadow's claws whizzed harmlessly over her
head. Scowling back at Evan, he sheepishly shrugged. She'd forgotten he had his hand on her shoulder. He was scared, she told
herself, nothing else. Despite her assertion, doubt began to rise to
the surface.

After taking a moment to switch her dagger so the blade
side was up, Isabella sprang up from her knee. She drove the dagger upward with all her force, driving the point toward the center
of the shadow's chest. It connected with the core, and Isabella
felt the familiar resistance and heard the comforting pop. This
time intense feelings of relief and gratefulness flowed out. Isabella
smiled as the air cleared and the thoughts she had been having
about Skia and Kimi, although still fears, no longer had hold of
her.

Lifting the dagger to put it away, Isabella noticed that the
topaz had something strange about it. There seemed to be one

black fleck she hadn't seen before. Along with that, there was a second one that was pulsing, but it seemed dimmer than the first, faded, really. Isabella didn't have the time to think of the implications of that new inclusion because as soon as the last bit of shadow fell, the cave began to shake. First, it was slight, almost imperceptible, but soon the rumble became a deafening roar. With the sounds of cracking stone all around them, Isabella needed to think fast.

"Get across to that wall!" Isabella pointed, breaking Evan's reverie. He scrambled to the wall, but as he did, the floor beneath him gave way and he tumbled out of sight, calling Isabella's name.

"Evan, are you alright?"

"Sure," he said, faking a laugh, "maybe you want to come and join me?"

Not sure if she wanted to, Isabella hesitated. After a moment, the choice was taken from her as the small ledge she'd found herself standing on gave away. Isabella tumbled down, expecting to land on the jagged rocks, but instead feeling herself be caught. For a moment, Isabella didn't know what had happened, then she looked into his eyes again, drinking in the deep green pools of hopeful energy. For his part, Evan stood there, holding her tightly.

Isabella giggled. "Thanks."

"Don't mention it," he said, staring at her face.

The ground shook again and the rocks on the floor above them began to crumble down.

"Let's get someplace safer," Isabella suggested, and Evan put her down.

NINETEEN

The dagger provided enough light to see the room they'd fallen into, but not enough to see past the openings in the walls. There were two, well, three if you counted the one they had fallen through in the ceiling: one in the wall in front of them and one to their left. Isabella walked to the one in front of her and tried to see down as far as possible. The passageway looked more like a hallway than a cave, but there were no doors or turns as far as the light went. The other passage, also looking more like a hallway, had two openings, one on the right about halfway to where the light reached, then another on the left at the edge of the light.

Isabella reached into the inside pocket of her jacket to take out the dream catcher. It was all well and good to explore a strange cave to rescue someone, but once they're saved, it's better to get out while you can. Sticking her hand in her pocket, Isabella closed her eyes and drooped her shoulders. She pulled out her empty hand. Only then she realized that when they went from the mountain to the forest, she had been so focused on not falling to her death that she'd left the dream catcher in the tree.

"Which way leads us out?" Evan asked, looking over her shoulder as she looked down the two passages.

"Not sure." Isabella considered her options. "I went into the cave heading west, so it would figure that we could leave heading east."

"How do we tell which way's east?"

Isabella reached into her pocket and pulled out the compass Rumi had given her. She rubbed her thumb over the filigree pattern on the case before carefully opening the compass. The needle seemed to rock back and forth for a moment, then began to spin counter-clockwise. Evan, standing next to her, slumped his shoulders.

"It was a good idea," he said.

"Something must be interfering with the needle." Isabella closed the compass and returned it to her pocket. "Maybe there's something magnetic down here."

"Or maybe this is just a dream, and compasses don't work in dreams."

"Gonna pinch yourself again to find out?" Isabella smiled back at him. She couldn't be confident in the dim light, but it looked like his face turned a pale red before he moved to look down one of the passages. Curiosity got the better of her. "I think we should go this way," Izzy said as she began down the path to their left, her shoes slipping a little, "those doors look interesting."

"Are you sure?" Evan's footsteps splashed behind her on the thin layer of water covering the floor.

"Got a better idea?" she asked.

Isabella took the lack of answer to mean that he didn't, so she went to the first of the two doors, opened it, and shone the light into it. The room inside was laid out like a bedroom of sorts. There was a sleeping area made of a pile of pine needles and some skins. A rough table and chair were set along the other wall, but nothing looked like it had been used recently, and the water on the floor had soaked the makeshift bed. Evan caught her shoulder as she went in to search the room, but Isabella ignored the gesture. Instead, she walked over to the desk. The dust covering its surface was thick, her breath causing big dust-bunnies to tumbleweed around on it. The air smelled sour in here, like rotting hay. On the table, buried in the dust, was a small key.

"What's that for?" Evan asked in a whisper.

Isabella shrugged and pocketed the key. If there was one thing she'd learned the last time she was here, it was that you never knew what would end up being useful. "Who knows," she answered, not bothering with the whisper, "but I don't think we need to worry about someone missing it. Doesn't look like anyone has been here in a while."

"Still"—he was hesitant—"stealing it?"

"It's not stealing if no one misses it." Isabella began to walk out of the room, taking the light with her.

He followed her out into the hall and down toward the next room, saying, "I don't think you understand the word stealing."

Now that they could see further down the hall, past the next door, the hallway curved to the right. A rumbling sounded far away, but it caused bits of stone and dust to filter down from the ceiling. Brushing the dust from her forehead, Isabella splashed into the second room. It was a pantry from the looks of it, but most of the food was spoiled or rotten. She saw potatoes that had long sickly-looking toppers coming off them and some small red piles of mush that were probably once apples. The rest of the food was even more unrecognizable, mounds of mold and fungus.

"Want to take anything from here?"

"I hope you're trying to make a joke"—Isabella scrunched up her face in disgust—"because gross."

Evan didn't answer. He hung by the door, waiting for her to explore the shelves. It smelled terrible in there, like stale and rot and death. Though it wasn't bad enough to make Isabella want to vomit, it did make her a little queasy so she soon joined Evan back in the hall and turned round the bend. After a few steps, she paused.

"Did you say something?" Isabella asked Evan.

"No, why?"

"I think I hear something." She closed her eyes, focusing her efforts to hear.

"Is it something bad?"

She shushed him again, and he rolled his eyes and crossed his arms over his chest. Ignoring his tantrum, Isabella tried to listen harder to the sound she was hearing. It was faint, but it sounded familiar. Continuing down the hall, Isabella stopped at a four-way intersection. The sounds got louder and more distinct. First a call for help, then crying, another call, then yelling at someone. There was more than one voice coming from different directions.

Isabella tried to focus on one of them at a time. First there was a woman's voice, calm and collected and pissed off. It was threatening to disembowel the person who trapped her. Another voice, quieter but from the same direction, sounded pompous even as it complained about being in prison, which the voice called incarcerated.

"Wren?" Isabella said the name quietly at first, then again louder, calling out, "Wren?"

"Isabella," Wren called out, "get me out of here!"

"Where are you?" Isabella splashed down the hall toward Wren's voice, the water now ankle-deep.

"Izzy?" Another voice, familiar still, but one she hadn't heard in a long time. "Izzy, is that you?"

"Finn?"

"It's me," Finn's voice called from the opposite direction. "I'm trapped."

"Iee iee!" Tucker called out. "Iee iee, help me. Shadows have me."

"Busy Izzy," her father called from down the last hall. "Be careful, get out of here. It's not safe."

Isabella froze. How could all four of them have ended up here? How could she save them? The questions bludgeoned her, the next hitting before the last was finished, giving her no time to answer. She stood still, listing to each person plead their case, call for her to help them, or else run away. Wren was formidable and deadly. She'd be good to help get the others out, but then again Finn was resourceful and loyal. He'd insist that they get everyone out. Her father was, well, her father, and after seeing him fight the shadow congress, she was sure he'd give even Wren a challenge, but he was telling her to get out. Tucker was helpless, but as much as she loved him he was also useless in this situation; less than useless because she'd have to worry about him getting hurt or worse. Maybe he was safer in the cell.

"Izzy," Evan called out, "come here. I found something."

The water was steadily rising. Her boots were leaking, but the water wasn't over the top of them yet. She let Evan lead her from the intersection into a room down the hallway where her brother was calling.

"In here." Evan pulled her into a small room. The only thing of note was a wooden ladder that led up to a trap door. "I bet that leads out, or at least up." The ground shook again. "We can get out of this water. There's nothing down here."

"Can't you hear the people calling for help?"

"I told you already, I don't hear anything." His hands were on the ladder already. "Come on, I don't want to drown down here. The water's getting deeper." The ground shook again, and the water started dripping into Isabella's boots. "And with these earthquakes, I don't want to be down here when this place caves in."

"But my brother's down here, and my father. I need to save them!" There was a thought forming in the corner of her mind, but she couldn't quite place it. "If they're down here, *they'll* drown. I can't let that happen. Wait here for a minute, I'm going to get my brother. He's little. You can help him up." Isabella rushed out of the room and back into the hall, sloshing through the water as she went. "Tucker? Dad? Wren? Finn? Where are you? I'm coming."

"No," her father's voice yelled, farther away than before. "Find the ladder and get out!"

"But Tucker—"

"Your mother can't lose all of us. Go, find the ladder."

Tucker yelled out next as if he hadn't heard what their father had said, or perhaps because he had. He was closer than her father and his voice rang out, "Iee iee, I need you. Help me. Too much water."

"I'm coming," she called back. The rising water helped to make her decision easy. Tucker first, then if Evan was still by the ladder, get him up there, then back for the rest. She wasn't going to lose anyone else. She wouldn't fail them like she failed Rumi.

"Izzy," Evan said as he grabbed her left arm, his grip tight on her skin, "where are you going?"

"I have to save my brother." The ground shook hard, small stones beginning to plop into the water around them. "Go back, stay by the ladder and wait for him. I'll be right back. He's close."

"Your brother's not here." He tugged at her arm, pulling her back toward the room with the ladder. "We have to go now before this place collapses."

Something about the whole situation felt strange to Izzy, but she still couldn't place it. Evan tugged at her arm, but her brother was calling for help. Evan said something about shadows and dreams, but there weren't any shadows here; she'd feel them coming.

"No." She jerked her arm from his grasp. "They're here."

Sprinting through shin-deep, almost knee-deep, water was not an easy task. At this point, though, Isabella was running on adrenaline fumes. Evan splashed behind her. He was probably right; this was dangerous, and when she found her brother there was no telling if she'd be able to get him out, nevertheless get back for everyone else. Isabella couldn't think about that. That line of thinking would only lead her to despair. Ultimately, her course was simple: get Tucker out and then get back for the rest, all before the water, now solidly knee-deep, turned the place into an underground river.

She ran down the hall, calling after her brother from time to time to gauge the distance between them. Evan was gaining on her, and she knew he'd try to stop her again if he caught up. She paused briefly to call down a side path to see if Tucker was there. He called back, the sound seeming to come from the central passage, so Isabella left the doorway and waded down the hall. The water was slowing her down, making it harder to get to her brother.

"We need to go," Even panted. "Everything ... is falling apart ... trust me ... the ladder."

"You don't understand. My brother needs me." Isabella pointed down the hall. "Can't you hear him."

"No, Izzy." Having recently caught his breath, his voice was serious. "I don't hear anyone calling. You're hearing things, and you're going to get us both killed."

"No," Isabella said, "listen. There it is again."

"Izzy, no one is calling out your name. Did you hit your head when you fell? You're acting really strange."

"I got this." She paused for a minute, thinking how bizarre the situation was. The ground rumbled again, this time longer than the ones that had come before. Isabella stretched out her hand to steady herself on the wall. "I got this."

TWENTY

The tremors were getting more frequent, but at least the water had stopped rising for now. The splashing of the stones tumbling into the water was another story. Isabella was sure what she was doing was dangerous, perhaps even stupid, and her father would be angry, but she was determined that he would get the chance to be mad about it.

"Tucker," she called out, "I'm coming, little buddy."

"Help me," his voice trembled, "I scared Iee iee."

Her heart beat faster as she pushed through the water.

Evan waded up to her. "Izzy," he panted, "we need to get out of here. What are you going to do when you get to your brother?"

"I'll get him out." She turned a corner and saw a hallway lined with openings, at least ten on each side. Isabella went to the first doorway and shone the light in. The room inside was cluttered with cardboard boxes, falling apart with their contents piled next to them. Old shirts and water bottles, shoes, and blankets, each with varying degrees of mold or mildew covering their surfaces. One pair of shoes had a small mushroom growing out from the ankle.

The next room across the hall was also packed with boxes, but this time they were wooden crates turning black with mold. A sound from inside one of them caught her attention. "Tucker?"

"There's no one in there," Evan said. "Who are you talking to?"

Isabella ignored him. She could hear her brother, not in this room maybe, but she could tell they were getting closer. There was another sound from the back of the room, and Isabella crept inside. The crates were labeled with pictures of animals: birds, foxes, bears. Each container had one animal image on it, but they were all nailed shut. She knocked on one crate and heard a dull thud; something was inside, but there was no reciprocating knock and no air holes, so whatever was in there was probably not alive. Still, she felt compelled to see what it was.

Looking around, Isabella spotted a crowbar on top of a box with a picture of a fox on it. Her heart leaped in fear as she approached the crate, feeling a tug inside her. The water seemed to flow against her, pushing her back harder the closer she got to the crate. Evan followed closer to her, seeming not to notice the pressure of the water. He grabbed the crowbar before she could get it. First, he held it out of her reach and looked fiercely at her as if he was planning to keep it from her, but then his features relaxed and he handed her the crowbar.

"It's not like I could stop you if I wanted to," he said, "so see what you need to see, then can we go?"

Isabella jammed the bar under the lid of the box it had been resting on and pulled it down. The nails complained as they pulled free. There were rust flakes on the metal and they left brown rings where they had been in contact with the wood. Inside the box was a taxidermy animal, a small red fox. Tears welled in Isabella's eyes as she pried off the front of the crate to get a better look. Scanning the fox quickly, her eyes paused briefly on the engraved plate at the front of the base. Under the four letters of the fox's name, the word 'Companion' was engraved in italics, and Isabella's heart dropped.

"No." The word was barely a whisper.

The fox's fur was a sleek red; no mildew or mold had touched her. The dark nose looked moist and cold but felt rubbery and dry, almost artificial, when Isabella touched it. The fox was posed in a defensive stance that Izzy had seen before, front right paw forward, the left slightly bent, ready to move quickly when needed. But she wouldn't be moving anymore. Her head was down and her mouth was open to show her canines. It was not the pose that Isabella wanted to remember. Isabella would have liked to see her curled up, nose under her tail like she was sleeping; instead, glass eyes stared forever at some final fight Isabella wasn't there to help with.

"You've seen," Evan said, looking at the frozen fox, "now let's get out of here. That thing gives me the creeps. Besides, there's nothing down here."

Isabella clenched her fists, closed her eyes, and chewed on her bottom lip. Her tears—and there were plenty she wanted to shed—turned red inside her as her sadness burned off into a rage that she focused on Evan. "Shut up," she growled at him. "Ever since I came down to save you, and don't forget for a moment that's what happened, you've been whining and begging me to climb that stupid ladder. You want to climb it out of here? Go ahead, and good luck with whatever is up there. Good luck in the pitch blackness because I am going to find my brother before something like this happens to him or worse." She turned to face him, her breathing quick. "And *that thing*"—she pointed over the shoulder—"was a friend of mine, so back off." She pushed her way past, leaving Kimi frozen with her eternal snarl inside a half-open box in the darkness. Leaving the room, Isabella brushed her arm over her eyes and the heel of her hand over her cheeks.

"Tucker," Isabella's voice shook as she called out. "I'm coming."

This time there was no reply. She stopped to listen. Someone, presumably Evan, came sloshing up and stopped a few feet behind her but she didn't want to see him. Isabella strained to hear anything, but when her repeated calls were met only with silence, she fell to her knees. The water soaked into her shirt, sending a chill through her she hardly noticed. Instead, she imagined the millions of possible reasons her brother hadn't returned her call. Could the water be deeper where he was? Could it have been over his head? Neither question had a good answer.

Isabella shivered on her knees. It was all too much for her; the water, Kimi, her brother, there was nothing she could do about any of it. Feelings of helplessness and frustration began to flood her consciousness. She was not some hero from a movie or some special girl who could save the world. She was an ordinary kid who didn't know what she was doing and struggled in geometry, like everyone else in her class. Her mind grabbed onto that thought. Geometry was the most frustrating subject. It was supposed to make sense, but it was just formula after formula and never any real numbers. You can't have math without numbers. It doesn't work that way.

The water rippled around her and when Evan's hand fell on her shoulder, she tensed up. He brought her back to the miserable situation. Kimi gone, her brother gone, next her father, and all because of her failings. Evan's grip tightened and he ground his teeth. His breathing was a forced calm, and she thought he was trembling slightly. He must be feeling the same way I do, she thought, and then again, if he was feeling the same way—

"How do you feel right now?" Isabella asked, hoping for, but not expecting, an answer.

"How do you think I'm feeling? I can't get you to leave these tunnels because you're chasing some sounds that I can't even hear, but it's not like I can do anything about it."

She tested her hypothesis. "So would you say you were frustrated? Maybe feeling a little hopeless?"

"I don't know," he snapped at her. "I told you how I feel."

Isabella stood up and hope surged through her. The third possibility why her brother hadn't called out was that there was a shadow nearby, and maybe he was hiding from it. She rushed down the hall that was once again filling with water as the walls rumbled almost constantly around her. She didn't investigate the rooms anymore. Instead she opened up her emotions. The hopelessness and frustration were more robust now, and though they were hard to overcome, they were clearly coming from outside.

They were not her feelings right now. She was mad, and she was sad for Kimi, but she was determined not to fail her brother.

"Wait up," Evan called behind her, coughing loudly as he wheezed in the thickening air.

"Quiet," she snapped back at him, "there's a shadow up here, and I want to get the—" Isabella skidded to a stop, a process made both more complex and simpler by the rising water. While the water slowed her, it made the floor slippery, causing her to almost lose her footing and go under. She pushed her back against the cool stone wall to her right, a doorway past her shoulder. Evan copied her movement, ending up on her left, and leaned his head back against the wall.

"In there," she whispered. "Shadow."

"How do you know?"

"I saw him." She scrunched her face indicating he was asking an obvious question. "Besides, these emotions you're feeling aren't yours."

"They feel like mine." Evan crossed his arms.

Isabella rolled her eyes. "Well, they're not," she said, ending both the debate and the conversation.

Peeking around the corner, she could see the back of the shadow. This one was bigger than the one she'd killed earlier, but the wispiness made it seem thinner, more transparent. On the other side, in a small cage, Isabella could see someone cowering. It had to be Tucker, but he must have been standing on something because his head and chest were above the water. She pulled her head back and leaned it against the wall. Her brother was in there, alive, and that was something—for now.

She imagined where the shadow's core would be floating in the massive, roiling body. Taking a deep breath, she looked around the corner again, this time focusing on the shadow and trying to ignore her brother, who must be terrified. The shadow was thin, with short tendrils shooting out along the sides, but Isabella could imagine the size of them trained on her brother.

She scanned the back of the shadow, letting her anger over Kimi and the fear for her brother center her. At the base of the shadow's neck, above where the shoulder blade would be on a person, Isabella saw the darker core. It was small, no bigger than a dime, but with some luck she knew she could hit it with a well-placed slash. She could always throw the knife, but there was no guarantee the gem would stay lit, and the darkness would definitely give the shadow an advantage, assuming that it could see in the dark. Izzy couldn't see in the dark and didn't want to take the chance they could. Besides, if she missed then she would be unarmed, and even if she hit it there was still a chance of injuring her brother on the other side.

Isabella took a step into the room and put her fingers to her lips. The light would give her away, but she hoped that the shadow might be too occupied with its captive to notice. Realizing the flaw in her plan too late, she pushed her way through the water into the room, the splashing sounds a clear giveaway in the confined space. The shadow turned and seemed to thicken in substance as it drew in the tendrils it had wrapped around her brother.

"Let him go," she commanded.

"What can you do to me, little girl." The shadow's voice was breathy and lingered on some of the sounds. "You are not your father. There is more of your grandfather in you."

"You don't even know my grandfather," she scoffed. "He was never a Dreamweaver."

The shadow made a wheezing sound that approximated laughter. "It's you who doesn't know, child."

Splashing in the doorway caught her attention, and Evan stepped through, shaking his head slowly. "No," he said, "no, this can't be."

Isabella moved her focus back to the shadow. She flipped the knife in her palm and crouched into a fighting stance. "Enough of this," she said, pouncing forward.

Her blade passed through the shadow harmlessly. Its massive claws slashed out where Isabella was and caught her in the back before she could get out of the way. Fortunately, her coat took the brunt of the attack. She shrugged out of her jacket, which sizzled as it hit the water, and readied herself for another attack. This one was closer to the mark but left her vulnerable to a counter-attack. She spun quickly, diving under the water and coming up on the other side of the shadow, whose swing was still following through the water where she had been moments before.

With the shadow bent over trying to reach the floor of the room with his attack, Isabella could get a better hit on the core. She felt the familiar tug as she pulled the knife free of the roiling body. For a moment, she heard a shriek, then the shadow condensed into a handsome older man who nodded and, with a flash of gratitude, disappeared.

Isabella heard Evan gasp and mutter, "How?" but she ignored his question to focus on getting her brother out.

It looked like Tucker was in some sort of cage. There was an obvious door, but there didn't seem to be any latch or lock holding it shut. Tucker shook the bars and begged Izzy to open the cage. A complicated series of switches and levers seemed to be connected to a chain running through several gears along the top of the cell. Isabella pulled on one of the levers. It tightened the chain and caused Tucker to cry out. Isabella looked closer at her brother and noticed his hands were now outstretched on either side of him, attached to a set of chains by shackles. She quickly pushed the switch back into place and the chains slackened again, allowing him to lower his arms.

Isabella closed her eyes and took a trembling breath. The wrong lever could hurt her brother, but if she did nothing then would drown in the still-rising waters. There were five levers in front of her. She could pull each of them separately, she considered, but if she did, one of the levers could do far worse to her brother than pull at his arms. Considering the ramifications, she decided against randomly pulling levers. Instead, she traced each of the chains that looked to be running to the levers. Two followed the first chain up to her brother's shackles. Two others went off into the wall to her left, one high and one low. She pulled the lever for the higher chain. The door to her brother's cage opened slightly, but someone screamed in the distance.

"What was that," Evan said, looking into the hallway. "It sounded like someone in pain."

Isabella ignored him. Getting her brother out was the most important thing. She pulled harder on the lever that had partially opened her brother's door. The scream came back, the pitch higher and this time edged with pleas to stop.

"Stop!" Evan came over to her and tried to take her hand off the lever. "You're hurting someone else to get him out."

Tucker's cage was not open enough for her to get in and free him. She pulled her arm out of Evan's grasp and glared at him. "Don't," she snarled, then pulled the lever again. The scream came once more, louder and more pained, but then it stopped and Tucker's door fell to the floor with a loud clang.

"I can't believe you did that." Evan stood unmoving, watching Isabella move toward the cage door. "Do you even care if you hurt that person?"

She turned on him. "What did you want me to do? I'm not a hero. I needed to save my brother. Nothing else matters."

"A lot of horrible things happened because people were trying to help someone else." Evan ground his teeth. "I thought you were different, but you're not."

Isabella ignored him and turned to Tucker. "Come on," she said softly, "let's get you out of those." She walked up to Tucker and touched his shackles. At her touch, they fell away, and he started giggling. Taking a step back, she looked at her brother's face.

"Oh Iee iee." Tucker's voice sounded mocking, "I'm so ... not here." As he faded from view, Isabella heard a laugh. It wasn't her brother's, but it was familiar even if she couldn't place it. There was something more going on here, but she didn't know what. With the rising water, figuring it out would have to wait.

Stunned, she stood in the cage, the rising water now up to her ribcage, and thought about what happened. That laugh. Why did her brother fade away? If it wasn't him, then Isabella really didn't know what was going on. Then the realization about the person in the next room hit her, and her knees wobbled. When she had thought her brother was in danger, the other person didn't matter, but now that she knew it hadn't been Tucker in the cage, what did that callousness say about her. Isabella considered the question as the ground shook around her, sending ripples throughout the room.

"The rumbling," she whispered.

"We need to leave," Evan said as he placed his hand on her shoulder and gently guided her out of the room. "This whole place is going to come down on us."

"But it was him—" she said, her mind scrambling to make sense of what she'd seen and done.

"I don't know what's going on, Izzy," Evan said, his voice sounding softer than usual, "but I'm pretty sure that wasn't your brother."

"No, no, you're right, he wasn't—" Isabella's eyes shot wide open and she gasped. Turning on her heels, she ran to the next room over, where the screaming had come from, and tore open the door. She didn't wait to check the room or make sure there were no shadows. One question kept circling in her mind. What had she done?

The room was mostly empty. A long table lined the right-hand wall alongside a cage similar to the one her brother—or the shadow pretending to be her brother—had been in. The table was covered with several contraptions that threw monstrous shadows on the wall in the light coming from the hilt of her dagger. In the cage was a boy about Isabella's age, bloodied and bruised. He

shied away from the light when she came in and started whimper-
ing and muttering, begging her not to hurt him anymore.

The cage was made of metal, but it looked like the side
was held together by ropes. Isabella could see a few places where
the bindings looked darker, places the boy must have unsuccessfully tried to untie the cords himself. Isabella approached the
cage slowly, wading through the deepening water. The boy in the
cage pushed himself against the bars in the far back corner, holding his hands in front of himself and shaking.

"It's alright," Isabella said, putting the blade to the rope.
"I'm going to get you out of here." Splashing in the doorway told
her that Evan had followed her. Glancing over her shoulder and
confirming her suspicion, Isabella returned her focus to cutting
the ropes.

"Are you sure that's a good idea?" Evan asked from the
doorway. "Remember what happened last time."

Isabella shook her head and kept cutting. The top rope
fell into the water and she moved on to the middle one. "Doesn't
matter." She looked at the shivering boy in the cage. His blond
hair was tinted red and matted against his forehead and he had a
cut on his right arm that looked painful, but it was his eyes that
haunted her the most. The terror showed through them, but Isabella couldn't tell if he was afraid because he was trapped or if he
was afraid of her. "It'll be okay," she said calmly, "we're going to
get you out of here."

After the second rope splashed into the water, Isabella
pulled on the door. The top came away, but not enough to
squeeze through. Letting go of the metal door, she felt under the
water until she found the third rope. She blindly sliced at it with

her dagger; the wet fibers were less brittle than the other two, but eventually she cut through it. The metal cage door swung quickly through the water, but the boy didn't move from the back of the cage.

"It's okay," Isabella said, trying to coax him out, "I'm not going to hurt you. I'm releasing you."

"Just grab him and let's go," Evan called from the door. "The water's going to get too deep to touch the floor soon."

"I'm Izzy," she said, ignoring Evan and reaching into the cage. "Take my hand. I'll get you out of here."

Tentatively, the boy reached out. The scratches on his hands looked raw and recent, so Isabella was careful not to touch them, hoping not to cause him any more pain than she had already inadvertently done.

"My name's Eli," he said, allowing himself to be led from the cage into the open room.

"Eli, this is Evan." She gestured over to Evan who was still in the doorway, the water now up around his knees.

"Good to meet you," Evan said, looking over his shoulder toward the ladder. "Can we go now?"

Evan followed them back down the hall they'd come through, away from the levers and cages and past the room with Kimi. Isabella looked longingly into the room, hoping to catch a final glimpse of her friend whose death had sealed both their fates. Now she knew. She knew why Kimi hadn't come, and she knew she would never become a Dreamweaver. Her shoulders sagged, her hands fully submerged in the water and causing the yellow gem in the hilt of her dagger to eerily illuminate the undulating waves. As much as she wanted to simply give up and collapse, there was no question this was a dream trap. She had to get the two boys out.

As they approached the turn in the hallway, something in the water caught her eye. She stopped suddenly. Evan bumped into her back, nearly knocking them both over in the process.

"Come on," he pleaded, "the water is going to be too deep for us to get out soon."

"Hold on." Isabella walked to the wall in front of her. Evan followed her, but Eli kept his distance. Keeping the dagger beneath the water, she pointed the hilt into the corner. Tucked into the corner of the wall, Isabella saw a hint of color in the otherwise gray stone. The air around her filled with dust as another rumble shook the ground. Isabella examined the waterline as the undulations caused almost a tidal effect. Between the waves, she was able to see a slight hint of blue. "That's it," she said and started to feel around in the corner.

"Izzy"—Evan grabbed her arm and began to pull her away from the corner—"we don't have time for this."

"For this we do," she said, not bothering to explain what was going on. After groping around for a while, a couple of times the water splashing into her nose and eyes, Isabella finally found the smooth metal of the door handle. A brief spark shot through her hand. "Eli, come over here. This is our way out."

"What are you doing? That's only going to lead down." Evan pulled her again, causing her to lose contact with the doorknob.

She pulled out of his grasp again. "No. This is the way out, trust me."

"The ladder is our way out—"

As he was speaking, Isabella turned the knob and threw open the door. She heard a rushing sound like someone had popped a water balloon attached to a hose, and Isabella felt her feet being pulled out from under her. She reached over and grabbed Evan's arm, pushing him under and through the door. He disappeared with the water and Isabella felt the relief of having gotten him out safely. Bracing herself against the wall to avoid being pulled in after him, she reached out for Eli.

"Hurry up," she called over the rushing water, "I'm not sure I can hold on much longer."

Eli was backing away from Izzy and the blue door, shaking his head.

"This is the way out," she pleaded, flattening herself against the wall to avoid being pulled through the door.

Eli shook his head more firmly and fought against the water pulling at him. He turned around and began moving down the way they were headed. As Isabella watched him, calling after him, she felt the guilt of her actions start to overwhelm her. In freeing who she thought was her brother, she had hurt this stranger. Now because he didn't trust her, he was going to be trapped in here forever, probably as a shadow.

The water pulled at her, trying to force her out of the door after Evan. She remembered she'd escaped the first dream trap through one of these doors. It had been safe on the other side, but when she'd come out with Tucker, they'd been surrounded by shadows. Isabella was torn. If she followed Evan, Eli would undoubtedly be made a shadow in here, trapped and suffering in the dream world forever. If she followed Eli, there was no guarantee that Evan would make it out safely; he had a better chance than Eli, but nothing was certain.

Cursing under her breath, Isabella pushed off from the wall and began to fight her way against the current. She'd done what she could for Evan. Eli was in greater danger. Each step became more difficult than the last, the water pushing against her and trying to force her out. Twice she lost her footing and plunged beneath the surface, coming up sputtering for air. Despite the water pressure and the speed at which it flowed through the door, the level never decreased in the hall.

The ground shook again, knocking Isabella to her knees, the water washing over her head. She tried to get to her feet, but the water's pull increased like a hole had been torn in the side of the cave. Her lungs burned and ached to inhale as Isabella scrambled for something to stop her from sliding back and through the door. The loose stones rolling with the water across the floor complicated things. Her vision began to darken. She swallowed to keep from inhaling. The water roared in her ears and pushed at her limbs. She frantically searched the ground for something to grab, knowing she couldn't hold her breath any longer.

The roaring of the water increased in pitch, turning into a ringing in her ears. Then suddenly, the pressure stopped. The rocks along the floor stopped moving, settling where they were, and Isabella pushed off the ground, breaking the surface of the water with a gasp. Her lungs ached and her head swam. Leaning her back against the wall for support, Isabella rested her hands on her thighs. The water was up to her waist now, despite whatever had happened with that door. She hoped that Evan was alright, wherever he ended up.

Once her legs stopped shaking, Isabella started off after Eli, hoping that he had fared better than her with the rushing water. Coming around the corner where the room with the ladder was, Isabella noticed a soft glow emanating from above. She ducked in and looked up. The trap door was open, and there seemed to be light coming through.

"Eli," she called up the ladder. Only silence answered her but she started climbing anyway. Chances were good that he'd gone up as Evan had mentioned that was where they were going. The water had also begun to rise quicker, and Isabella couldn't swim. If Eli was still down there, there would be nothing she could do for him anyway. With each rung of the ladder, her heart pounded harder in her chest. Wren and her father weren't there either, she told herself; like Tucker, they were simply shadows trying to trick her. It had to be true or she was abandoning them, and that would be too much for her to take.

At the top of the ladder, the room was dry but empty. A set of wet footprints left the room and headed down the hall to the right. Figuring it was as good a trail as any, Isabella followed the wet footprints until they stopped in front of a closed door. The door itself was wooden, old white paint chipping around the edges of the frame. She expected a sort of shock like in the first dream trap as she tentatively reached out for the handle, but all she felt was cool, damp metal. The door creaked on its hinges as she slowly pushed it open. "Eli," she said softly, "are you in there?"

A figure moved furtively in the darkness of the room. As Isabella lifted the dagger, the weak yellow light barely reaching the far wall, she saw Eli stacking boxes trying to reach another trap door in the ceiling. This one was blue.

The ground shook savagely and the boxes Eli had stacked toppled over. He threw the one he had at the toppled stack and muttered something that Isabella couldn't hear. Taking a step into the room, her foot splashed in a puddle. Hoping it was not what she feared, Isabella turned around to see a wave of water about four inches high moving toward her. Stepping into the room, she pushed the door closed, hoping to stem the flow.

She grabbed a box and started helping Eli build his tower to escape. After seeing Kimi's taxidermied body in the other room, Isabella didn't want to even think about what was in these boxes. When the third box was in place, the water was beginning to seep around the door frame a foot off the floor. Isabella shuddered at the thought of what would happen if that door gave way. The stack of boxes was still only eight feet high. Eli's fear of her seemed to lessen as they worked in relative silence, Isabella placing the boxes while Eli handed them up to her. When the stack was within reach of the ceiling, Isabella pushed open the blue door. She could hear birds chirping and the air smelled fresh on the other side, but she couldn't see anything.

"We're there," she called down to Eli, "climb on up."

Eli mounted the first box awkwardly, and the whole pile began to shift. Grasping the lip of the trap door, Isabella steadied the tower as best she could while he climbed the remaining boxes until they both knelt at the top. A tremendous cracking sound startled them, and Isabella jumped, accidentally kicking the box Eli was perched on. She shot her hand out, grabbing his right sleeve as the door gave way and a cascade of water crashed into the lower boxes. The tower faltered, and Isabella, hoping her grip on Eli would be strong enough, propelled herself through the trap door and into the darkness beyond.

Isabella lay on her back, panting and drenched from head to foot. She sat up and took off her right boot, emptied the water out, put it back on, and repeated the process with the left one. Having lost her coat, she shivered in her wet clothes. Beside her lay Eli, breathing heavily and coughing. Evan, unfortunately, was nowhere to be seen. The sun was still high in the sky, and she waited for the now-familiar sound.

Eli sat up and looked over at her. "How did you know?"

"I've had some experience." Izzy shrugged as she scanned the branches.

When the sucking sound came, Isabella remembered the sound the cottage had made as it disappeared the fist time she escaped a dream-trap and sighed. It was over. Thinking back to the other dream traps, not everything—if anything—had been real in there, but that didn't change her choices when she thought hurting Eli could save her brother. The memory made her shiver and, pulling her legs up to her chest, Isabella rested her forehead on her knees. She couldn't deal with this. In time, maybe she could, but now there was too much to get done.

TWENTY-ONE

Isabella gave herself a few minutes to collect her thoughts. The memory of her brother trapped in the dream world had driven her to make the choice she had, but it wasn't just that. Seeing Kimi, or seeing something that looked like Kimi, mounted on a plaque, made Isabella feel hollow. She shivered again and tried to push the thoughts out of her mind. Kimi was alive; no matter how real that had seemed, Kimi had to be alive.

Still holding her knife, Isabella stood up to put it back in the sheath. She noticed that the pommel was still glowing faintly, except now two dark spots, one of which was pulsing slowly, were encapsulated in the stone. She watched the light fade; the pulsing dark spot faded with the light until only one spot was left. There seemed to be a connection between the light and the dark spots in the yellow stone at the base of the dagger, but Isabella couldn't figure it out. She also didn't know how those spots got there. When the thing first started glowing, there was one, then there were three, and now it's back to one. Shaking her head, she sheathed the knife and looked around.

Eli glared at Isabella. "Don't think that makes us even."

Isabella didn't say anything. She didn't want to talk. What she'd done to him was wrong, but it was to protect her brother, or at least who she thought was her brother. Evan had tried to make her stop, and that made her feel uncomfortable. Then again, Kimi had done the same thing in the first dream trap that she'd been stuck in, but Kimi knew more than Izzy.

She looked at Eli, still sitting in his puddle. His blond hair looked darker now and it fell about his face, plastered down to his forehead lopsided and over one of his eyebrows. He brushed it back and looked up at her with his hazel eyes. He looked sincere, but something about him put Izzy on edge, something slightly off.

"I know it was you who did this." He motioned to his bruises and cuts. "How do you think you're any better than those things?"

"Shadows."

"Whatever, those shadows," he scoffed as he pushed himself off the ground. Eli stood quietly and looked around. "Either way," he continued, "we should leave before they come back."

"They won't." Isabella was scanning the trees, hoping to catch a glimpse of her dream catcher, but she didn't see anything.

"How can you know?" Eli's voice was pleading. "We should leave just in case."

"There's no need." Isabella looked down at him again and forced a smile. "That was what's called a dream trap. The shadows set them up to lure people in, make more shadows or something."

"Oh"—he didn't sound convinced—"but still, I think we should—"

"We are not going anywhere," Isabella snapped at him. "I lost something out there, and I'd come with someone." The look on his face was a cross between fear and surprise, and Isabella closed her eyes, took a deep breath, and tried again. "I'm sorry, Eli. I was on a mission when I heard someone yelling down there." She looked at the sky. She couldn't tell exactly what time it was, but she noticed it was late afternoon at least. "It's time-sensitive, but I couldn't leave you in danger. You're safe now, well, safer at any rate, but I need to keep going. To do that, I need to find my friend."

"Friend?" a voice from the trees asked.

"Skia!" Isabella was genuinely excited to hear his voice. "I was hoping you'd still be here."

"Where else would I have gone?" Skia scampered down a nearby trunk, dragging something behind him. "Besides, I thought you could use this."

"My dream catcher." Isabella reached down and took the dream catcher from the squirrel. It was a little beat up—one of the crystals was missing, and a bit of the webbing was frayed— but it looked still intact.

"I'm sorry," Skia said as Izzy examined the dream catcher. "It was hung up on a branch, and I think I might have damaged it getting it down."

Isabella tucked it into one of her back pockets. "Don't worry, thanks for getting it for me. By the way," she said, motioning to the boy sitting on the ground, "this is Eli. He was trapped in the cave."

"It was a dream trap," Skia said. "I was trying to warn you."

"I know. "Isabella looked at Eli. "But if I hadn't gone in, he'd have been caught in there when it collapsed. There was another person down there. Did you see him come by?"

"I'm sorry, no," Skia said.

"I would have gotten out," Eli said defensively. He kicked a stone into the trees but kept his eyes averted from Skia.

Isabella rolled her eyes. "Come on, when I found you, you were trapped in a cage."

"I was fine until you came along." He crossed his arms over his chest and stared at Izzy.

Isabella turned to Skia, not wanting to think about the truth of his statement. "I'm lucky that I'd been in one before, or I would never have found the door."

"Wait a minute!" Eli raised his eyebrows. "Who found the door."

"I found the first one," Isabella retorted.

"Maybe you should tell your friend what happened before you found that door." Eli stalked over to the edge of the trees and leaned against a trunk in the shade. "Your friend here's got some anger issues, squirrel."

"What happened?" Skia asked as he climbed a trunk and hopped to Isabella's shoulder.

"Nothing," she said as the squirrel nuzzled into her neck. "I missed you too."

"I mean, if you call not caring who you hurt because you have an agenda nothing, then sure," Eli spat.

"Isabella?" Skia leaned out to look at Izzy's face. "Are you alright."

"Fine." Isabella rolled her eyes, but she could feel the tears threatening to begin all the same. "None of it was real anyway."

"Your actions were real," Eli said from his spot by the forest.

"Shut up," Izzy snarled at him. "You weren't there, and when I got you out of that cage, you ran. If I didn't chase you down, you'd still be in there, so I think we're good."

"That's not how I remember it." Eli took a step toward Isabella, but Skia spoke up before they could continue their argument.

"You're right, though, Izzy," Skia said. "Nothing in a dream trap is real unless you bring it in there yourself. The shadows have never been that creative. They prey on your own insecurities, or they magnify their own. What you see in there is your subconscious. It's strange to find two people who share the same experience in a dream trap, but it happens sometimes. I've never been in one, but from what I can understand from the books, dream traps aren't so much tailored to an individual but are more like those ink blot things that Wesley said his psychiatrist uses with him. There's a blob of ink on a page, then you try to see what you think it means."

"But your actions, what you do, that's still you," Eli added.

"Theoretically, maybe. It depends on how you see your actions. If you think things are fated to happen, you could argue that nothing we do is our fault, or if you think that our past helps decide our future, then maybe. I like to think that it's a bit of both. But either way," Skia added when he felt Isabella's shoulders tighten, "dream traps are set up to bring the worst out of whoever gets trapped."

"I don't want to talk about it," Isabella said, putting an end to the conversation. "Did you find anything while I was in the trap?"

"I did." He gave an excited chitter and hopped off her shoulder, taking off down a path that led back around the front of the cliff face.

"Where's he going?" Eli asked.

"Only one way to find out," Isabella said and took off after Skia. When she rounded the corner, she heard Eli's footsteps behind her. Part of her wished he would leave, but until he did, or until he woke up, Isabella needed to look out for him. For all his complaining and the general annoying nature he had, she had caused most of his injuries to save her brother. She could afford to give him the leeway to take out some of his anger toward her, as long as he didn't take it too far.

As Isabella rounded the cliff, she noticed that the vines and the cave she'd gone into weren't there anymore. She'd expected as much, given what happened to the cottage that had been her first dream trap. Eli didn't seem to notice as he jogged behind her.

"Over here," Skia called from a similar-looking cave.

This time the vines clearly were morning glories, and the smell reminded her of her grandmother's house on summer afternoons. The trumpet flowers were big with purple petals that faded to white and then yellow as they neared the center. The ground preceding the cave looked churned up like someone had struggled there, and there was a low noise coming from inside.

"Another dream trap," said Eli when he'd caught up. He stood with his arms folded in front of him and scowled at the opening.

"Not this time," Isabella said as she smelled the vines, "right, Skia?"

"Not that I can tell."

"Still," Eli continued, "I'm not going in there."

"That's fine," Isabella said as she found her pack that she'd left on the ground before going into the dream trap. She put the dream catcher in and pulled out a dry sweater, changed in the clearing, and tossed a piece of jerky to Eli. "I'm going in."

"Why?" Eli's incredulity was evident in his voice. "Haven't you learned your lesson?"

Isabella smiled as she rummaged through her bag. She wasn't sure what she had in there to help them, but she pulled out the map and unrolled it. "So, Skia," she said as she pointed to the northern section of the map, "where do you think we are?"

Isabella and Skia reviewed the map while Eli paced behind them, eyeing the cave warily. For her part, Isabella watched him out of the corner of her eye. She wasn't sure what to make of him; one moment he seemed terrified, and the next he was lashing out at her. It seemed like he wanted to get as far away from here as possible, but he wasn't willing to go out on his own. That made sense to a point as he had been alone in that cage for who knew how long, but that in itself was another thing; she'd found him, but she still didn't know if he belonged here or if this was all one long, lousy dream for him, and he'd wake up at any moment.

"So now that you know where we are," he said once Skia and Izzy had stopped examining the map, "can we go?"

"No." Izzy eyed the cave as she oriented herself with the compass. "I have to go in there and check it out. If this is what Skia thinks it is, then her friend is inside and I need to rescue him."

He glared at her. "I've seen your help. Whoever's in there would be better off without it."

Isabella didn't answer. Instead, she packed the map away, pulled out some jerky for herself and, slinging the backpack over one shoulder, began toward the opening of the cave. The pack's weight shifted as Skia leaped onto one of the dangling shoulder straps and climbed to rest on top of the bag, but she didn't hear Eli follow. Shaking her head, Isabella walked into the darkness for a second time that day.

WENTY-TWO

The walls of the cavern looked like they'd been smoothed out by water centuries ago. Stalagmites collected along the path, so tight together in some places that Isabella needed to take her pack off to squeeze through, while stalactites made columns lining the passageway. The opening was wide enough and relatively unobstructed by vine, and a sickly green light was still able to seep into the cavern. Skia, not wanting to get separated from Isabella, stayed mostly on her shoulder, but the little squirrel was shaking. Isabella felt that sense of urgency again, a vague uneasiness that she needed to do something quickly, but she wasn't sure what that something was.

"Are you sure this was a good idea?" Skia asked. "Maybe Eli was right to not come in here."

"You want to rescue Wesley, right?" Isabella didn't need an answer to the question, which was good because Skia didn't give one, although he did stop complaining about going into the cave.

They picked their way farther into the darkening cavern. Isabella kept checking the pommel of her dagger, hoping it would light up again, but so far it hadn't done anything. She was beginning to get worried that they weren't in the proper cave. Skia had been very light on the details of his weaver's entrapment, but Isabella hadn't given it much thought until now. She'd been so focused on getting to him so they could help her find Kimi.

"How did Wesley get trapped anyway?" she asked.

"Honestly, I don't know."

Isabella stopped in her tracks. "What do you mean you don't know?"

"I wasn't with him when he went into the caves," Skia admitted. "I don't like confined spaces or darkness, so he suggested I stay out in the trees and keep watch."

"So you don't even know he's in trouble?"

"Of course I do." Skia sounded insulted. "Every companion knows when their weaver is in trouble. Some weavers can even tell if their companions are in trouble, but most can't. We get a feeling in our stomachs like we need to get to them as quick as possible. It's as if we're late for something."

Isabella considered what Skia had said, and while it didn't help the current situation, it at least confirmed that Wesley was actually in trouble. But something still bothered her about it all. Skia was helpful enough, but there was something that he wasn't telling her.

"Do you hear that?" Skia asked, leaning forward and digging his nails into Isabella's right shoulder.

Isabella winced and lost her train of though. "Stop that, it hurts." She shrugged her right shoulder and, when he relaxed, added, "And no, I don't hear anything."

"It's faint," he whispered, "listen. I think there's a woman in pain down there."

Isabella stood listening, but she didn't hear anything until the ground began to shake. Immediately, she thought about the dream trap, but in both cases the companions had seemed to instinctively know to avoid them. This shaking was accompanied by a loud rumbling, and then with the sound of a book being dropped on a desk—a big book in a small room— the ground stopped shaking and the faint light went out.

There were several moments of darkness while Isabella tried to get her bearings. Skia dug his nails into her shoulder again, and Isabella was confident that when this was done she'd have scratches all over. No way to explain them to her friends the next time she changed for gym. The darkness in here was different from the one in the dream trap. There it had been an empty feeling, but now the darkness weighed on her as if the air had grown heavier without the light to hold it up.

"What are you doing?" Skia pushed under Isabella's hair and shook gently against her neck.

"Going to see what happened at the entrance," Isabella said. "Eli was out there, and I want to make sure that he's alright."

"There's something about him that I don't like."

"Yeah," Isabella replied, feeling the same way, "but until I know what his deal is, I think we should keep an eye on him. Besides, I needed to help him get out of there."

"I still don't want to go back there. Usually, big noises mean danger."

She drew her dagger, holding it defensively pommel side up. As a faint yellow glow began to emanate from the stone in the pommel, Isabella felt her shoulders relax slightly. At least they weren't going to be trapped in complete darkness.

Isabella felt her hair move as Skia pushed out from under it and tentatively climbed down her arm toward the dagger. "I've never seen one of these in real life," he said, his previous nervousness forgotten in his excitement, "and you know how to make it work."

"One of whats?"

"A raka stone." He reached out tentatively to touch the stone, then rested his small paw on it. "I've read about them in the library, but I never thought I'd see one in real life. There are said to be only seven left after the Great Purge. Let's see, you have one charge left on it right now. Were they there when you got it, or can you charge it too?"

"I don't even know what you're talking about."

Skia climbed back up Isabella's arm and settled gently on her shoulder. "You need to be careful about who sees you doing these things," he said quietly, as if he were afraid someone would hear them. "I should have realized when you used the dream catcher. The Council, they got rid of your kind in the Purge, and there hasn't been one seen here since."

Isabella stopped again. "What are you even talking about?"

"About eighty years ago, there was a civil war among the Dreamweavers. From what I heard, it boiled over into the waking world too."

"Do you mean World War Two?"

"I don't know." Skia shrugged, and Isabella started back toward the entrance again. "Here it was called the Great Purge. It began when the Council of Dreamers was set up to regulate the weavers. They were tasked with balancing the power between the two sides. The problem was a group of weavers refused to accept the rulings that were being passed down. At first, they kept to themselves and did what they always did, helped the dreamers, but soon they began to disappear.

"At first, no one noticed. I mean, things happened, but it soon became evident that only the dissenters were vanishing. That's when they went underground. They avoided the capitol, went into hiding, and came out only to help the dreamers, but that wasn't enough for the Council. They deemed them too powerful, too unbalancing, and outlawed the use of charms. They determined that anyone caught using charms would be stripped of their companions, thus depriving them of their ability to work within the dream world. When weavers and companions are separated too long in the dream world, their companion goes through the shivering. Nobody wanted that, so the Council's plan basically worked. The Samskara, that's what they called the charm users, petered out. Some tried to rescue their companions, but they failed and were imprisoned. The rest just didn't come back.

"That blade is the only one of its kind made. If I'm right, that's the Samsa'raka. I think it means something about cycles and the moon in one of the languages in the waking world. An old language, I think, the same one the charm users took their name from. This blade was once used by the leader of the Samskara until she was lost to the shadows. She was one of the first stalkers born of the Great Purge, and the legend goes that the Samsa'raka was stolen from her by her second, a hunter who abandoned their people after the Great Purge and disappeared. Supposedly, it uses the sun much like the moon does and reflects the light. It also takes something from the shadows it kills. Not the shadow itself or anything like that, but the part that makes them shadows. In freeing them from it, the Samsa'raka absorbs power that can then be used to aid the wielder, if they know how to use it."

"So if this is the—"

"Samsa'raka," Skia filled in.

"Then you're saying that anyone who held it could make this light thing happen?"

"No," he chittered excitedly, "just the opposite. Only a Samskara should be able to use it, and even then only a few of them can even use a raka stone. They're basically illegal in the dream world, or using charms and trinkets is, so don't let anyone know about this."

"Eli's already seen it, and we need light, so if Wesley is here then he'll see it too."

"Don't worry about Wesley," Skia said excitedly, "he'll be as fascinated by it as I am. He'd be more likely to try to study you than turn you into the Council."

"You don't seem to like the Council." Isabella was starting to notice a trend in the squirrel's admonishments. "What's so bad about keeping order? My dad works for them from time to time."

"He works *with* them sometimes," Skia corrected. "There's a difference."

"But you said the Council sent you and Wesley on this mission. Don't you work for them too?"

Movement in the darkness ahead distracted Isabella from their conversation. Something lumbered, lurching from stalagmite to stalagmite. Tightening her grip on the dagger, Isabella tried to angle the light better without letting down her defense. All they could see was a vaguely human-shaped shadow against the darkness, and it was getting closer. The sound of gravel crunching beneath feet echoed through the passage. It stumbled forward and yelped.

"Hello," it called, "Izzy? Is that you?"

Skia tensed at the voice, but Isabella relaxed. "It's Eli," she said, then, loud enough for Eli to hear, "It's us. Hold on, we'll come to you."

Eli was leaning against a stout stalagmite when they arrived. He rubbed his left knee and had a cut above his right eye. His face was puffy and red, and he was filthy. He sighed piteously and said, "I told you coming in here was a bad idea."

"You didn't need to follow us," Skia snapped back at him.

"Calm down," Isabella said, stroking the squirrel, "no need for anyone to get nasty. What happened?"

"I'm not sure," he replied, looking over his shoulder. "I wasn't planning on following you, but when the sun started to go down, the trees began to look like a cage, and I wasn't about to go there again. So, I figured I was safer with you than waiting alone to see how you were going to mess this up."

"How generous." Skia turned around on Isabella's shoulder.

"You're welcome to come along," Isabella said, ignoring Skia's outburst.

"Thank you," he said pointedly to Isabella. "When I came in, I tripped over something, and then there was this terrible grinding noise, then *boom* and darkness."

"He must have tripped some trap or something," Skia said, rejoining the conversation.

"First, we need to check out this door," Izzy said as she started to walk toward the entrance.

"Really?" Eli's shoulders slumped. "I just came from there."

"That was our way out." Isabella walked past Eli and continued toward the entrance, assuming he would follow. "We need to see if it still is." The closer they came, the more concerned she became. The pale green light that had been shining through the cavern's entrance was dark now, which Isabella considered could have been from the setting sun. When they arrived to find a large metal door blocking their path out, the reason for the darkness became clear. Isabella tried to shine the light around to see the trap that sprung the door, hoping for some sort of handle that might allow them to open it again.

"I swear it was somewhere near here that I tripped," said Eli, sounding desperate.

"I believe you," Izzy comforted. "I wanted to see if we could undo it with the same thing that set it off."

They had similar luck when it came to finding a release latch or lever. The stone around the newly lowered metal door was smooth and damp. The door itself looked to be made of four-foot by four-foot square pieces of steel, bolted together at the seams. It rose beyond the reach of the light emitted by the raka stone. Isabella sheathed the dagger and tried to lift the metal door.

"What are you doing?" Eli asked. "Do you think you're Captain Marvel or something?"

"You know who Captain Marvel is?" Isabella asked, surprised that someone in the dream world knew about movies or comics from the waking world.

Eli scoffed. "Of course I do. What do you think I am, a denizen or something?" The way he said *denizen* made Isabella uncomfortable. She was going to ask what he was, but Skia interrupted.

"There it is again," Skia chittered, pulling some of Izzy's hair to get her attention.

Standing up and turning to face the darkness of the cave, Isabella pulled the dagger out again. The light, which had dimmed while it had been sheathed, surged again. This time two of the dark spots pulsed. One settled and the other faded, leaving Izzy with one spot left in the stone. This time she heard it too. Skia had said he'd heard a woman scream, but now Izzy knew what he had actually heard, and she was sure it wasn't a woman's scream.

TWENTY-THREE

The sound reverberated through the room, one moment sounding like it came from in front of them, the next behind. Isabella struggled to follow it, with the help of Skia who rode on her shoulder. Eli, for his part, stayed behind them, and she had to keep looking back to make sure he didn't get lost. She wished he'd walk next to them; there was room for him to, but every time she asked he'd come up by her, then fall back again as if having her in front of him might protect him from any harm that lurked in the darkness.

"I think the sound is coming from over here." Isabella lifted the pommel of her dagger, casting a warm yellow light that cut through the darkness. The light showed a pathway through one of the walls in the cavern, but it was hard to tell from across the stalagmite-covered floor. The air in the cavern was cold and wet, making Isabella glad that Skia had decided to ride on her shoulders and drape his tail across the back of her neck. Still, she wished she hadn't lost her favorite jacket.

"Are you sure?" Eli asked. "It's so hard to hear where things are coming from. These stalactites are making it hard to go that way. Maybe we should take the easier path back there. That's probably where whoever we're looking for would have gone."

"They're stalagmites," Isabella corrected, "and even if they went that way originally, this is where the sound is coming from."

"But how can you be sure?"

His constant doubting was beginning to annoy Isabella, and she found herself wishing that he'd wander off and leave her alone. She turned toward Eli, his face taking an eerie, sallow look in the yellow light cast by the raka stone. "I don't know, but I do know this is right. The closer I get, the surer of it I am."

"It's not Wesley," Skia chimed in from Isabella's left shoulder, "I know that much."

"And we'll find him, I promise." Isabella felt like she was losing control of the situation, but an urgency was driving her toward the sound. "We need to check this out first. That scream sounds like someone is in trouble."

"Just because someone's screaming, doesn't mean you'll help them," Eli mumbled under his breath, a fact for which Isabella was glad because it meant she could ignore it. He complained more than anyone that Isabella had ever met, and it had started grating on her about twenty minutes ago.

"Stay close," she said, ignoring his mumbling, "I think I found a path through here."

The three began to pick their way through a tangle of stalagmites, many of which were covered almost entirely with a slick film that came off on Isabella's hands as she tried to use them for balance. The same slick water dripped onto their shoulders and hair from the stalactites hanging unseen above them in the darkness. When they arrived at a clear area, Isabella felt as if she'd been rolling around in mud.

"This place is disgusting," Isabella said as she once again wiped the sliminess from her hands on her almost-soaked-through pants. "I was not planning on caving today."

"And I was?" Eli's voice came from the darkness behind them, and Isabella turned to see him emerging from the pathway she'd found. "Whose bright idea was it to come in here?"

"Whose bright idea was it to follow me in?"

"I can't even tell how we got here," Eli continued, ignoring Isabella's retort. "How are we going to get back?"

"Doesn't matter."

"Says you. It matters to me."

"In case you forgot, you followed us in here. There is no way out back there. It's like my father always says, 'If you can't go back, might as well keep going forward'."

"Your dad must get lost a lot," Skia chimed in.

Isabella's shoulders tightened and her jaw clenched at the comment. Who did Skia think he was, insulting her father. The squirrel didn't know her father, and Izzy was insulted at the insinuation from someone who had come for his help. The quiet chittering on her shoulder caught her by surprise and threw her off.

"Relax," the squirrel said, "I was kidding around. It's sound advice. I couldn't imagine that there are a lot of instances when one can't go back and needs to *always* say such advice."

Isabella's shoulders relaxed, and Skia continued.

"I mean *always*, that's like at least daily, right? Oops, got trapped in a cave again. Well, if you can't go back, might as well keep going forward. Oh, wow, avalanche. Whelp, if you can't go back, might as well keep going forward." Isabella was smiling at the increasingly crazy situations Skia was coming up with. "Not another volcanic eruption, well can't go back—"

Isabella was laughing by the time the Skia stopped his scenarios. "Okay," she said, wiping the tears from her eyes, "I get it. I get it."

"Are you two done?" Eli didn't sound as amused as Isabella felt, but the laugh had done her some good.

"Yeah." Isabella was still smiling at the thought of her father shrugging his shoulders at a volcanic eruption like it was a glass of milk Tucker spilled at dinner. "Let's go. It's this way."

As Isabella picked her way through the stalagmites, the sound of the screaming became more distinct and the urgency that drove her on became more pronounced. There was someone that needed help, and Isabella felt compelled to help them. It was a strange feeling to her. She'd helped other people in the dream world before— like Evan when he was cornered by a shadow— but she'd never felt this urgency before now. Skia was holding tightly to her shoulder, occasionally suggesting one path or another but otherwise coming along for the ride. Eli was silently trudging behind them; the silence was something Isabella was both surprised and ecstatic about.

"Listen"—she stopped for a moment—"it sounds close now." They had entered the mouth of the passage Isabella spotted earlier, but the sound hadn't changed until now. The occasional scream sounded both scared and hoarse. "We're almost there, Eli." Isabella turned, expecting to see him trudging as dejectedly as he had been since, but instead she was looking down an empty passage. The shadows of the stalagmites punctuated the light from her raka stone. "Eli, follow my voice. We'll wait for you."

"You told him to stay close," Skia offered.

"I know." Isabella didn't want to stop, but she wouldn't want to be left in the dark either. "Where do you think he went off to?"

"Maybe he had to pee."

"Do people pee in the dream world?" As soon as the question came out, she felt her face flush. Skia chittered on her shoulder. "That's not what I meant, I just … it's just that when I'm dreaming—and this is the dream world—so I … I don't know." Her face grew hotter as she tried to explain away her ignorance.

"It's still a world," Skia offered through his chittering. "People are still people. They eat, sleep, fall in love, have children."

"You mean there are people who are born in the dream world?"

"Not often, but there are."

"How do they grow up? I thought people living here were in some sort of holding pattern."

"No"—Skia stood up on Isabella's shoulder—"time works differently in here, but people age. Only the Council is eternal, until they decide to leave the Council. Then they age too."

The whole thing was getting too confusing for Isabella, and while she was curious about Skia meant by time working differently, rescuing whoever was trapped needed to take priority. "Eli," she called again. The sound of water dripping and the occasional screaming sound, a sound that was starting to grate on Isabella's nerves, were the only thing she could hear. "Eli, come on, this isn't funny. I want to get going."

"You don't think something happened to him?"

"Like what?" Isabella asked. "There weren't any huge chasms or anything."

"I don't know. Maybe a shadow got him."

"He would have complained."

"Ugh, not again," Skia imitated Eli's annoyed tone, "another shadow in this dark place. Izzy, couldn't you take care of this for me?"

Isabella smiled in the darkness. She felt wrong for doing it, but she was mostly sure that hadn't happened. "I didn't feel any shadows come up. They have this emotional leaking."

"Emotional leaking," Skia chittered. "I've never heard it described like that. It's apt, but still."

"I don't think he's coming." Isabella strained to see through the darkness beyond the small area lit by the raka stone. "I don't want to abandon him in here, but I don't want to stand here forever either. I need to find where that screaming is coming from."

"I'm not sure if this will help you make up your mind"— Skia moved behind Isabella's neck to her right shoulder—"but as we've gotten closer, I can feel Wesley down here. We're going in the right direction. Whatever is screaming isn't him, I'm not sure it's a person, honestly, but he's past it, and not far past it either."

"That's good, but leaving Eli because we're close still isn't right."

"There's another thing too." Skia's voice sounded pained. "It's been a while since I left Wesley. It took me three days to find you."

"Okay?"

"And we've been traveling for three days."

"Which means?"

"Well, if a weaver and their companion are separated for six days—"

The realization hit Isabella like a waterfall; she had been so worried about the amount of time in the dream world apart from Kimi that she hadn't properly thought about Skia being separated from Wesley. "The shivering."

He drooped his tail across Isabella's neck, and his voice dropped a little. "I can feel it. At least, I think this is what it would feel like. No one's ever come back to say."

"Eli!" Izzy shouted into the darkness. "We need to get going. There's not a lot of time. Yell, if you need help, and I'll come to get you." Isabella and Skia stood in the slightly yellow glow fighting back the cavern's darkness and strained to hear anything that might be Eli. Water dripped into puddles below the stalactites in rhythmic consistency, and the occasional unseen animal scurried over some smaller gravel littering the floor, but nothing sounded loud enough to be Eli. "I don't want to leave you here," she called into the darkness again. "Where are you?"

Part of her wanted to go back and search for Eli through the maze of stalagmites, but if he didn't respond to them, there was little hope of finding him. Then there was Skia; he'd come for help, and now they were close, but so was his shivering. Eli had been demanding since the beginning in the dream trap, but that didn't mean she could abandon him in the darkness. Besides, Isabella told herself, if the roles were reversed and he'd hurt her, regardless of the reason, she wouldn't be ready to forgive him either. Kimi had never left her, even after all the trouble Isabella had given the poor little fox. Isabella squeezed her eyes closed at the thought of never seeing Kimi again, which was becoming more and more likely. When she had last seen her, the fox had been infected by a shadow, and while Izzy had used honey to begin fighting the infection, she didn't know if Kimi had been able to get the help she needed after Isabella had left.

"Isabella." Skia's voice was beginning to sound weak. "We need to do something."

"I know." Her own frustration was coming through in her clipped response. Taking a deep breath to calm the feeling rising in the pit of her stomach, Isabella knew that she needed to do something. Although waiting was the easy choice, she thought it was probably the wrong one. Looking back in the direction of the screaming, Isabella began to have a sneaking suspicion about what it sounded like. Turning back toward the cavern, Isabella cupped her hands around her mouth and called out, "Eli, we're going to move on. I'm sorry, but it's a matter of life and death now." She waited a moment and thought she saw movement in the shadows near the edge of the cavern but couldn't be sure.

Isabella took another deep breath, frustrated tears beginning to gather at the corners of her eyes. First, she hurts him, and now she's about to abandon him. If they turned back and searched for him, Skia might go through the shivering and who knew what could happen to the person screaming deeper in the cave, but saving them meant abandoning Eli to whatever this cave had lurking in its darkness.

"I'm sorry," she called into the darkness. "We'll come back. We'll find you." She turned and started toward the sound of the scream once more, adding under her breath, "I promise."

Despite Skia's earlier agitation, the squirrel was quiet now as he draped over her shoulders. They'd been traveling through the tunnels for a while, but knowing how long was difficult down here. He'd become still a few turns after they'd lost Eli, and Izzy was beginning to worry that they would be too late when the tunnel they'd been following ended abruptly, and Isabella, not seeing the precipitous drop, tumbled forward into the darkness.

TWENTY-FOUR

The darkness was so complete that Isabella was unsure at first if she had even opened her eyes. What she was painfully sure of was the cold. Her right arm, pinned under her body, ached dully and her wrist was throbbing. Using her left arm to push herself up, Isabella sat on the cold stone floor of the cavern and looked around. Her head, throbbing in time with her pulse, swam in the complete darkness, increasing her disorientation.

"Skia?" she called. Her voice, small and hollow, echoed back to her. Thinking of how silent the little squirrel had become over the past few minutes, Isabella felt her chest tighten. "Skia, are you alright?" She reached out and ran her fingers over the rough pebbles that littered the floor. "Make some noise. I can't see you."

Her echo called back hauntingly in the darkness, but besides the sound of the gravel beneath her fingers, a heavy silence pervaded the air. It was the type of silence that falls before someone gives you bad news, the silence felt like an impending disaster. Not wanting to stand up and accidentally impale herself on a stalagmite, she moved to her hands and knees and began crawling around. Getting her hands on the dagger meant light, and with light came hope, but until then all she had was action. Scouring the floor, Isabella ran her hands lightly across the sharp gravel and jammed her finger into something solid. Feeling around the edge, she realized that it must be where she'd fallen from.

Using the wall as a guide, Isabella slowly stood up, waving one hand over her head to avoid cracking her already aching skull on some low-hanging stone. She worked her way to standing beside a steep stone wall. Running her hands up the face of the wall, Isabella hoped to be able to grab the edge and pull herself back up, but couldn't reach even after she tried to hop up, sending a sharp but manageable pain shooting from her left knee. In fact, the wall seemed to be made of almost polished stone with nothing that could pass as a handhold, not that she thought her wrist could take any sort of a climb. She leaned against the wall and let out a loud sigh.

"Great," she said to the darkness, "now what?"

Listening for her echo to ask itself the same question, she heard the screaming sound again. She'd been chasing that sound ever since first hearing it, and now, standing in the complete darkness, it sounded closer than ever. The throaty, hoarse sound, vaguely feminine, had something about it that seemed desperate, and now that she was closer, it also sounded familiar. It was like a voice from another life, almost forgotten, calling her from the darkness, and she decided that there was nothing to lose in trying.

"Kimi," Isabella called out tentatively, "is that you?"

There was another scream, louder and more desperate, but no words. Disappointed, but with little else to do, Isabella began to work her way toward the sound. The darkness wasn't letting up, but Isabella could at least begin to tell a direction when she focused on the cry. Moving first along the wall, scuffing her feet on the loose gravel in case Skia lay somewhere on the floor in her path, she made her way down the passage. When the cry seemed directly opposite her, she tentatively moved from the wall and worked her way across the room, arms held out before her. When her palms touched the cold smoothness of another wall, Isabella stopped to listen again.

The sound seemed to have moved to her left, so she moved left along the wall until she felt a corner. Rounding the corner carefully, feeling with both her hands and feet to avoid any more surprises, Isabella worked her way further into the darkness. She felt horrible about leaving Skia behind, but after her futile search and with no response to her calls, there was little else she could do. The cry grew louder and the feeling of urgency became almost unbearable.

"Hello?" Isabella cried out, hoping for a response. "Do you need help?"

"Finally." The voice was filled with relief. "Is it you?"

Isabella's heart felt like it was going to leap out of her chest, and tears began to spill from the corners of her eyes.

"It is, it is," she repeated until her mouth caught up to her brain. "Kimi, I thought I'd never see you again."

The little fox's voice was close as Kimi said, "You're telling me."

Dropping to her knees, she frantically searched the floor for her friend. She moved from side to side, sweeping her arms around the floor in front of her. She was so thrilled to have found Kimi that she didn't notice when she skinned her knuckles on the wall. After a fruitless search of the floor, she called, "Where are you? I can't find you."

"I'm up here," Kimi answered. "I'm in some sort of cage, but I can't open the latch."

"Is it locked?"

"How should I know, "she said hoarsely, "I can't even see my tail in front of my face."

Isabella worked her way up the wall near Kimi's voice. "I was hoping you could see. Don't you have good night vision or something?"

"Even night vision requires a little bit of light. Besides, I'm not sure it would matter. Latches and doors aren't my thing."

"Right"—Isabella remembered the fox's comment from when they first met in a dream trap—"no thumbs."

"Funny girl." Kimi's voice was droll and tired, but there was an edge of a smile in it too that gave Isabella some hope for them. "Now, are you going to help me out of here, or should I go back to screaming?"

"I thought that was you," Isabella said as her hands found the corner of a small cage. "How'd you get in here?"

"I thought I'd vacation in some dark hollow while I pined your leaving so I wandered in here."

"Really?" Isabella felt horrible for not being able to come back and check in on Kimi, but despite trying she'd been unable to until her dad brought her to the cabin to train. The thought that her being away had driven Kimi to such a state broke her heart.

"No," Kimi chuckled in response. "Why would you think that was true? I was out helping Delson round up some shadows and a stalker caught us. Did you think I crawled underground when you didn't come back?"

"Of course not," Isabella lied.

"How did you get down here?" Kimi was moving around in the cage and her fur brushed up against Isabella's hand. "Do you have a torch or a light or something?"

"Remember that dagger Ajay gave me last time?" Isabella said as she felt around the cage for a way to get Kimi out.

"No, I was a little distracted with fighting a shadow."

"Well, he gave it to me when I came after you. I guess the stone at the end of the handle is something called a raka stone. It lights up in the darkness."

"Think it might be useful now?"

"Yup." Unable to find a door, Isabella worked at the rope-like material tied at the corners of the cage. "Too bad it's somewhere in the room back there where I fell."

"Could you get back to the room?"

"Probably, why?" She managed to work one of the ropes off a corner of the cage. "Got it. I think if I get one more off, I can get you out."

"If you get back there, I might be able to smell out the dagger for you. If it has a raka stone, you can't let that fall into the wrong hands."

"What do you mean?"

"If a stalker got their hands on that thing, even if one of the Samskara got it, there would be no end to the trouble it would cause. It's best if we bring it back to the Council of Dreamers as quick as possible."

"We'll talk about that," Isabella said, grunting a little as she loosed the last rope on the corner of the cage and pulled the side apart slightly, "but first, let's see if this is good enough for you to get out."

Fur and ribs slid across Isabella's knuckles and she felt a slight breeze against her face as Kimi leaped past her, landing softly on the floor. Isabella couldn't see her, and the soft pads of her feet made it impossible to hear her either.

"Kimi?"

"Right here." Isabella felt a slight pressure on her leg and reached down, lightly touching the fox's tail.

Lowering herself to one knee, she reached out and pulled the fox into a tight hug. "I missed you, and I'm so sorry. I misunderstood everything last time, everything. I was so stupid." The words flowed out of her as she cried into Kimi's soft, musky fur. "I know you have no reason to forgive me, and you said you wanted nothing to do with me, and I understand, but I don't want you to go through the shivering. That's just, I mean, I can't." Isabella's words dried up.

"Are you quite done?" Kimi's tone was imperious, but she didn't struggle against Isabella's hold.

"I'm sorry." Isabella released the little fox and sheepishly smiled into the darkness. "I didn't think I'd ever see you again, and I could hardly stand that after I realized everything, but then I read about the shivering in one of my dad's books. The thought of you going through that broke my heart." Something clicked in Isabella's memory and her hand went up to her mouth. "The shivering. Skia! We need to find him."

"Slow down." Kimi's voice was even. "Who's Skia?"

Isabella quickly recounted the story of the past few days in the dream world, from her failed attempts to call Kimi all the way through to finding this cave and losing everyone she was with. When she was done, it felt like a weight had been lifted from her shoulders. Well, maybe not so much lifted entirely, but enough so that, for the first time since she began her journey, she felt like she could manage. The sense of urgency was gone too, that nagging pull to go deeper into the dream world that had worked on her so profoundly that she wouldn't have been able to stay at the cabin if she'd known there was an army of shadows out there. Knowing Kimi was safe helped, but now they had to save Skia from the same fate.

"Sounds like he's wherever you dropped the dagger," Kimi said at the end of Isabella's story.

"Right, but I looked."

"You only used your eyes in the darkness. When we are blind to the way, first we need to find some other way to see."

"Not sure what you mean by that, but I called out to him too. Nothing." Isabella could feel the weight begin to resettle on her shoulders. She crossed her arms in front of herself and grabbed each shoulder with her hand, squeezing as if physically holding herself together. "What if we're too late?"

"If we're too late," Kimi said calmly, "then we're too late. An unfortunate thing about being fallible is that we make mistakes. Sometimes our mistakes get someone hurt, sometimes they help someone we didn't intend to help."

Isabella thought she heard an edge in Kimi's voice and bit her lip for a moment before she said, "Looking for you wasn't a mistake."

"But finding me was."

"No," Isabella said, finally understanding the urgency she'd felt ever since first coming back through the waterfall. "I don't think it was."

"You knew I was—"

"Not exactly," Isabella interrupted. "I didn't know you were in a cage in this cave, but I did know something, or rather I felt something." She was quiet for a moment, trying to figure out how to say what she wanted to say and not sound crazy. "I think I felt you calling."

"Don't be ridiculous," Kimi scoffed. "You can't feel sound."

"Not exactly, no, I know that." She chewed on her lip and searched the darkness for the right words. "When I first came through the waterfall, after my dad pulled me out of the water, I felt this urgency, like I needed to do something. It was like when you get busy legs. I don't know if foxes get those, but I do, so that combined with this feeling in the back of my mind like I'd forgotten something important, like my books for school or something."

"I'm not sure what half of that means"—Isabella could hear Kimi shifting uncomfortable at her feet—"but if it's anything like when there's a badger in your den, I get that all too well."

Isabella chuckled. "Like I had a badger in my den. I think that was you calling out for help."

"Right." Kimi sounded skeptical. "This is fascinating and all, but don't we have to save a squirrel from shivering?"

"That does sound a lot less dramatic when you put it like that," Isabella mused while she traced her way back toward the drop-off. "Do you think you can find the dagger and Skia?"

"I'm a nocturnal predator," Kimi said, the imperious tone back in her voice. "How do you think I hunt?"

Afraid she might have insulted her companion, Isabella didn't ask what she meant by that and instead made a mental note to read up on foxes. If she was going to be a Dreamweaver, which was possible again now that she'd found Kimi, she needed to know more about her companion. Besides, that way she could avoid putting her foot in her mouth as much.

The trip back was uneventful, but this time when they got to the doorway, Kimi asked Izzy to wait and let her try to get the lay of the land without all the clomping around. Isabella tried to follow Kimi's progress, but her eyes refused to adjust to the lack of light and she couldn't even hear the light-footed fox scampering around the room. When a light clattering sounded at her feet, Isabella jumped, banging her shoulder into the rough stone of the wall.

"Sorry to startle you," Kimi's said, her voice tinged with the edge of a laugh, "but the knife is by your foot."

Isabella bent down to pick it up. The handle of the dagger felt the same, but no light came from the raka stone. "I think it's broken," Isabella said, tapping the pommel of the dagger to no avail. "It's not working."

"Don't look at me," Kimi said, her voice coming from deeper in the room. Then, "Got him!"

Isabella could feel the familiar frustration rising within her. The stone in the dagger's hilt had lit up before and in the dream trap, so why didn't it work now? She could imagine what Kimi thought about all of this. Another failure. She screwed up her face in the darkness and concentrated on the edge of the stone. Light. Light. Light. "It's not working," she growled under her breath.

"I have the squirrel." Kimi's voice was muffled. "Would you take him?"

Isabella bent down and took the slightly damp squirrel who lay limply in her hand. Having Skia unconscious was not ideal, but at least he was still. She knew it wouldn't last; if the shivering started, the convulsions would too and by then it would be too late. She needed to get the light working on the dagger, but the harder she tried, the more hopeless it felt. Kimi waited patiently at her feet, but Isabella could hear her shifting back and forth on the gravel floor. She rested Skia on her shoulder and placed her free hand over the raka stone, hoping that would help. Nothing changed.

"Come on." She could hear the tears threatening in her voice. "Why won't you light? Light. Light. Lightlightlight." Isabella was screaming at the dagger, and it took considerable willpower not to simply throw it against the wall. "I can't," she sighed in exasperation, "I'm sorry, I just—"

"Sure you can." Kimi sounded so calm and assured. "You've done it before. You can do it again."

"No, I can't," she snapped at the fox. "I'm trying, but nothing's happening."

"You said it's a raka stone?"

"That's what Skia said."

"What color?"

"What do you mean what color?" Isabella couldn't believe that Kimi would care about color at a time like this. "Why does it matter?"

"It matters if you want it to work."

At a loss for other options, Isabella tried to remember the color of the stone. She thought it was an orange or something like that, but when Kimi rejected orange as an option, she threw up her hands and guessed yellow.

"Yellow is the color of topaz," she said. "That means it will need you to think about love or purity."

This was ridiculous. "I can't. How can I think about love when Skia is going to start convulsing any minute?"

"You did it before," Kimi added.

"Not helpful." Isabella rolled her eyes. "I know I did it before."

"What were you thinking of then?"

"I don't know." Isabella wracked her brain. "I was trying to find Wesley. Maybe it was Skia's love for Wesley that made it work. Maybe I didn't do anything."

"Maybe," Kimi agreed.

"That's it then." Isabella sank down against the wall and sat in the cold, damp earth that made up the floor. "I've failed, again."

"You're giving up?"

"What do you want me to do? I'm not my father."

"Well, that's obvious."

Isabella started at the matter-of-fact tone in Kimi's voice. "What's that supposed to mean?" She'd taken Skia's limp body off her shoulder and was stroking it gently.

"Well," Kimi said, putting a paw on Isabella's knee, "you are a fourteen-year-old girl, and he's gotta be pushing forty or something. That, and I'm not a wolf."

"Oh." Isabella appreciated Kimi's attempt at a joke, but she didn't feel the humor. "I thought you meant his motto."

"Didn't know he had one."

"I told Skia about it while we were on our way here. 'If you can't go back, you might as well keep going forward'. It's stupid, I know, but—"

"Sounds like good advice to me," Kimi said, leaning her weight against Izzy's leg. "Especially now when there's not much else we can do. You were able to find me without the light. What's the worst thing that can happen if you keep going forward?"

Isabella stopped stroking Skia and began to gently stroke Kimi's fur. She thought about what her father would tell her, how disappointed he'd be that she had failed someone who'd come looking for his help, but he wasn't there, and she was. She smiled, enjoying the warmth of Kimi's side on her wet, dirty pant leg.

"Izzy." Kimi's voice was barely above a whisper.

She looked down at the little fox. For the first time since they'd been reunited, she really looked at her. There was something both powerful and fragile in that petite frame, the delicate curve of her snout darkening near the pointed tip. Her ears were perked up and twisting back and forth as if listening for something. Her body and tail were plush and warm, but the spindly legs looked like they could be snapped like a twig if she wasn't careful. Running her hand down the fox's fur, she paused at the discolored stripe on her haunch. The last time Isabella had been in the dream world, Kimi had rescued her from the shadow congress and had been cornered and wounded. This patch must be reminiscent of that.

"Does it hurt?" Isabella asked as she traced the lighter-colored fur with her finger.

"Can you see it?"

Isabella smiled sadly. "It's noticeable, I'm sorry. Does it bother you that people can see it?" Kimi stood up and turned to face Isabella. "It doesn't look bad if that's what you're worried about."

"You can *see* it," Kimi repeated, but this time it wasn't a question.

"What?" Isabella stood up quickly, almost dropping Skia in the process, but catching him at the last moment. "I can see you." She lifted the dagger, the stone in the pommel glowing fiercely.

"You did it!" Kimi yelped, almost hopping vertically. "How'd you figure it out? Did you think about your father?"

Isabella had thought about her father, she remembered that, but it had been fleeting. She had been focused on something else. "Must have been," she said, smiling down at her friend and companion.

"What now?"

Isabella looked down at Skia's limp body in her hand, then back over her shoulder at the small cliff she'd fallen from earlier. "Well, we can't go back—"

TWENTY-FIVE

As bad as Isabella felt for Skia, she was happier having found Kimi. The little fox's presence made her smile and seemed to make the darkness a little less oppressive. The tunnel they were going through wasn't simple; between the narrow squeezes and underground springs that seemed to zigzag along the path, Isabella was relying on Kimi's sense of smell more than the light from the raka stone in the pommel of her dagger. A few times when the tunnel got too narrow, she would have to pass Skia through the opening to Kimi on the other side before clambering through herself. Now she was filthy and wet and cold, but there wasn't anything she could do about it except go forward. She found herself repeating her father's advice to herself several times.

"The scent is strong here," Kimi said, looking up over her shoulder from the ground. "We must be closing the distance."

"Why're you formal all the time?"

Kimi didn't respond. Although Isabella was glad to be back with the fox, her patience was waning and some of the little things that Kimi did—the formal way she talked, the slight condescension in her voice, even the way she'd sprint down offshoots, then run back to say they were dead ends—were beginning to grate on her. Kimi didn't rise to the argument, probably for the better, if Izzy was honest with herself. Instead, she just kept up with what she was doing.

"Are you sure this time?" Isabella knew she was whining, but there's only so much a person could take. "You've said we were close for the last four turns."

"We have not gotten farther away, have we?"

Isabella rolled her eyes and mocked Kimi, then immediately regretted being childish. Kimi, again, ignored the slight and instead bolted down another offshoot of the tunnel. The first few times, Isabella would chase after her, but now she gave in to her tired legs and sat in the wet gravel of the crossroads waiting for Kimi to return and tell her it was yet another dead end. She held Skia's limp body in her lap and stroked it softly, wondering, not for the first time, how much longer the little guy had.

"I'm sorry," she said softly to the prone squirrel. "We're doing our best, really we are. This place is a maze, but Kimi is something else." Isabella looked down the path Kimi had run down. The spring bubbled up by the entrance of this offshoot, like it did for many of them, and seemed to flow down it. "If anyone can find him, Kimi will. I need to thank you for helping me find her. I'd given up hope, well, mostly given up hope." She was silent for a while, listening to the trickling water and trying to hear Kimi's paws splashing her way back. Sighing, she added, "If it wasn't for you, I'd still have been at the cabin. Maybe my dad and Vígolfr would be back, maybe not, but I wouldn't be here, and

Kimi would—" She still couldn't bring herself to finish that sentence.

A flickering light further on down the path caught Isabella's attention and she stood up, carefully transferring Skia to one hand and preparing to defend herself with the other. She shifted position so she was inside the entrance to the offshoot, closest to where the light was coming from. She figured that would give her the best opportunity to surprise whoever was coming down the path. Her heartbeat pulsed rhythmically in her ears and her hands began to shake, causing her shadow to shiver along the wall behind her. Her shadow. The light. These concepts hit her with a suddenness. If she had a shadow, if the dagger was making light, then it would give away her position. "How do I get this thing to go out," she grumbled under her breath. Failing to come up with a solution, she jammed the hilt into her hip, hoping to block enough of the light that she'd not be noticed, but also hoping that it wasn't too late.

Plunged into darkness, the light coming down the passage she had been on flickered brightly off the damp stone walls. Closing her eyes, Isabella tried to reach out to Kimi like Wren had said she could do with Mentu, but nothing happened. The light on the walls was getting brighter so Isabella backed along the passage, trying to get deeper and avoid being noticed. Waves of fear washed over her, and before she could stop herself, she broke out in a run down the offshoot toward where Kimi had disappeared. Isabella pulled the dagger away from her side, trying to get a little light to guide her, figuring that the torch or whatever made that light would conceal her escape, but the raka stone had gone out. She counted it as a mixed blessing and, sheathing the dagger, she ran her hand along the wall so she could find her way back. After a short distance, the wall gave way to open air, and Isabella, who'd been leaning on it like a crutch, tumbled into a puddle, dropping Skia and soaking her knees the rest of the way through.

Scurrying to put her back to the wall in this new passage, Isabella tried to calm her breathing before she hyperventilated. After a moment, she remembered Skia and felt around, thankfully finding him next to, rather than in, the puddle. With her breathing under control enough to slow her ragged breaths, Isabella peeked around the corner of the passage and back down the tunnel. At first, there wasn't anything she could make out except a slightly flickering glow by the crossroad she'd been sitting at earlier. Then suddenly the light was blindingly bright, and she ducked her head back around the corner. The light didn't do much to illuminate where she was, but it didn't lessen either, so Isabella took three slow breaths to work up the courage and then looked back around the corner.

Standing in the crossroad of the central passage was a figure, blotted out almost entirely by the torch they carried in their left hand. Isabella was on the verge of calling out and coming out of hiding, happy to see another person down here, but the light flickered again and seemed to dim a few times. Then she heard voices echoing down the passage, but they were too distorted for her to make out what they were saying. There was clearly more than one voice, but Isabella only saw one person. The torchlight changed again—not a flickering, but more a steady dimming as if something was blocking some of the light. Squinting into the light, she could make out a second figure, almost translucent in the light from the torch. Isabella watched as the figure seemed to grow. She felt the fear and worry moments before she realized what she was looking at. It was the same fear that had made her bolt down the passage, only this time it wasn't as strong.

Pulling her head back around the corner, Isabella leaned her head against the wall, pulled her knees up to her chest, and hoped that the shadow stopped before it got to her. There was no doubt now that calling out would have been a mistake, probably a fatal one for both her and Skia. Maybe even Kimi too. Isabella worried that Kimi would come barreling back at any moment to tell her that it was another dead end. She scoffed in her head. Truer words, she thought.

Then she closed her eyes and tried to think about Kimi again. She imagined the little fox scampering through the puddles, but then she corrected herself. Kimi wouldn't scamper. Slink, maybe. She pictured her slinking down the passage, carefully nosing the air and the ground respectively. What was she smelling that Isabella couldn't? Perhaps body odor. That made her glad she didn't smell it, but maybe it was something else. Pheromones? Those were a thing, or maybe it was more straightforward than that. Whatever Kimi was sensing, Isabella tried to get her to stay there, sit down, take a nap, anything as long as she didn't come back through the passage. Stop, stop, stop. She tried pushing those words through her mind, imagining them as a ball moving through the water, like when her father forced her to go to the beach last summer. Stay there. She imagined the ball floating away, then getting snagged up on something and stopping. Sitting there, huddled against the cold stone wall, swallowed by darkness with water soaking her socks and back, Isabella shivered both from the cold and the fear freely flowing around the corner like tentacles from some dark underworld, cathulu-esque creature, and she waited.

Not far from where Isabella sat, there was a young man, a little older than her, huddled against the darkness. He sat quietly, legs crossed, hands resting on his knees, statuesque. He was beginning to think that no one was going to come. They knew where he'd gone. Heck, they'd sent him there to remove the threat. There was a shallow chuckle from his still form as if something both disgusted and amused him.

He'd tried to escape several times now, but the knots holding his cage together were too strong. Besides, the darkness was keeping him where he was. He'd had a torch when first coming in here and thought he was doing good by helping some blond kid who had stumbled into the camp. It was against the rules to help the wanderers, but this one seemed different, and almost no one objected. Besides, he wasn't the first one that had helped some random person they'd met wandering around.

Technically they didn't know precisely where he was. Honestly, he wasn't sure either, but they knew the direction he'd gone. And although they hadn't officially sanctioned this, they hadn't forbidden it.

His shoulder hitched and he felt something warm slide down his cheek. He allowed himself enough movement in the darkness to wipe the wetness from his face, then returned to his waiting. Someone would come for him. He felt a little relief that his guards had finally left him alone, either assuming he was no longer a threat or called away; the reason didn't matter. He closed his eyes again and took another breath. He hadn't needed to see his guards to know what they were. Shadows. The emotions flowing from them were strong too, stronger than any others he'd felt recently. Something was up and, try as he might, he couldn't handle them by himself. Someone would come for him. They had to. He didn't want to think about what would happen if the shadows came back and decided they were tired of guarding him.

⚶ TWENTY-SIX ⚶

Isabella held her breath as the fear swelled within her. Closing her eyes, she focused on her breathing. Her legs wanted to run and her lungs wanted to scream, but doing either would undoubtedly draw attention to her, so she inhaled, counted to three, then exhaled. She focused on staying calm until a calm began to permeate the area and the light reflecting off the dampness of the cavern walls began to dim. She waited until the darkness was complete again, blind though it made her, and listened to the dripping water and the slight trickle of the spring flowing. Sitting in the dark, Isabella felt drained, exhausted. And while she should get up and go search for Kimi, she leaned her head back against the cavern wall and closed her eyes.

A small wet nose nuzzling against the side of her hand roused her, and she realized that she must have fallen asleep. She had no perception of time in the darkness, not that time seemed to make much sense in the dream world in general, but at least she knew the difference between night and day when she could see outside. Underground, there was no difference; everything was night.

"Hello?" Izzy's voice was gravely and lethargic. Clearing her throat, she tried again, "Hello?"

"Good," Kimi's familiar voice sounded quietly in the darkness, "you're awake. We're close. Come on."

"Close to what?"

"Someone needs help. I didn't talk to him because you were screaming in my head to stay put. Could you not do that again, by the way? It was rather distracting."

"Wait"—Izzy's eyes shot open—"you heard me?"

"Yes," replied Kimi, evidently annoyed, "but let's not again, alright?"

"Sorry, but there was a shadow here," Isabella explained, "and I didn't want you to run into it."

"Thank you, but I can handle myself." Kimi nosed at her hand again. "Now come on, it could be that rodent's weaver."

Isabella followed Kimi, maintaining contact with her tail in the darkness because she didn't want to use the dagger and risk drawing attention to them. After a short walk through the gently twisting passage, they emerged into an area lit from above. Squinting against the dim light, Isabella tried to see, but she needed to let her eyes adjust after complete darkness before the dim light wasn't blinding.

When the glare subsided, Isabella could see that they were stood on a small outcropping of stone surrounded on three sides by a vast underground lake. Rain from outside came through a hole in the ceiling, pattering down in the center of the pool. The water itself was emerald green and looked both shallow and fathomless. Above the pool, in a cage dangling over the water, sat a man, probably in his mid-twenties. He was rail-thin but not emaciated, with a hawklike nose and a sharp chin. He sat with his legs dangling in the air out in front of the cage. His hair—Izzy couldn't tell if it was dark brown or black—was hanging in his downturned face and his shoulders were slumped. For a moment, Isabella thought he might be asleep, or worse, but suddenly his head shot up and he squinted into the darkness.

"Who's there?" His voice was weak, but there was a defiant power behind it. "If it's you again, *stalker*"—he seemed to spit the word as if it left an unsavory taste in his mouth—"I've already told you all you're going to get."

Isabella wasn't sure what to say, or if she should say anything at all, so she waited to see what he would do. In her hands, Skia stirred as if he was having a bad dream. Hopeful that this could be Skia's weaver, she took a few steps until she stood at the edge of the water. Looking down, she could see movement in the untold depths. The water, still and inviting on top, seemed to teem with life below the surface, long shapes twisting and intertwining beneath. Isabella wasn't sure what they were, but she'd seen enough movies to know not to trust that whatever was down there would be friendly.

Looking back up at the cage, she called out, "Wesley?" Her voice was shaking and sounded about as strong as a summer breeze.

"Who are you?" he called back. He shifted, pulling his legs back in the cage, and then knelt on the bottom bars. "Another stalker?"

"Skia brought me," Isabella called up, "he said he needed help rescuing his weaver. Is that you?"

The young man scoffed. "He's been gone too long. Why are you tormenting me?"

"But I—" Isabella remembered the feeling when she'd thought she was going to lose Kimi, and tried to figure out a way to convince him. She was still unsure if Skia was going to wake up; he'd stirred when they'd first come into the cavern, but since then, he'd lay silent and still in her arms.

"Besides"—it sounded as if he were talking to himself—"you're not Allan Shaw."

"No," Isabella called up to him, "but I am his daughter."

There was silence from the cage as he considered what she had said. It was too high to reach, but Isabella's eyes followed the rope up from the cage to the ceiling and then down to the wall beside the door. She'd begun to formulate a plan by the time he said anything.

"His daughter?"

"Yes, and I have Skia here, but he's not doing well."

"That's why he's not blathering on?"

Isabella smiled. "He does like to talk. I think I have an idea. Hold on." She set Skia down by the door where the rope was tied off, Kimi hovering nearby. "If I can lower you down enough, you can swing back and forth. If we time it right—"

"I'll land on the peninsula. Brilliant."

"And if you don't, you'll land in the water," Kimi offered, "and I'm not sure she'll have the strength to pull you out again."

"Then I guess we'll have to get it right the first time," Isabella said.

"Or I'm fish food."

"Or"—a voice from the doorway made Isabella jump—"you could leave him there."

After her initial shock, Isabella realized who it was. "Eli! I'm glad you found us."

"You don't even know why he's trapped up there," Eli continued, walking out into the dim light of the cavern. "Maybe it's a trap."

"It's not," Wesley called down, "I was investigating some shadow activity up there and fell through the hole in the ceiling. The cage was anchored up there, and when I fell in, it unlatched and swung down here. The top closed when it did, and there you go, a bird in a cage."

"So you say." Eli shrugged his shoulders.

"But Skia said—"

"That's another thing," Eli continued, "what *do* you know about Skia. He showed up wherever you were and asked for your help, so you followed him into this dark cavern to what? Rescue some guy you don't even know? What if I told you that I know Skia lied to you?"

"Look, kid," Wesley called from the cage, "I don't know who you are or what you're doing here, but how about we talk about this down on the ground?"

"I'm not going to lift a finger, Samskara," he said, leaning against the wall opposite the rope.

"Samskara?" Isabella looked back and forth between the two.

"I was almost positive when I saw you with that squirrel, but seeing him, I know for certain. You told me you were a weaver, good for you, but if the Council of Dreamers hears that you helped a Samskara"—he pointed up to the cage—"then forget about being a weaver. Why do you think that rodent came to get you? There was no one else who'd help it."

"Skia went to get her father," Wesley called down, his voice wavering a little.

Eli motioned to the group. "And he clearly decided not to come, else he'd be here."

Isabella remembered how Vígolfr had come and pulled her father away before Skia had managed to secure his help, and for the first time wondered if that was by design and not a coincidence. If Eli was right and Skia had lied to her, she could be helping someone who had essentially tried to destroy everything she wanted to achieve. Her father, Wren, Finn, all worked with the Council. Looking up, she saw Wesley kneeling on the wooden bars of the cage, hands grasping them with a mixture of hope and trepidation.

Kimi, who had remained a quiet observer of the interchange, looked up at Isabella expectantly. She had been in a cage too, tied tightly and hidden away in the darkness. If it hadn't been for Skia, whether he'd lied or not, Isabella wouldn't have found the little fox. She owed the squirrel for that. Besides, Isabella looked at the boy as he leaned against the wall, what about Eli? He was in a dream trap, got hurt, she helped him get out, and then he complained a lot. That was about it.

"How did you find us?" Isabella asked suddenly. It was a question she was asking herself, but her voice, ringing clear through the cavern, surprised her.

"I took the easier path," he said smugly. "You know, the one I tried to get you to take."

"Good thing you ignored him," Kimi said loud enough for Izzy to hear.

Isabella looked between the two of them. "Doesn't matter," she said. Nobody moved. The falling water made ripples in the center of the pool and the silent serpentine creatures below glided smoothly together. The cage creaked as Wesley shifted uncomfortably on the bars. Then she repeated, louder, "Doesn't matter."

With a confident, determined step, Isabella walked to the edge of the water and looked down once more. There was no way to tell how deep it was or how big those things down there were. She didn't even know what they were. She looked up at Wesley. "I need you to start that thing swaying." She nodded over at the rope. "I'll get ready to loosen it when I think I have the timing down." She sighed. "But Kimi was right. We only have one chance to get this right."

"You're making a mistake," Eli said from his place on the wall.

"Maybe so, but nobody deserves to be trapped like that. Wesley," she said as she began to unwind the rope, "start swinging."

Wesley stood carefully on the bars of his cage then, grasping the front and the back, he began to shift his weight back and forth. There was little change at first, but each shift brought an incrementally larger arc to the cage's movement. Using the peg the rope was tied on as a brace, Isabella tried to let out the rope little by little, increasing the arc farther still. Eli and Kimi both watched in silence as the cage swung farther over the water, then closer to the land, then back over the water. Isabella counted the timing of the swing, her arms shaking from the weight despite the brace. The rope slipped through her hands, evoking a grunt from Wesley. Her palms burned as she struggled to regain control of his descent. Looking over her shoulder, she could see Wesley holding on, his momentum cut in half because of the slip.

"It's not working," she called back to him, "I can't keep holding it."

Getting up on shaking legs, he began shifting back and forth again. "Don't give up on me yet," he called out, "just a little more."

"I'm not sure—" Isabella's arms were shaking, her palms screamed, and sweat was beginning to drip into her eyes. "—I can't keep this up."

"Just a little more." Wesley swayed. "Now!" he yelled, and Isabella dropped the rope, turning around quick enough to watch the cage slam into the ground at the edge of the peninsula with a sickening crack. Wesley was thrown to the ground, and as he struggled to keep his balance, the cage with its now unattended rope, teetered backward and, almost in slow motion, tumbled back into the water, taking Wesley and the cord with it.

Running to the edge, Isabella watched as the rope tore through whatever held it to the ceiling and flung farther out into the pool. The cage and a flailing Wesley sunk into the swirling mass below. Isabella's hand shot to her mouth and she choked out a cry. Kimi leaned against her side, also silent in quiet respect.

"I told you it was a mistake." Eli's smug voice from behind her tore at Isabella's heart and she turned toward him, fists clenched at her side.

"How could you." She struggled to get the words out, tears streaming freely down her cheeks as yet another failure burnt itself into her heart. "You could have helped you little—"

"Little what?" Pushing away from the wall, he walked to the center of the opening; the darkness behind him seemed to swell. "I warned you, Isabella Shaw, Dreamweaver wannabe. You had to be heroic. Three times I tried to save you"—he glared at her, and his voice rose with each word—"three. But no, you needed to save him. You needed to stick your damn nose in where it doesn't belong, didn't you? Now you'll have to pay the price too, not just that annoying companion of yours."

Isabella stepped back, her eyes widening as he continued. The room seemed to be filling with a suffocating fear and hatred.

"Yes, I know all about you and your daring escape at my shadow congress. Oh, that got you. Yes, that little get-together was mine; I was going after your father and that damn pain in my ass apprentice of his. My shadows need to eat, and with your father out of the way, my nightmares can have all the food they want. They can gorge on the sleepers, easy pickings."

There was splashing in the water behind her, but it was the movement behind Eli that worried her. They seemed to materialize out of nowhere, but Isabella knew they were coming. Three shadows loomed over the spindly boy, but he didn't react to the emotions pouring off them: the fear and hatred, the anger, the regret. Isabella was buffeted by them, wave after wave, and she felt her knees begin to buckle. This was her fault. After all, if she'd been stronger, she could have held onto the rope longer. Wesley would have been safe and Skia would live. If she'd been a better Dreamweaver—if she'd been a Dreamweaver at all—she'd have saved him.

Movement by the wall caught her attention, breaking her roiling self-pity. Skia, seemingly revived, launched himself at Eli's arm and latched his sharp claws into him. Screaming, Eli flailed, throwing the squirrel off toward the water. Scurrying up Isabella's pant leg to his place by her ear, Skia snarled at the boy and his shadows. Kimi, paws planted solidly apart, lowered her head and let out a series of high-pitched warning yelps. Her teeth were exposed, ready to strike. Isabella bent her knees. There was no way out of this. Her back against the water and she could hear the churning in the center, but she refused to imagine what was happening beneath the surface. She drew her dagger—the Samsa'raka if Skia was to be believed—and dropped into a fighting stance.

TWENTY-SEVEN

At first, no one moved. The tableau seemed to be set like a chessboard waiting for the first player to take their turn. When that move was made, both sides leaped into action. One of the shadows, ordered by Eli, drove forward, cascading hopelessness in front of it. But this time, Isabella was prepared. When she felt the emotion buffeting her like a hurricane wind, she took an even, deep breath and squeezed the handle of the Samsa'raka. The jewels in the handle bit into her palm, but she ignored the pain. The stone flared briefly but otherwise did nothing.

Kimi, spurred by the advancing shadow, launched into the air, teeth gnashing at the shadow's right arm. While she passed through and landed safely on the other side, the shadow's arm dissipated momentarily before the dark swirling mist reformed, the new appendage sporting long, glistening black claws. Eli laughed and sent his other two shadows forward. With one shadow between her and Kimi, Isabella swiped her dagger diagonally across its midsection as Skia, pushing off from her shoulder, propelled himself through the head. For a moment, the shadow wavered, then coalesced into the shape of an old woman. Her sad eyes looked at Isabella, and then she nodded and disappeared. Isabella prepared to face off against the next one.

With both her friends on the shadow's other side, Isabella struggled to oppose the hopelessness and anger concentrated on her. The shadow in front of her wavered once again, and Isabella prepared to move forward through where it was. The shadow seemed to draw other shadows from the air around it, from the water, and from the cavern itself, toward it into long tentacular appendages. Two of these wrapped around itself, increasing the creature's bulk, then the remaining three shot out toward Isabella.

Too slow to get out of the way, Isabella was pierced through her right shoulder, the tentacle leaving a smoldering hole in her shirt. The smell of burnt flesh wafted up to her nostrils, but she refused to drop the knife. She swiped up to the right, drawing the blade through the tentacle, and it pulled out of her shoulder. The blade sliced through the misty darkness, but this time the tentacle did not grow back. Instead, the shadow pulled back, drawing the hopeless feeling with it before driving forward with the remaining two tentacles outstretched, pressing the emotion more forcefully before it.

Overwhelmed, Isabella stumbled backward, her foot slipping from the edge of the outcropping and making a splash in the water. Not being able to swim, falling in would be the end of her. She stumbled forward, careening toward the shadow. Kimi barked and Skia hissed, but she couldn't see around the shadow in front of her. Stopping Eli would stop this; he was the ringleader, the man behind the curtain, and it was time to get back to Kansas. Flailing her arms for balance she couldn't find, Isabella crashed to the ground in front of the shadow. The emotional charge was almost unbearable this close, and while she knew these were not her emotions, she found tears of frustration and hopelessness forming in her eyes and clouding her vision.

Looming above her, seeming to have grown taller, the shadow raised its taloned hand and was raking it down through the air when Isabella felt something pulling her toward the water. The shadow was forgotten in her fear of drowning; Isabella twisted and kicked, trying to free herself, but whatever had her was powerful. Her fingertips hurt from scraping at the loose stones that should have been underfoot, but still she tried to find purchase. Calling to Skia and Kimi for help, Isabella looked back in time to see her ankles disappear beneath the water. She couldn't tell what had her, but she imagined the slithering serpentine creatures below dragging her down. She could feel several smaller ones squirming on her ankles.

Kimi was the first to arrive, but still not getting to her until she was up to her waist. The shadows stood by watching, and Eli laughed. "I see the darkness has its own plans for you." He didn't leave or come closer, just smugly leaned against the wall. "I would have preferred to see you suffer a little more. You would have made a fabulous shadow eventually, but at least you will no longer be my problem."

Isabella wasn't listening; she was trying to keep her head from going under as the constant pressure pulling on her legs increased. Eli walked over, seeing her knuckles turning white as she gripped the last bit of ledge, barely keeping her head afloat. "Having some trouble?"

"Help me," Isabella cried. "I can't swim. This thing is going to drown me."

Squatting down in front of her, Eli looked down at Isabella, ignoring Kimi's growls as she pulled on Isabella's sleeve. "You'd like me to help you? Didn't you *abandon* me in the caves? We'll come back for you, I promise," he mockingly imitated her voice. "A hollow promise. Besides"—he shrugged, smiling down at her—"letting you drown saves me the trouble of doing it myself."

Risking letting go for a moment, Isabella swiped at Eli's ankle, hoping to either use it to pull him in or pull herself out, preferably both. Instead, what happened was the pressure on her legs increased, and she lost her grip. Her chin slammed down on the stone edges of the outcropping and the world blinked into darkness.

The shadows had been gone for a while, mused the boy in the cage. Was it possible that they forgot about him? No, he reminded himself, you're not that lucky. He heard voices, but in these caverns, voices could be coming from anywhere. They could even be a figment of his imagination. How long did it take for you to go insane from solitude? He couldn't remember, but he'd been here for a while. There was no telling why they were keeping him alive; it wasn't like the shadows to take prisoners, but these served a stalker.

He thought about the blond kid he'd tried to help, the whole reason he'd been landed in this mess. It should have been a routine extraction. Something had felt strange about it, but he'd chalked that up to never having gone in alone before. Typically, there was someone with him, and damn if he didn't miss that someone right now.

"They'll be coming for you," he repeated out loud. It had become his mantra, understandably so given the hopelessness that covered everything when the shadows were around. "They'll come for you."

So here he sat, motionless, in a wooden cage. He took a deep breath in, held it a moment, then breathed out. In the distance, someone screamed, calling for help, but he didn't know the voice. Any other time, he'd run to their aid, but what could he do from in here? Besides, he was unarmed. The stalker had made sure of that, the boy he'd come to save. He scoffed at himself. Some help. "They'll be coming for you. They'll be coming—" Somewhere in the back of his mind was an echo of a long-forgotten memory. He thought about carriages going down mountain passes. He breathed again and sent his hope that whoever was screaming found the help they were looking for.

"She's waking up." The voice was vaguely familiar, but Isabella couldn't place it. She shifted, her blankets bunched uncomfortably beneath her. "Hurry, get her some water."

"Leave me alone," she grunted and curled herself into a ball, wondering why her room was so cold.

"Are you sure she's not dreaming?" another familiar voice said, and Isabella wondered why so many people were in her room. She didn't remember planning any sleepovers. Regardless, she had a splitting headache and her jaw felt like she'd chewed on an iron pan. This was not going to be a good morning. "I think she's coming to."

"Coming to what?" Isabella was annoyed at being woken up and sat up quickly, intending to surprise whichever of her friends were talking about her while she slept. Sitting up quickly was a mistake. The world swam in front of her eyes and her vision narrowed. Squeezing her eyes shut, she cradled her head in her hands and tried to fight nausea that threatened to relieve her of the last thing she'd eaten. "Oh God, what happened?"

Nobody said anything, and for a moment, Isabella thought that she had imagined the voices from before. When the nausea subsided, she risked opening her eyes to the world. It took a moment to place herself. She could feel cold dampness clinging to her body, and there were three shapes in the darkness in front of her. Her eyes focused first on the fox, and a name floated beyond her memory. The other two came into focus moments later: a young man and a small squirrel. She looked at the man and asked her question again, "What happened?"

"You look out of it," he replied, seeming to ignore the question. "Are you okay?"

"Answer my question first." Images flashed in Isabella's mind: a wooden cage, going into the cave with a boy and a squirrel, but not this boy. The fox walked up to her, strange behavior for a wild animal, but something about it felt good. It sniffed her hand, looked up at her, then hopped into her lap. Kimi. The name popped into her head, along with Skia, the squirrel. Absentmindedly she began stroking the fox's back as she amended her question toward to boy. "Who are you?"

"My name," he said, standing up, Skia on his shoulder, "is Wesley, and I owe you a debt of gratitude."

"And an apology, I think," Isabella added, rubbing her chin. "I seem to remember this is your fault." The pieces were starting to come together again: the cave, Kimi, the fact she was supposed to be training to be a Dreamweaver like her father, but he'd got called away.

"Yes," Wesley said, rubbing the back of his neck with his left hand, "I couldn't think of another way."

"You could have let me handle them." Isabella still didn't trust her legs, and Kimi seemed comfortable, so she stayed sitting for the moment.

"You were so badly outnumbered. It was the only thing I could think of. Once I landed in the water because you dropped my cage—"

"Rescuing you, but okay."

"When I landed in the water, I realized that the shock had broken some of the wooden bars. I was able to get a hole big enough to squeeze through. And it turned out those snake things, they were common anguilliformes."

"Angluia-what?"

"Anguilliformes, eels. Harmless most of the time, and they were leaving me alone, so I figured the best course of action was a strategic retreat. I think it was Joseph Stalin who said 'it takes more courage to retreat than advance'."

"I'm going to go on a limb and say two things. The first one is that Stalin is probably not the person you want to emulate, and the second is that you're not from around here."

"You mean the dream world," Wesley chuckled. "Of course not. I'm a weaver, like you." He motioned at Isabella's lap and the sleeping fox.

Isabella looked down at the fox resting contentedly. She wanted to be a weaver, but things hadn't been shaping up very well for her lately. Kimi shifted into a more comfortable position, and Isabella decided not to correct him.

"This here is Skia, my companion." He smiled brightly at the little squirrel perched comfortably on his shoulder.

"Yes," Isabella said, now fully recovered from her blackout, "we met. Remember, we came to rescue you."

"Oh yeah." Wesley chuckled nervously. "I don't want to seem ungrateful about that, but did you happen to have a plan to get out of here? That blond kid—"

"Eli."

"That's his name? Okay, so Eli and his band of shadows are on the other side of the water. I'm sure there's a way around this that doesn't involve swimming, and I for one don't want to be here when they find it."

"I had planned on walking out the same way I came in originally, but that door closed, so to speak. So as of right now, no, but I'm open to ideas," Isabella explained.

"If there is no way back," Kimi said, uncurling and stretching before getting off Isabella's lap, "then go further forward."

Isabella looked down at the little red fox and smiled. Having Kimi next to her felt right, like something that had been missing in her life was finally found. "Forward it is then."

"Wait," Wesley said, "you think we should go deeper? As in, down there." He motioned to an opening filled with darkness on the other side of the room, and Isabella nodded. He looked around himself and, crossing his arms over his chest, held his shoulders. "But there is light here. There's got to be a way to the surface from here."

Isabella looked up at the ceiling. There was indeed an opening, but it was a long way up. "I know Skia is a good climber" —she looked at the squirrel who was as unnerved about going deeper underground as his weaver—"but I'm not sure he can pull any of us up there, and if I'm not mistaken, you don't have a rope."

Wesley looked around nervously. "I can't see down there. How do we know it's safe?"

"I can guarantee you that it is not safe," Kimi said, eyeing Wesley pointedly.

Isabella remembered her first meeting with the fox on her last trip to the dream world. Kimi's matter-of-fact nature had led Isabella to think the kind fox was her enemy. Turns out, the truth can be a harsh friend at times. Wesley seemed to take the fox's words better than Isabella had initially, but then the Kimi had shown up with Isabella and Skia, and he trusted Skia. "Besides"— Isabella tried to make her voice sound cheerful—"we have this."

She pulled out the dagger Ajay had given her when she'd met the hunter in the forest under the ash tree.

"How is a dagger going to—" Wesley's words stopped short as the yellow topaz on the back of the dagger began to glow faintly. He walked over, not taking his eyes off the dagger. "Is that —" He reached out as if to touch it but then drew his hand back. "It can't be. The Samsa'raka was lost years ago. Stolen."

"I'm not sure what you're talking about stolen." Isabella drew the dagger back toward herself, warily eyeing Wesley. "You seem to know what it is though, care to share?"

Wesley took Isabella's cue and stepped back to give her space. "I don't know much, just what I've read. Honestly, I thought it was a legend." Wesley leaned against the damp cave wall. "It belongs to the Samskara, a group of helpers." Noticing Isabella's confusion, he clarified, "Helpers are like weavers, but without companions. The elders of the Samskara were said to make and use charms that could accomplish feats even the best weavers could not. Eventually, the Council banned the use of charms by weavers, most of whom didn't care because they couldn't use them anyway, but the Samskara refused to stop. Because of that, were sanctioned by the Council of Dreamers. The Samskara went underground, and some say they used their charms to co-op the shadows' free wills and encouraged them to band together against the Council and weavers. That lead to the Great Purge and the eradication of the Samskara. The Council confiscated the remaining charms and destroyed them.

"The Samsa'raka"—he motioned to the knife that Isabella held—"was never found during the Purge. Legend has it, a young Samskara took the knife and used it to raise an army of shadows that plagued the dream world, launching an attack on the Capitol, the seats of the Council of Dreamers, and ravaging the surrounding villages. The Samskara who wielded it convinced a few hunter bands to side with her, and for a time the world was on the verge of collapse. Then suddenly, everything stopped—the blitzes on the Capitol, the village raids by the shadows—and the world settled back into an uneasy balance. The Samsa'raka disappeared from the legends, and the shadows seemed to disband."

"But what about the shadow congress?" Images of huddling over her younger brother, surrounded by writhing shadows, rose unbidden into Isabella's mind.

"Shadow congress?" Wesley's eyes grew wide.

"Yes," Kimi said, breaking into the conversation, "several moon cycles ago."

"About a year now," Isabella corrected.

Kimi nodded. "In your waking world, but here time works a little differently. Anyway, the Council of Dreamers caught wind of a gathering of the shadows, like in the times that immediately followed the Great Purge, and they started calling it a shadow congress. They sent your father"—she nodded to Isabella—"to settle the matter."

"From what I remember," Isabella said, raising her eyebrow at the fox's modesty, "you did more than your fair share."

"I was there for other reasons," Kimi replied, looking up at Isabella with a knowing glance before continuing her explanation.

Isabella didn't hear what Kimi said next because she was too focused on the implications of the words the fox had just said. A new wellspring of hope rose in Isabella, warming her chest and catching her breath. If Kimi hadn't been there to take care of the shadow congress, could she have been there to help save Tucker? And if that were the case, Isabella wondered what that meant for her and Kimi. Was there still a chance for her to become a true Dreamweaver? Wesley's question brought Isabella back to their conversation.

"So, does that mean they're uniting again?"

"Who's to say," Kimi concluded.

"This history lesson is great and all," Isabella said as she started toward the entrance to the passage leading deeper into the cave, "but it's not like any of this is going to matter unless we get out of here." The raka stone flared up momentarily as Isabella neared the edge of the passage, and something glinted on the ground a few feet away. "What's that?"

"What's what?" Skia asked, still perched on Wesley's shoulder.

"Down the path." Isabella walked through the opening and began down the slightly declining passageway. "Something caught the light from the stone. I'm going to take a look."

"Wait," Wesley called from behind her, but Isabella was done talking.

Kimi, seemingly in agreement with Isabella, sauntered to her side. "I thought we'd never get moving."

Isabella chuckled good-naturedly at the fox and continued toward where she'd seen the glint on the ground. It was farther in than she initially thought, but the sound of gravel crunching behind her made it clear Wesley and Skia were following. As hope of finding whatever had caught the light before began to fade, the stone flared again and Isabella saw more definition of the object.

There seemed to be two pieces of long reflective material about a yard down from where she was now. They were haphazardly discarded in the middle of the passage, and as Isabella drew closer, they took on more definition in the dim light from the raka stone.

"Are they what I think they are?" Isabella bent down as Kimi drew closer and sniffed at the handle of one of the swords lying on the ground. Something about them seemed familiar. The blades— both curved with a fatter section in the middle—were clearly well cared for and appeared only recently discarded. Beside them, was a harness that Isabella picked up. The leatherwork was impressive and well cared for. It was clear that the harness worked as a sheath to stop the swords to someone's back. With a little adjustment, Isabella strapped the harness to her back.

"Izzy," Kimi said as she looked up, wide-eyed, "I spent some time with Finn's clan of hunters while I was healing. Do you remember Finn's confidant?"

"These aren't—"

Kimi sniffed the handle again. "I'm afraid they are. There's no mistaking it."

"Cool looking swords." Wesley came up behind them. "Some sort of kilij if I'm not mistaken."

Isabella ignored Wesley's comment, picking up the swords and looking closer at the finely etched blades. "If he's here, we need to find him."

"We need to get out of here," Wesley insisted. "Remember your friend Eli and his shadows?"

Isabella turned at looked square into Wesley's eyes. "Yeah, but if Delson is here then Finn might be here too. He didn't abandon me when I needed him, and I'm not going to leave here until I'm sure he's safe."

"If these are his weapons, then what does he have to defend himself with?" Wesley asked.

"Izzy," Skia seconded, "Wesley has a point. If he doesn't have his weapons, then there's a good chance the shadows have already taken him. I'm sorry."

Isabella slid the swords into the harness and turned back toward the darkness ahead. "You do what you want, but I came here to rescue you. I'm not about to run away when I know someone else might be in trouble."

"Isabella," Wesley insisted, "you don't even know if he can be rescued."

"And I'm not going to give up until I do," she said defiantly as she began down the passageway.

Kimi watched Isabella walk away, took a deep breath that seemed to fill her with new energy, and bounded after her. Wesley didn't follow immediately, but as the darkness began pressing itself into the wake of the passing raka stone, a shiver ran down his spine. With hunched shoulders, he trudged after Isabella.

~~TWENTY-EIGHT~~

O ver here," Wesley called from behind Isabella. "I think I see some light down this passage."

They had walked down the passageway for a while, but the lack of sunlight made determining exactly how long tricky. Wesley hung back a few feet from Isabella, but she noticed that he typically stayed within the circle of light cast by the raka stone in her dagger. There was still one speck of darkness in the stone, but Isabella noticed it was getting smaller the longer she used the dagger. The specks in the stone seemed to be indicating some sort of power level or charge that was left, and as proud as Isabella had been to figure that out, she was equally disturbed to realize it was almost empty and she still didn't know how to fill it.

"I don't care," Isabella called over her shoulder. "Go on, Kimi, lead the way. We are not leaving here without Delson."

Kimi put her nose back to the ground and continued following Delson's scent. Skia had been pacing across Wesley's shoulders, clearly more agitated as they descended deeper into the caves.

The sound of Wesley's hurried steps caught up behind her. "Look," he said, his voice quivering in the growing gloom of the cave, "I get that you want to rescue the hunter, but they understand the risks they take. They know that hunting shadows is dangerous."

Isabella continued forward without acknowledging Wesley. Her shoulders tensed at what he was suggesting. The thought that a weaver would be so callous, so heartless, had never occurred to her. She knew that Wren had endangered Finn and Delson and the whole hunter clan, but that was different. That was trusting them in a fight, not abandoning them to the shadows. Seething inside, Isabella quickened her steps.

"Your raka stone is fading," he continued. "You need to recharge it before the light fades completely. If it gets too dark, we won't be able to see the shadows when they approach. We'll be captured, and then who will help your friend?"

"I don't think she's listening to you, Wes," Skia said from his shoulder.

"What was your first clue?" he snapped back.

A wry smile arched on Isabella's face, but she was not going to let his fear stop her from doing what she thought was right. If she ran out of light, she'd follow Kimi; the fox didn't seem to need the light anyway. If they came across a shadow, she'd do her best. That was all she could do. She told herself again that going forward is your best choice when going back isn't an option.

"Listen, Isabella, we need to be smart about his. Plan not react. Your friend might already be dead."

Isabella closed her eyes and took a deep breath, but it didn't help. Spinning on her heels, she took three steps toward Wesley and Skia and put her face inches from his. Her chest heaved and her muscles tensed. Next to her, she could hear a low warning growl coming from Kimi, mirroring her own emotional turmoil. For a moment, she didn't say anything, but Wesley took an involuntary step backward anyway.

"If you want to go, then go," she said through clenched teeth. "I will find Delson, I will rescue him, or I will die trying. He would do no less for me or for your sorry disgrace of a weaver self, for that matter. So, if you want to go, go." She stepped closer and Kimi's growl became louder. "But if you're going to follow me, then shut up." Spinning once again on her heels, Isabella walked away, fists clenched and chest pounding.

For a moment, Wesley stood without moving, looking at the fading light of the raka stone. Looking back over his shoulder, he could still see the light from the side tunnel, but he had no way of knowing if it was a way out or just a place where the light crept through a small hole.

"That was terrifying," Skia said.

"She's going to get herself killed." Wesley looked after her, the yellow glow of the raka stone creating a sort of halo effect on the cave walls around her. "They're gonna be pissed if I let her."

"So, we should follow her, right? I mean, we can't bring her back to the rest if we let her get killed."

"And we'd lose the Samsa'raka."

"Again."

"Not helpful, Skia. Okay, then we don't have much choice. That's why I let myself get captured in the first place."

"What are you going to do when she figures out what's going on?"

"Let's hope she doesn't." Wesley began to move forward, a shiver running down his spine. It was cold in the cave, but cold he could handle. He wasn't sure if he could handle what lay ahead, what he'd gotten himself into. "Because I'm not sure I can handle her."

"At least she's not trained yet, Wes."

"True," he sighed. "But I'm not sure that's going to matter." Shaking his head, he added, "If we help her save this hunter, maybe we still have a chance to get her on our side." He increased his pace to catch up with Isabella and Kimi before the light faded too much to follow.

"Looks like they decided to follow after all," Kimi said, the amusement evident in her voice. "That was an impressive display back there."

"I lost my temper." Isabella shook her head. She hated when she lost her temper; being out of control scared her.

"You stood up to Wesley," Kimi countered, "and stood by your friend."

The sound of footsteps behind them indicated that Wesley had caught up with them. She heard his breathing, slightly ragged and clearly winded from trying to catch up. Skia had said he was a bookish guy, not in the field that much, which explained how he'd let himself get caught. Kimi's soft footfalls whispered along the gravel floor of the tunnel, but Wesley's sounded like a herd of elephants. Sneaking up on whoever was holding Delson was not going to be an option. If he was still alive, that was.

Isabella closed her eyes and focused on listening to Kimi. The light from the stone in her dagger's handle was getting dim. As much as Isabella didn't want to admit it, Wesley was probably right. Without the light, fighting any shadows would be much more challenging. Isabella stopped and raised her chin. Wesley, who must not have been paying close enough attention, bumped into her from behind, immediately fumbling with an apology, but Isabella shot him a glare and put up her hand to hush him.

Something was off in what she'd heard. There was a soft sound under the footfalls of her companions, almost like a voice, or a couple of voices, reverberating off the walls of the passage. She closed her eyes again, focusing on hearing what was happening up ahead. Wesley's breathing sounded too close, too loud, but she tried to tune it out. Kimi brushed against her leg in the dark, and Skia shifted on Wesley's shoulder. Then everything came into focus. There were two voices.

The first voice sounded over-friendly as it said, "Your protestations are useless."

"Nothing is useless as long as I draw breath." The second voice was weaker than the first, possibly further away.

The first voice laughed humorlessly. "It is inevitable that they will come."

"Nothing is inevitable"—the second voice was angry now—"they don't even know I'm here."

"That's not what my spies tell me, hunter."

The second voice said something that Isabella couldn't quite make out, but it sounded venomous nonetheless.

"Did you hear that?" Isabella asked Wesley.

"Hear what?"

"The talking." She shushed him again and tried to hear more. "I lost them, but they were clear as day. Two people. One of them was a hunter. It had to be Delson."

"I don't know what you're talking about. There is no talking down that way. These caves can play tricks on the mind," Wesley warned. "If anything, it could be a dream trap."

"We're going to investigate anyway. If there's even a chance Delson is down there, we can deal with whatever else we run into."

"Have you ever been in a dream trap?"

"Yes"—Isabella shrugged her shoulders—"have you?"

"Well, not exactly," Wesley stammered, "but I've read a lot about them, and from what I can tell—"

"Which is exactly nothing if you haven't actually dealt with one," Isabella interrupted and let the subject drop without missing a stride.

It was impossible to tell how far they walked or how deep they'd gone, but the air felt heavier, denser somehow. The light from the raka stone faded beyond use as anything more than a beacon for Wesley to follow, as long as he stayed close enough that the darkness didn't swallow it. The companions found themselves so close together that Wesley stepped on the back of Isabella's boots a couple of times before she warned him back, but offered him her hand to hold to keep from being separated. Her other hand she had out in front of her, low enough to feel the top of Kimi's raised tail. Isabella was beginning to second-guess her decision to continue forward in dark silence, but she followed Kimi's resolute movements. The little fox had proved her value several times when Isabella first found herself lost in the dream world looking for her brother. At the time, she had doubted Kimi but now she wondered what would have happened if she had trusted this little fox. No use second-guessing, she figured, but plenty of use avoiding the same mistakes twice.

They traveled down the passage for a while longer before a faint light emanated from around a corner up ahead. Kimi's tail twitched and Isabella stopped moving forward. The four of them stood listening for the sounds of talking that Isabella had heard earlier, but there was nothing any of them could hear now.

"What do we do now?" Skia was the first to break the silence, but the little squirrel kept his voice low.

"One of us is going to take a look around the corner," Kimi responded, her voice sounding as tired as Isabella felt.

"I'll go." Isabella started toward the corner, but Wesley grabbed her by the arm to stop her. "What?" she asked as she turned to face him.

"Why are you going? It could be a trap, remember?"

"All the more reason for me to go." Isabella rolled her eyes. "I've actually dealt with one before."

"Right," Skia added, "but I'd be quieter, better I go than you."

"But you don't know what Delson looks like," Isabella protested, "you wouldn't be able to recognize him."

"Would it matter?"

"What's that supposed to mean?" Isabella scowled in Skia's direction. She knew the squirrel couldn't see her, but she hoped that the scowl sounded in her voice.

"Not what you're thinking," Skia chirped back. "Just, would it matter to you if it was a stranger in the cage? Would you turn around at this point if it wasn't Delson?"

Isabella almost retorted, then felt herself deflate. Skia was right. After all, she wouldn't turn around if it wasn't Delson. It didn't matter if it were some stranger trapped in this desolate darkness. She was here, and she would do her best to rescue whoever it was. "You're right," she said after a pause, "it wouldn't matter."

"Oh great." Wesley's frustration was apparent in his lowered voice. "So now you're all against me?"

"No one is against you, weaver," Kimi said, a patience Isabella was unfamiliar with in her voice. "Your companion has simply accepted the situation as it is, something I would recommend you do soon, or this may go poorly."

With a sigh of resignation, Wesley fell silent. Skia scurried off his shoulder and passed Isabella and Kimi. The three of them waited in the darkness. Skia was a logical choice—he was small and quiet—but Isabella didn't like sending someone else into danger when she could help it. Time stretched on and the light around the corner flickered, faded, and brightened again. Someone coughed, and there was a muffled noise.

Wesley rose to his feet and began pacing before asking, "What is taking Skia so long?"

"Be patient, Wes." Isabella tried to relay a calm she didn't feel. She had been wondering the same thing, her nerves beginning to fray. Something felt off, but she put it down to the disorientation of the heavy darkness.

"Something's wrong." His footsteps stopped pacing back and forth and he began to walk past Isabella and Kimi. "I'm going to get him."

"No," Isabella hissed as she stood up to grab him before he passed; she didn't know why, but the whole situation was beginning to get on her nerves. "He'll be back."

"They don't call it being squirrelly for nothing," Kimi chimed in as she stretched awake from the short nap she'd taken.

"You don't know him." Wesley pulled on his sleeve, his voice raised slightly in an angry whisper. "He likes to curl up by the fire. He's not one for adventuring."

"Could've fooled me," Isabella countered as she kept her hand on Wesley's arm. Part of her wanted to comfort him, but she could feel herself grabbing harder than she intended. "Do you forget that he traveled all the way to my father's cabin to get me? Alone. He's got more in him that you give him credit for."

"Still," Wesley said, leaning sullenly against the wall, "he should be back by now."

"Aww," a voice said, accompanied by a quiet scuff of gravel behind them, "how cute. You're worried about your little rodent."

With the last syllable, a torch flared to light, momentarily blinding them.

Isabella and Wesley shielded their eyes from the light and began to back toward the corner where Skia had gone to investigate. Kimi, having scrambled to her feet with the flare of light, was backing up with them, letting out a low warning bark. The anger flowing toward the three of them made it immediately clear what they were facing, but as their eyes adjusted to the light, they could only see Eli clearly. Behind him, the air swirled in darkness, swallowing the light from the torch he'd lit.

"Don't look so surprised," he sneered at Isabella. "You didn't think that little stunt before was going to stop me? Besides, I know your kind. You wouldn't leave your friend behind."

"What is your issue?" Isabella took another step back. This one hand she held the dagger in front of her, while the other she used to feel along the wall.

"You have something of mine," Eli said, motioning toward the dagger with the torch he held.

"That's not yours," Wesley said before spitting on the ground between them.

"Oh"—Eli tilted his head at Wesley, smiling—"are you trying to say it belongs to you? What makes you any better than me?"

"We help people," Isabella answered back, "you ... I don't even know what you do, but it's not helping."

"Oh, like you helped that girl? Now, what was her name, Tumie? Runi? Whatever, it doesn't matter now, does it? I mean, it's not like she made it out of the dream world. To the shadows with her." He laughed as if he'd made a joke. "I mean, my shadows did take her after all. Such a powerful weaver you're turning out to be, Izzy. So successful and astute."

"Don't listen to him, Izzy," Kimi said, standing by her side with her ears pinned back.

"That's fine." Eli shrugged. "I was done talking anyway. Get them." He pointed his empty hand toward Isabella and Wesley. The darkness behind him swelled and swirled past him, giving the torchlight the same color and movement as the light from around the corner.

TWENTY-NINE

With the passage lit by Eli's torch, Isabella was able to see the advancing shadows coagulate into three distinct shapes. Each shadow quickly reached the top of the passage—at least a foot farther than Isabella could reach—and filled about half the width. As a result, one seemed to advance quicker than the others.

A choked cry sounded to her right, something that could have been an apology, but it was drowned out by the crunch of footsteps fleeing in the direction Skia had gone—the direction opposite the shadows. Not wanting to take her eyes off the shadows, Isabella assumed that Wesley had run off, abandoning her and Kimi to whatever these shadows could dish out.

The leading shadow reached out with a clawed arm, ribbons of darkness dripping from the talons as they glistened in the firelight. The Samsa'raka seemed to pulse with energy, but its light faded almost instantly and the stone went cold and dark in the hilt. The carvings on the blade, on the other hand, seemed to shine a pale yellow. Swirls and symbols ran the length of the lustrous silver, but Isabella didn't have time to examine them closely as the first shadow advanced, lashing out with its glossy black claws. Isabella jumped back. She avoided the claws touching her skin, but her shirt was not as lucky; three lines raked across the front, the edges ragged.

Isabella countered with a slash across the right arm of the shadow. The dagger caught the shadow where a person's wrist would be, slicing a section away. The hand and claws of the creature dissipated before they fell to the ground. The symbols on the blade flared once, then settled brighter than they'd been before. The shadow screeched in pain and lunged at Isabella, but Kimi was quicker than it had expected. She sprung, teeth bared, and ripped through the shadow's leg, causing it to shift as she pulled some of it with her. The slight shift in the shadow's movement was enough that Isabella could push against the wall of the passage, dodging the slashing claws of the creature's left arm.

The shadow swirled in front of Isabella, whose back was still to the wall. The mass of blackness, almost palpable, teamed with emotions that Isabella had to fight to avoid falling prey to. She'd realized last time that oppressive emotions were a shadow's most potent weapon. Those emotions were pushing against her now, feelings of hopelessness and unfocused anger. Isabella stared into the shadow, losing herself for a moment in its depths. A shudder ran down her spine and her arms dropped to her sides. She felt so alone: Kimi's growls sounded so far away, and Wesley had run off.

"That's right," the voice said, breathing on her, "there is no point to this."

Isabella closed her eyes and, exhaling, relaxed her shoulders. Opening her eyes again, she could see that the shadow had reformed, its claws dripping decay like a salivating animal. It moved in closer, but Isabella didn't move; her head was bowed and her face held an expression of hopelessness. Kimi started pulling on her pant leg, but Isabella didn't respond.

"Move," Kimi growled. "Izzy, you need to move."

The shadow moved in closer to Isabella, the swirling darkness now inches from her nose. A cool mist emanated from the creature, but Isabella didn't seem to notice. Her head was lowered and swayed back and forth, trancelike, but her eyes were open and searching. The burnished blade flared slightly, then settled back so dim the symbols were almost unidentifiable.

"Give it up, fox," Eli said from behind the other two shadows that had advanced slightly. "Can't you see your weaver is too weak to withstand my shadows? I overestimated you, pulling three of my shadows from the world. I could have sent these two after some dreamer." He sighed. "Live and learn, I suppose."

"You're smug for a traitor." Kimi shifted her focus to Eli, backing away from the shadow and Isabella. She slowly moved around the distracted shadow.

"Calling me a traitor," Eli said with a laugh, "when you're going to walk away from your weaver when she's in need?"

Kimi slunk forward toward the two shadows guarding Eli. Her ears were pinned back and her mouth open to show her teeth. "I suppose it could be seen like that if you don't know any better."

"Oh, that old lie about shadows and stalkers?" Eli laughed again. "You think if you take me out, my shadows dissipate. You poor little neophyte, taking the word of your precious Council as gospel."

The shadow in front of Isabella raised a dripping claw as if savoring the distress she was in. A drop of decay fell onto Isabella's shoulder and began dripping down the sleeve of her shirt, leaving a sizzling line in the cotton. Isabella didn't react. Her chin lifted slightly, but her head kept swaying and her eyes continued to rove over the shadow.

"You're not going to throw me off," Kimi said, edging over to the side while keeping her eyes on Eli.

"If you take me out"—he shrugged—"which I highly doubt, my shadows will simply roam free, spreading their devastation as they see fit. They follow me because I help them, simple as that."

"Nothing is ever as simple as you think." Kimi lunged at one of the shadows guarding Eli but was swatted aside. She slammed into the wall, falling limply to the floor.

"Not going to throw you off, eh?" Eli chuckled. "Apparently, that is exactly what we're going to do." He motioned toward the prone fox, and the other two shadows began to close the distance.

Suddenly, Isabella's head snapped up, her right arm, holding the dimly glowing blade, following suit. The instant the blade began to move, it flared with a blinding glow. Eli let out a startled gasp at the sudden movement and brightness, dropping his torch which sputtered out on the damp floor. The light from the blade glowed bright enough to see without the torchlight, and shadows danced on the wall. Isabella brought the dagger straight up into the middle of the shadow, having found her spot at last.

The blade found its mark in the dark center of the shadow, causing a popping sound as the shadow seemed to fall to form a young man with disheveled hair and a scruffy face. He was thin with hard features and shook as he wrapped his dirty arms around himself. Then, as the blade flared again, he looked at Isabella for a moment and sighed. His features softened and a light came back into his eyes. He smiled, bowed his head, and faded away to nothing.

"H-how..." stammered Eli in the warm yellow glow. The two shadows that had been slowly advancing on Kimi drew back, letting out a hissing sound.

In the corner of her eye, Isabella caught sight of Kimi. The already small fox looked somehow smaller laying on her side. Isabella knew better, though. That fox was bigger than anyone could imagine. She was brave and steadfast and clever, all the things that Isabella wished she could be but never seemed to measure up to. She could see the slight rise and fall of Kimi's chest in the light of the Samsa'raka's blade, so she kept her focus on Eli and his remaining shadows.

"You're a w-weaver," he continued to stammer, "you can't —"

Isabella had no clue what he was talking about, but she could tell he was shaken by what he'd seen, and she wasn't about to lose that advantage. "I can, and I did. Stick around. You can find out what else I'm capable of," she said threateningly.

Without waiting for a reaction, Isabella lunged toward the remaining two shadows. While she missed the darker ball, the dagger sunk deep into the shadow closest to her and managed to pull a sizable section out of its side. The shadow reeled and shrieked in pain and fear as it swirled in a chaotic dark vapor. Isabella saw Kimi begin to stir, but the second shadow noticed it too and began to flow quickly toward the fox.

"No, you don't." Isabella slashed the dagger at the shadow advancing on Kimi but missed her mark, stumbling to the floor.

Eli, who had taken a step back when Isabella advanced, crossed his arms in front of himself and laughed. "Very impressive."

Not rising to his attempts to draw her focus away from the fight, Isabella raked the floor with her left hand, pulling up some gravel and small stones. She threw them at the second shadow, but they didn't dislodge the denser ball that seemed to shift inside. Pushing off like a runner on their mark, Isabella ran headlong into the shadow as it loomed over Kimi's now shifting body, willing her companion to open her eyes and help in the fight. Isabella's footing slipped and she flailed her arms as she tried to regain her balance. The dagger clattered from her hand, plunging the passage into darkness as her left knee slammed into the floor, causing a jarring pain to shoot up her side. She extended her arms, trying desperately to grab anything and steady herself.

Her right hand closed on something cool and smooth, but it didn't stop her forward momentum and Isabella hit the ground hard, banging her left shoulder into the wall of the passage. The ball in her hand burned with cold, but something kept Isabella from dropping it. Her entire arm began to ache and burn. Her breath started coming in short gasps, but despite the pain she couldn't will her hand to open.

There were sounds of movement to her left and Isabella shied away, expecting the sting of the shadow's claws to descend on her shoulder at any moment. Instead, she felt a cold nose and warm fur nudge something hard and smooth into her left hand. It didn't take long before Isabella realized that Kimi had brought her the Samsa'raka. The moment her hand closed on the hilt, the blade blazed with a golden fire. In the newfound light, Isabella saw that her right arm was swollen and black. The darkness seemed to shift and move further up toward her shoulder. In her palm, held open despite feeling closed, was the shadow's core, still linked to the shadow standing before her by a thin thread of darkness.

Isabella met the shadow's cold yellow gaze, and slowly closed her hand around the cold, marble-sized core. Squeezing her palm tightly around the core, numb to any feeling, she heard the familiar pop. The shadow screamed and fell away to leave the shape of a small child. She couldn't have been more than seven, and her eyes went wide before she too faded from the world.

The last shadow began to advance. Intense pain lanced through Isabella, emanating from her right arm. She doubled over, gasping for breath. Lights flashed behind her eyes as she fought to stay conscious. She heard Kimi shuffling behind her, then the small paws pounced on Isabella's back, lightly digging their nails through her shirt. The now-familiar breeze of Kimi launching herself at a shadow brushed past Isabella's hair, and the tell-tale popping sound told Isabella that Kimi had found her mark. The distant crunch of footfalls fading away signaled that Eli had fled, and although she knew they should give chase, Isabella felt exhaustion overtake her. She collapsed onto the ground and the blade fell from her hand, plunging them both into the darkness once again.

The damp had soaked into Isabella's clothes by the time she was finally able to push herself off the ground. Her right arm ached and hung uselessly by her side, but her left arm was strong enough to push her to her knees and use the cave wall to stand up. When she touched her right arm, it felt swollen and stiff. Pain lanced from the place her fingers probed and shot down her arm.

"Kimi," she whispered, "are you alright?"

"You're finally awake." There was concern in the little fox's voice.

"I can't see anything. Do you know where the dagger is?"

The sound of metal dropping on stone by her boot answered her question. Isabella picked it up and looked at the faint light the stone gave off as soon as her hand touched the handle. The stone now had two black specks in it and gave a weak yellow glow. The blade, which had flared so brightly when the shadows attacked, was back to its lustrous silver color, the symbols almost indiscernible from the rest of the metal. Knowing she wasn't going to like what she saw, Isabella angled the light onto her injured arm. The skin of her hand was black and glistening, swollen and stretched taut.

"That doesn't look good," Kimi said, her voice dry but concerned nonetheless.

"Doesn't feel good either." Isabella didn't want to think about what it all meant. She knew she was in the dream world, but the last time she had been injured in the dream world, it had followed her to the waking world. She'd spent a week in an air cast for her ankle. She was afraid to think what this might mean for her. Something similar had happened to Kimi the last time they'd been together. Isabella had used honey as a disinfectant, but there was little hope of finding honey in a cave, and Kimi's scratch hadn't looked as bad as her arm did now. That was a later concern though. For now, she needed to rescue Delson and get out of this cave. "Let's go. There's not much we can do about it here."

The two moved slowly down the passage in the direction Skia had gone to investigate and Wesley had fled. Isabella kept the light from the raka stone low enough so she could make out shapes but hopefully not angled enough to give away their position. They may have taken care of the shadows, but Eli was still out there, and who knew how many shadows he had at his disposal down here.

As they neared the corner, it looked like a stone moved along the edge of the wall. At first, Isabella was ready to throw something at it, but then she remembered that Skia should be down this way somewhere.

"Skia," Isabella said, careful to keep her voice low, "is that you?"

"Izzy, Kimi, it's good to see you. Where's Wes?"

"Your guess is as good as mine," Kimi answered. "The coward ran the minute the shadows struck. Left us to take care of them ourselves."

"It's not like that," Skia protested.

"What was it like?" Kimi glared at the other companion with disdain. She held her chin high and her tail straight back.

Her fur, typically lustrous and pristine, was matted with mud and plastered to her body, but the regality with which she held herself in the damp gloom of the cave made Isabella smile.

"He's not a fighter," Skia scrambled to explain as he climbed Isabella's right pant leg. "Not all weavers fight the shadows. There are other ways."

"Ridiculous," Kimi scoffed. "How can you help the dreamers if you don't help them beat their shadows back?"

"There are times when running is better than fighting." Skia sniffed Isabella's hand on his way by and flinched before commenting, "That's not good."

"Let's go." Kimi started moving forward, having had enough of the conversation.

"Wait, Kimi"—Isabella turned her head to the squirrel who had taken up a perch on her shoulder—"let's hear what Skia saw before rushing in. Maybe we can get a plan together."

Kimi sat but didn't come closer. "If you want to listen to him, Izzy, I'll wait, but I'm not going to trust the words of a coward's companion."

"Wesley is not a coward." Skia's tail twitched erratically behind him, tickling Isabella's ear. "I told you, not all weavers need to fight."

"What else do weavers do?" Isabella was curious. Up until now, all she'd seen of the weavers were Wren and her father; both fought the shadows and both were at the shadow congress when the battle came.

"Nothing else," Kimi answered Isabella's question. "The Council of Dreamers even fights the shadows when they're needed."

"Not everyone follows the Council's edicts," Skia said. "There are those who—"

"The rebels." Kimi stood, the hair on her back raised and her ears pinned back. "Traitors," she spat.

"What rebels?" Isabella looked from Kimi to Skia. "What are you two talking about?"

"A group of cowardly traitors who ignore the Council's rules. They're one step above the stalkers, if you ask me. They don't always help the dreamers. They choose who to help and don't care who is sacrificed to get what they want." Kimi turned her head toward the corner. "I should have known when that coward was willing to sacrifice Delson to escape with his own sorry hide."

"It's not like that." Skia was almost whining now. "That's the Council's propaganda, Izzy. You have to believe me."

Isabella shook her head. "I don't know what to believe, but right now, it doesn't matter. We have to rescue Delson and find Wesley so we can all get out of here. Rebel or not, no one deserves to fall to the shadows."

"Take notes, Skia," Kimi said. "That's how a real weaver sounds."

Isabella smiled despite their situation. A real weaver. She wasn't sure if Kimi was right, but it sure felt good to hear. "Now, tell me what's around the corner so we can make a plan."

THIRTY

As they rounded the last corner before light could be seen ahead, Skia urged Isabella to stop. The dark tunnels were putting them all on edge, but Skia seemed to be taking the brunt of it. Losing Wesley for a second time might have had something to do with it. Isabella was trying to be understanding, but the squirrel's insistent chattering in her ear was grating on her nerves.

"What is it now?" she said, hoping the annoyance she felt didn't come through her voice.

"I don't think we should rush in there." Skia had made the same request at least three times since the fight with the shadows in the tunnel.

Isabella fought to keep her voice even. "You told us it was a hunter in a cage. No shadows. We're safe."

"Right, but that was then. Things might have changed."

"Skia has a point," Kimi said, "as much as I hate to admit it."

"So, let's sit here for a moment and—"

"And wait for more shadows to come?" Isabella said, cutting the squirrel off and moving forward again. "Would it change things if there were shadows there? Would we shrug our shoulders and head home?"

"No," Kimi answered, "but it wouldn't hurt to have a plan when we get in there."

"Right," Skia agreed, "a plan and an escape plan. We can't help anyone if we don't have a way to get out safely."

"I get what you're saying"—Isabella stopped for a moment and looked down at Kimi, Skia joining the fox on the floor —"but I have a plan. I go in there, we save Delson, then we all get out." She smiled. "So let's go."

Without waiting for Kimi or Skia to argue, Isabella turned on her left heel and ran down the passage toward the room where, if Skia was right, Delson sat trapped. She knew her plan sucked, but there were times in life when people needed to take action first and think things through after. This felt like one of those times.

There was no doubt that Kimi would be following right behind her, but she didn't know what Skia would do. If she was honest with herself, she wasn't sure it mattered. She felt terrible about her ambivalence, but Wesley had proved unreliable and Isabella didn't hold much hope for his companion. Kimi would be a little annoyed at her for pulling that trick, but there actually was a plan. She'd charge in, putting anyone who was in there on the back foot, then Kimi could come in and they'd already be off-balance. It wasn't a great plan, but it was a plan. She knew that Kimi and Skia would've objected, so she'd decided not to tell them.

With each footfall, pain shot through Isabella's right arm and shoulder. The skin on her arm was beginning to feel tighter, and she had little doubt that the swelling had continued. The future of her arm, her own future, honestly, was unknown, but Isabella tried not to dwell on that thought. Dwelling on that wouldn't help Delson, and it wouldn't help her. She pushed forward, hoping that her plan, as flimsy as it was, would be enough to get them through this one more time. She could hear Kimi's nails catching across the gravel floor and knew that at least part of the plan was going to work. She'd get there before Kimi caught up with her. She glanced over her shoulder, trying to catch a glimpse of Kimi, knowing that the little fox's bravery seemed almost contagious.

"Izzy!" Kimi's voice sounded concerned, but Isabella kept running. "Izzy, stop! It's a tr—"

Isabella's left foot caught a stone sticking up from the floor, and she lost her balance, tumbling forward uncontrollably. She landed hard and twisted as her left palm hit the floor. Her body angled to the right and she came down hard on her already throbbing shoulder. Unable to stop herself, she felt her head hit the unforgiving ground.

The glaring fluorescent lights and the sounds seemed wrong to Isabella. The walls in the room were white, and there was a strange mechanical beeping noise. Isabella rubbed her eyes in the dry, cold air. It felt like something was pulling on her right arm, but she couldn't see anything. As her eyes adjusted to the brightness, she heard a door open and footsteps falling hollow on a hard floor.

"Oh, good, you're awake. You had us scared there for a bit," an unfamiliar voice said from the doorway.

Isabella tried to turn her head, but something around her neck kept her facing the ceiling. Her throat was dry and her voice cracked when she first tried to speak.

"Don't overdo it, sweetie," the voice said. "You were in a pretty bad accident."

Isabella tried to piece things together. She'd been going camping with her dad. There was a pickup that'd run a stop sign, but her dad had been able to stop in time, hadn't he? "No," she managed, her throat like sandpaper.

"Hush, hush." The doctor was standing over her now. Looking up, Isabella could see a man, probably in his late thirties or early forties, his dark hair beginning to gray around the temples. He held a paper cup with some ice chips in it to her lips. "Take some of this. It'll help. They had to intubate you in the ambulance. We took the tube out last night, but you're going to have a sore throat for a day or two still. The cool ice will help."

The ice chips felt good going down, soothing her dry throat. "How's my dad?" The words came out strained and rough, but the doctor seemed to understand.

"He's alright." He moved around to the end of the bed and looked at her chart. "He and your mom have been here off and on, but they had to go home and take care of ... your brother, is it?"

"Tucker, yeah." Isabella didn't remember the accident, but she felt bruised and sore.

His smile was warm and confident. "I'll give them a call so they can come down and see you. Things are looking good, but I don't like the look of that infection so I want to keep you here for a few more days to monitor it."

"What happened?"

"We were hoping you could tell us a bit about that." He moved to adjust something on the IV attached to her right arm. "Your dad said you were camping?"

"The truck that almost hit us—but, no, Dad stopped in time. We were in the woods, around the fire."

"What's that?" the doctor stopped what he was doing and looked at her with concern.

"Nothing"—she shook her head—"just that we almost got hit by some guy driving a pickup truck on our way to the camp-site."

"Well, the ambulance picked you up from the woods, so you must have made it there at least. I overheard the police questioning your father. He said something about a fire?"

"We were sitting around the fire." Isabella tried to make sense of the fragments of memory. "There was a waterfall by the cabin."

"Afraid not," the doctor said, smiling at her sadly. "There was no cabin by where you were found. Did you fall by the river? Is that how you hit your head?"

Isabella squeezed her eyes shut and the image of a cave flashed in her mind—moist, cold air, stalactites—but when she opened her eyes again, she was in the hospital room. "I was running."

"Did someone hurt you?"

"Yes." Isabella felt confused. She remembered being attacked, but she couldn't put the pieces together.

"The police wanted me to look into it," he said, pulling up a chair from the other side of the room. "They mentioned that your brother went missing last year. Ran away, I think they said. Then you went missing. You were injured then too."

"I don't—" Isabella vaguely remembered something about that, something about an ash tree and a fox. "Kimi, something about Kimi."

"Right, Kimi LaPei. The police said that she'd found you and your brother in the woods when she was going for a walk. You were both shivering. The police suspected abuse back then, but there wasn't enough evidence." The doctor leaned in close to Isabella, and for a moment she thought she could see the door right through his lab coat. "Look, before I call your parents, you can tell me. Was it your father who did this to you? Do you feel safe at home?"

"What?" Isabella's head felt like it was spinning. "No, well, I mean yes—I mean—"

"You're safe here." The doctor put a reassuring hand on Isabella's right arm, but it felt like his hand was on fire. She winced and tried to pull her arm away, but she couldn't. "I promise, I won't hurt you. I took an oath when I became a doctor. Do no harm. You're safe. We can protect you and your brother."

"No." Isabella shook her head, squeezing her eyes closed again. The smell was wrong; it wasn't the antiseptic smell of a hospital. The air was cool, but it was moist in her nostrils and there was a hint of something else in it. It smelled like dirt; not the good dirt like when she'd help her mother with the garden, but something darker, earthier. Something else was wrong too. Under the electronic sound of the beeping machines, there was a shifting noise as if someone was adjusting the way they were seated on a gravel floor.

The doctor's voice brought her back to the room as he said quietly, "I promise you that you can tell me."

Isabella looked around the room. She knew it didn't feel right but couldn't put her finger on why. Her arm was aching, throbbing up to her shoulder, and it was cold. She lay in a hospital bed, covered with a blanket, but she was shivering. She felt dampness soaking up through the blanket and something cold and hard digging into her side.

"Can I take this thing off?" she asked, gesturing to the uncomfortably tight neck brace.

"Let's leave it on for a little bit more," the doctor said, flipping absently through her chart. "Are you sure everything is alright at home?"

"Everything's fine at home," Isabella answered. "It was an accident."

"If that's how you truly feel." The doctor stood up, looking at Isabella with concern. "Your parents are on their way, so they should be here in an hour or so. I'll come back and check on you before they get here, in case anything changes." He smiled a sad smile, then left Isabella alone in the sterile room with the mechanical beeps and an uneasy feeling that something was wrong.

When the girl had come around the corner, running like someone on a mission, he thought she was coming to rescue him. She had his swords, the ones that Eli had tricked him away from when he feigned injury in the tunnels. The underhanded stalker had taken advantage of his generosity. He'd spent the last few days kicking himself for his own stupidity. Finn was always telling him that he was too trusting, but Finn was one to talk.

The girl looked vaguely familiar, but he couldn't place her. He'd been about to call out to her, but when she tripped and fell, her head coming down hard on the floor of the cave, he knew that she wouldn't be answering him any time soon.

She needed help, and he was a hunter with the Champion. He needed a way out of this cage if he was going to make that happen. A dark stain began to spread across her forehead from where she banged her head on the stone floor, matting down her hair in places. She'd have one heck of a headache when she woke up. What he was worried about were the shadows that seemed to be condensing around her. He'd seen this before on his shadow hunts, usually with one of the walkers or a denizen. The Champion had called them shade traps, and while he didn't know much about them, he did know that they were bad news. He needed to help her get out of it, or the head wound would be the least of her worries.

"Hey," he called to her, his voice barely above a whisper in the hope of not alerting the shadows guarding him, who seemed to have disappeared for now. "Hey, you got to get up!"

The girl on the ground mumbled something about a fire and camping. She was delirious or dreaming, but she didn't seem to hear him. He had to find another way to get to her. Standing up, he grabbed hold of the cage bars and began to shake them, hoping he could loosen the hinges or something, but it was no use. The cage was made of some strengthened wood, the sides wrapped together with thick ropes, and he didn't have anything to cut them. The knots, although visible, were all on top and out of his reach. The cage seemed to be connected to the floor by some sort of latching system that he couldn't figure out. "Come on," he called out in frustration as the girl shifted on the cold stone floor.

"Kimi," she mumbled, but then the words became unintelligible.

He knew that name. Ajay had brought a small red fox named Kimi to their camp to recuperate after the battle with the shadow congress. He'd said it was some weaver's companion. Finn had spent a lot of time with her. When he'd asked Finn about it, he mentioned some girl he'd helped before the battle with the shadow congress. If this was that girl, then she was a weaver. If the shadows got her, things would get a lot worse around here.

After the doctor left the room, Isabella tried to push herself up off the bed, but her body felt unnaturally heavy and the room began to spin. She took a slow breath and lay her head against the pillow. Her eyelids grew heavy and a chill ran through her body. She fought the coming darkness, willing herself to move, shift position. Pain lancing through her forehead and her right arm made her gasp for breath, but she managed to shift onto her left side. Her newly exposed back felt wet and cold when her hospital gown, stuck to her skin, was exposed to the air. Using her right leg, Isabella reached out toward the edge of the bed. If she could get her leg over the edge, she'd be able to use it to pull herself up into a sitting position; from there, maybe she could stand and get out of here.

She looked over toward the door, willing the doctor and any nurses to stay away, and took a deep breath. Something about her room, about her whole situation, felt wrong, and she was not going to lay around and let other people tell her what to do. The doctor's story about being found in the woods with her brother by someone named Kimi had the edge of truth in it, but the feeling that rose in Isabella's chest when she said the name told her that it had more meaning to her than a stranger who found her. Besides, accusing her parents of abuse was something Isabella couldn't even imagine.

Closing her eyes, she inhaled deeply, the scent of moist dirt again filled her nostrils as she readied herself for the pain that was sure to come as she stood up. The burning behind her eyelids beckoned her to give in to sleep, but Isabella pushed the urge aside and opened them again. She hooked the heel of her right leg on the side of the bed and pulled herself closer. The room swam again, but she squeezed her eyes closed and took another steadying breath. With another pull, she could get herself to the edge of the bed with both legs hanging over the side. The weight still pressed on her, but she could use her good left arm to struggle into a sitting position.

When she righted herself, her vision began to narrow and darken. Afraid she would pass out and fall to the floor, she tried to place her head in her good hand, but the neck brace was in the way. She reached behind her neck and undid the Velcro, then placed her head in her hand and waited for the feeling to pass. Her feet dangled above the floor, which seemed much farther away than it should, but Isabella pushed off anyway and readied herself for the shock of landing.

The pain was what she'd expected. A couple breaths steadied against the side of the bed later, and she was able to stand straight. Outside the door, people were moving around. She looked for the switch to turn off the monitor, hoping to avoid the alarms that were sure to go off if she pulled the cables out like she'd seen done in the movies.

Isabella questioned her sanity. She was in a hospital, injured, and could have a concussion. Paranoia was a symptom of head trauma, wasn't it? Her face felt wet and sticky, but when her hands came away, they were clean. The mechanical ticking and beeping sounds seemed to swell around her, threatening to overwhelm her consciousness. She searched the machine for an off switch but couldn't find one. Instead, she traced the cord coming out of the back to the wall and pulled the plug, but nothing happened. The machine continued to beep incessantly and the displays continued to show her heart rate, which was beginning to increase.

The buttons on the machine looked like they were labeled, but Isabella couldn't tell what they said. There were five oval buttons down the left side of the screen, and a dial. First she tried the dial, but it didn't seem to do anything so she moved onto the buttons. Usually, she thought, a power button is on the top or the bottom of things, but not knowing anything more than that, Isabella made a choice. She pushed the bottom oval and held her breath, waiting for the alarms to start going off, but they didn't. The machine didn't turn off either, but the beeping stopped, which was enough for her.

Switching to the more immediate problem of the IV attached to her right arm, Isabella considered her options. She could try to pull the cords out of the machine or out of her hand. As bad as the idea sounded, leaving a needle in her also didn't sound great. She'd seen it done in movies, and it always seemed to work out for them. She carefully peeled back the tape holding the tube to her arm. It pulled a bit at the tiny hairs, but it was simple enough. Shifting her attention to the large patch of tape on the back of her hand, her stomach turned over. She knew there was a needle in her hand, and she hated needles. Looking at the patch of tape covering it, with the tube coming out, made everything seem more real to her. She picked at a corner of the tape and readied herself to pull at it.

A loud screeching sound echoed through the hallway and heavy footsteps ran past her door, a dark shadow falling over the window as the figure passed. Isabella felt her heart rate jump as the shadow seemed to trail behind the figure for a moment. More shouting came from the hallway, and Isabella realized that what-ever was going on out there was the best cover she was going to get for her escape. She pulled at the tape, not thinking about how the adhesive would pull on the sensitive skin at the back of her hand. The needle was visible with the tape off and she gently pulled it out. A small bubble of blood followed the needle out, but Isabella ignored it in favor of her next problem: where to go once she got into the hallway.

The door to her room was unlocked. Before throwing it open and making a run for it, Isabella peeked around the corner. A group of nurses and doctors seemed to be trying to corral a small red fox who'd somehow gotten into the hospital. Seeing it, Isabella smiled. She'd always loved foxes, but something was dif-ferent about this one. She stepped out into the hall, looking at the red fox as it scurried through the legs of a doctor, its tail making his lab coat billow out behind him and hang in the air for a mo-ment before falling back down impossibly slowly.

"Hey!" A harsh voice behind her made her jump. "You should not be out here."

Isabella turned to see her doctor standing in the hallway, his coat wafting in a breeze that didn't exist. Tensing, Isabella looked back over her shoulder at the group trying to wrangle the fox, then back at the doctor standing in front of her.

"Look, I know it can be scary sometimes, but trust me," he said, his voice softening as he took a step closer to her, "you're safe here. Just get back into your room and we'll take care of this vermin." He stood in front of her. His arms were positioned to catch her if she ran as his knees bent as if ready to chase her.

Isabella felt tears begin to rise unbidden to her eyes. She felt confused and unsure what was happening, as if someone else's emotions were being forced on her. An intense self-loathing washed over her, combined with a feeling of inadequacy. Despite the awareness that these were not her own emotions, they felt so real. She raised her eyes to the doctor and leaned her head to the right slightly. His eyes looked strange, as if a yellow glow were struggling to get out. Not a golden yellow, more of a sickly one in the whites surrounding his irises. The image of a boy, bruises covering his chest and arms, the smell of the antiseptic of a hospital, and the sound of a beeping heart monitor flashed through her mind. She found herself wanting to comfort him, this man who stood before trying to stop her.

"It's okay," she said. "It wasn't your fault."

The doctor faltered; his white coat seemed to darken and writhe for a moment before it settled back into a lab coat. "You're injured." His voice sounded less sure of itself. A new wave of insecurities washed over Isabella, but this time she was able to keep them from affecting her. "You've taken out your IV. You're going to get hurt."

Isabella felt her own confidence reemerge. "No. No, I don't think I will." She smiled at the doctor, who looked less threatening and more scared. She looked over her shoulder again as one of the nurses grabbed the fox by its tail and began to pull it back toward one of the open patient rooms. Isabella glanced back at the doctor and smiled before saying, "I have to take care of something."

Without waiting for his response, she pivoted on the ball of her right foot and pushed off toward the group at the end of the hall. She knew the doctor would chase her, but Isabella hoped she'd have enough time to get to the fox first. Deep in her heart, Isabella knew she would need to help it if they were going to get out of here. There was no logic behind that feeling, but the sheer strength of it made logic unnecessary. Isabella knew that fox. She didn't know how or why, but that fox was a part of her.

Ignoring the throbbing in her arm and head, Isabella sprinted toward the nurse who was still pulling the fox's tail. The fox was trying to turn and snap at the woman, but there was little it could do. Every time it turned, the nurse used that moment to pull it closer to the open door, presumably trying to trap it inside. Isabella's footfalls echoed through the noisy halls, impossibly loud in her own ears, but she closed the distance without any of the other doctors getting in her way. The closer she got, the less sure Isabella was of her plan. The nurse was big, outweighing her by at least eighty pounds, but Isabella was hoping she would be off-balance from pulling the fox.

The cold of the floor was a shock to her foot with each step. It felt almost damp, but Isabella was glad that they hadn't put some sort of slipper on her; she could get traction with her bare feet. She dropped her good shoulder and, throwing caution to the wind, barreled into the woman dragging the fox. For a moment, time seemed to stand still. Isabella felt her shoulder sink into the woman's side, almost like it wasn't even there, but then there was a slight resistance and the woman screamed, let go of the fox, and stumbled backward into the room. Isabella lost her balance too, so committed to rushing the woman that she hadn't put any thought into how she'd stop her momentum. She found herself tumbling over the woman and landing in a throbbing heap in the hallway between her and the fox.

The fox, freed from its restraint, spun to face Isabella and the woman on the other side of her, ignoring the other doctors and nurses in the hallway around it. Close up, they seemed less substantial somehow, like trees reflected in a puddle. The nurse, who was heaving her bulk back to a standing position, stood facing the opposite wall. To her amazement, Isabella watched as the woman seemed to invert herself and turn around without moving. The hair on the back of the woman's head began to part, first making room for her bulbous nose to poke through, then separating further as her chin and eyes seemed to materialize on what was once the back of her head. Her joints, seemingly bending against nature, inverted themselves as well, and before Isabella could process what she was seeing, the woman stood leering down at her with malice and hatred in her eyes.

The vicious snarling and guttural cries of the fox brought Isabella's attention back to the little creature. Its eyes burned with a ferocious inner light and saliva wet its jaws, but Isabella wasn't afraid. She knew instinctively that the anger wasn't directed at her. When the fox, its nails struggling for purchase on the cold linoleum floor, began to move forward, Isabella didn't shy away. Without thinking, she turned slightly to offer her back to the fox as a platform for it to launch itself at the nurse. Small pinpricks on her back reminded Isabella of something she couldn't entirely place and the angry call of the fox carried over her head as it barreled directly at the center of the nurse's chest. Isabella marveled at the bravery of the small creature.

Her wonderment didn't lessen when the creature seemingly passed through the nurse and landed, skidding to a stop on the other side. Isabella rose to her feet, feeling new strength flooding through her. She faced the nurse, ready to dodge out of the way if the woman attacked. But instead of the large nurse, Isabella faced a wispy dark shadow, insubstantial at the edges and with a hole in the middle that was slowly closing up from where the fox had passed through it. Tendrils of more substantial darkness seemed to drip away from the shadow, sizzling the ground where they hit and causing the linoleum to darken and peel at the edges of the tile.

The shadow let out a shriek of rage and lunged at Isabella, its glistening claws cutting through the air and dripping decay as they descended on her. Isabella tried to dodge out of the way but tripped on a metal cart she hadn't noticed. She tumbled over it with a loud clatter. The shadow's claws slammed into the wall, causing the drywall to mold almost immediately. Streaks of wet blackness dripped toward the floor. The shadow raised its other claw and brought it down toward Isabella as she lay tangled in the metal cart on the floor.

Unable to get away, Isabella readied herself for what was coming. She thought of her parents' love for her, of her brother and his smile that could fill the room. Then more images came to mind: a boy with a bow and arrow and a goofy grin, a woman in a sweater with a kitten on it, holding some sort of giant bird, and the fox, limping through the forest, looking up at her. Everything seemed to snap into place, and as the shadow's claws descended on Isabella, she raised her throbbing right arm to ward off the coming blow and called out to Kimi, her companion, for help.

The boy in the cage willed the prone girl to get up as one of Eli's shadows loomed over her. He'd had a moment of hope when, seemingly from nowhere, Kimi came bounding in and leaped off the girl at the shadow. He'd seen her do that before. This had to be the girl who Finn had brought to their camp back when the Champion had agreed to help the weavers take on the shadow congress. He vaguely remembered her showing up in the middle of the congress as the tide of the battle shifted in their favor. Kimi had pulled a similar move then, too, and managed to dislodge one of the shadows from the hill.

This time, although the shadow was knocked back, it didn't chase the brave little fox. Instead, it shifted its focus back to the girl. Standing over her with its claws raised, the boy knew that the shadow would strike her down and drag her into its thrall if something didn't stop it. He'd seen it happen before, and he didn't care to see it again. Searching the floor of his cage, he found a stone about the size of his fist. He was never good at fighting from a distance; that's why the Champion had suggested the swords. They seemed to suit him, but they were not an option now. He had one chance to help her but he knew it'd be a long shot. He'd have to aim it between the bars of his cage and still manage to hit the shadow. Thought was the enemy here; action was what was needed.

Drawing his arm back to the opposite side of the cage, the boy cleared his mind, as he'd been taught, and visualized the stone flying through the space between the bars and directly into the shadow's claws, displacing them enough, he hoped, so they wouldn't strike the girl. He took a deep breath, held it for a second, then released it slowly and let the rock fly. He managed to clear the bars of the cage and the rock flew true at the shadow, but instead of striking the claws as he'd hoped, it passed high of the descending arm and clattered off the wall.

Thankfully it was enough. The shadow, startled by the sudden noise, struck at the wall, drawing large chunks away as its deadly claws slashed. Then the shadow raised its other arm and brought it down toward the prone girl. He could see Kimi pushing off toward the shadow to take another pass at it, but the boy knew she wouldn't get there in time. He searched the floor for another stone but couldn't come up with more than a handful of gravel.

The girl on the ground shifted, raising her right arm to ward off the shadow's attack—an effort he knew would be futile— as she called out to Kimi. He could tell her arm was already injured as dark tendrils seemed to have wrapped themselves around it, but her voice sounded strong despite her dire circumstances. He'd seen others in her position cower and cry out in anger or stand resigned to their fate, but she was different. Her voice was firm, her posture defiant. This was someone who could have made a difference in the world. He cried out as the claws descended on her arm, willing himself to honor her fight by being witness to it, regardless of its inevitable end.

The boy raised his chin as the shadow's claws fell mercilessly on the girl's arm and readied himself to witness her transition. But instead of seeing the fading of a once vibrant person, what he saw baffled his mind and made him question everything he'd ever known about the shadows. Instead of the rot swiping through her arm and spreading over her body until she was nothing more than a wisp of darkness, the claws met her arm and stopped. They struggled against each other, strength for strength, and the girl pushed the shadow's claws back. He dropped to his knees and held the bars to steady himself. Swallowing back tears of joy and hope, he let out a cry of triumph as the girl rose to her knees, pushing back the shadow's deadly claws with only her arm.

Isabella felt the claws touch her skin, but she didn't feel the shattering pain she'd expected. She felt pressure and a burning sensation, yes, but she resisted giving into it. Pain burst through her shoulder, but it wasn't more than a dull ache and she managed to push back against the decaying darkness. The shadow shrieked at her, its yellow eyes burning with malice, but Isabella forced it back still.

From the corner of her eye, she could see the doctor approaching her, but he looked stunned at what he saw. Whether it was the shadow woman or her own resistance, she wasn't sure. Kimi also moved in the background, crouching behind the attacking shadow. Isabella pushed back on the shadow's claws and raised herself to one knee, then the next. The pressure grew, but so did her own strength. As she got one of her feet beneath her, she heard a triumphant call, but it seemed distant, on the edge of her consciousness. Feeling around for the tray from the metal cart, or something else she could use to defend herself, Isabella's hand closed on something cool and solid. The handle in her hand felt smooth and well worked. Closing her fingers around it felt comfortable and familiar.

Heedless of the other arm now descending on her, Isabella ducked under her right arm, bringing it and the shadow's claws over her head. A painful drop fell on her cheek and sizzled, but Isabella ignored the pain and continued, twisting her body and bringing her left arm up at an angle to arc through the midsection of the shadow. The edge of the Samsa'raka—for she knew now that that was what was in her hand—hung for a moment in the shadow's core before it continued through with a light popping sound. The shadow's descending claws faltered before dropping harmlessly to its side. Isabella continued her pivot and ended facing the attacking shadow again in time to see it coalesce into the form of a rail-thin woman with a sad smile and watery eyes. Moments later, the woman faded from view, and Isabella saw the doctor standing in the doorway to the hall, his lab coat billowing out behind him in smoke-like tendrils. His hands seemed to be elongating, each finger ending in a glistening black nail.

Behind her, Isabella heard Kimi call to her. Looking over her shoulder, she could see a blue door to one of the cabinets in the room. Isabella pivoted again on the ball of her right foot and rushed to the door. Grabbing its handle, she wrenched it open and pushed Kimi through as the little fox tried to turn and fight the coming shadow. Without waiting, Isabella dove in after the fox and tumbled out onto all fours in a dark room, her fingers sinking into the dirt on the floor, the cool, wet air filling her lungs. In front of her stood Kimi, her muscles tensed. She was staring off to Isabella's right, a low growl coming from her throat.

ᴄᴇ THIRTY-ONE ᴐᴇ

Looking into the gloom of the cavern, Isabella took in her surroundings. Behind her was the entrance she had charged through before falling into the dream trap, but in front of her was a shape moving through the darkness deep within the cavern. Between them and the dark shape was a boy in a cage. He looked at her with wide blue eyes and a slack jaw. His blond hair, swept neatly back out of his face, was tied behind his head with a string of some kind. He had high cheekbones and sharp features. His broad shoulders were covered with a smudged leather vest.

Isabella walked toward the cage, Kimi at her side. The fox kept its eyes on the shadowy form working around the wall. "Delson, right?" Isabella squinted to make out more of his features in the darkness.

"Yeah," he said, his voice guarded. "You look familiar. And is that Kimi with you?"

"It's a pleasure, hunter," Kimi said, momentarily pausing her growling to address Delson. "Though perhaps not the best circumstances."

"You can say that again," he chuckled, "but you're not that girl Finn brought to the camp last year, are you? You're a weaver, I thought she was—well, I guess I don't know what I thought she was."

Isabella smiled and examined the cage. It was made of wood with a solid-looking lock about the size of her first. "I brought these for you," she said, taking off the harness and handing him his swords.

Delson took them through the bars and sheathed them behind his back. "How did you do that?"

"Do what?"

"With that shadow." His eyes searched in the darkness for some explanation. "You pushed back its claws with your bare arm?"

"You saw us in the dream trap?"

He shook his head. "No, but one moment you were lying there unconscious with a shadow about to slice you to ribbons, and the next thing I know you put up your arm and pushed the damn thing back. I have never in all my life seen anything like it. You're amazing."

Isabella smiled at the exuberance that Delson managed despite being trapped in a cage. "Your guess is as good as mine," she said, "but let's keep our guesses until we get out of here. Any idea where the key is?"

Delson half smiled and pointed sheepishly up toward the ceiling above the door. Isabella followed his finger and saw the faint glint of a metal key suspended from the ceiling, halfway between the wall and the cage and about twenty feet above the ground. A path hugged the wall and ended abruptly when it was level with the key, but it was still about five feet away.

"And maybe we hurry," Kimi offered, "before whoever that is gets here."

Delson looked over to where Kimi was focused. "That will take whoever it is a while still. There's a thin ledge that way. Wesley and I came in through there before Eli captured us. He'd said the Council sent him to investigate this cavern for shadow activity. Did he make it out?"

"Let's get you out first, then we'll figure the rest out," Isabella said while looking at the path and the key. "Kimi, I have an idea, but I'm not sure you're going to like it."

Looking back and forth between Isabella and the approaching figure, Kimi asked, "Am I going to have to guess the idea?"

"How far can you jump?"

"Not that high," she scoffed.

"How about from that path to the key?"

"And how do you expect me to land?"

"I'll catch you."

"No," Delson chimed in, "I'm not worth it. A weaver is worth three hunters at least."

Isabella ignored his protest. "What do you say?"

Kimi walked under the dangling key, then over to the entrance of the path. She turned to Delson. "How did Eli get the key up there in the first place?"

"He sent one of his shadows."

~ 302 ~

"Figures." Kimi studied Isabella for a moment. "You sure you can catch me?"

"Wouldn't suggest it if I wasn't."

Kimi sighed. "We could use that cowardly squirrel right now."

"I trust you, though," Isabella said, meeting the fox's greenish eyes and smiling.

"So be it," Kimi said with a sigh, "but if you don't catch me—"

"I will," Isabella promised.

Kimi moved toward the narrow path ascending the wall in a gentle arch, her feet sure against the loose gravel that fell skittering to the ground as she moved upward. She needed to leap over missing pieces in several sections but made it to the top with little difficulty. Standing on the slight outcropping opposite the key, Kimi moved to the edge and looked down. From where Isabella stood, she saw a thin muzzle of the fox poke over the edge and look down toward her. Kimi let out a high-pitched whine.

"I'm ready when you are," Isabella called up.

"This is a bad idea," Delson said behind her.

"Do you have a better one? If not, then be quiet and let me concentrate."

Delson fell silent and looked on in utter amazement at what he was watching. To watch a weaver and their companion work was something that most hunters only saw in combat, but they were working to save him and he felt unworthy of the risk. Despite that, he knew better than to be an annoyance. That was Finn's job, after all. He smiled to himself, thinking of how angry Finn would be for having missed this.

"When you're ready," Isabella called up, "try to knock the key down, and I'll catch you." She looked around her to make sure the ground was clear where she assumed Kimi would end up.

"For the record," Kimi called down, "this is a bad idea, but here we go." The sound of Kimi's paws skidding on gravel came from above, followed by a loud shriek as the fox launched itself off the ledge toward the dangling key. Gravel rained down on Isabella, who shielded her eyes with her arm. High above her, Kimi's red fur arched gracefully through the air toward the key. Time seemed to slow for Isabella as she focused on the graceful creature seemingly suspended in the air above her. As she neared the key, Kimi opened her jaws and snapped them closed around it. Her momentum carried her body past the key, but she held on with her teeth, causing the chain the key was suspended from to sway wildly. Kimi let out another whine and began jerking her body, trying to dislodge the key.

The swing was making it harder for Isabella to position herself where she thought Kimi would land. Every time she thought she was in place, the chain—and Kimi with it—would swing in a new direction. Isabella found herself almost running back and forth, trying to make sure Kimi didn't hurt herself in the fall. She loved that little fox. She was a part of her, and Isabella was not about to let her get injured now she'd found her again.

Isabella saw Kimi was swinging toward the cage and moved to stand in front of it. Kimi let out another whimper and jerked one more time, causing the chain to rattle loudly and swing wildly in the opposite direction. Isabella saw Kimi come unhitched from the chain and begin tumbling through the air toward the path that she'd just ascended. She was going to hit the wall before she made it to where Isabella could catch her. Running toward the path, Isabella regretted ever suggesting this crazy plan, each step reminding her that her arm was not in great shape to begin with. As her feet landed on the incline, she saw that Kimi would hit the wall about a foot higher.

Pumping her legs as fast as she could, Isabella raced up the incline until she was level and then turned and pushed off, intent on keeping her promise to catch Kimi. She twisted to face the flying fox and the two made contact in mid-air. Isabella wrapped her arms around the small creature, Kimi's musky smell filling her nose, and arched her body to try to soften the blow as best she could. Eyes closed, she prepared to hit the stone. When the impact came, she rolled into it while using her body to protect Kimi, who was curled into a ball in her arms. As they skidded to a stop, Isabella could feel what had to be hundreds of scrapes along her back from sliding across the gravel, but she had managed to avoid hitting her head and crushing the fox, so she counted that as a win.

She lay there for a moment with Kimi in her arms, catching her breath and trembling slightly from the exertion. Isabella opened her eyes and stared up at a figure standing over her. Immediately her hand went to the dagger in her belt and held it out in front of her, warding off the latest threat.

"Whoah, slow down." The young man standing over her, hands raised in surrender, looked down at her from under his shaggy hair. He flashed her a big goofy smile. "Just thought you might want some help up. That was a heck of a save, Izzy." He extended his hand down to her.

Reaching up to grasp his hand, Isabella felt a wave of relief. "Finn," she said, "how'd you get down here?"

"There's an entrance probably a mile or so down that passage." He motioned with his chin over his shoulder as he helped Isabella to her feet. "You look like you've been through it down here. Think you could put that away?" he asked, looking at the dagger.

Isabella chuckled and sheathed the dagger in her belt once more.

"Saw what you and Kimi pulled off to rescue Del. Impressive feat." He nodded his head to Kimi, who'd stopped growling once she realized who it was.

"I think it was you who said we'd be unstoppable if we ever worked together," the little fox said, holding her chin up. Her green eyes seeming to glow in the dimly lit cavern.

"That I did," he agreed proudly.

"Um," Delson said, still confined in the cage, "I'm glad you're all good and everything but I'm still trapped over here."

Isabella smiled, realizing that she was still holding Finn's hand and staring at him. His eyes were enchanting, so full of carefree warmth and attention that looking into them felt like home. Reluctantly letting go of Finn's hand, she walked over to the lock on Delson's cage. "I'm sorry, Delson," she said, shaking her head in embarrassment at her distraction. "Let's get you out of there." Isabella slid the key into the lock with a satisfying click and pulled on the door. The hinges, resistant to moving, complained loudly, a noise which echoed through the cavernous space.

Finally free of his confines, Delson nearly tackled Isabella with an exuberant hug, tears and laughter mingling in his expression. He kissed her quickly on the cheek and then, releasing her, turned to Finn. "You came." His shoulders hunched down, but his head was pointing up at Finn, tears glistening in his eyes.

"You doubted me?"

"No." He exhaled and ran to Finn, enveloping him in a powerful hug. "Not for a moment." Delson rested his head on Finn's shoulder, his own shoulders quivering slightly in the glow. Finn returned the hug, stroking the back of Delson's hair. Delson looked up at Finn, who wiped a tear away from his cheek with his thumb. Delson tilted his face up to Finn's and then leaned in, their lips meeting. Both closed their eyes and seemed to let out a sigh of relief.

Isabella felt awkward watching the romantic moment between the two. Awkward, and a little jealous. She'd imagined Finn had come to help her again, as before, when she needed guidance. But there was no mistaking what she saw.

"You didn't know," Kimi said, standing next to her. It was something between a statement and a question. The fox's voice held more understanding than Isabella imagined could be in such a small creature.

"No," Isabella said, biting back her disappointment.

"It wouldn't have worked anyway." Kimi looked up at Isabella. "You're from different worlds."

Isabella smiled halfheartedly and looked back past the cage, hoping to get a better view in the growing light. Beyond the cage, the floor of the cavern seemed to drop away. A rope attached to the back of the cage dangled over the edge, disappearing into the darkness below. Beyond the darkness was a narrow ledge, barely a foot wide, that traced the wall on the opposite side and led into another passage opposite the one Isabella had entered.

"That's the way out," Finn said, putting his arm around Isabella's shoulders.

She felt her muscles tense as he did. She didn't want to be mad at him, but she couldn't help it. She knew that he had never suggested that they could be anything more than friends, but she still felt cheated, like she'd lost something. Knowing those feelings wouldn't help, she moved from under his arm and turned to look at both of them. Finn looked surprised, but Isabella cut off anything he was about it say.

"We need to find Wesley and get out of here. Delson, did he come through this way before you saw me?"

"No." Delson steeled his features and squared his jaw. He seemed to go through a transformation; all emotion was gone, and his shoulders were back. This was the Delson Isabella remembered from the battle with the shadow congress. "Nobody has come through since the shadows left me here." He indicated the passage Isabella had emerged from. "We'd gone that way before we were separated."

"Since when do the hunters work with the rebels?" Kimi asked.

"What?" Delson took a step back, "You mean—"

"That explains a lot," Finn said, walking over to stand with Delson. "After you left, Wren came by to ask for some help clearing a shadow den. She'd wanted you and I to go, but when the Champion said you were on a mission with another weaver, she said there were no weaver missions in the area. She still wanted me to come, but I declined."

"You turned down a chance to work with a weaver to come after me?" Delson's hard edge seemed to falter for a moment.

"What do you think, you dolt," Finn said, smiling at him and punching him lightly on his arm.

"Look, I'm glad you're here," Isabella interrupted, "but now's not the time. So, if Wesley didn't come through here, there has to be some other passage back there. That's where we go."

"Wait a minute," Delson said. "If Wesley was a rebel, why are we going after him? The weavers have been at war with the rebels for as long as I can remember. Since when are weavers working with the rebels?"

"I'm not a weaver," Isabella said, turning to head down the passage back into the darkness she'd come from.

"Could have fooled me," Finn chuckled.

Isabella spun on him and marched the four steps until she stood directly in front of Finn. Her fists were balled by her side and she could feel the tension building between her shoulder blades. "Nobody asked you," she barked in his face. Finn's eyes went wide, and she pressed the advantage. "I promised his companion that I would help him, and that is what I am going to do. That's what I did before I came to rescue Delson, and we got separated. Now he's missing again, and I don't want to hear about your stupid conflicts and loyalties. If you want to go help Wren, go. If you want to get out of here with Delson, then go. Nobody asked you to come here, nobody asked you to help, and nobody is asking you to follow me. But I am not leaving anybody in this dark and oppressing place. If you have a problem with that, if that makes me not a weaver, then so be it."

Not being able to think of anything more to say, Isabella turned her back on Finn and began to move away. When he grabbed her arm and turned her around, she almost slapped him, but he took a step back, letting her go in the process.

"I never said I wasn't coming," Finn said, a look of seriousness in his eyes that she'd only seen once before. "And if you ask me"—he put his hands up in a conciliatory gesture to forestall her interruption—"I know you haven't, but if you did, not being willing to leave anyone behind makes you more of a weaver than any I've met, Isabella Shaw."

Isabella didn't trust herself to answer, so she nodded curtly, turned back toward the entrance, and began to walk. A slight scuffling of gravel behind her preceded Delson jogging up on her right-hand side. "Quick question," he asked.

"What is it?"

"Why is that dagger on your belt glowing?"

Not until he asked his question did Isabella realize that the cavern had been getting lighter the whole time they had been talking. Looking down at the Samsa'raka, the stone in the hilt was pulsing a yellow light that seemed to grow stronger with each beat. She looked at the dark passage before them and moved her hand to the handle of the dagger. Delson drew his swords and she heard Finn behind them readying his bow. Something small flew at her from the darkness and Isabella leaped out of the way in time to see Skia streak past them in a panic.

"They're coming," the little squirrel chirped in terror. "They're right behind us."

"Where's Wesley?" Isabella asked as soon as she realized it was Skia.

"He's right behind me." The breathless squirrel climbed Isabella's pant leg and perched trembling on her shoulder, chittering nervously. "We need to get out of here."

"Back to the cavern," Isabella called to the group as she heard the crunching of running feet on the gravel floor of the passage. "There's no room to fight them in here."

"Look out!" A panicked scream came from the darkness ahead of them before Wesley emerged, pounding down the passage. "There's too many of them. We need to run."

ᖰᨆ THIRTY-TWO ᨆᖰ

As Wesley pushed past the group, the raka stone in the hilt of Isabella's dagger flared a bright yellow, exposing several shadows gliding after him. The shadows' tendrils lashed out in front of them, attempting to grasp Wesley before he could escape. When the light of the raka stone flared, the tendrils drew back into the bodies of the shadows. They seemed to falter for a moment until they were driven on by something behind them. Then they pushed forward into the light, closing the gap between them and Isabella's friends.

"Back to the cavern," Isabella called out again, backing away quickly while holding the Samsa'raka defensively in front of her. "Go, now."

The sound of retreating feet on the gravel stones cleared the way for Isabella to turn and run back to the larger area where her friends could help ward off the coming shadows. As she passed into the cavern, the light of the raka stone illuminated the whole room. Stalactites hung from the ceiling over a gaping area where the floor seemed to have fallen away or been eroded by water. At the edge of this area sat the cage where Delson had been imprisoned. Along the wall leading away from the passage the group had emerged from was a thin walkway skirting the cavernous opening in the floor. Isabella hadn't been able to see the bottom the last time she'd looked, and she didn't have time to investigate it now.

Moments after rejoining her companions, Isabella felt the surge of emotions that always came before the shadows arrived, inexorably pushed toward them like the water with the tide. Delson stood ready for a fight. His sea-blue eyes looked like steel, missing their joyful exuberance. He'd drawn both swords, holding one before him and the other above his head, pointed at the entrance; he looked like a jungle cat ready to pounce on its prey. Finn had dropped to one knee and nocked an arrow. He aimed dead center of the passage, hand back in line with his jaw, which seemed as taut as the bow string he held. Wesley was the only one who didn't look ready to fight. He had no weapons that Isabella could see and seemed to be frantically searching in the satchel he had been carrying with him. Isabella hoped he was looking for a knife or something. She turned toward the passage, making sure that she sidestepped enough to be out of Finn's way.

The shadows reached the entrance and began to pour into the cavern. Their edges blurred into one and another, making it hard for Isabella to see how many there were. The emotional onslaught washed over the group and Delson gasped. Tendrils of shadow wove above and behind them as they began to flank the group. Delson struck first, swiping his sword against the shadow who tried to edge around the right-hand side of the group. His sword swiped off the arm of the first shadow. It swirled, replacing the limb almost instantly. Finn loosed an arrow into the entrance, piercing one of the shadow's eyes and drawing it through and out the other side. Almost instantly, the shadow reformed.

"They're working together," Wesley called out from the middle of the group.

"Like the congress?" Finn asked, nocking his third arrow and taking aim.

"Don't know, I wasn't there." Wesley kept rummaging in his bag. "I've never seen this level of cooperation before."

Isabella struck out at the shadow in front of her, raking the dagger across three tendrils reaching toward her. The severed limbs fell, dissipating before they reached the floor. "Fascinating," she said, slashing at another shadow advancing on Wesley, "but we could use a little help here, not a lesson."

Kimi leaped to Isabella's left, latching onto a claw from one of the shadows about to strike Isabella. She managed to pull the hand away before the claw came off in her mouth, and she let it clatter to the floor. Isabella swung the dagger at the shadow before it could strike at Kimi with its other tendrils. Feeling the now familiar resistance of a hit against the shadow's core, Isabella put her weight into the follow-through until the resistance gave in. The shadow, poised to slice Kimi's back, faded briefly into a young girl about Tucker's age, holding a small stuffed fox and crying before it faded completely. Isabella stared at the vacant space, the sounds of the battle fading to the background. She tried to imagine what had turned that poor girl into a shadow and what would happen to her now.

A pressure on her right arm caught her unawares and threw her sprawling to the left. She looked up to see a large shadow, its claws pushing through the air on its path toward her. She felt her arm for what she was sure would be a horrible gash, but there was nothing except cold, swollen skin. Pushing herself up, Isabella took stock of their position. There were at least ten shadows arrayed around them, and their small band had shifted and closed ranks so they were standing in a shrinking circle closer to Wesley, who still searched his bag.

"Got it!" he cried out triumphantly. "Skia, get over here."

The squirrel, who'd been pulling small bits of shadow away at ground level, climbed on to Isabella's shoulder and leaped at Wesley. He ducked his right shoulder, deftly catching his companion. After catching the squirrel, Wesley brought out a small lump of brownish stone from his pack and held it to his heart.

"I thought you were getting a weapon," Finn called out incredulously, "what's a lump of coal going to do for us?"

"Better." Wesley grinned. "Smokey quartz." He closed his eyes and Isabella could feel a cool breeze pull lightly past her toward Wesley. He lifted the quartz into the air above his head and called out, "*Saha Nau Bhunaktu*". The quartz began to emanate a grey-brown smoke, and Wesley brought it down to his face and began to blow and turn in a complete circle. Whatever the mist was seemed to push at Isabella's right arm, but she pulled it into her chest and readied a strike with her dagger against the shadow in front of her. As she pulled her dagger back to strike, the shadow reeled back, clawing wildly at the mist Wesley had blown. The shadows continued to be pushed back until they seemed to be consumed by the mist and disappear.

"How'd you do that?" Finn called out from the rear of the group, his exuberance coming back full force.

Seeing that the threat had ended, Delson sheathed his swords and turned to Wesley. "I thought you said it wasn't a weapon?"

"It's not." Wesley wavered on his feet. His eyes seemed to struggle to remain open. "Temporary ... Need to ru—" Before he was able to finish his sentence, he and Skia collapsed to the ground, his quartz slipping from his hand and clattering on the floor.

"You heard the man," Finn said, moving to scoop up Wesley. He threw him over his shoulder in a fireman's carry and began to move to the ledge leading to their way out. Kimi picked up Skia by the scruff of his neck and began to trot after Finn. Delson waited with Isabella, who looked down the passage where the mist was still suspended in the air.

"They're people," she said. "Did you know that?"

"Who are?"

"The shadows. I see them when I kill them with the dagger. They seem almost thankful for it."

"I don't know about that, but we should get going." He looked over his shoulder at Finn and Kimi who were working their way along the ledge. "I don't know what Wesley did, but he said it wouldn't last."

"Go with them." Isabella started moving toward the passage. "I need to see something."

Delson drew his swords. "Nope, I'm not leaving a weaver alone in this blasted place."

Isabella sighed and looked between the passage and the ledge. Kimi was safe and Finn was bringing Wesley to safety. She looked at Delson standing there, weapons drawn against whatever foe stood in their way. His loyalty surprised her, not because he seemed cowardly, but because he was willing to follow her regardless of her plan. "You don't have to."

"I suppose"—he smiled at her, a glint of mischief in his eyes—"but how would I explain to the Council what happened to you if I run. A hunter keeps his promises."

Isabella motioned toward the ledge. "You have. Wesley is getting out of there safely."

"Not that promise, but thanks for helping me with that one. The last time Wren was in the camp, after the battle with the shadow congress, she asked Finn and I to promise to help you if you were ever in need. Finn didn't hesitate, so neither did I."

"You didn't even know me." Isabella squinted at him in the fading light of the raka stone.

"Finn did," he chuckled. "That boy doesn't trust easily, so when he agreed without hesitation, so did I."

"You love him, don't you?"

"Finn?" Delson looked at the shadowy figure on the other side of the cavern and smiled. "Yeah, I do."

"You sure you want to follow me back in there? You can still catch up to Finn and Kimi. You look a bit banged up."

"You're one to talk, weaver."

"Call me Izzy," she said.

"What's the plan then, Izzy?"

"I need to rescue Eli."

"Eli? That guy's a stalker. He's the one who tricked Wesley and I into getting trapped here in the first place. He captured Kimi and almost captured you too. Why ... How do you plan to rescue him. He's evil."

Isabella looked at the mist. "No, he's lost like these shadows. I felt it before when we were in a dream trap together."

"One he put you in, no doubt."

"You're not wrong," Isabella conceded, "but I feel like he can be saved."

"I gotta say it again, you are nothing like any weaver I've ever met, Isabella Shaw," Delson said, a mixture of awe and confusion in his voice.

"You don't have to come," she said again, looking at Delson. His exuberance glowed brightly behind his eyes, soft now like where the ocean and the sky meet. "There is no shame in making sure Wesley gets out safe."

"He's safe with Finn and Kimi. It's you I'm more worried about right now," he chuckled. "Actually, after seeing you handle those shadows, that's not even it. I don't want to miss whatever crazy plan you have in mind next. Finn's going to be wicked jealous."

THIRTY-THREE

W e're getting closer." Delson pointed down a side passage with his sword. "Just down here, I think."

"How do you know this place so well?" Isabella held the dagger up, letting the growing light from the raka stone cast its glow in front of them. "I thought you were locked up down here."

He motioned at her dagger. "I don't, but if my prediction about that dagger of yours is right, that stone gets brighter as we get closer to the shadows."

"I was beginning to think the same thing," she agreed. "So, around the next bend then." She chuckled to herself. "Guess there's no sneaking up on them."

"Never is," Delson admitted as he put his back against the passage wall and peeked around the next corner.

"What do you see?" Isabella moved next to him, imitating his position.

"It's light in there, so they may not have seen the dagger," he whispered. "Eli's there, along with three shadows. What's the play?"

"I'm going to walk out there and talk to him," she said. "You stay here in case things don't go well."

"They won't."

"Don't be so negative." She punched him lightly in the arm.

Rolling his eyes, he motioned her forward and moved closer to the wall, hoping to stay out of sight. Isabella stepped into the middle of the passage, still hidden from the view of Eli and his shadows, and straightened her ripped shirt. She could feel butterflies in her stomach, like when she was supposed to give a presentation at school. Her friends had always told her to calm down, that it wasn't life or death, but this time it very well might be. Closing her eyes, Isabella took a deep breath and stepped forward confidently. She stood there for a moment, looking at Eli. His blond hair covered his eyes before it flared out in wispy curls above his eyes. He had a friendly face when he wasn't trying to kill her, but there were sadness and fear behind his eyes.

"There you are," he said without looking up. "Come to join me finally?"

"No." Isabella's voice sounded small in her own ears. She cleared her throat. "No," she repeated a little louder, "I've come to save you."

Eli laughed and looked up. He had a pleasant laugh, relaxed and easy. "I'm not sure you understand the situation here."

"I get it"—she stepped forward—"you feel trapped here. You think that there is no way out for you, that you are beyond redemption, but you're not. No one is beyond redemption." Isabella looked from him to the shadows. "These are not your friends. They will never give you the companionship you're looking for."

He stopped laughing and put his hand on his chest. His bottom lip quivered slightly and he raised his eyebrows, causing them to disappear beneath his shaggy hair. "You can't mean—are you sure?" His voice sounded small, vulnerable, and Isabella pressed her advantage.

"Come with me and I'll show you." She walked across the floor until the only thing between them was a raised stone platform Eli had been using as a table before she came in. Isabella reached her left hand out for him to take, her right cradled against her body.

Eli extended his hand across the table. His eyes seemed to water slightly as a look of hope washed over them. "After everything I've done?"

"Nobody is beyond redemption." Isabella smiled at him. "There are people who will help you. I want to help you."

For a moment, Eli held his hand out, fingertips shy of touching Isabella's extended arm. Then, like a switch had been flicked , he dropped his arm and laughed a rueful and cruel laugh. "You should have seen yourself," he scoffed. "'Nobody is beyond redemption'," Eli said, his mimicking voice filled with mock concern. "'Come with me and I'll show you'." He covered his face with his hands and pretended to cry. "How did you see this working out there, Izzy? You thought you could come in here and get me to give up my ... my what? My *evil ways?* That sort of melodrama is perfect for you, right up your alley." He walked around the stone platform and leaned against it, facing her. "You can come out from back there, Delson."

Isabella turned to see Delson step out from the passageway, his swords still drawn but not ready to fight. Isabella eyes widened. "You're not—"

Eli answered for him. "No," he snarled, "he has his *honor*."

Delson held up his hands. "I swear, Izzy, I'm not working with him."

"Not that he didn't have the chance." Eli stepped toward Isabella and reached for her right arm. She pulled it back away from his grasp. "Though it looks like you will be soon enough. Maybe he will come to help me then."

"I will never work with you and your shadows," Delson said, spitting at the ground in front of Eli.

"Whatever," he replied, turning his back on them and walking back around the stone table. "As for these things"—he motioned to the three shadows that lurked at the far wall of the room—"I don't think they're my friends. My servants, maybe, but not my friends. You'll see soon enough."

"What's that supposed to mean?" Isabella drew her dagger. "I've taken out your shadows before. I can do it again."

"You think so small." Eli shook his head. "When I said you will find out, I didn't mean I was going to demonstrate my control. There's no real need for that. You've seen it already. Neat trick that coward friend of yours pulled to take out my army, though." He bobbed his head from side to side, looking up at the ceiling, "Though you do know it's temporary, don't you?"

Isabella didn't answer his question. "Get to the point."

"Oh, don't look angry all the time. I meant when I said you'll see that you're going to become one of my shadows. Well, if not mine, then someone's at least. That arm"—Eli motioned to her right arm where black tendrils had begun wrapping their way up to her shoulder—"you can feel it, can't you?"

"I don't know what you're talking about." Isabella squared her shoulders to Eli and raised her chin.

He rolled his eyes. "Okay. There are two ways someone becomes a shadow in the dream world. Either you die and can only think about powerful emotions like hate or sadness or regret— that's the way most of you weavers know about—or you could do it like that." He motioned to her arm again.

"You know what that is?" Delson asked from behind Isabella.

"I do, my astute hunter," Eli's said smugly. "And I know how to stop it."

"You have to tell us." Delson stepped forward, lifting his swords.

Eli laughed and waved a hand dismissively. "I have to do nothing of the sort, and unless you can muzzle that dog of yours, Isabella, I will have to release my own."

Isabella looked over her shoulder at Delson pleadingly. He lowered his swords but his muscles were still clearly tense. She turned back to Eli. "Why say you know how to fix it if you're not going to tell us?"

"Now you're starting to see things clearly. You came down here to save me, but I don't need saving." He gestured to the docile shadows behind him. "I have everything under control here. Once your friend's little smoke trick wears off, I'll have my army back. I'm nothing if not patient. You, on the other hand, seem to need some saving." He motioned to her arm with a nod of his chin. "I'd be willing to share what I know in exchange for you joining me. I can take or leave your hunter friend here. And your companion, for that matter."

Isabella crossed her arms in front of her chest. "I thought stalkers didn't have companions."

"A common misconception perpetuated by that corrupt Council of Dreamers. Oh, don't look so surprised. I bet that backward group of superannuating biddies and buffers didn't even tell you about the rebels and why they are at war, did they? Did they even say they were at war?"

"Maybe they have." Isabella knew she was bluffing. She'd never even met the Council, but her dad and Wren worked with them, so they couldn't be bad.

"You've never even met them, have you? Honestly, you're better off for it. Watch out for them." He leaned forward, spreading his hands on the raised stone between them. "Don't trust them implicitly like most of the weavers do. They have no loyalty"—he nodded toward Delson—"to the hunters or to the weavers. They're as likely as not to burn you when they find you've been working with the enemy."

"I'm not working with you."

"Not me, your rebel friend Wesley. You don't think I know a weaver's charm when I see one? That stone he used, that's banned by your Council. All the charms are. They are the old ways, the ways of the uncivilized, so they say. That dagger of yours," he said, pointing at the Samsa'raka, "that's one of the worst. The Shadow's Dagger, they call it. If they see you with it, they will burn you and your friends, and all because they're too weak to use charms. They're afraid of those who can; they're afraid that those like you could become more powerful than the whole Council of Dreamers combined.

"That's why I want you to join me. You have some power behind you, Isabella Shaw, and a lineage. You're not quite as powerful as me, but in time—well, in time, who knows. They will try to strip you of your power, and if you don't play their games, they will take even more. They're not the good guys you think they are."

"Oh," Isabella said, "and I suppose you are?"

"No, but at least I don't pretend to be something I'm not. Join me and I will cure that pesky little infection of yours. Together we can destroy the Council of Dreamers and live in the dream world like royalty."

"Izzy." Delson's hand was on her shoulder.

"No," she said, sheathing her dagger, "I don't want that. I want to help you."

"Then help me." Eli jumped up on the raised stone and looked down at them, his fist held in front of him in triumph. "Help me to destroy the corruption that is rotting this world from the head down. Help me destroy the Council of Dreamers."

"I won't do that."

He looked at her for a few seconds. "A pity," he said, lowering his arm and turning his back on them. "When you change your mind—and you will—come find me." He jumped down from the table and moved through the shadows aligned at the other end of the room. "If you manage to get out of here, that is. I believe that mist must be wearing off by now. I'd go if I were you."

When Eli left the room, his shadows began to advance on Isabella and Delson, their movement measured and unhurried.

"Let's get out of here." Delson pulled Isabella back the way they had come. "You tried your best. If we don't get out of here before Wesley's mist wears off, we might not get out of here at all. Remember that shadow army is between us and the exit."

"I know." Isabella kept her eyes on the back wall where Eli had departed. There must be a passage back there somewhere, but the shadows were between them. "I think he knows something he's not saying."

"I don't doubt he does, but we'll have to find it out some other time."

"What about my arm? I don't want to become a shadow like them."

He looked between the advancing shadows and the passage they'd come from. "If he knows a way to fix it, then there's a way. Nigel will know, but first we need to get out of here. Come on."

THIRTY-FOUR

A s Delson and Isabella charged around the corner into the central passageway leading to the room where Delson had been imprisoned, Eli's shadows were still advancing. In front of them was the mist where Wesley trapped the shadow army. Beyond that was their best chance at escape.

"Quick, once we get through the mist, those shadows won't be able to follow us." Delson glanced over his shoulder at the shadows before picking up his pace.

"If it holds," Isabella whispered, feeling her stomach tighten as she neared the mist. Something about it looked different than when they'd gone through the first time, as if it was reaching out for her somehow.

"It'll hold."

"How can you be so sure?"

"'Cause if it doesn't, we're done for," Delson said with what Isabella thought was almost excitement.

"Great," she mumbled under her breath as Delson disappeared into the mist. She could feel pressure pulling her toward the mist and she leaned into it, allowing it to help her speed up a little. She shadows behind her continued to advance, heedless of the mist they were about to run into. When Isabella broke the leading edge of the mist, the feeling of being pulled forward transformed into running through waist-deep water. The mist pushed back against her legs and torso, but what she felt most was the pulling on her right arm; the one she'd crushed the shadow's heart with earlier, the one Eli had called infected.

The mist made everything look insubstantial, hindering her view. She could see a shape that must have been Delson running unimpeded through the mist and almost through to the other side, but the other shapes were what drew her attention. She'd expected to see the writhing masses of the shadows that had attacked them on the ledge, but instead what she saw were vague shapes of people. Many of them stood, a couple sat down, but one or two seemed to fight toward the edge of the mist where Delson was emerging.

Isabella struggled forward, her progress seemingly less hampered than that of the shadows trying to get through, but unquestionably more so than Delson's. Her legs burned from the exertion and her chest heaved as she breathed through the thicker air. The closer she moved to the other side, the more pressure she felt pushing back against her. Her right arm trailed behind her, pulling so awkwardly back that Isabella thought her shoulder was going to dislocate.

"Izzy?" Delson's voice sounded far away, muffled by something. "Izzy, where are you?"

She tried to call back, but she couldn't make any noise. As hard as she tried to call out to him, to say she was right behind him and that he shouldn't worry, she couldn't make her vocal cords cooperate. She opened her mouth and soundlessly called his name. A tightness cinched her chest; this feeling, the pressure, was the same as her recurring nightmare, the one her father used to protect her from as a child. She'd never been able to call out when she was in the shadowy whirlwind.

Her pulse quickened. The air grew thicker around her, pressing on her face like the mist was becoming solid and cementing her into place. Frantically, Isabella tried to grab at anything she could get ahold of, but the mist pushed back, pinning her right arm uselessly behind her and giving her nothing to grasp with the left. Her eyes darted around the shifting pale haze, but she couldn't see anything to help her. Some forms nearby began to move in her wake, wandering in her direction as if dreaming.

"Izzy, I'm coming back to get you," Delson's muffled voice called out from the other side of the wall of white.

Isabella tried to scream again, calling for him not to come in after her, telling him to leave, to get out while he could before the mist broke and the shadows were released. Once again, her screams were silent even to her own ears. She could feel helplessness trying to overcome her, dragging her to the ground like the shapes around her, trying to get her to give up the pursuit, to give up on trying to escape, to give up on trying to stop Delson from going back toward the shadows waiting for them where they'd entered the mist.

"Izzy," Delson called, his voice sounding like it was coming through water, "take my hand if you can. I can't see you in there. Call out if you need help."

Isabella tried to call out to him, tears of frustration building in the corners of her eyes. She stopped pushing against the mist and stood still. The mist pressed in on her, trying to pull her down toward the ground, but she refused to let it. Around her, the figures had stopped moving too. They settled, as passive as they were before. Isabella clenched her fists and squeezed her eyes shut. She willed the growing panic in her chest to release its suffocating pressure. She pictured her friends in her mind, reliving everything they had done for her. Wesley, collapsing after he released the fog. Skia, skittering down from the tree with her dream catcher when she'd forgotten it. Finn, carrying the prone young man down the narrow path to safety, the one who had led her across the river to find her brother the last time they were together, who believed in her to do the right thing even when she was wrong. Delson, standing bravely by her side despite the dire odds. And Kimi, brave and loyal Kimi. How many times had that little fox refused to abandon her, even when Isabella scorned her and pushed her away? Isabella took a deep breath, fighting to pull in each molecule of air that seemed to resist her lungs. She wouldn't let them down, not after everything they'd done for her. Nobody else would endanger themselves to protect her. After everything she had done, she would not let this stop her. Isabella released the air from her lungs in a scream of pride and defiance.

"I can hear you!" Delson called, his voice still far away but with an edge of joy. "Grab my hand."

Isabella saw a hand extend into the mist. It was faint and seemed far away, but it was there. When she screamed, the pressure of the mist released her; the air came easily to her lungs and her limbs were free, but the release was only temporary. Almost as quickly as it had let her go, it pressed back around her, building slowly. She took advantage of the time she had and pushed forward. The pressure continued to build as she neared the edge but Delson's extended arm, shoved into the mist, was now visible up to his elbow.

As Isabella grabbed his wrist with her left hand, he mirrored the action and she heard him grunt from the other side. "I can't pull you out," he said, panic beginning to edge into his voice. "I don't know what to do, Izzy. I can't pull you."

Isabella pulled on her right arm, which the mist had dragged behind her again. The pressure was excruciating and her muscles burned by the time she brought the arm even with her body. Ignoring the ache and the pressure, Isabella continued, stars bursting in her vision from the exertion. Her right hand landed on Delson's forearm, causing goosebumps to rise on his skin immediately. He released her wrist when she pulled her left arm from his grasp. Reaching further up, he extended his arm toward the mist's edge, which all but solidified in front of her. The mist darkened around her right arm like the sky before a summer storm. Isabella pulled herself up Delson's arm, inching forward, the pressure growing with each movement until she burst through the other side. Tendrils of mist followed them, seemingly reaching for the shadow around her right arm but dissipating before they reached them.

Isabella pulled with such force that when the mist released her, she and Delson tumbled over backward, knocking into the cage that had been holding him and making it topple over the edge of the cliff. She landed on top of him. His swords, sheathed to his back, scraped across the stone floor with a loud grating.

"Thank you," Isabella said once she pushed herself up to stand with her hands on her knees, concentrating on catching her breath.

"I didn't do anything." Delson stood as well, but he seemed much less winded by the experience. "What happened in there? Did you get attacked?"

"What do you mean?" Isabella looked up at him, her breathing coming back to normal. "The pressure in there was crazy. It was like those dreams when you're trying to scream but you can't."

"There was no pressure in there." Delson raised an eyebrow at Isabella. "You don't think it had something to do with that, do you?" He motioned to her right arm, which was now wreathed in a wispy shadow.

Not wanting to think about what that might suggest, Isabella ignored the question and looked toward the narrow trail Finn and Kimi had left on. "Think they got out alright?"

"I would imagine so." He moved to stand beside her, their backs to the mist and the shadows beyond, looking at their escape. "I guess there's only one way to find out, right?" Delson took one step toward the ledge and stopped suddenly. Isabella saw a look of shock cross his face before he fell forward. "Shadows," he cried out, scrambling against the ground to keep from being pulled back into the mist.

Isabella turned to see the mist writhing with five tentacles of shadows that had forced themselves toward the edge. One was at the exact place that she had gotten out and had one tentacle wrapped around Delson's ankle, pulling at him. A second tendril was trying to latch onto the same leg. Pulling her dagger from its sheath at her belt, Isabella swept at the shadow latched onto Delson's ankle. Slicing through it with ease, the severed section began dissipating instantly, but the pant leg around which it was wrapped had all but disintegrated, burning sections of Delson's ankle in the process.

The shadow screamed and struggled through the mist, clawing at the ground around it, looking for something to pull on. Isabella saw the shape of a thin man inside the mist, but where he'd managed to emerge she saw the writhing shadow. She shook her head sharply and looked again, but what she saw didn't change. Trying not to let herself get distracted, Isabella swiped again as one of the tentacles lashed out toward her arm.

Having righted himself and drawn his swords, Delson stood beside her, defending against a shadow emerging to her right. This one had managed to get one arm and half of its torso entirely free, but inside the mist Isabella saw a young, curvy girl with long hair. She returned her attention to the shadow emerging from the mist just in time to defend against a swipe from its now free claws. With most of its body out, the shadow seemed to be having an easier time extricating itself. The mist itself also seemed to be receding as the shadows fought their way to the edge.

Not having time to consider what that meant, Isabella swung her dagger to the left and defended against a third shadow that had fully emerged. This one had brought its arm up from below Isabella's guard, but she was able to draw back and deflect the glistening black claws as it swiped up at the underside of her left arm. The first shadow, seeing an opportunity, lunged at her from the right. Raising her arm to ward off the blow, Isabella felt the impact of the shadow's claws on her skin. While it burned, she was able to push it back.

Delson was having similar difficulties with the shadow pressing the attack on him. He deftly defended the onslaught of claws and tentacles with his two curved swords, but he could not push the shadow back. Instead, he was being pushed back toward the edge of the cliff, inch by inch, as he sidestepped the flurry of slashing claws aimed at him. Seeing their dire position, Isabella tried to use the raka stone as she had before to push back the shadows. Focusing her concentration on funneling power into the stone, Isabella was encouraged as the yellow glow pulsed outward, making the shadows draw back momentarily before the light faded into a dull throb, the power seemingly drained from it.

With the fading light, the shadows, their number increased to four now with a fifth beginning to emerge from the shrinking mist, closed the distance. Their shrieks of pain and sadness were almost palpable in the growing darkness as the dagger's glow continued to ebb. Delson let out a cry of pain as one of the tentacles wrapped around his exposed wrist seemed to sizzle, and his sword clattered to the ground at his feet. Isabella, faring better than Delson but being pushed back as well, swung ferociously with her dagger in her left hand, using her right like a shield to keep from being overwhelmed.

The shadow wrapped around Delson's wrist wrenched him viciously to the right, away from Isabella. Seeing this from the corner of her eye, Isabella lunged after him, grasping at the shadow's tentacle with her right hand. Her foot hit something solid that skittered away toward the edge of the cliff and disappeared. When she connected with the shadow, she clenched down and pulled it toward her, hoping to free Delson from its grasp. The shadow turned its glowing yellow gaze on her, surprise and fear showing in its burning eyes. When Isabella plunged the dagger at the heart of the shadow, it released Delson and jumped out of the way.

Now free, Delson swiped at the distracted shadow with his remaining sword, landing a solid blow at the shadow's core, causing it to dissipate and leaving Isabella holding nothing but air. Delson and Isabella turned their backs to each other, defending against the slashing claws and tentacles of the four remaining shadows. At the edge of the mist, Isabella could see more shadows beginning to emerge. They were not going to be able to fight them all. She looked toward the ledge. It was their only hope of escape, but it too was blocked by emerging shadows. Two new ones were clawing their way from the mist directly onto the path between them and their exit.

Two shadows launched a coordinated attack at Delson, one from the right grabbing at his leg and the other from the left slashing at his head. Isabella, fending off three different shadows now, noticed too late that Delson had only seen one of the incoming attacks. While he raised his sword to protect his head, the shadow attacking from the right latched on to his already injured leg and pulled him to the ground again. His hand slammed down on a stone, the force knocking the sword from it and sending it to the edge of the cliff. Delson, refusing to give up, kicked at the shadow but could only push away small wisps. With some struggle, he managed to free his leg, but he couldn't stand. Pushing himself backward with his hands and one uninjured leg, he fought to get back to his sword that was teetering half over the edge of the cliff.

Seeing he was about to be overwhelmed, Isabella made a vicious arch with her dagger, successfully pushing back two of the three shadows advancing on her, and rushed to Delson's defense. A shadow loomed over him, its claw raised in gleaming triumph as Delson blindly tried to find his sword in the now almost lightless cavern. The shadow brought its glistening claws down, decay dripping like saliva from a rabid dog's jaws onto the ground. Isabella jumped between them and, raising her right hand, grabbed what she assumed to be the shadow's wrist. The shadow's look of triumph faded as it failed to move its arm through Isabella's grasp. Her burning muscles strained and shook as she struggled against the shadow's strength, but she was able to fight him to a stalemate.

One of the shadows to their right moved in toward Delson. Isabella watched helplessly as it lashed out one of the tentacles at Delson's hand, wrapping around his wrist as he was about to grasp the hilt of his sword. It wrenched at his wrist, trying to drag him closer to the edge of the cliff, and successfully knocked the sword off in the process. To the left, the shadow Isabella hadn't managed to push off with her previous slash pressed the attack and caught her in the side while she struggled against the shadow whose arm she held. The claws cut sharply into her left side, causing Isabella to cry out as a wave of pain and nausea washed over her. Her stomach lurched and she felt a cold sweat break out across her entire body. The pressure of the shadow's arm she refused to let go of drove her hard to her right knee. Isabella weakly mounted a counterattack against the shadow who'd sliced into her, but it easily avoided her blade and began to close the distance for another attack.

A high-pitched snarl rang out from their right, and Isabella saw the familiar flash of red lunge through the shadow that she was struggling against, drawing a large chunk with it. The shadow screamed in anger, but the pressure weakened and the shadow that had managed to slash Isabella's side turned to face the newcomer. Kimi skidded to a stop about two feet from the group, her mouth open and letting out her sharp warning barks. She locked eyes with Isabella for a second, and it almost looked like the fox was enjoying herself.

Taking advantage of the brief distraction, Isabella plunged the dagger at the shadow looming over her, landing a strike directly at the dark, swirling center. The familiar pressure that eased with a slight pop told her the hit landed home. The arm she held seemed to solidify into the pudgy limb of an older man, his flesh pale and clammy. The eyes, once filled with malice and hatred, softened to the sad grey ones of a man who regretted so much in life. Then the image faded, like an afterimage on a screen, and she was left holding nothing.

The light of the raka stone flared brightly as the shadow faded and Isabella focused on pushing the shadows back with the light. As the pulsing yellow grew in intensity, the shadows closest to her and Delson drew back and cried out in pain. The one holding Delson released its searing grip, depositing Delson with his head and arms hanging over the edge but his torso still on solid ground. He rolled himself back fully from the edge. Isabella, reaching for Delson, called for Kimi to come. As she did, something whizzed past her right shoulder and into the descending hand of a shadow. The hand was redirected as the arrow clattered off the stone floor. A second arrow followed it, and then a third.

Knowing that retreat was the only logical move, Kimi ran to defend Isabella who was helping Delson to his feet. He leaned heavily against her, his left leg held slightly above the ground as he was clearly unable to put weight on it. The slashes in Isabella's side burned. She gasped as the pain flared with Delson's added weight, but she did her best to ignore it.

"Just leave me," he begged. "I'm only going to slow you down."

Isabella ignored his request. Ignoring the pain, she put her right arm around his back and under his right arm. "I can't carry you, but I'm not leaving you. Now let's go." With that, she started to move toward the ledge. The pulsing yellow light of the Samsa'raka, held high in her left hand, did an excellent job of keeping the shadows at bay. Kimi kept close between Isabella and the shadows, backing up while snarling and snapping at any who ventured too close. Any shadow that Kimi couldn't deter was met with an arrow loosed from Finn's bow across the chasm.

They had to slow down as they moved across the ledge, backs against the stone wall and the chasm in front of them. Isabella struggled not to be pulled forward over the cliff each time Delson's leg refused to hold him up, pushing his weight onto her. The shadows, kept at a distance by the light of the raka stone and Finn's arrows, congregated at the mouth of the ledge but were advancing slowly across it themselves. When Isabella got to the other side and handed Delson off to Finn, he put a small stone in her hand and called for them to follow him. The group moved quicker now that they were off the ledge, but Isabella knew that the shadows would as well.

ℭ𝔢 THIRTY-FIVE 𝔢ℜ

After getting to the other side of the ledge, Finn led the group down a series of tunnels ending in another large cavern. Part of the ceiling had caved in, leaving an opening to the outside. Fresh air and the sound of birds chirping, something that Isabella had not realized she had missed, filled the space. In the cavern's center was a large lake and in the middle of the lake, dangling from the hole in the roof, was a rope-ladder. Isabella thought back to middle school gym class where everyone had to climb the rope net hanging from the gym ceiling. She quietly thanked her luck that she'd never had a problem with that particular exercise.

She looked to the stone that Finn had placed in her hand. It had a glassy, translucent quality to it. Under the almost polished-looking surface, an opaque orange color mixed with lighter swirls of a dull pink. On their way down the tunnels, Finn had explained that Wesley had given him the stone for her to use if they had to collapse a tunnel or something. Isabella was to hold the stone to the waist of her pants, say some gibberish, then place the stone on the ground and run. As she held the stone now, Delson leaned heavily against Finn at the edge of the water.

Kimi walked and sat down beside her. "So, what's the plan?"

"I don't know that I trust whatever this is." Isabella turned the stone over in her hand several times.

"He did save us back there against the shadows," Kimi reminded her.

Isabella looked back at the rope-ladder. "Right, but then he collapsed. What if that happens to me?"

"Then we'll get you out of here."

"And how do you intend to climb out?"

Kimi looked over her shoulder at Finn. "I guess I can allow the hunter to carry me. He's been faithful so far."

"You don't trust Finn?"

"It's not so much that," Kimi said, looking up at Isabella with intelligent eyes. "The hunters always have revered weavers and their companions. The Council fears that if they get too comfortable around us, that reverence might wain and they could become less reliable."

"You've been to the council?"

"Vígolfr mentioned it before you and I met, when he and your father realized our connection."

"Weavers know who is connected to a companion?"

"Not usually." Kimi looked down the passage. There was a cool breeze coming their way, and the passage was eerily silent. "But maybe we have this conversation later?"

"Right." Isabella looked back at Finn and Delson, then down at Kimi. "So, if I'm going to do this, why don't you go back by Finn. I don't want to trip over you when I run."

Kimi nodded and turned to walk to the edge of the water. As she did, she brushed her tail against Isabella's leg. The contact made Isabella smile and a tension she'd been unknowingly holding in her chest relaxed. They had bonded; Isabella was sure of it. Any residual doubt about their relationship washed away with that brief but affectionate gesture. They would be fine.

Refocusing on the crystal, Isabella tried to remember the words that Finn had said. They were moving fast as he said them, there were a lot of a's and hard consonants, but Isabella thought she remembered them. She held the stone in front of her waist, took a deep breath, and tried to say the words. She was almost sure she had gotten them right, but she didn't feel anything. She placed the stone on the ground in the middle of the entrance and ran back to the water's edge. Expectantly, she counted off three seconds, then five, then ten. Nothing happened.

"Did I get the words wrong?" Isabella looked at Finn.

"I don't think so."

"Then why didn't it work?"

"Did you hold the stone in front of you like Wesley said?"

"I think so."

They looked at the small stone in the middle of the passageway.

"Did he say how long it would take?" Delson asked.

Finn shrugged. "He said to run, so I assumed that meant it would be fast."

"Why does he think I could even use it?" Isabella asked. She was torn between going back to get the stone and just trying to get out.

"You can use the Samsa'raka," Kimi answered. "You can do this too. They are the same."

"Weavers' charms?" Finn's eyes went wide. "They're real? The charms, I mean?"

"What do you think that smoke thing Wesley used before was all about?"

"That's crazy!" Finn grinned widely. "I gotta see this. Go on, Izzy, give it another try."

Isabella walked over to the stone and picked it up. She tried again but still didn't feel anything. "I think I should feel something when I do this." She looked back at the group. "What am I doing wrong?"

"Got me," Finn said with a shrug.

"What about Kimi?" Delson asked.

"Companions cannot use charms," Kimi said, shaking her head.

"Right," Delson said, "but Wesley called Skia over before he did that whole smoke thing. What if you need to be in contact with your companion?"

"No." Isabella shook her head. "I don't want to put Kimi in that kind of danger. What if something goes wrong and I blow myself up."

"If that happens," Kimi said, walking over to Isabella, "then we're all dead."

"I don't know that you're going to have much choice anyway," Finn said.

"Are you sure?" Isabella looked down at Kimi, a tightness in her chest at the thought of the fox getting injured. "This could be dangerous."

"When is it not?"

Isabella glanced back over her shoulder at Finn and Delson. "Finn, if we go down like Wesley did, promise me you will get Kimi out of harm's way first."

"I'll get you both out," he said, settling Delson on the ground.

"Promise me you'll get Kimi first."

Finn closed his eyes and took a deep breath. "I promise."

Isabella nodded curtly. A promise from Finn was a promise kept. She knew that much. The cool breeze coming down the path was getting stronger, bringing with it the edge of the emotional wave that came from the shadows. They were coming, and they were close. She looked down at Kimi. "Okay, are you ready?"

"To the end, my weaver." The fox curled her tail around Isabella's leg and took a defensive stance, eyes narrowed and looking down the hall.

Isabella picked up the smooth stone. It felt cold in her hands, lifeless. For a moment, she thought about what would happen if they failed, if the shadow army caught them there. Delson was injured. Finn would be able to climb to safety before the shadows got him, but he wouldn't. He hadn't left her and Delson before and he wouldn't do it now. He'd insist that she go, but she wouldn't go without Kimi, and she wasn't sure she could carry the little fox with her side as it was. They would face the shadows together, the four of them, and they would lose.

Isabella held the stone to her waist again. She closed her eyes and took a deep breath, then in a loud and confident voice, said the phrase as accurately as she could, *"Kim samavartataagre, yaachate sanhRi."* As the last echo of her words faded, Isabella felt the stone begin to warm in her hands. As it did, a wave of fatigue washed over her, the room wavered slightly, and she felt like she couldn't breathe. Her eyes widened in panic and her vision began to darken at the edges. Knowing she had to set the stone in place before it burst, Isabella forced her body to move. Like in a dream, she stepped forward, breaking the connection with Kimi's tail. The little fox dropped to the ground.

Isabella heard the scuffing sounds of feet moving across the loose gravel floor at the edge of her awareness. Finn was keeping his word. She forced herself to take another step, her body moving impossibly slow. In front of her, down the passage, she saw the shadows coming around the last corner. The Samsa'raka flared a searing yellow for a moment and then went out, its energy spent. The shadows didn't falter in their advance. Knowing she needed to move quickly didn't change the fact that she couldn't. The stone seemed to pulse with heat, growing hotter and heavier like it was drawing something from inside of her. With each pulse, Isabella felt herself weaken, her vision narrowing a little at a time. She stood in the middle of the passage, facing the army of shadows alone. She bent down to place the stone in the middle of the floor.

Standing up was no easier than walking with the stone had been, but one thought circled in her mind. Run. She pushed off with her right leg, expecting to move quickly now that she'd set the stone down, but it was like running through deep, shifting

~ 345 ~

sand dunes. Isabella could feel the shadows' emotions on her back as the heat from the orange stone continued to pulse. Someone was calling to her, but Isabella couldn't make out the words. Run, she told herself. Run. One foot in front of the other, Isabella pushed through the resistance until a large rumble, followed by a concussive shock, knocked her to the ground. The world went black.

When Isabella opened her eyes, she was propped up against the wall, cold stone against her back. Kimi lay beside her, breathing slowly and evenly.

"You're up!" Finn's voice was filled with relief.

"What happened?" Isabella tried to push herself up from the floor, but everything hurt.

"You did it," he said as he grinned at her, his eyes filled with gratitude and excitement. "It was amazing. You were standing there with that stone, like before, but then you started moving forward. No lie, though, it was like you were in slow motion or something. When Kimi collapsed, I feared the worst, but you were unstoppable. You moved forward and the air in front of you was all ripply, like water when you throw a stone in it. Then the shadows were there, and—"

"Finn," Delson called from the edge of the water, "let her be. She was there, you know."

"Sorry." Finn smiled and shook his head, but his eyes were still wild with excitement. "Nobody back at the camp is going to believe this. It was crazy."

Isabella touched her side, expecting it to come away red with her blood or black with decay. Instead, it was covered with a translucent amber with some green flecks mixed in.

"Oh," Finn said, "that's the salve we put on those scratches. Nigel put it together after the fight with the shadow congress. You know, based on what you did with Kimi."

Isabella placed her left hand on the little fox, tracing the white strip where she'd been slashed while helping Isabella save her brother. A tinge of guilt washed through her, but the fox seemed to relax with the contact.

"Seems those bees had fed on some nectar that helped with the shadow infections. Nigel had us gather them and has been cultivating them ever since. Now he makes us all carry some of that salve in case we get hit with the shadows. It's saved several hunters that would have been turned before. I put some on Delson too, but he insisted that I save most of it for you. Once we get up, Ajay will have his and we can put more on that stubborn bit of a bollix."

"You'd do the same, rumbly muppet," Delson jibed back at him with a chuckle. "Besides, the burns are not as bad as those slashes."

Isabella pushed herself up from the floor. "Thank you both, for everything. Now how are we going to get out of here?"

"Now that you're up and moving, think you can climb that?" Finn motioned to the rope-ladder. "I'll carry Del."

"Unfortunately," Delson grumbled.

"You know you'll like it," Finn quipped back.

"Yes," Isabella said as she smiled at the two of them, "I can climb." She stretched her sore muscles. The blast had knocked her unconscious, but there wasn't much change in the light above. Looking at where the entrance was, Isabella was surprised to see a pile of rubble completely obscuring the door. "Can they get through that?"

"How do I know?" Finn shrugged. "Until today, I didn't know you weavers could blow stuff up with rocks. Either way, we should get out of here now that you're moving."

Isabella watched as Finn walked over to Delson and helped him stand before they hobbled through the water to the rope-ladder. The water was only about waist high at its deepest and became shallower under the ladder, presumably where the stones from the opening had fallen. She watched as Finn lifted Delson over his shoulder and then began to climb. The muscles in his arms strained and he was moving slowly, but he made progress.

Isabella shifted her attention to Kimi, who had woken during their short conversation and was stretching herself. "Well, that was new," she said after she finished.

"Are you alright?"

"Oh yes." The fox sat down and watching the swaying rope-ladder with suspicion. "Apparently I collapsed, but I feel fine now. Tired, but nothing a little more rest won't fix."

"Good." Isabella followed Kimi's gaze to the rope-ladder. "You can't climb, can you?"

"No," she said. "No thumbs, remember."

"Right." Isabella looked at Finn struggling under Delson's weight. He would come back down for Kimi if she asked him to, but Delson was the second person he'd carried up that today. Besides, he wouldn't always be there to help them. She looked around for something to make a basket out of to carry Kimi up, but there was nothing but stones and water in the cavern. "Okay, I have a plan."

"You do?" Kimi sounded suspicious. "I'm not going to let you tie that rope to me. I will not leave you down here and be hauled up that thing like a sack of grain."

Isabella laughed. "Don't worry, Kimi. No one is going to haul you up from the end of a rope."

The shifting sound of rubble drew their attention to the entrance. The stones on their side looked secure, but that didn't mean the shadows weren't trying to get through. If they could grab someone's arm and try to drag them off a cliff, they could move rocks.

"Whatever you're going to do," Kimi said, the fur raising on her back, "I think you better do it quickly."

Isabella sat down on the ground and took off her boots. Then, standing up, she unbuttoned her pants and started to pull them off, thankful for the bike shorts she typically wore under them when camping.

"I'm not sure now is the time for a wardrobe change," Kimi quipped. "What are you doing?"

"You'll see." Isabella enjoyed that, for once, she knew something that Kimi didn't. Once Isabella had worked her pants off, she put her boots back on and waded through the water to the rope-ladder. It swung wildly as Finn struggled above her, grunting with the effort and grumbling to Delson about something she couldn't quite hear. Isabella pulled the end of the rope-ladder from the water to see how much there was available. Satisfied that she could cut off a length of rope and leave enough to reach the lower rung, Isabella used her knife to cut off about five feet, leaving the frayed end swaying above the water.

She came back out and tossed the rope on the ground next to her pants. Kneeling on the cold stone floor, Isabella started by spreading out her pants and rebuttoning them. "My dad did this on a road trip one time when he wanted us to go for a hike but forgot a backpack. I laughed at him then, but I guess he was on to something," she explained as she tied the ankles of her pants together with the middle of the rope. She doubled the knot and then brought the ankles up toward the waist. She strung the rope through her belt loops on either side and tied it off at what would have been the back of her pants. Smiling, she stood up and showed Kimi what she had done. "Voilà, a backpack. You get in here, and I'll carry you up myself. It won't be comfortable, but it will work."

Some of the smaller stones tumbled down the pile of rubble as Kimi said, "Not that I have much choice, do I?"

Isabella shrugged and smiled. "Not really. Trust me?"

The little fox stood up and raised her chin, looking straight into Isabella's eyes. "Implicitly."

Isabella held the waist of her pants open for Kimi to climb into. She fit most of her body in, but her front paws and head stuck out the top. Isabella carefully tightened the rope around the pants' waist so the ride wouldn't be too rough, then slipped it on her back. Kimi's weight rested below Isabella's shoulder blades, and the pressure was comforting as she put her hands on the rope-ladder to begin pulling them both up to the sun. Finn was almost through the hole above when Isabella grabbed hold of the bottom rung. Hand over hand, Isabella worked her way up the ladder. Without the extra weight of the ladder in the water below, it swayed more violently than the net in gym class, but she tried to push her feet against the side ropes to hold it steadier. Her arms—the right more than the left—and side burned, but Kimi's weight against her back gave her the motivation she needed. Kimi was trusting Isabella with her life, and it was a trust she would not betray.

A shadow moved over the hole, blocking part of the light. Isabella's heart sank momentarily until a thick, familiar Hindi accent called down to her from above. "Resourceful little weaver," Ajay's unmistakable baritone laugh filled the room, echoing through the cavern. "First-class."

Isabella didn't answer, afraid to take her concentration off the rope-ladder. The muscles in her arms quivered with each pull and her thighs were beginning to burn.

"Don't mean to be a *pakau*," he called down to her, "but those shadows are making short work of your little rock pile. "*Jaldee se*, hurry it up. I'm here if you need a hand, but Finn is *thaked* out from his climb. Del's not a light guy."

Isabella pushed forward. Knowing Ajay was up there looking down on them gave her hope. Worst case, he could pull them up, but Isabella was determined to finish the climb herself. When she reached up and felt the edge of the rock that made up the ceiling of the cavern, she closed her eyes and took a deep breath.

Once she was on solid ground, her muscles quivering from the exertion, Ajay pulled the ladder back up and turned to the rest of the group. "Avert your eyes, you lousy bunch of *vellas*. Give the lady some privacy." Crossing his arms, he moved toward them, using his body to block their view of Isabella as she put her pants back on.

THIRTY-SIX

Finn lay on his back in the sun, eyes closed and limbs splayed out on all sides. He looked worn out, and, at a glance, he could be mistaken for sleeping. Delson sat against a rock in the full sun while Wesley, with Skia on his shoulder, put some of Nigel's salve on Delson's wounds from the shadows. Ajay had coiled the rope and was attaching it to one of the two packs leaning against a tree at the forest's edge near the entrance to a path. Isabella sat in the grass a little apart from the group, knees pulled to her chest and her right arm resting on them. Kimi was curled up next to her, and Isabella absently pet her with her left hand.

"You are all *pāgala*," Ajay said with his baritone laugh. "I used to think it was Finn, but guess I was wrong."

"I've heard the stories, big guy," Finn said without opening his eyes, "you're no better than the rest of us."

"Don't lump me in with the rest of them." Delson winced as Wesley touched a particularly tender wound. "I'm only here because the Champion sent me."

"About that," Finn said as he propped himself up on his elbow and looked at Wesley, one eyebrow raised. "How did you ever get the Champion to agree to help a rebel?"

"He's a rebel?" Ajay's shoulders tensed, and his hand went for the sword strapped to his back. "You lying piece of—"

"Hold back, Ajay," Delson held up his good hand. "Wesley came through for us in a pinch. He saved our skin down there. He may not be a weaver, but he's not a bad guy."

"Can't trust 'em." Ajay closed his massive hand around the hilt of his sword.

Wesley stood up and raised his hands in defense. The salve that he'd been helping Delson with made his palms glisten in the sun. He took two steps back, putting some distance between himself and the latest threat.

Isabella stood up and Kimi stood with her. "Ajay, put that away."

"With all respect, little weaver"—Ajay stopped with his blade half out of its sheath—"you don't understand their kind." He spat the word 'their' at Wesley like it was a curse.

"Then explain it to me." She moved to stand between Ajay and Wesley. Kimi stood beside her, her tail swishing slowly back and forth.

"The rebels are one step away from stalkers," he said, but he didn't pull his sword out further. "You can't trust them. They're *bina samaan ke*. They have no honor."

"Now wait a minute," Wesley said as he took a step forward, still keeping Isabella between him and Ajay, "you have no right to say that."

"I have every right." Ajay pulled his sword the rest of the way, squaring his shoulders to Wesley. "You may have these three fooled, but I am not naive. You rebels are after one thing, and I will make sure you do not get it."

"Hold on here." Isabella felt a chill run up her spine. Things were not going well. She turned so they could see both Wesley and Ajay. She didn't know who to believe. Ajay had proved he was trustworthy from the beginning. He helped Tucker and he'd given her the dagger that had saved her many times. Wesley had run at the first sign of trouble, but he'd come back and risked his own life to help them when he didn't have to. Without him, they would not have gotten free of the shadows or the cave. But if she thought about it, what did she really know about either of them. "Put that thing away"—she motioned to Ajay's sword—"can't you see he's unarmed and half your size."

"Don't let him fool you. They're crafty buggers," Ajay replied, not backing down.

Isabella tried a different tact. "Wesley, what were you doing down there in the first place, and why did you need Delson?"

"Like you'll get a straight answer from that one." Ajay pointed with his sword at Wesley but lowered it and waited to hear his answer.

"I'll give you a straight answer," Wesley replied as he looked at Skia.

"I think they've earned it," Skia said, climbing down from Wesley's shoulder but not leaving his side.

"Though please, Ajay, I'd prefer to tell it without the threat of death on my head."

Isabella nodded at Ajay and pointed to his scabbard. The big man scowled but slammed his sword back into the sheath. "I make no promises, which is more than his kind deserves."

"I'll take what I can get," Wesley said. "Ajay is not entirely wrong to distrust the rebels. There are a lot of them who are little better than stalkers, but there are a lot of weavers who some might say are worse. I was a weaver once. I spent hours in Central Library, studying the Great Purge and the history of the shadow wars. I wanted to be a historian. Actually, I'm studying history at the Pacific Lutheran Uni—" He looked at Isabella and bit his lip, realizing that he may have said too much. "Anyway, when I was in the library in the Capitol, there was this one book shoved back behind one of the shelves. It was about weavers' charms."

"See," Finn interjected, "I told you weavers' charms were real."

"That's the thing. I had been told they were only legends," Wesley continued. "Turns out that before the Great Purge, some of the weavers used to use charms."

"Like that stone you made the smoke with?" Delson asked.

"Exactly!" Wesley's eyes were wide with excitement. "But the Council of Dreamers banned the use of charms."

"With good reason," Ajay said, standing with his arms crossed and frowning down at them all. "None of you are old enough to remember the rebellion and the Purge. You wouldn't understand."

Finn looked at Ajay with a puzzled expression. "That was like sixty years ago, wasn't it?"

"Closer to eighty," Wesley corrected.

"How old are you, Ajay?" Finn sat up, studying his friend.

"Not a topic for the moment," Ajay answered, dismissing the question and turning to Wesley. "So, I haven't heard one thing come out of your mouth about why I shouldn't rid the world of your filth?"

Finn stood up and moved closer to his friend. "Ajay, calm down, man. This isn't like you."

"This is not one of your stories, Finn," Ajay snapped at him. "Kindly adjust, boy." He closed his eyes and took a deep breath before opening them again. Isabella saw the kindness she remembered. "I'm sorry, Finn. You do not yet know things that you will learn in time, but for now, trust me. Now, Wesley, continue."

Wesley's excitement was more subdued, but it began to bubble under the surface of his words as he continued talking. "I didn't know then, but after the Council had banned the use of charms, they destroyed all of the literature on them and their benefits. They took one of the early weavers' weapons against the shadow armies and basically threw it out the window. Because some of the weavers who used the charms had become powerful stalkers, they claimed that using charms was too powerful. Said it corrupted the weaver and made them seek more power, turning them from their true purpose.

"With the defeat of the great shadow armies, lead of course by some of those stalkers, in the last shadow war, most of the weavers didn't argue. After all, there were only a handful of weavers who could use charms anyway. Most either didn't bother to learn because of the propaganda against it, or weren't strong enough. You all saw what the smoky quartz did to me. So, it became a bit of a lost art. Then came the Great Purge.

"Once the Council of Dreamers outlawed the use of charms, it was only a short step to use the prejudice and fear of the denizens and the weavers alike to feed a public outcry against the charm users. That led to several years of violence and the near elimination of all charm-using weavers. Most were killed, but some had it much worse. Their companions were torn from them in a ceremony, essentially barring them from ever entering the dream world again."

Isabella looked down at Kimi. She had used the dream catcher and the Samsa'raka. She had even used one of Wesley's stones. A shiver ran up her spine as Wesley explained the creation of the rebels, the eventual war between the rebels and the weavers, and how it had ended in a stalemate. Ajay seemed to relax some as Wesley's story went forward, but Isabella felt the opposite. With each revelation, she felt the tension building between her shoulder blades.

"The few that were able to hide their ability eventually banded together and continued their work fighting against the shadows and the nightmares. They became known as the rebels. We stay hidden from the Council because they have vowed to wipe us out, but the reason is not what you think it is, Ajay. I know you trust the weavers, and most are good people, but the Council is not among them. There's a prophecy in the book I found that day in Central Library. It's common knowledge amongst the rebels and used to be for the weavers as well, but they erased all records of it; at least they thought they did. It goes:

When the shadows rise, the ancient house succumbs
in darkness, the citadels will fall
and woven dreams unwoven threads straddle barriers
and cross the bounds of endless night.
Then the lost arise to gather the splinters
of a shattered world and transcend the light."

The group sat silent for a moment after Wesley finished. Isabella's shoulders were in a knot, her arm ached, and her head spun. She'd heard a little about the Purge, but the thought of the Council turning weaver against weaver scared her. She knew that her family was connected to the Council of Dreamers somehow and that her dad worked with them. That would mean her family was implicit in this.

Ajay stood, arms crossed in front of his broad chest, face impassive. Finn looked as shaken as Isabella felt. He was standing, shoulders and arms relaxed, but his mouth was slightly open as if he had something he wanted to say but couldn't get the words to come out. It was Delson who spoke first after letting out a whistle. "That's a heavy load to lay down. If that's true, then what does that mean?"

"I'm not sure anyone understands it yet. At least, none of us do."

"Right," Delson clarified, "but what does it mean for us?"

"It means that you've been taken in by another tall tale," Ajay said.

"I understand if you don't want to believe me," Wesley said as he scanned the group with his eyes, "but you need to get

Isabella and Delson to your apothecaries quickly. That salve is fascinating stuff, reminiscent of some I've read about in the rebel's books, but it's not as good as what one of your apothecaries could do. For obvious reasons, I'm not going to be coming with you. I ask you one thing. I know you don't owe me this, but I hope I've earned a little of your trust. Please don't tell the Council about me, about us. They think the rebels have been wiped out, and we'd prefer to keep it that way."

"You want us to lie to the weavers, to the Champion?" Ajay was incredulous. He shook his head and walked over to the bags, turning his back on Wesley and the rest of them.

"Not lie, exactly, but omit some of the facts. They need to know about this shadow army that Eli is building and about this cave, but I'm sure he will have moved on by the time they get back here. Please, keep me and the rebels out of it."

"Wesley saved us down there when we were facing that shadow army," Isabella said, "so I think he's earned this. I'll keep the secret. Delson? Finn?"

"I promised the Champion to keep you safe, even if we didn't know you were a rebel at the time." Delson shrugged. "If what you're saying is true, I guess keeping my mouth shut helps me keep my word."

"I've never seen anything like what he did down there," Finn said, awe in his voice, "so I'm going with Izzy on this one. What do you say, Ajay? Wesley did save our lives."

"You're all *pāgala*. I make no promises to those who cannot keep their own." Ajay shouldered his pack and began down the trail toward the hunters' camp.

Wesley looked after him, shoulders slumped in defeat, and sighed. "It was a big ask and he has no reason to believe me. I will go back to the rebels and let them know that I might have given away our existence."

"What will they do to you?" Isabella asked.

"To me?" Wesley laughed and shook his head. "Nothing, they're not like that. We'll beef up our security, add sentries. We know that every mission may end up in our being found, but we need to keep going. The shadows are building strength and the wanderers are in trouble. Everyone is." Wesley began to leave in the opposite direction to Ajay, but then he stopped and turned around. "Isabella, don't trust the Council of Dreamers, at least not fully. There's something brewing, and I don't think they're clean in all of it. If they ever learned about the Samsa'raka or that you are a charm user, I don't know what they would do"—he looked at Kimi and then back at Isabella—"but I don't think it would be good."

"Well," Isabella sighed, "I haven't met them yet, so maybe it won't be an issue."

"You will, weaver," he said, "and the less they know about your abilities, the better."

"Izzy." Finn had helped Delson to his feet and shouldered his pack. "We've gotta get moving. I want to catch up to Ajay before he gets to the camp."

"If you care for Isabella at all," Wesley called to them, "then you'll keep her secret like you promised to keep mine."

"Don't worry about her," Finn called back, "she wouldn't leave Del in that cave. If anyone wants her, they'll have to go through us to get her. Come on, Iz."

"Iz?" Isabella raised her right eyebrow and scrunched her face in disgust.

"Yeah," Finn smiled back, unperturbed, "I'm seeing if it fits."

Isabella shook her head. "It doesn't."

"We'll see," Finn said with a shrug before he continued down the trail.

She was about to retort when Wesley grabbed her by her left elbow. "One more thing," he said, lowering his voice. "The fewer people who know about whatever it is that happened to your right arm, the better. The Council will see it as a threat and will probably strip you of your weaver status. If the hunters can't rid you of it, get them to promise to keep it a secret."

"Eli said that it would eventually turn me into a shadow." As she stood in the sun, Isabella could feel the throbbing of the shadow encapsulating her right arm less, but it was still there.

Wesley looked at it. "Could be, but there's got to be some way to fix it. I don't know what it's going to look like in the waking world. I've never read about anything like this, but Skia and I will find out for you. And if you're ever in need, you are always welcome among the rebels." Skia climbed up on Wesley's shoulder, and Wesley began to run in the opposite direction, leaving Isabella and Kimi standing alone in the clearing.

"Well, that was ominous," Kimi said, looking up at Isabella.

"Can we trust him?"

"That's a good question."

"Can we trust any of them, Kimi? Do we really know any of them?"

"We know Finn and Delson." Kimi looked down the path.

"That's a start," Isabella said and gave Kimi a pat on the head. "And I can trust you."

"Well, I should hope so," the fox replied with mock incredulity in her voice, "after all I've done for you." Kimi swished her tail and walked imperiously toward the trailhead. Smiling, Isabella followed her loyal fox and her friends.

The walk back to the hunter's camp was quiet, with each of the five lost in their own thoughts. Ajay waited about a mile down the path, but as soon as the rest caught up, he re-shouldered his pack and stormed off down the trail. Delson leaned on Finn for support, but even their exuberance seemed to have been dampened by Wesley's tale.

Isabella worried about Ajay. He seemed to be adamantly against the idea of keeping Wesley's secret, and he had no real reason to trust him. She wanted to trust that Ajay would do the right thing, she wanted to have him on her side in whatever was coming for the future, but there was a lot about the big man she didn't know. Finn trusted him, but Ajay's reaction to Wesley seemed to surprise even him.

Picking up her pace, Isabella moved up to walk next to Ajay. He looked down at her but didn't change his pace. They walked for a while like that before Isabella spoke up. "I never got the chance to thank you properly for taking care of Kimi for me last time."

Ajay looked at Kimi and then smiled warmly at Isabella. "It was my pleasure, little weaver."

"You can call me Izzy, you know."

"I know," he replied before looking off in the distance, seeming to get lost in his thoughts again. They walked again in silence for a while, then he asked, "Do you trust him, little weaver?"

Isabella thought about it for a moment before answering. "I don't know," she said honestly. Ajay raised his bushy eyebrows at her but didn't respond, so she continued. "Wesley saved us in the cave when he could have run, but he lied to you guys, and he's the reason Delson was down there in the first place. So no, I don't know if I trust him. But I also don't know much about the Council, and if what he said about the Council letting the purge happen— helping it, even—is true, then I don't think I can trust them either."

"You don't trust easily, do you?" Ajay smiled and turned to look down the path. "Is there anyone you do trust?"

"I trust Kimi. I trust Finn and Delson."

"Good that," Ajay said with a nod. "They are loyal to a fault."

"And I want to trust you."

Ajay stopped for a moment, scowling. He took a deep breath and blew it out, then closed his eyes and shook his head. "Do not give your trust where it is not earned, little weaver. I am not as worthy of it as they are."

"You protected my brother and you saved Kimi. That's deserving of trust."

He tilted his head slightly while looking down at her. "You saved the little fox, but I understand your point." Ajay shrugged off his pack and pulled out a shirt. "Take this. Wrap your hand." Ajay watched as she awkwardly wrapped his shirt around her hand. It was loose, and there was a sleeve hanging from her wrist, but Isabella was pretty sure it wouldn't fall off. Ajay chuckled and shook his head. "Let me help." While he expertly rewrapped her hand, he said, "I will keep your secrets. But I do not do it for the rebel. I do not trust him."

Isabella looked at the wrapping on her hand; it left her fingers free to move but contained the shadow tendrils that twisted up her arm. "Why do you hate the rebels so much?"

"That is a long story for another time."

They continued the rest of the way to Nigel's hut in relative silence. The camp was active, but not like the last time Isabella was there. Groups of hunters sat around various fires or at rough tables set out in front of what looked to Isabella like a food cart from a fair. The smell of cooked meats and stew made her stomach rumble as she tried to remember the last time she'd eaten.

Nigel's hut smelled like the inside of Isabella's grandmother's potpourri bags. The walls were covered with bunches of dried herbs and flowers and there were several shelves lined with bottles containing liquids, all labeled in elegant cursive. A wooden table with various herbs and some small blades sat against one wall; a doorway into another room was on the opposite wall. Through the door, Isabella heard someone singing softly to themself.

"Nigel," Finn called out when they entered. "We need some fixing here."

The singing abruptly stopped and the person in the other room cleared their throat. Isabella heard footsteps before seeing a thin man, probably in his early to mid-twenties, his short brown hair fading down until it was shaved by his temples and around his ears. He had metal-rimmed glasses with round lenses resting on his hawkish nose. His eyes were a light blue and his skin was pale with some freckles. His face lit up when he saw Finn and Delson, but a cloud of worry surfaced when he noticed Delson's injuries and Isabella with her arm wrapped in Ajay's shirt.

"Did you use the salve I gave you?" he asked, coming into the room and wiping his hands on the apron he wore. His voice was soft and had a slight British accent.

"We did," Delson said, "and it's working wonders."

"Get him over here, Finn." Nigel motioned to a chair he had moved closer to the fire burning in a stone fireplace on the back wall of the hut. "Let's get a look at those wounds, shall we?"

"No." Delson pulled away from Finn's shoulder and leaned against the table, making one of the bowls rattle a little in the process. "Isabella first. The weaver takes precedence."

Nigel turned to Isabella with a gracious bow. "I'm sorry, miss, I did not notice your companion when you came in. I will, of course, tend to you first, but don't you have better apothecaries in the Capitol than that of a simple hunter?"

"Nigel, you're the finest around and you know it," Finn said.

"You're too kind, Finnegan, but you're also mistaken," Nigel smiled. "I will see to your injuries before sending you on to the Capitol with some of our hunters to assure your safety. May I say first, thank you, and it is a pleasure to finally meet you. When Ajay brought Kimi to me before, she was quite well recovered because of your quick thinking. I made that salve based on what you did to save your companion. You have saved many of our hunters since then because of it. Now, what seems to be the problem?"

Isabella looked at Ajay, who stood in front of the closed door, then at Finn and Delson, who nodded. Slowly, Isabella unwrapped her arm, revealing the wispy shadow that seemed to extend up her forearm, wrapping around in two strands from her palm. Nigel gasped and stumbled back a step, knocking into one of the shelves and making the bottles on it clatter against one another.

"Blimey, what is that?" Nigel's face paled and his eyes were wide. One of his well-manicured hands, with some dirt under at the edges of the nails, was held to his thin chest.

"We were sort of hoping you could tell us," Ajay said.

"I've never..." He stepped forward and reached toward Isabella's hand. "May I?" Isabella nodded, and Nigel reached out to touch her arm. His hand went through the shadow and touched her skin, then he pulled it back quickly. "Cold," he muttered.

He turned her hand over and looked at her palm where there was a dark circular mark about the size of a golf ball, and the two lines of shadow met. One went out between her thumb and pointer finger and wrapped around the back of her hand, while the other went toward her wrist on the other side before wrapping around. "How did this happen?" he asked.

"I was fighting a shadow," Isabella said. "I overbalanced on an attack and fell right through one. When I landed, I had the shadow's core in my hand and it was looming over me, so I crushed it."

"With your bare hand?" Nigel stepped away and began searching his drawers for something. "And you didn't die?"

"I passed out, but Kimi had my back."

"So that's a thing," Nigel said before he cried out in triumph and held up a pair of thin leather gloves. "My predecessor, Jacques, told me about something like this. Some new hunter once did something similar, but by the time he got back to camp, he was babbling incoherently and in the throes of a massive fever. Jacques treated these gloves with something he called Shadow's Bane. It's actually called Wolf's Bane, or aconite, and its poisonous if injected, but it helps treat shadow wounds. That's what I used to help Kimi the rest of the way." He handed Isabella the gloves. "Put these on and they should keep the shadows at bay. It won't cure this, though."

"What happened to him, the hunter?" Delson asked.

"Well," Nigel said, looking at Isabella with sympathetic eyes, "Jacques said he eventually faded into a shadow, and they had to kill him. But I don't know what will happen with a weaver. You lot tend to be ... different. The Council will know better."

"We can't tell the Council," Isabella said as she looked Nigel in the eyes, daring him to contradict her.

"You need to tell the Council," he insisted. "If you don't, I will."

"What if we asked you really nicely to keep this one secret?" Finn asked, smiling his big goofy smile.

"Did you not hear me when I said the last person turned into a shadow?" Nigel glanced around the room at everyone, his eyes stopping on Kimi who sat imperially at Isabella's side. "We need to tell them. They might be able to help her."

"There's something I need to check out first." Isabella put her left hand gently on Nigel's wrist. "Please, at least for a little bit."

"What did the Champion say about this?" Nigel looked to Finn.

"We're not really planning to tell him."

Nigel looked pleadingly to him. "Ajay, you've been here longer than I have. Please tell me you're not in agreement here. Talk some sense into them, will you?"

Finn and Delson looked to their friend as he leaned against the door to leave the apothecary. Ajay sighed deeply and closed his eyes, shaking his head. "I'm sorry, Nigel," he said at last, "but I'm with them for now. The little weaver wants to keep this quiet. I don't like it, but she's earned it, don't you think?"

Nigel looked from one face to the other again, eyes searching for something. At last, his shoulder slumped and he looked at the ground. "This is going to come back to bite us all. I hope you know what you're doing."

"So, you'll keep quiet about this?" Finn asked, the joy in his eyes shining brightly and his smile beaming across his face. "From everyone. Nobody outside this room is to know."

Nigel sounded defeated as he said, "Nobody outside this room would believe me."

Finn rushed the man and embraced him in a warm hug. Nigel patted him gently on the back and then pushed him away.

"Enough of that, Finnegan." Straightening his glasses that Finn had knocked askew, Nigel turned to Isabella. "But you must promise me that if this gets worse, you will tell someone."

"I promise."

"Alright." Nigel pointed to the gloves in Isabella's hand. "Put those on. Nobody should see your arm. When this goes south, and it will go south, I will tell everyone you forced me into keeping my mouth shut."

"That's fair," Ajay said, then turned abruptly and left the hut.

After Nigel tended to Isabella and Delson's wounds, they left him sitting by his fire, head in his hands. Isabella felt guilty for causing such conflict between Finn and the other hunters, but something about Wesley's warning was eating away at her. Finn and Delson escorted her out of the camp to a clearing about half a mile down the trail. They still needed to report back to the Champion, but the four agreed that Isabella didn't need to come. Her presence would make things more challenging to explain, and weavers didn't answer to the hunters, so the Champion wouldn't expect her anyway.

"You going to be alright getting back to wherever you're going?" Delson asked when they stopped to say goodbye.

"Yeah." Isabella pulled out the dream catcher that Rionach had given in her in the town by the lake when she'd first come to the dream world. "Weavers' charms."

Finn's eyes widened. "No way! You mean that you can—"

Delson chuckled and shook his head as he put his arm around Finn's shoulders. "You're such a child, Finnegan."

Finn turned and gave Delson a kiss on his cheek. "But you love it."

Isabella focused on her father's cabin in the woods, the little pond, and the rolling hills beyond the wooden paddocks. She felt a pang of homesickness for the place despite not having spent much time there. With a deep breath to clear her mind, she spun the dream catcher out into the clearing. Once again, it seemed to hang in the air and pick up speed. Blue sparks shot out from the edges as it expanded, showing the cabin and the pond on the other side.

"Weavers' charms, that's fierce," Finn said.

"Weavers' charms," Isabella said, looking back at the two of them. "I guess that makes me one of the rebels after all."

"Isabella," Delson said, "if I've learned one thing about you, it's that nobody else gets to define you. Most weavers would have left me for dead. The rebels got me into that mess, but you came back for me. For what it's worth, I think you're better than both of them."

"Whatever you are," Finn added, "we got your back when you need us."

"I know." Isabella went over and gave them both big hugs before she and Kimi leaped through the glowing ring of light and landed in the field outside her father's cabin. She turned around and watched as the swirling ring began to close on Delson and Finn, standing with their arms around each other, waving to her. Isabella smiled and blew them a kiss. Then, picking up the fallen dream catcher, she stuck it in her pocket. She and Kimi walked to the cabin, hoping her father would be there and they could go home.

❦ THIRTY-SEVEN ❧

S o what are you planning on telling your father?" Kimi asked
as they walked across the soft green fields that surrounded
the cabin.

"I don't know." Isabella reached down and picked a purple
morning glory that was growing on the corner of the paddock
fence. "I trust him. I mean, he loves me and all, but he's working
with the Council. He's likely to turn me into them if he thinks it's
in my best interest."

"What if it is?"

Isabella sniffed the flower then tossed it in the air. She
watched as it floated gently to the ground and nestled among the
blades of grass. "I don't want him to make the choice for me.
What if he decides that all this is too dangerous and somehow
makes it so I can't come back? I'd miss you."

"I don't know," Kimi said. "It's a lot quieter when you're
away."

The two walked in silence the rest of the way to the cabin. While they were still a way from the porch, the door opened

and Isabella's father stepped out. He smiled and leaned against the support for the porch roof. Vígolfr walked out next to him and sat down.

"Well, here goes nothing," Isabella said to Kimi as they approached the porch. "Remember, nothing about Wesley, the charms, or my arm."

"What can we tell him?"

"The shadow army," Isabella said with a nod. "The Council should know about that."

"If you say so." Kimi didn't sound too sure of the plan, but she didn't argue.

When they got to the bottom of the stairs, Isabella's father came down and enveloped her in a big hug. He apologized for being called away but said he couldn't give any details about his mission other than he had to eradicate a hive of nightmares. They sat on the steps looking out over the pond and talked for a while. Vígolfr curled up by the door and Kimi went in search of something to eat in the grass.

When Isabella told him about her adventures into the caves in search of a lost dreamer, a white lie she used to avoid telling him about Wesley, he leaned back and looked up at the roof, silent for a moment. Isabella's heart sank. She expected him to say that things in the dream world were getting too dangerous and that she was too young, or some other crazy reason why she shouldn't be there. Steeling herself for the coming argument, Isabella planned out various responses in her head so she'd be ready when the time came.

"A shadow army?" he asked after a while. Running his fingers through his thinning hair, he let out a breath. "That's ... unusual."

"I know what you're going to say," Isabella said, deciding a preemptive strike would be the best. "And before you do, there's something I need to tell you."

"Okay." His voice was guarded, but he raised his left eyebrow at her.

Isabella dove into her strongest defense. "You're not going to stop me from coming here. I have every right to be here, as much as anyone else. I have made friends I can rely on when things get difficult, and Kimi and I are a team. If you stopped me from coming back, what would become of her? Think about it. That wouldn't be fair. I know it's dangerous and I know that there's something strange going on with the shadows. But I can take care of myself. I don't need you to protect me."

While Isabella spoke, her father drew his eyebrows together, causing the space between them to furrow. His eyes narrowed and he held her in his stare. Isabella typically flinched from that look — not because her father ever hit her, but because it was the look that preceded one of his talking-to's, and those typically followed her majorly messing something up. But this time, Isabella held his gaze and looked directly into his eyes as she made her case.

"Are you quite finished?" he asked, his tone daring her to continue.

"And another thing," she forged on despite his demeanor, "I came in here by myself last time. I don't even think you could keep me out if you wanted to. I will come back here, I will be a

Dreamweaver, and nothing you say is going to stop me." Isabella stopped. She could hear her heartbeat in her ears and could feel the sweat beading between her shoulder blades. She'd never spoken to her father that way, never stood up to him like that. This was something that mattered. This wasn't extending her curfew or something she wanted at the store; this meant something.

When she finished, her father stood up. Vígolfr stood with him and they both walked down the stairs to the edge of the pond, leaving Isabella alone. Confused, she sat and watched the two of them as they stood by the water. Having finished her snack, Kimi came over to Isabella and hopped up the steps next to her.

"That went well," the little fox said. "What'd you do to scare them off like that?"

"I don't know."

"What did he say?"

"Nothing." Isabella was at a loss. "He just got up and walked away."

"Think you should go check on him?"

"Do I have to?"

"It would probably clear a few things up."

Knowing Kimi was right didn't change Isabella's reluctance to hear what her father had to say. She'd crossed a line, she knew that, but it was a line that needed to be crossed. "You know, Kimi," Isabella said as she pushed herself to her feet, "sometimes I hate when you're right."

"Sometimes?" Kimi asked as she followed Isabella over to the edge of the pond.

She stood next to her father in silence for a bit, both staring at the little waterfall and the pond it fed. She had said what she wanted to say, probably not as eloquently as she would have liked, but now it was out there. She waited for him to speak next. In the silence, she picked up a small stone and skipped it across the water's surface, watching the ripples expand everyplace it touched.

"This pond wasn't always here," her father said, looking at the waterfall. "This used to be a cliff. I would climb it when I was a kid. Everything seemed so much bigger then, you know. My Far-far would get so mad at me. He'd tell me that I was going to fall and break my neck, then how would I ever take care of my wolf pup—Vígolfr was a pup then," he chuckled. "This was you. This waterfall, the pond beneath it, you created this. This place, the cabin, the dream world, even Kimi. Nice to finally meet you, by the way." He bowed slightly to the fox who returned the gesture.

"All of this is as much a part of you now as your skin or your hair. I wouldn't try to take this away from you, even if I could. No, this is where you belong, at least some of the time. And you're right, you are going to need friends because it is dangerous here. Like this pond, like the stone you skipped across the top, you will leave your mark on this place. And that mark is going to spread out in ways that you could never imagine. Ripples. If you save a dreamer, or, God forbid, fail to save one, you will create a chain of events that nobody can possibly predict, both in this world and the waking world. It's a big responsibility."

He sighed and looked down at her. "I want to protect you. Every fiber of my being wants to take you away from here and protect you from the nightmares like I used to when I'd weave your dreams. But I can't. Your speech back there—which, by the way, let's try to be a little nicer next time, eh?— made that abundantly clear. What I'm saying is this: I can't wrap you in bubble wrap and protect you from everything that's coming your way, and from what you've already told me, there seem to be some big things in your future. What I can do is be there for you when you need me, Vígolfr and me. You understand that, right? I will always be in your corner. It's important to know who to trust. I'm your dad, even here, and I want you to know that you can tell me anything."

When her father finished talking, he held out his arms to hug her. Isabella felt a tinge of guilt for not telling him about the rebels and her arm, and for keeping the Samsa'raka a secret, but whenever he was here he worked for the Council of Dreamers and she needed more than his word that he indeed was on her side before she let him in on the stuff that mattered. The guilt continued to fester in the back of her mind as she hugged him, but Isabella did her best to push it back.

"We have to get going for now," he said. "I think your mom's going to be worried about us. And if I'm not mistaken, young lady, tonight is a school night." He cuffed her playfully on her right shoulder and Isabella did her best to hide the wince of pain. "But tomorrow night, I'm going to have to let the Council know. They'll probably want to talk to you about it. I wanted to wait a bit before I brought you before them because you are much younger than the average initiate, but if what you said about the shadow army is true, they need to know. Since you were there, you'll be able to answer their questions a lot better than I will."

Isabella's heart sank. She thanked her luck that she'd resisted the urge to tell him everything after his impassioned speech. Looking down at the gloves Nigel had given her, Isabella wondered what other ripples her time in the dream world had caused. A chill ran through her as she imagined what her hand looked like beneath that glove in the waking world.

After saying farewell to Kimi and Vígolfr, Isabella cleaned up in the cabin before she and her father traveled back to the waking world to pack up their unused campsite. As they were packing up, her father asked about the gloves she was wearing. Not sure what to say, Isabella settled on a half-truth and told him they were a gift from some hunters she'd helped. He'd smiled, nodded, and dropped the subject. Still, the cab of the truck was filled with tension on the ride home, so Isabella put in her headphones and leaned her seat back. The trip to the dream world was exhausting, and she didn't want to talk and accidentally tell her dad about the rebels or that she could use charms. Instead, she closed her eyes and, although it was only late afternoon, the rumbling of the engine and all the time in the fresh air made her drowsy. Mentally noting the irony of being tired after spending so much time in the dream world, Isabella decided not to fight it and she quickly fell into a dreamless sleep.

Isabella was still wearing the gloves on Tuesday when she returned to school after the long weekend. It amazed her how the world rolled forward as if nothing had happened, and for the most part, nothing had for most of them. Isabella felt as if something had shifted inside her. Her friends were still infatuated with Evan, the new kid in school, but when Isabella saw him, there was something about him, his mannerisms or the things he said in class, that reminded her of Eli when he wasn't trying to kill her. Maybe it was the fact that he was in the dream trap when she found Eli, but that wasn't his fault.

Sitting with her friends at lunch, Isabella began to wonder why nobody had mentioned the gloves she was wearing, not even the teachers. She was about to say something when she noticed her friends giggling and looking behind her. They had talked about nothing else all day except how Evan had asked her out last week and how it was all around school that she'd turned him down to go camping with her dad. Based on their giggling, Isabella was sure Evan must be coming up behind her. She closed her eyes, trying to tamp down the unfair annoyance that had begun to develop whenever Evan was around. It wasn't his fault that he reminded her of a stalker, which she could never tell her friends anyway. She rubbed her itching palm on her knee and waited for him to come up behind her before she got up to throw her trash away.

"Oh!" Isabella pretended to be startled by Evan's presence. "I didn't see you there."

"I know," he said, smiling at her. "I'm good at sneaking up on people when I want."

"So, you wanted to sneak up on me?"

"Sort of." He smiled shyly, a gesture that didn't seem in his nature. "You've been avoiding me all day."

"Sorry," Isabella said, trying to sound off-hand, "didn't realize I was."

"So, pizza this weekend?" He looked around the lunchroom; Isabella looked around too and noticed that several pairs of eyes were on them.

"I guess," she replied with a shrug. She didn't want to—she wanted to try to get back into the dream world and talk with Kimi to figure out what was going on—but everyone was watching, and if people were already talking about her blowing him off last weekend then doing it again would make rumors start. Better to go and try to have a good time.

"Cool," he said. "Catch'ya later." He walked back to his table and started talking to the other guys he was sitting with.

Isabella went to throw out her trash without even looking at her friends. She didn't want them to think that getting pizza with Evan was anything more than two people eating pizza, but when she got back to the table they were buzzing with excitement over what they christened as a date. Isabella let herself get caught up in the excitement. He was cute, and a date with him could be fun. It wasn't his fault that he reminded her of someone else.

Later that day, as she was getting out of History, Isabella saw Evan at his locker and decided she'd repay the favor of sneaking upon him. He was focused on something on his phone when she walked up and put her hand on his shoulder. He dropped his weight from under her hand and turned, pivoting on his right foot. He didn't bring his hands up, but Isabella wouldn't have been surprised if he'd been ready to before he recognized her.

She'd seen hunters moving like this when they sparred, but she'd never seen it in the waking world.

"Sorry," he said, his cheeks turning a dull pink. "You shouldn't surprise people."

"You're one to talk," Isabella shot back. "You snuck up on me first, remember?"

Evan began to respond, but Isabella cut him off. "Don't worry about it. Let me see that." She reached out and took his phone from his hands. He protested, but she ignored him. She didn't like that he seemed to think he had the upper hand when it came to what her friends had convinced her was a date. She punched her number into his phone and hit send on an empty text. In her pocket, her phone buzzed with an incoming text message. She handed his phone back to him. "Now you have my number," she said as she walked away without looking back.

That night, Isabella felt good. She'd taken control of the situation at school and was looking forward to her date that weekend. Evan had texted her later that night saying how surprised he was by the way she'd given him her number. They chatted back and forth for about an hour, then she told him she had things to do and the texts stopped. As she was getting ready for bed, Isabella realized that she hadn't taken the gloves off at all since she'd come back from the dream world.

Standing in the glaring lights of the bathroom, Isabella looked down at her hands. She felt her heartbeat thudding in her chest. The last time coming back from the dream world, she had a dislocated shoulder and a twisted ankle. This time, for the most part, things were fine. Nigel's medicine had done wonders for the minor scrapes and bruises, but the shadow infection in her hand was another story. Her palm had itched for most of the day, and now that she was looking at it, the itch was back and worse than ever.

Slowly, she worked the glove off, pulling out her fingers first and then drawing it over her hand. She drew in a quick breath as she saw a small irregular circle of darker skin in the middle of her palm. She'd half expected the shadowy tendrils that wrapped her arm in the dream world to still be there, but while she was relieved to see they were not, something about the mark disturbed her. As she looked at it, the spot seemed to move on her palm and spread. Isabella quickly put the glove back on and looked at herself in the mirror. She was marked by the shadow. She didn't know what that meant, but if Eli was right, nothing good was going to come of it.

EPILOGUE

The room behind the council chambers was sparsely furnished. It had many purposes and had had many lives in the centuries since the Council had been established to govern the dream world and the Dreamweavers. Today, it was a war room dominated by a large wooden table. On the table, weighted down with items that seemed to be readily at hand, the map of the dream world was spread out, a dagger on the southwest corner and an empty glass to the northeast. A plain-looking stone and a small statue kept the map from curling at the other corners. There were red pins in several places on the map, and a small pile of papers sat on the edge of the table.

Councilor Harris was looking down at the map, his thick arms crossed over his broad chest. At the side of the room, his companion, a large brown bear, lay resting. Councilor Merin stood flipping through the papers, a red-furred mink curled on the table next to her.

"I'm not sure it's going to work, Paloma," Councilor Harris said, pointing to a red pin in the southern area of the map. "If what Allan said is correct, the stalkers are amassing an army here, and I'm getting reports from some of the weavers of increased shadow activity up in the north-east as well."

"I understand your concern, Oliver, but this strategy has kept the shadows at bay for the last five decades." She absently pet the mink who shifted comfortably under her hand. "There is no reason it won't continue to do so."

"But the prophecy," Councilor Harris continued. Although he was deferential to the mocha-skinned woman, he refused to back down. "When the shadows rise and the ancient house—"

"Enough." The tone of her voice left no room for question. "Don't quote that worthless prophecy to me again. We rid ourselves of such foolish superstition when we removed the books on charms from the library. Unless you forgot, we are in the Citadel."

Harris's voice sounded tense as he replied, "No, I haven't forgotten."

"Besides, we have more pressing matters to attend to. Namely Allan Shaw and his daughter, Isabella."

"She's too young to have found her companion." Councilor Harris walked over and leaned against his bear. The bear grunted slightly but didn't move.

"Too young or not, it seems that she has found her companion, which means she will need training."

"I guess Allan's apprentice Wren could be convinced," he said as he walked back to the table. "I think we have her out in the west at the moment. We could call her in. She's been a great asset lately. And didn't you shortlist her for the next council slot?"

"I did," Councilor Merin confirmed with a nod. "The hunters tell me she's taken a liking to this girl."

"Wouldn't that be a good thing? Besides, she won't let anything slide. She tough and loyal. It could do that Shaw family some good to have someone bring them under the rule of the Council for once."

"Except I am looking for a more permanent solution to the problem the Shaw family represents."

"We could simply ban her," Councilor Harris suggested. "Sever her connection with that fox and be done with it. It's barbaric but effective."

"A possibility, I suppose, but we need Allan ... for now." Councilor Merin picked up her mink and placed him on her shoulders. "No, I have someone in mind who will make Wren and Mentu look like those kittens from her obnoxious sweaters. We need someone special to train young Isabella Shaw, and I know just the person." Councilor Merin walked gracefully from the room, leaving the door open behind her.

Oliver Harris stood at the table watching the councilor leave. He looked over at Roth, his brown bear companion, then walked to the window overlooking the city and watched as the people below continued to go about their days. The thoughts of sacrifices he had made to be here surfaced in his mind—sacrifices Allan Shaw had refused to make—and wondered if it was worth it. If the prophecy was indeed coming, if the citadels were about to fall, everything he had abandoned to protect this place might have been given up in vain. He sighed and called to Roth as he walked from the room, following Councilor Merin. With a grunt, the brown bear lumbered to his feet and trudged after his weaver.

Thank you for joining Isabella on her second journey into the dream world.

Keep your eye out for the next installment of Izzy and Kimi's adventures in Dreamweaver Diaries BOOK THREE:

Until then, sign up for my mailing list so you don't miss the updates, and get access to the official **Dreamweaver Diaries Choose-Your-Own-Adventure** to discover if you have what it takes to become a Dreamweaver!

www.ericjohnsonwriter.com

ABOUT THE AUTHOR

Eric Johnson spends his days chasing after one of those diabolically bipedal entities we often refer to with the innocuous moniker of "Pre-Schooler" or waking in the wee hours of the morning to quiet someone's nightmares or weave them a pleasant dream. Otherwise, he is correcting papers, planning lessons, climbing trees, remodeling his home in the woods, reading in the groggy wastes of the middle of the night (since those aforementioned entities don't sleep), or drinking black, dark roast (or something with a little more bite). Sometimes he even gets some writing in there too.

You can also read his poetry in a full-length collection titled *The Conditions We Live*, published by Unsolicited Press.

To find out more about Eric and his work, or sign up for the mailing list at www.ericjohnsonwriter.com